FOREVER TOUCHED

FOREVER TOUCHED

A TOUCH OF VAMPIRE

BECKY MOYNIHAN

BROKEN
BOOKS

Published by Broken Books
www.beckymoynihan.com

ISBN-13: 979-8-9883737-3-5

Cover design by Becky Moynihan
Cover model by Ravven
www.depositphotos.com

To the dreamers:

Keep wishing on stars and believing in happily ever afters

CONTENT WARNING

This book contains mature themes of abuse, addiction, prostitution, and sexual violence. Recommended for ages 18+

PROLOGUE

EVERETT

Blood and lust saturated the air.

The heady concoction pulled at my senses, urging me to indulge in my baser instincts. To join the sway of sweaty bodies undulating on the dance floor and select an eager partner.

Only here could predator and prey so freely mingle. Although our DNA was vastly different, we looked the same on the outside, which was the only reason why humans didn't run screaming from the establishment. Yet an instinctual part of them knew that they were surrounded by danger, a feeling too powerful to resist. The thrill of it kept them here—and kept them coming back.

The allure of the forbidden was a seductive song, eclipsing the beat of the sensual music pulsing through their bones.

It was the same with every vampire-owned nightclub.

The promise of pleasure drew humans and vampires alike. It was a mutually beneficial arrangement, one I'd partaken in countless times myself.

Blood and sex with no strings attached was an offering few vampires could turn down. As long as the humans were willing and left with no memory of being fed on, these nightclubs were allowed to legally operate without fear of being shut down.

This one was different, though—or so my father suspected.

Sighing impatiently, I checked the time on my phone again. Not even ten o'clock. This was going to be a long night. From my spot at a velvet-cushioned booth tucked in the darkest corner of the club, I heard a human female giggle. I glanced up, my dark mask hiding the slight movement.

Not a day over twenty, the girl being led off the dance floor wore a skimpy black dress that barely covered her breasts and backside. Even through the shadows, fog, and red pulsating lights, I could make out her eager expression. She'd done this before. Probably many times. That dreamy, somewhat glazed look in her eyes told me everything.

She giggled again, teetering forward with her mask knocked askew. The male holding her hand tugged her past a dark screen and into a private alcove—or not so private. My night vision easily cut through the gloom and penetrated the thin screen, revealing the pair. They were already entwined, kissing and pawing at each other. Despite the sensual music pulsing through the air, I could even hear their feverish moans and sighs of pleasure.

Instead of looking away in embarrassment, I openly watched the display, waiting for the male to make his move. I didn't have to wait long. The greedy bastard only lasted seconds before tugging the girl's head back and plunging his fangs into her neck.

Her startled cry quickly morphed into one of ecstasy. At the sound, a burning need seared my throat, making my mouth water. There was a bar in the opposite corner of the club, but I'd chosen not to indulge tonight. One drink would quickly turn into several, and if I went down that road, I too would be pulling a girl behind a screen.

Impatient once more—this time with myself—I swallowed the hunger and refocused on the entwined pair. The male was taking full advantage of the girl's eagerness, hiking her short dress up to her waist. When he slipped his hand between her thighs, she gasped and arched against him. I continued to watch the erotic display, not surprised when the vampire fumbled to undo his pants seconds later.

Stifling an eye roll, I kept my gaze trained on the pair as the male whipped out his dick and frantically thrust inside the girl. I flicked a glance at my phone on the black cushion beside me, then sneered when the male orgasmed less than a minute later.

"Overeager whelp," I muttered. He hadn't even let the girl finish.

The couple parted soon after that, the male hastily slipping out to no doubt pursue another partner. The girl stumbled out more slowly, looking unfocused and high as a kite.

Dismissing them both, I leaned back against the booth cushion with another impatient sigh. This was a waste of my time. I had better things to do than watch vampires and humans barely past the age of maturity hump each other. Besides the required masks to gain entrance, this club was no different than the others. Sure, it was more exclusive, strictly catering to Venturi and their drothen—who seemed drawn to this place simply for that fact. The anonymity and exorbitant entry fee were also a bit strange, but I'd seen no evidence of foul play.

Everyone here was rich, horny, and looking for a good time. Despite the masks, I even recognized a few of the males. They were indulging in their baser instincts, nothing more. That wasn't a crime, so long as the rules were being followed.

My phone buzzed, and I reached for it.

Anything? the text from my brother said.

Dead end, I quickly typed in reply, then rose from my seat. *Tell Father that I'm headed back.*

I was about to hit send and leave as quietly as I'd arrived when the music suddenly stopped. I looked toward the dance floor just as a bright beam of light illuminated a masked figure dangling high above the ground. Decidedly female, she sat on a large silver hoop that was attached to the ceiling via a chain.

At the sight, the crowd below looked up and froze. *Everything* froze. No one moved, barely even breathed, as the female hung suspended in the air. The fog billowing around her started to thin, and when I saw that her graceful legs were bare, I lifted my eyes, curious to see the rest of her.

She wore a two-piece sequined outfit, one that left little to the imagination. I couldn't help but notice her body, lithe but shapely in all the areas I enjoyed looking at. Her top openly displayed a generous amount of cleavage, and I paused to appreciate the view. My gaze dipped to her taut stomach next, to a glittering diamond pierced in her navel. Further intrigued, I sought out her face.

What I saw stole the breath from my lungs.

Her features were ethereal. There was no other word to describe such otherworldly beauty. Flawless olive skin. Full red lips. Thick black lashes that not even a mask could hide. High cheekbones and almond-shaped eyes spoke of partial Asian descent, possibly Japanese. Her hair was her most striking feature, though. Dark at the roots, the sleek strands lightened to a silver gray, cascading like a shimmering waterfall to her petite waist.

A slight smirk drew my gaze to her lips once more. Even from across the room, I could see the amusement dancing there. The confidence. Her audience was captivated, and she knew it.

She suddenly let go of the hoop and fell backward. Silver hair and sequins flashed as she arched through the air in a freefall to the ground.

My heart stopped.

I couldn't scent her from here, but if I had to guess, I'd say she was human. A fall from that height could badly injure or even kill her.

The crowd beneath her parted as she fell, but they didn't attempt to catch her. A sudden need to save her struck me. The need was so strong that I was halfway across the room before I could think better of it.

Time slowed. I reached for her, using my supernatural speed to beat her descent to the ground. Yards away from catching her, she abruptly twisted. Faster and faster until she spun like a top. Before she could smack into the ground, something jerked her to a halt. I slowed, confused. She kept twisting, her legs spreading in an upside down split. As they did, I finally saw it. The silk silver fabric wrapped around one of her ankles.

I quietly swore.

The fall had been an act. One that I'd fallen for hook, line, and sinker.

Her body twisted once more, her spine gracefully arching as she caught the fabric, contorting herself in half. At the impressive move, the crowd unfroze. Several males wolf-whistled and hollered their appreciation. She continued to spin, holding the pose for several seconds.

I watched, unable to look away. Not wanting to. I was wholly captivated by this intriguing female.

As if she could feel my gaze, she turned her head and our eyes collided. Once more, I was struck by her ethereal beauty. This close, the silver mask couldn't hide the color of her eyes. Dark brown around the edges and bright amber at their centers. They were like bursts of sunlight, so intense that I was struck dumb. I gaped at her like a fool, completely forgetting where I was.

Everything about this female drew me in. She was the flame, and I was the helpless moth. And she knew it. Her lips tilted into that amused smirk once more. As her body twisted away from me, she threw me a wink.

At the flirtatious gesture, my cock went rock hard, straining against my pants. Like a besotted idiot, I drifted closer, overcome with the desire to touch her. Something about her screamed forbidden. She was adorned head to toe in silver, which should have turned me off. But the "untouchable" vibes only made me want to touch her more.

My legs carried me closer, close enough to touch her. But before I could make contact, she curled into a ball and shimmied up the silken fabric. I swallowed my disappointment, stepping back so I could watch her climb up to the silver hoop once more.

When she reached it, she began to dance, in a way I'd never seen before. Using the hoop and fabric, she glided through the air, sensually contorting her body in ways that made my blood heat. She moved with the fluid grace of a vampire, and yet, I was still fairly certain she was human.

Enraptured, I watched her for who knew how long. The music picked up again and so did the dancing. Bodies gyrated around me, but I didn't move from my spot. I continued to watch her, unaware of how much time ticked by.

The spotlight on her suddenly winked out.

I jerked, as if jolted from a trance. Then blinked. Just once, but that was all it took for her to disappear. Fog shrouded the air once more, so thick that the flashing red lights couldn't penetrate it. The hairs on the back of my neck stood up, and I strained to catch a glimpse of her. But, no matter how hard I searched, she was nowhere to be found.

"Where is she?"

I hadn't meant to say the words out loud, but a male vampire nearby heard them and slurred, "Star always vanishes at midnight. Where she goes, no one knows."

He laughed, the sound crazed enough that I knew he was blood drunk. No one had recognized me yet, including him, despite my sloppy attempt at staying hidden. The mask helped, and picking out individual scents was nearly impossible in a place like this. Still, I'd lingered too long. Time to pull my own vanishing act.

Slipping past the drunk vampire, I made for the exit, careful not to make eye contact with anyone and give away my identity.

The nightclub might not be the den of secretive activity my father suspected it was, but I knew one thing for certain.

I was definitely coming back.

CHAPTER 1

ADALYN

"Adalyn!"

The all-too-familiar shout dispelled my dream, and the images scattered before I could commit them to memory.

Sighing, I rubbed my eyes and struggled to clear the fog from my tired brain.

"Adalyn, *now*," the shout came again, more demanding this time.

"Coming." My reply came out as a dry rasp, but I knew Mistress could hear it. Forcing my stiff limbs into action, I pushed myself into a sitting position. My head promptly pounded, and I grabbed it with a muffled groan.

You okay?

As the concerned words flitted through my mind, I cracked an eye open to glance at my nightstand. A brown mouse with a white streak on her chest stared back, her round black eyes blinking up at me knowingly.

Yeah, I quickly reassured my familiar through our telepathic connection and reached out to stroke her tiny head with one finger. *Just had a busier night than usual.*

She nuzzled my finger, flooding our bond with sympathy. *You need more rest. And food. Don't forget that you're mortal, Ada.*

I snorted, which further irritated my parched throat. *How could I forget when my body painfully reminds me of that fact every day? Don't worry, Pepper. I brought in really good money last night and kept a little extra for myself. I'll splurge and buy a huge breakfast.*

When she eyed me skeptically, I rose from the bed on unsteady legs and started to dress.

Promise? the little mouse pressed as I exchanged my pajama bottoms for a ripped pair of jeans.

Shimmying into them, I looked over my shoulder at her. For such a small creature, she was really good at calling me out on my bull. *I'll do my best, Pep. You know how busy I am. I forget to eat sometimes.*

She twitched her long whiskers at me in annoyance. *You don't forget. You just give all your money to* her.

I pursed my lips and turned away, not bothering to reply. We'd had this conversation more times than I could count, and it always ended the same way. I was feeling lousy enough already without adding guilt to the mix, so I ignored my familiar's judgmental stare and threw on a torn oversized sweater.

"ADALYN!"

Wincing at the shrill scream, I hurriedly slipped on my sneakers and called back, "Coming!"

At least drink some water. You sound like you have laryngitis.

Stifling an eye roll, I walked the three steps to my little bathroom and switched on the sink faucet to guzzle some water and splash my face. Neither made me feel better, but I threw Pepper a saucy look anyway and crooned, "Happy?"

She huffed a perturbed squeak. *No. Be careful.*

My smirk widened. *Always am. But be careful yourself. That stray tabby has been sniffing around here again. He tried to sneak inside last night.*

Pepper somehow managed to look indignant, lifting her pert pink nose into the air. *I'm no ordinary mouse, Ada. I can't be bested by a stupid tomcat.*

Despite my exhaustion, a laugh burst from me.

"Adalyn Elise Starr, this is your last warning. You have five seconds to get your butt up here!"

Instead of giving in to a shiver of dread, I blew Pepper a kiss and whispered, "I'll bring back some cheese from that deli you like so much."

Sharp cheddar, please! she called as I whirled and beelined for the basement stairs.

Taking them at a run, I made it to the top in three seconds flat and yanked the door open just in the nick of time. A figure in a black satin robe greeted me on the other side, a matching satin scarf wrapped around her golden hair. The tall regal woman didn't look a day over forty, but she was much, much older. Old enough that using a *phone* to shout at me wouldn't even cross her mind.

At the sight of me, she frowned, which caused her ivory skin to heavily crease.

"I'm—" I started, but she raised a jeweled hand for silence.

"You know how I feel about punctuality, Adalyn. A slothful spirit is not only unattractive but highly disrespectful. I rely on you to complete errands during the day, and the sun already rose half an hour ago."

"I know, and I'm sorry, but—"

"*No* excuses," she said, her tone sharpening. "Own your mistakes and accept the consequences like I've taught you."

I bit my tongue to keep a retort at bay and lowered my chin a notch in submission. "Yes, Mistress. I'll—"

"Not be paid today."

I felt the blood drain from my face, even as I nodded my understanding.

She shoved a handwritten list at me and a wad of cash, which I

3

gingerly accepted. "I want you back no later than noon. Georgina and Octavia should be up by then, and I want you to supervise their dance lessons again. Octavia especially needs help." Biting my tongue once more, I nodded and turned toward the kitchen door. Before I could make my escape, she stopped me in my tracks with a stern, "Have you forgotten something, Adalyn?"

Schooling my expression, I faced her with a blank look.

She huffed in annoyance. "We've been over this countless times. Every morning, I need to know if you've seen or heard anything new at Dreamscape."

"But the cameras—"

"Can't pick up everything. Details, Adalyn. *Details.* You've been given a once-in-a-lifetime opportunity. We pay you well and expect your full cooperation in return. You should be grateful for this job."

"I *am.*"

"Well, if it's proving to be too much for you, I could always tell Heath that you can't handle it."

"No," I replied, a little too quickly. Her lips twitched into a faint smile. "I can handle it. I really am grateful to have been given the opportunity."

She raised a manicured eyebrow expectantly.

Ignoring my lingering headache, I quickly racked my brain and said, "We have a new prospect. He watched me dance for two hours last night and was definitely interested."

Her brown eyes started glittering with an excitement I'd seen many times before. "And? *Details*, Adalyn. What did he look like?"

"Um, he was tall and dressed in dark colors. His hair was black, but since he wore a mask, I'm not sure if his eyes were blue or green."

"Venturi?"

"Definitely. He carried himself like a noble."

"Did you flirt with him? Let him touch you?"

"I . . . I winked at him."

"Winked? That's *it*?"

"Yes, Mistress."

The excitement faded, replaced with an ire that made me want to shrink back. She stepped into my personal space and roughly grabbed my chin to hiss, "Is that all? Tell me the truth, Adalyn."

A familiar pull tugged at my mind, forcing me to say, "That's all I know. I swear."

She let go of me with a disgruntled huff. "Sloppy work. I'll have to dock your pay again for potentially losing us a client. Now leave before I get any more upset. And don't forget to wear your hat."

She didn't have to tell me twice. Tugging the baseball cap from my back pocket, I jammed it on and slipped out the door before she could find another reason to punish me. The moment I stepped outside, warmth from the early morning sun greeted me like an old friend. I paused to greedily inhale the fresh, salty-sea air.

Inside the old Victorian-style mansion, the curtains were always drawn, the air chilly and drenched in the coppery scent of blood. My room in the basement was even chillier—since my mistress rarely bothered to "waste money on heat," as she put it. As a vampire, the cold Maine winters didn't bother her. The same went for her two grown daughters. I, on the other hand, woke up each morning frozen as a popsicle.

Thankfully, the weather was finally starting to warm up. June was my favorite month here in Glassport, Maine. Everything was blooming, and the tourists were starting to make an appearance. That meant more humans at Dreamscape Lounge, which meant more vampires, which meant more *money*.

This month was also a reminder that another year had passed.

That time was still relevant, despite how frozen it felt. In less than two weeks, I'd be twenty-one years old.

The only downside of being reminded was that I'd been here for six whole years. Six years that I would never get back.

As a sudden chill worked its way up my spine, I shook the thought off and turned toward the carriage house that had since been remodeled into a garage. The structure desperately needed a new paint job, but I didn't dare bring it up to Mistress. I already had a big enough to-do list on my hands. Literally.

I quickly scanned the list before tucking it into my pocket, along with the cash. For three females, they sure drank a lot of blood. My once-a-week trip to Bangor for fresh blood was now becoming *twice* a week. Pulling out my keys, I unlocked the garage door and headed for the freezer stocked full of ice packs. I grabbed several and dropped them into a cooler, then popped the trunk of my car to place it inside.

Well, it technically wasn't *my* car. There was very little that I actually owned, but since I was the only one who could go out during the daytime, Mistress had given me permission to use it almost exclusively. The vehicle was a forest green 1960s Aston Martin, one that had been collecting dust for years before I came along. I'd had to tinker with it for countless hours before finally getting it to run again.

Even though the car wasn't really mine, it still made me feel independent when I drove it. Like I could simply take off and never come back.

If only.

Banishing the impossible thought, I hopped into the driver's seat and started the engine. It rolled over easily, thanks to my constant tinkering, but I grimaced at the high-pitched squeal the garage door made as it lifted. I made a mental note to replace the rollers soon, then carefully eased out of the garage. If either Octavia or Georgina heard me leaving, they'd bombard me with texts, adding to my already long errand list.

Thankfully, no texts came in while I steered away from the seaside property and turned onto the road that would lead me to Bangor. As soon as the coast was clear, I whipped off my hat and tossed it on the passenger seat. Cranking the music, I rolled down my window and basked in the feel of the wind stirring my hair. These precious moments on the road were the only ones I had to myself, and I made the most of them the only way I could. The music effectively drowned out my thoughts, while the wind swept away any lingering traces of the world I lived in.

It was a ruse, though. A temporary band-aid fix.

As much as I yearned to leave this life behind, I couldn't. I was stuck. For how long, I didn't know. If Mistress kept finding reasons to dock my pay, I'd be here *forever*.

Feeling another shiver creep up my spine, I gripped the steering wheel and stomped on the gas. The wind whistled through my ears, whipping long silvery strands of hair across my face.

I wouldn't be stuck here forever, I firmly told myself. I'd take matters into my own hands if I had to. It wouldn't be hard. In fact, it would be easy. Easier than breathing.

With a mere thought, I could make this all go away.

But I wasn't ready to pay that price. Not yet, anyway. I'd been stuck here for six years, but I could last a little while longer.

By the time I arrived in Bangor forty minutes later, my mood had darkened considerably. Knowing that I wouldn't get paid for the next twenty-four hours definitely made it hard to stay positive. Mistress knew just how to pull my strings. Robbing me of the ability to pay off my debt was the number one way to secure my obedience. I wouldn't be slacking off anytime soon.

Grabbing my hat, I made sure it was sitting low on my head before leaving the car. Bangor was a big enough city that I easily blended in without being recognized, but Mistress didn't like to take chances—not when it came to me. I was lucky she even let me drive into the city by myself.

Scurrying from one place to the next, I quickly knocked off the to-do list, saving the blood supply store for last. As soon as I was finished, I'd make good on my promise to Pepper and indulge in a large breakfast. My stomach growled at the thought of finally being filled, and I hurriedly entered the store to collect my order.

As usual, a human manned the shop—at least during the daytime hours. Vampires like my mistress and her daughters couldn't tolerate the sun and, therefore, mostly slept during the day and went out at night. Since they hadn't been born as vampires like Venturi were, life wasn't handed to them on a golden platter. They had to work for a living like the rest of the world, not that Georgina or Octavia had ever worked a day in their lives.

The Faircrofts were *made* vampires, also known as Feltore. They weren't royalty or even nobility, even if they wanted to be. Still, their mansion was as close to Sanctum Isle as it could get while remaining on the mainland. I'd never stepped foot on the island where most of the Venturi lived and probably never would. Only a few Feltore were allowed to mingle with their kingdom's elite, and the Faircrofts had been trying for decades to infiltrate that exclusive circle.

They still were, but not for the same reasons anymore. Everything had changed six years ago when Mistress lost her husband. Unfortunately for me, I was stuck in the middle of their scheming and knew far too much.

But, despite how desperately I wanted to leave this life behind, I understood their motives for getting close to the vampire elite.

Understood and agreed.

Which was why I was able to set aside my own dreams and focus on the task at hand. I'd seen the human male dozens of times before, but when I entered the shop, he greeted me with a blank look. Thralled to forget. Most of the humans who fraternized with vampires were, including the humans who visited Dreamscape. It was the only way to ensure that the vampire's existence remained a secret. Even witches practiced spells of forgetting on humans. The fewer of them who knew about supernaturals, the better.

"You here for an order?" the human asked me, skipping pleasantries.

Nodding, I held out my cooler for him to take. "Order for Margaret Smith." I wasn't allowed to speak the Faircroft name in public, but my presence here had never been questioned before. Blood had become a lot more accessible for the past six years, and vampires were encouraged to visit establishments where blood was freely given. It cut back on attacks that often led to human deaths. Fewer human deaths meant less chances of vampire exposure.

I understood this plan and actually agreed with it, but the word "free" was a joke. Blood was *expensive.*

When the human male returned with my cooler now stocked full of blood bags, I was painfully reminded of that fact.

"That'll be two thousand," he said, holding out his hand.

Shocked, I pushed back my baseball cap to gape at him. "Two thousand? There must be a mistake. It's usually only fifteen hundred."

He shrugged. "Business has been slower than usual, so our prices increased."

"But . . . but I don't have two thousand with me."

He shrugged again and lowered his hand. "You can come back later, or I can just cancel your order."

When he moved as if to return the blood bags, panic fluttered in my chest. "No, that's okay. I have the money. Here." I dug into my pocket and pulled out the extra five hundred he needed. As he took the money and handed over the cooler, my stomach growled miserably. Sighing, I exited the store with my precious cargo. Pepper would be upset that I'd sacrificed my well-being yet again, giving up the only money I had to ensure I stayed in Mistress's good graces, but what other choice did I have?

The only way I was going to pay off this blood debt was with sacrifice. Nothing short of giving up my soul would make Mistress free me of my indenture.

By the time I made it back to Glassport, I could barely keep my eyes open. Witches needed food and sleep the same way humans did, and I was running dangerously low on both, especially after the longer than usual night I'd just had. Mistress rarely kept the fridge stocked with anything but blood, so chances were I wouldn't get anything to eat until after I'd earned some tips this evening.

Tips that weren't mine to keep tonight, I reminded myself. Still, I couldn't perform my duties if I starved to death. I'd keep just enough to buy a sandwich and save a few scraps for Pepper. Just the thought of a sandwich made my mouth begin to water.

Ignoring my aching stomach and burning eyes, I lugged my purchases into the house and began to put them away.

Ada.

At the gentle admonishment in Pepper's tone, guilt flooded me.

I tried. I really tried, Pep. I'll catch a quick nap and eat tonight, though. Promise.

Her resigned sigh whispered through my mind. *You can't keep going like this.*

I know, but I'm tougher than I look, I told her, trying to lighten the mood. When annoyance trickled through our connection, I changed the subject. *Hear anything interesting this morning?*

Nothing of importance, but Thing One and Thing Two have a guest over. He's still here.

At the news, my amusement over her nickname for the Faircroft sisters quickly faded. *Again?* I glanced at my phone and scowled. They should be prepping for their dance lesson right now. If they kept me waiting too long, I wouldn't have time for a nap before heading over to Dreamscape. Tempted to start on my household chores early, I banned the idea and shut the fridge with an extra loud *snap*.

Rules were rules. Straying from my predetermined schedule wasn't an option unless I wanted to be punished again.

My mood took a nosedive, and I marched from the kitchen before I could check myself. Dimly, I heard Pepper warning me to stop, but I was too annoyed. Too tired. Too *hungry*.

Those two needed a wakeup call, and I was the only one who would do it. Their *mother* certainly wouldn't. She allowed them their every whim, spoiling her daughters every chance she got. And when they inevitably screwed up, *I* took the blame for it.

Well, not today. Today, I needed to follow the rules, which meant *they* needed to follow the rules. Time for some tough love.

Not bothering to be quiet, I stomped up the stairs to the second floor and stormed toward Octavia's room. I whipped open the door without knocking, then squinted through the darkness to find the space empty. Turning on my heel, I crossed the hall to Georgina's room, once again jerking the door open without a knock.

The moment I did, I desperately wished that I hadn't.

Several candles had been lit around the room, illuminating the luxurious space enough to reveal three forms tangled together on the massive four-poster bed. A male was in the middle, flat on his back and stark naked. The sisters were draped on either side of him, both feeding from his neck and equally naked. Octavia was feverishly pumping his dick, and before I could look away, he orgasmed with a groan, spilling a stream of cum onto his stomach.

The second he was finished, Georgina removed her fangs from his neck and straddled him. Before his shaft could soften, she sank on top of it, impaling herself balls deep. As she began to ride him, she crooned, "Have you come to watch, troll?"

I hastily stepped back, but before I could close the door, her voice cracked like a whip through the air.

"*Stay.*"

I started to shut the door anyway. Her golden curls tumbled forward as she looked over her shoulder and met my gaze.

Immediately, I felt the *pull* as she opened her mouth and ordered, "Come inside and close the door."

Against my wishes, my feet crossed over the threshold, my hands betraying me as they shut the door. Satisfied, Georgina resumed her ride, bouncing up and down with abandon as her younger sister continued to feed from the male's neck. After a minute, she ordered him to fondle her breasts, and he readily complied. Feeling left out, Octavia grabbed one of his hands and placed it between her legs. As he began to rub her clit, she moaned into his neck and roughly grabbed his hair.

Agonizing minutes later, all three of them were panting heavily, on the verge of release. Like a domino effect, they reached orgasm one after the other, starting with Georgina. She dramatically threw her head back and screamed, digging her nails into the man's chest. Scratch that. *Claws.* As dark blood pooled on his brown chest, he loudly groaned out another release. Octavia followed suit, releasing his neck with a shuddering gasp as she came against his fingers.

I stood quietly, waiting for them to finish. Georgina languidly moved off the male, only to bend over and lap up the blood on his chest. My stomach lurched, but I forced myself to watch anyway, my expression carefully neutral.

This was punishment for daring to think my opinion meant anything in this household. It was my own stupid fault for coming up here.

This wasn't the first time the sisters made me watch them having sex. They were attached at the hip and shared everything, including men. The first time I'd been exposed to their kinky love life, I'd only been fifteen years old. I'd cried then, but I'd never cried since. The less I reacted, the less ammunition they had.

Thankfully, they never forced me to join them. Even now, when I looked the same age as them, I knew they wouldn't cross that line.

They despised me too much, especially Georgina.

She finally looked over at me with a self-satisfied smirk and purred, "Enjoy the show? I know how much you love watching."

Knowing I wouldn't reply, she made a show of stretching like a cat before grabbing a pink satin robe and slipping from the bed. The entire room looked like a tornado had swept through it. Clothing, shoes, and other accessories littered the floor, even though I'd just cleaned it yesterday.

As she sashayed toward me, slowly pulling on her robe, she said, "Octavia, take care of our guest."

Octavia lifted her head with a pout, reaching up to wrap a strawberry-blonde curl around her finger. "But I always do it. Why can't you?"

"Because I need to take care of our *other* guest."

At the evil glint in her dark brown eyes, dread shivered up my spine.

Octavia huffed but did what she was told, forcing the man to look at her as she thralled him to forget certain aspects of their coupling. "You were never bitten . . ." she started, pricking her finger with a sharp black claw so she could smear blood over the bite marks on his neck. The puncture holes immediately began to seal shut.

"You're late for your dance lesson," I told Georgina, hoping to distract her. No such luck.

"I don't remember hearing about a dance lesson today." She lifted a hand and slowly licked the blood from her claws. "Do you, Tavia?"

"Nope," her sister chirped.

"Sounds like you made a mistake, troll. I think a punishment is in order." Pausing to examine her claws, she let them recede back into her skin before tapping her chin in thought. "What do you think her punishment should be for barging in on us, Tavia?"

Octavia let go of the man to clap her hands with glee. "I know, I know! Make her dance *naked!*"

I stiffened.

Georgina rolled her eyes. "So juvenile."

I started to relax but should have known better.

"Well, troll? You heard her. Strip and start dancing."

A groan pushed at my throat, but I swallowed it. As far as punishments went, this one was rather tame. And by dancing for them, I was technically still "helping" them with their lesson. It would be humiliating, but my days of feeling self conscious were long gone.

Before she could force my cooperation with thrall, I started to undress. Georgina looked on with amusement, watching until I was completely nude before her. "When's the last time you ate, troll?" she sneered, reaching out to poke one of my ribs. A sudden violent urge to grab her finger and break it ripped through me, but I balled my hands into fists and kept still.

At my stubborn silence, she scowled, looking like a younger version of her mother.

"Well? We're waiting. Dance, already." She flicked her fingers at me impatiently and stepped toward a chaise lounge to drape herself across it.

"How long should I dance for?"

I should have known better than to ask.

"Until I tell you to stop." That evil glint returned.

Gritting my teeth, I started to dance. Slowly at first, then faster when Georgina demanded it. I danced and danced, losing myself to the movements, to the rhythm until the room and its occupants melted away. Music wasn't necessary. I created my own, my body responding to each silent note.

At some point, their male companion left, but I kept on dancing. My feet flew over the hardwood floor as I leapt and jumped and twirled. My hair fanned out in shimmering strands, catching the flickering light of the candles.

I danced for hours. Danced until my feet ached and my legs turned to jelly. The room suddenly spun, faster and faster until I lost my balance and crashed to the floor. Stifling a yelp of pain, I struggled to rise, only to fall again.

After the third attempt, Georgina sighed and droned, "I'm bored of this. Dance lesson is over."

I barely heard her, my headache like a deafening drum in my ears. Somehow, I managed to pick myself up, collect my clothes, and leave the bedroom. How I got from the second floor to my room in the basement, I didn't know. All I remembered was falling onto my bed right before darkness swallowed me whole.

CHAPTER 2

ADALYN

His eyes were like green amethysts.

Pale and piercing.

They seemed to look directly into my soul.

Time froze, and for once, I didn't mind.

The longer he looked at me, the more I wanted him to.

I could bask in his undivided attention forever.

He suddenly reached up to remove his mask, and I held my breath in anticipation.

I wanted to see him. Needed to. He somehow felt familiar to me, like I'd seen him before.

He pulled on the black strings, undoing his mask.

My heart started to pound.

The mask lowered, and I caught the first glimpse of his face.

My heart pounded faster. Faster and faster.

Only a second more, and I would know who he was.

The mask lowered another inch . . .

Then abruptly vanished in a swirl of black smoke.

And so did he.

I awoke with a yelp, grabbing my index finger as it painfully throbbed like a second heartbeat.

I'm sorry, Ada. I didn't know what else to do.

"Pepper?" I mumbled with a groan, peeling my eyes open to check on my finger. "Did you just *bite* me?"

Shh, keep your voice down. The brown mouse rubbed her soft head against the injured finger as if to make it all better. *You've been out for hours. I had to reach you somehow.*

Why? Is it morning already? I spoke mind-to-mind, yawning so wide that my jaw cracked.

No, Ada. That's just it. You haven't finished the day yet.

My mouth shut with a sharp *click*. Oh no. I scrambled upright as fast as I could, earning me a perturbed squeak from Pepper.

"What time is it?" I reached into my pocket for my phone but found bare skin instead. What the—? Why was I *naked?* My head started to pound again as I racked my brain, finally remembering my little *dance* in Georgina's room. I must have passed out from pure exhaustion. Mistress was going to *kill* me.

No, she won't, Pepper reassured, picking up on my frantic thought. *She needs you too much.*

"*Needs* me?" Snorting, I dragged myself out of bed and began to dress. *My dad killed her husband. The only reason why I'm still alive is because it amuses her to have a warlock elder's daughter as her personal servant.*

Taking care of this house and its occupants isn't the only thing you do, Adalyn.

"Don't remind me," I muttered, grabbing my phone to tap on the screen. As the time glared back at me almost accusingly, I cursed and hurried my movements.

All I'm saying is that your abilities make you important. You're more than an indentured servant, and once you've paid off your father's blood debt to the Faircrofts, you have a bright future ahead of you.

If I survive that long, I cryptically replied.

Ada, she softly admonished. I paused to eye her on my bed. Even without a light on, I could pick out her tiny round body. That's how used to living in the darkness I was.

Sighing, I said, *You were right earlier, Pep. I'm mortal. That means I don't belong in this world. If I stay too much longer, I think it's going to kill me.*

She released a mournful squeak. *Then let me come with you tonight.*

I looked down to jab my feet into my shoes. *You know it's too dangerous. I can't risk your life.*

I'm immortal, Adalyn. Celestial spirit, remember?

But your body *isn't*, I inwardly snapped, pausing to glare at her. *You can still be injured or killed in this form. If you rejoined the celestial plane, I would truly be all alone, and I wouldn't survive that. I wouldn't want to.*

Oh, Ada.

I have to go, I quickly said and moved for the stairs before my emotions got the best of me. *I'll bring you back some food from the club. You have my word.*

You don't need to worry about me, Adalyn.

Pausing one last time, I looked over my shoulder at her. *Of course I do. You're the only thing I care about in this messed-up world. It's just you and me against those greedy bloodsuckers. Don't forget that.*

Pepper huffed a semi-amused squeak. *Oh, I won't. Be careful out there.*

My lips curved into a saucy smile. *Always am.*

Feeling a little less tired but still hungry as a bear, I hurried upstairs to start my afternoon chores. With the approaching sunset, the Faircrofts would be heading out soon. If I didn't have my chores done before then, Mistress would become suspicious and demand an explanation. Saying that her daughters made me dance naked until I passed out wouldn't end in my favor. She'd only see my weakness, not her daughters' poor behavior.

Spurred on by the unfairness of it all and my desperate need for food, I tackled my chores in record time. I was just finishing up a load of laundry when Mistress called out, "We're leaving, Adalyn. Make sure you're at the club promptly at nine."

"Yes, Mistress," I called back.

Hearing the front door slam shut, I turned to leave the laundry room with a basket of clean linens. A tall form in the doorway brought me up short, startling me so badly that I dropped the basket. The clean linens tumbled out and hit the floor. I quickly wiped the dismay from my face as Mistress looked down her nose at me and spoke in low tones. "And I expect you to secure us at least one new client tonight. There will be consequences if you don't."

"Yes, Mistress," I replied and lowered my chin in submission.

She turned to leave, tossing her golden curls over her shoulder as she said in parting, "Oh, and rewash those linens before you leave. Don't be late, Adalyn."

Biting my tongue, I waited for the front door to shut before gathering the linens from the floor and shoving them into the washing machine once more. Could this day get any worse? I was used to dealing with her impossible demands, but securing clients had never been a stipulation of my job.

As the only witch working at Dreamscape Lounge, my job was to be mysterious and alluring, to dance until my audience was wholly captivated. Most of our clientele were filthy rich and could go anywhere for their nightly entertainment, but many of them kept coming back to Dreamscape.

I did that. I kept them coming back. They wanted to see the witch who dared to dance for vampires.

That's how it had all started anyway. Dancing for hungry, horny predators night after night. Giving up my self respect and pride, piece by piece.

But that was child's play now. My other job—my *secret* one—demanded so much more from me. I'd accepted the job out of desperation, and the only thing I'd had to give up was the last of my innocence.

A small price to pay for my freedom. At least, that's what I kept telling myself.

But Mistress was never satisfied, always finding new reasons to extend my blood debt. Not only did I have to *entertain* the male vampires who'd become my clients, but now I was supposed to *secure* them?

"Why don't I lasso the moon for you while I'm at it?" I grumbled, allowing myself a moment of self pity. But only for a moment. I didn't have time to wallow, not if I wanted to survive this world.

An hour later, I hurriedly put away the clean linens still warm from the dryer and dashed out the kitchen door. I was cutting it close, but I would make it to Dreamscape on time. The club was thirty minutes away, situated on the outskirts of Bangor. It used to be a hotel, but three years ago, the building had been purchased by Mistress Faircroft and her new business partner, Heath Clancy.

Their main goal had been to set apart their club from the rest, allowing only certain humans and vampires entrance. Anonymity was key, hence the required masks. IDs weren't needed, only money. *Lots* of it. Enough that only the extremely wealthy could afford the place. In no time, the exclusive club had gained a reputation of being an "exotic" feeding den for the vampire elite.

Not only were the humans carefully culled to suit their rich tastes, but they could feast their eyes upon me. These days, nothing said *exotic* like a witch working in a vampire-owned nightclub.

Pulling around back, I parked and quickly sent Mistress an obligatory text that I'd arrived. I had my own keycard and let myself in through one of the back doors, taking the stairs as usual so I wouldn't run into any of our clientele. The club opened at nine, but I didn't make an appearance until ten. Which gave me enough time to get ready, being sure to closely follow my mistress's meticulous regimen.

She expected *perfection*. I was to look enticingly forbidden, the low-hanging fruit that begged to be plucked and consumed. But the clientele weren't allowed to *touch*. At least while I was dancing.

My stomach was painfully cramping by the time I reached my room on the third floor. Only a couple hours more of this torture, and I could finally *eat*. At least I wasn't scheduled for aerial dancing tonight. That took the most energy out of me, even though it was my favorite form of dance.

It always felt good to be so high above the creatures bent on destroying me.

Tossing my phone and keys onto the glass table just inside the door, I shucked off my clothes on the way to the bathroom. I'd been looking forward to this *all* day. After dealing with the Faircrofts for the past several hours, this slight reprieve was a little slice of heaven.

On my way over to the elegant clawfoot tub, I grabbed a toothbrush and got to work making myself "presentable." Mistress didn't care what I looked like during the daytime. In fact, the scruffier I looked, the better. Less chance of being recognized that way. But at night, not even a single hair out of place was acceptable.

I didn't mind this part of my day, though. Pampering myself. Scrubbing my skin so raw that I could almost feel *clean* again.

When the tub was adequately filled, I turned off the water and slipped inside. The temperature was just below scalding, exactly how I liked it. Despite the heat, I barely flinched. Submerging myself in hot water felt like I was melting the *taint* off my body.

If only it could melt away the taint on the inside.

Nudging the impossible thought aside, I rested against the tub and breathed in the lavender-scented steam. I let my eyes close, but falling asleep wasn't an option. After a moment, I forced myself into motion again, blindly reaching for my loofa on the cart beside the tub.

When I found a large hand instead, I yanked my eyes open with a startled squeak. A hulking vampire grinned back, snatching up my hand before I could pull it back.

"Good evening, Star. You're looking as beautiful as ever." The sandy-haired brute dipped his head and kissed my knuckles.

"Heath," I gasped out, shocked to find him kneeling beside my tub. "What are you doing here?"

"This is my club, Star," he replied, as if that was all the explanation I needed.

As he continued to run his lips over my knuckles, I tried to tug my hand back. His grip tightened.

"I need . . . I need to get ready." Silently cursing my stutter, I struggled to slow my racing pulse. Vampires loved nothing more than frightened prey.

"I can help you. My hands might be big, but I've been told they can be quite gentle."

At the insinuation, my blood ran cold.

"I think you should leave, Heath," I said before I could stop myself.

He tensed, and so did I. This was bad. This was *really* bad. I was an employee. A *servant*. One wrong move in this bloodthirsty world could cost me my life, and rejecting the club's owner was definitely one of them.

Not knowing what to do, I held still, barely daring to breathe.

After a moment, he slowly raised his head to look at me. He wasn't grinning anymore, but he didn't look angry either. More like amused that the little witch had attempted to defend herself. His cloudy gray eyes trailed over my face, then lower, boldly peering into the water to take in my naked body. I didn't move a muscle, not even to cover myself. Doing so would only make me look more vulnerable.

Finally, he met my gaze again and said, "Don't forget, Star. While you work under this roof, you're half mine. If I wanted to, I could order you into my bed with a few simple words. I'd have every right." He lifted his other hand and touched my cheek. I stopped breathing, willing myself not to pull away. To not so much as flinch. "It's no secret that I crave you. Watching you dance night after night for the past three years has been torture. But if I had even *one* taste, I know that I wouldn't be able to stop. I would take everything and leave nothing for the others, and that's just bad business."

At his confession, I inwardly recoiled. My body held perfectly still, but he must have seen the disgust in my eyes. Faster than I could blink, he grabbed my head and shoved me beneath the water. I screamed, lashing out with my arms and feet, but he was too strong. As the oxygen raced from my lungs, I grew desperate and willed magic to my fingertips. It readily flowed through my veins, coming to my aid. But before it could blast from me, it stopped.

Just stopped.

I was no longer in control of it. The magic didn't obey me. It obeyed *them*.

When I stopped flailing, on the verge of passing out, Heath finally released my head.

I popped back up, gasping and coughing as I struggled to refill my lungs. He pushed the wet hair off my face, and I flinched this time, but he didn't seem to notice. His grin was back, softer than before. Relaxed.

Content. He was *content*.

Apparently, he got off on drowning girls half to death.

"Shhh, it's okay, Star," he said in soothing tones, letting his fingers roam over my face, then lower. I stiffened all over, but knew better than to reject him a second time. Thankfully, he stopped at my neck, pausing to press his thumb over my racing pulse. "Mmm, I bet you taste exquisite right now."

My heart stopped as his fingers curled around my neck and slowly drew me toward him. I squeezed my eyes shut, bracing for what was to come.

Don't be afraid, don't be afraid, I ordered myself, waiting for the inevitable.

Warmth hit my throat as his breath fanned over my skin. He inhaled deeply, drawing my scent into his lungs. The hissing sound he emitted was almost my undoing. I balled my hands into fists, refusing to push him away.

I would survive this. I had no choice.

As his lips touched my skin, I couldn't suppress a tiny shiver of revulsion. At the same time, a sliver of anticipation cut through it. I violently shoved the feeling aside, hating it. Hating myself for even *feeling* it.

Sick. You're sick, I inwardly screamed at myself, feeling the angry burn of tears prick my eyes.

At the last second, Heath pulled back and gruffly whispered, "May that serve as a reminder, Star. I could drain you in seconds, and you wouldn't be able to do a single thing about it. Whatever you feel for vampires doesn't matter. The sooner you accept this life, the easier it'll be. And, who knows?" He paused to press his mouth to my throat, eliciting a small gasp from me. His lips wickedly curved against my flesh as he finished, "Maybe you'll even enjoy it."

With that, he let go of me and left as silently as he'd arrived.

CHAPTER 3

EVERETT

I was at the same booth as last night, tucked in a dark corner far from the heated press of bodies on the dance floor.

Gaining entrance had been the same. A black mask hid my identity, and a wad of cash allowed me inside with no questions asked. Anytime someone got too close, I warned them away with a dark look. No one dared bother me, but when the clock struck ten, anticipation flooded my veins.

This was the moment I'd been waiting for.

I didn't know why I was so interested in seeing her again. I'd been with countless beautiful women over the past two centuries, human and vampire alike. A gorgeous face no longer affected me—or so I thought, until last night. Her beauty wasn't the only thing that interested me, though. There was something about her. Something almost . . . familiar.

I hadn't scented her. Hadn't talked to her. Didn't know if she was human or vampire. I hadn't even seen the entirety of her face, and yet I *knew* her somehow.

The feeling had plagued me all day, so persistently that I'd had no choice but to return. I had to know who she was. Once I did, I could get her out of my system and leave this place behind. My brother wasn't the only one who'd steered clear of feeding dens for the past century. Being here chafed me in the worst of ways. The memories it dredged up were far from pleasant.

Still, I caught myself sitting straighter as I searched the place for the ethereal dancer adorned in silver. The one they called "Star." A fitting name, considering that she'd hung suspended in the air like one, dazzling everyone who looked upon her.

When I didn't spot her right away, I felt a strange sense of disappointment. Then frustration. Coming back here had been a waste. Time to leave before I made an even bigger fool of myself. I'd allowed my cock to dictate my actions, which wasn't like me. Not anymore. One girl had no business affecting me this way, especially when I was supposed to be on the hunt for more important things.

This place seemed harmless, though, as far as nightclubs went. I'd have to take my hunt elsewhere.

Just like last night, I rose from my seat, determined to leave this place and never come back. But as I did, the music stopped and a beam of light swung onto the dance floor. Not high above, but smack in the middle of the gyrating throng. My keen gaze shot to the crowd, racing over each face. None of them were her.

The crowd suddenly parted, creating a circle around an object rising from the floor. From *beneath* the floor. A hidden stage. And standing on the stage, grasping a silver pole, was Star.

At the sight of her, cheers and whistles rippled through the crowd. As the stage locked into place, leaving her several feet above the crowd, everyone froze again. Froze and waited in anticipation. She was wearing a similar outfit to last night, silver and sparkly. But it was somehow even more revealing, low in the front and barely there in the back, showing off her supple backside. Her silvery hair was down again, slightly stirring in an unseen wind.

As the crowd waited with bated breath, she slowly pivoted on her shiny silver stilettos, twirling around the pole until she was facing me. When she did, it was like a magnet drew her gaze directly to mine. I was still tucked in the shadows, but she found me anyway. As her eyes locked onto mine, the room and everyone in it disappeared. Despite my earlier pep talk to myself, I was ensnared once more, moving toward her before I could think better of it.

Come to me, her eyes seemed to beckon, filling with flirtatious amusement when I readily obeyed.

Before I knew it, I was at the stage, looking up at her like all the rest of the besotted idiots trapped by her beauty. Pathetic. *I* was pathetic. Apparently, I still possessed a healthy lust for flesh. There was no mistaking how much I wanted to get this girl alone and explore all she had to offer.

She was a distraction, one I shouldn't be indulging in right now, but I couldn't look away. Satisfied that she'd lured me in, she broke eye contact and swung around the pole again. When she lifted both legs and pressed her core to the metal like she would a lover, the crowd went wild. Money fluttered through the air and hit the stage. Every time she rubbed against the pole, the money came down harder.

Several of the people around me paired up and began to grind against each other, turned on by the erotic dancing. A female nearby tried to touch me through my pants, but I blocked her without taking my eyes off Star. I was aroused like the rest of them, but I had no interest in the people around me.

The only one I wanted was the silver-haired girl above me.

As if pleased by my undivided attention, Star paused to crook a finger at me. My pants tightened even more, and like an obedient dog, I placed my hands on the stage and leaned toward her. Smirking, she crouched with her legs spread wide. The crowd went wild again. Releasing the pole, she began to crawl toward me on all fours. The sight nearly made me come. Suppressing a groan, I watched her every move, thrilled to have her eyes solely on me.

When she came within touching range, I didn't reach for her like last time. I didn't want her to pull away again. Didn't want her to disappear. Holding perfectly still, I waited for her to come to me, trying to catch even the faintest whiff of her scent. But the air was too saturated with arousal and sweat.

Inches away from me now, she reached into her top and pulled out what looked like a keycard. In a blink, she slipped it into the pocket of my shirt. So swiftly that I didn't even feel it. Another blink, and she was back at the pole.

Seconds later, the spotlight on her winked out. Fog billowed into the air, and just like last time, she disappeared. Instead of searching for her, though, I slipped away and pulled out the keycard she'd given me.

306.

A room number.

My blood heated, filling me with even more heady arousal. She wanted a private audience with me.

Without a moment's hesitation, I veered toward the elevators. The hallway was dark, but I easily spotted the two male vampires standing guard. When I presented the keycard to them, the bulkier of the two held out his hand.

"Ten thousand upfront."

I paid him without question, and the pair wordlessly stepped aside. I kept my guard up, though, making sure to keep my face downcast as I entered the elevator.

Most vampire-owned nightclubs didn't have interior cameras—a protective measure in case the human authorities came sniffing around. But I'd already spotted a few in this place, so carefully hidden that I'd almost missed them. If one of them caught my face, my cover would be blown. Not that I minded anymore. After tonight, I had no intention of ever coming back.

I would allow myself one night of sinful indulgence. One night of letting lustful instinct call all the shots. Once I filled myself up on the silver seductress, I could move on and fulfill the task my father had set before me.

As the elevator opened onto the third floor, I cautiously stepped out. The hallway was clear, but I didn't lower my guard. Even a rendezvous such as this could be a trap. Other clubs offered private rooms, but experience had taught me to always expect ulterior motives. Not everyone who frequented feeding dens came for blood and sex.

With that in mind, I proceeded down the hallway slowly, keeping an eye out for possible threats. All was silent. I couldn't even hear the pulsing music from down below. They must have soundproofed the walls for optimal privacy, a fact that further stirred the blood in my groin.

I was going to make her scream tonight. Multiple times. Knowing that only I would hear it filled me with satisfaction.

When I found room 306, no one stood outside the door. I listened a moment longer, then stepped forward to knock.

Seconds later, a feminine voice from inside called, "Come in."

It was her. I was sure of it.

Grasping the handle, I opened the door. My senses were immediately bombarded by lavender and incense. Candles decorated the room, intimately lighting the space. As I entered the room, my gaze took in a kitchen and small living room. The decor was stylishly done in whites, silvers, and blacks, but my interest was only on one thing. I stepped inside and closed the door, boldly moving toward the bedroom. The door was open, and I wasted no time seeking out the female inside. As I darkened the doorway, I stopped and took in the view that greeted me.

She was sensually resting on the king-sized bed, propped up by a mound of pillows and wearing nothing but a mask and satin silver robe. The robe was open, draped over her in a way that revealed teasing hints of flesh. The luscious curve of a breast. A flat expanse of stomach. A shapely leg from heel to thigh.

At the sight of me gracing her doorway, that smirk of hers slowly made an appearance. My pants tightened to the point of pain. As if all too aware of the torture she was inflicting upon me, her smirk widened.

"Welcome," she said in sultry tones, eyeing me for a moment before straightening from her relaxed position. The move shifted her robe, allowing me a full view of one of her breasts. My mouth watered as I took in her hard nipple, already anticipating how it would taste. "Come," she continued, crooking a finger at me once more. "I won't bite."

At her teasing tone, my gaze went to her face again. I still assumed she was human, but the heady incense made it hard for me to scent her. I took a step forward, then another, wanting to know for sure. How I handled her tonight would depend on what she was. If she was human, I would have to be careful not to break her. But if she was a vampire, I could be rougher, allowing myself to indulge in her even more.

I stopped at the foot of the bed and inhaled, drawing in a plethora of smells. Lust and blood were the predominant scents, but I also caught hints of male. Several of them. I wasn't the first she'd lured up here.

Suddenly annoyed, I cut to the chase. "Are you human?"

She shook her head and pushed to her knees, allowing me an

unobstructed view of her pussy. I swallowed a groan, beyond excited that I wouldn't have to be careful with her. I would take her several times. *Hard.* That should help purge her from my system.

"Guess again," she said, slowly walking on her knees toward me. The robe opened even more, revealing both her breasts. The air stuttered from my lungs, and I could barely focus on anything else. She was a masterpiece, her body sculpted to perfection. I didn't know such perfection could exist. Of course it made sense that she would be a vampire. A body like that could only be immortal.

Still, I opened my mouth and uttered the word, needing to know for sure before I ripped that robe off her and consumed that gorgeous flesh with abandon. "Vampire?"

Her full red lips tilted into a roguish grin. She finished crossing the mattress and stood on her knees before me, her eyes almost level with mine. "Guess . . ." she whispered, tilting her face up to breathe the word in my ear. At the same time, she reached down and grabbed my throbbing cock, making me see stars. "Again."

With her this close, touching me this way, I could barely breathe, let alone think. Her words didn't register. All I could concentrate on was her hand slowly rubbing my dick and her breasts pushing up against me. My world narrowed to her, on the pleasure flooding my veins. When she used her other hand to undo my pants, I held still, enjoying her attention. I'd allow her a few minutes of control, then I'd take over.

As she freed my painfully hard erection and firmly gripped it, I let my eyes roll shut. She was skilled, no doubt about it. She'd probably handled many dicks, maybe multiple times a night. I felt a flash of annoyance again, but when she began to pump my shaft, thoughts of her touching other males fled my mind.

Allowing a small groan to slip free, I basked in the euphoria, knowing that I wouldn't last long. What she was doing felt *that* good. I hadn't felt this good in ages. Her hands were pure bliss, stroking my hardened length and swollen tip in tandem. As my pleasure built, so did my desire for her. I reached up to cup one of her breasts, fitting my other hand against her lower spine. At the move, I felt her stiffen. Confused, I let go of her breast and opened my eyes.

"Bite me," she breathlessly said, pumping me faster. Despite how close I was to orgasming, I hesitated, suddenly unsure.

Something was wrong.

"Bite me," she repeated, almost begging me now. She tilted her head back to expose her throat. My gaze dropped to the vulnerable column, and a new need coursed through me. A stronger one. An all-consuming one. One that I could no longer deny. I felt my fangs descend. On the verge of coming, I pushed aside my lingering doubts and gripped the nape of her neck, angling my head so I could puncture her throat.

Lust and hunger rode me hard. I opened my mouth and sank my fangs deeply into her flesh. She jerked against me, but I quickly infused the bite with my venom, easing the bite's pain. The stiffness in her body melted away, and she sighed in pleasure. Pleased with her reaction, I pressed my mouth to her skin and began to suck. Wanting to experience that delectable first taste of her blood, I held off my orgasm for a moment longer. Only a moment more, and my body could experience the full effect of what she had to offer.

I pulled her closer to me, prepared to thrust inside her the second I finished orgasming. She stroked me faster, knowing that I was teetering on the edge of release. I sucked her harder, drawing in a mouthful of her blood.

The instant the blood touched my tongue, I shoved her away with a hiss. She hit the mattress with a startled cry. Blood dripped from my mouth and onto the white duvet.

Spitting out the remainder of it, I glared down at her and snarled, "*Witch.*"

She stared at me with wide eyes, twin lines of blood dribbling down her neck. Pressing a hand to the puncture wounds, she blinked a few times before replying, "I thought you knew that."

"Of course I didn't." Ignoring the throbbing ache between my legs from not being able to finish, I quickly zipped up my pants. "What kind of sick joke is this anyway? Vampires don't come here to feed on *witches.*"

At the sneer in my voice, the confusion on her face vanished. She gripped her robe and tightly wrapped it around her body. "On the contrary. Vampires come here every night to feed on me."

I scoffed. "That's disgusting."

Her expression wiped clean of all emotion. "No more disgusting than you coming up here tonight."

I blinked, caught off guard by her candor. "You're right. It's disgusting that I so easily fell under your seductive spell. That won't be happening again. I'm done here."

As I turned to leave, she scrambled upright on the bed. "Wait."

I kept going, storming from the room. Now that my dick was no longer in charge, I could clearly detect the magic permeating the air like a bad omen. The metallic scent bit at my nostrils, and I flared them in frustration. How could I have so completely missed it earlier?

"*Wait.* You have pale green eyes. Like amethysts. I saw you in a—"

"You saw *nothing,*" I growled, jerking around to scowl at her. I expected her to cower, but she barely even flinched at my brusque tone. "I was never here, got it?"

She pursed her lips, then smoothed them into a smirk devoid of humor. "Sure. That's what the masks are for, right? Total anonymity. What you do here stays here."

At the slight judgment in her tone, I curled my own lips into a humorless smile. "And I'm assuming a witch masquerading as a *blood whore* would most definitely want to hide her identity. I bet your coven would cast you out if they knew. The shame of it would be too humiliating."

Her smirk faded.

Without waiting for a reply, I whirled and left her behind, hoping to never see her again. Tonight had been a terrible mistake. No one needed to know how epically I'd screwed up. If only I could wipe the memory of it from my brain. This night might have been a total disaster, but I doubted I'd be forgetting it anytime soon.

By the time I made it back home two hours later, I'd called myself every foul name I could think of. I felt violated in a way I'd never felt before. The memory of her hands on me. The lingering taste of her blood in my mouth. It burned me from the inside out.

Stalking up the steep flight of stairs to the front entrance, I barely acknowledged the guards before breezing past. No one greeted me when I barged inside, which was a good thing. My dark mood made me want to lash out at anyone who dared get too close.

With a burst of supernatural speed, I was on the fifth floor in seconds. I passed by my father's and brother's rooms without pause, not wanting them to see how upset I was. Besides, they were probably fast asleep beside their *wives*, happy as clams. No need to disrupt their blissful little bubbles with my foul attitude. It was better that I spend the rest of the night alone, if only to lick my wounds in peace.

But, as I eased open my bedroom door, I sensed right away that someone was on the other side. Sighing, I slipped inside and shut the door. Two heartbeats quickened at my arrival, and I turned to see a pair of housemaids in my massive bed.

"Your Majesty," they said in unison, both completely nude.

Sighing again, I muttered, "Let me guess. The king sent you?"

They bobbed their heads. "Yes, my prince."

I swept my gaze over them, but the earlier fire in my veins was gone. Looking at their supple bodies did nothing for me. It was like that witch had sucked all the life out of me.

Frustrated at myself all over again, I began to undress. Both human females eagerly watched. Their anticipation was usually enough to get me going, but not this time. I almost stopped and ordered them to leave, which only fueled my ire.

I wasn't going to let that *witch* mess with my head any longer. She meant nothing to me, and the brief moment we'd shared also meant nothing. I'd lusted after her. *Desired* her. But I hadn't known what she was. If I'd known, I never would have let her touch me. Never would have sunk my fangs into her soft flesh and tasted her blood.

At the memory, heat stirred in my blood once more.

Angry at my body's betrayal, I tore the last of my clothes off and joined the ladies in bed. They giggled at my arrival and shifted so that I could lay between them. As soon as I did, they began to kiss and touch me from the neck down, their interest mainly on my dick. The redhead leaned down and took me into her mouth, moaning breathlessly. Normally, I'd be hard and ready for her eager lips, but my body suddenly had no interest in her. She stroked and sucked on me, but I barely felt it.

The other female offered her throat to me. Out of desperation, I dragged her close and sank my fangs into her neck, pulling deeply. Her sweet blood filled my mouth, and I almost gagged. Star's didn't taste anything like this. Star's blood was rich, exploding with exotic flavors I'd never tasted before. Flavors I was suddenly craving.

My anger grew. To distract myself, I drank fiercely, swallowing mouthful after mouthful. All the while, the redhead continued to pleasure me. Closing my eyes, an unwanted image of *her* flitted through my mind. The thought of her sucking my cock immediately filled me with euphoria. My cock hardened and the redhead moaned, renewing her efforts. Holding onto that twisted image, I sought out my release, hating myself the entire time.

This was torture. Mindblowing, earthshattering torture. The longer I thought about Star in my bed instead of these two women, the more alive I felt. I hated it. Hated and craved it.

Giving into the moment of pure insanity, I rode the high that her imagined presence brought. Just like that, I was on the edge of release. Picturing that secretive little smirk of hers, a smirk meant only for me, my orgasm barrelled through me. With a groan, I swallowed another mouthful of blood and pulled out my fangs, falling back on the bed in pure bliss.

Seconds later, the bliss vanished as the redhead straddled my hips and tried to impale herself on my cock.

"Not tonight," I told her, ignoring her disappointed expression as I lifted her off me and stood from the bed. "I'm taking a shower. Return to your rooms, ladies. I won't need your services for the rest of the night."

Or ever, my mind whispered.

Scowling, I headed for my bathroom, in desperate need of removing this night from my body. I doubted nothing short of stripping the skin from my flesh could erase *her*, though.

Even then, I was pretty sure the silver-haired witch had somehow managed to imprint herself on me.

Deep enough that no amount of scrubbing would cleanse her from my system.

CHAPTER 4

ADALYN

The door banged open, and I jumped, dropping my sandwich.

As Heath stormed in, followed by Mistress, my stomach immediately soured. Before I could get up from the table, Mistress was in my face, shouting, "What did you do, you stupid girl?"

"I—"

My head violently flew back as she backhanded me across the face.

"Careful," I heard Heath caution, the word muffled as I nearly lost consciousness. "She'll be useless to us with a broken neck."

"She already *is* useless," Mistress hissed, roughly grabbing my chin to force my eyes back to hers. "Were you even able to get his name before he left?"

Blood dribbled down my cheek from where she'd struck me. One of her rings must have broken the skin. Despite the painful throbbing in my cheekbone, I struggled to focus, knowing how precarious my position was right now.

I'd epically failed to secure the new client, something that had never happened to me before. Once they tasted my blood, they were like putty in my hands. None of them had *ever* pulled away in disgust. My blood was like crack to vampires.

How *he* had managed to resist the pull, I had no idea. I'd done everything right. Seduced him, lured him in, made his darkest desires come true. I knew he'd enjoyed my touch and seeing me naked. Knew he'd wanted to consume me.

So how had everything gone so horribly wrong?

Half an hour later, I could still hear his condemning words.

Blood whore.

True, that's what I was. But he'd said the words with such contempt and disgust, like I was the most vile creature he'd ever met.

Clearing my suddenly tight throat, I replied to Mistress, "I'm sorry, but he didn't swallow my blood. I wasn't able to form a connection."

She bared her teeth at me in displeasure. "Heath told me the client spit it out. Why would he do such a thing?"

"I-I don't . . . He didn't realize I was a witch. I don't think he likes witches."

Mistress barked a humorless laugh. "It shouldn't matter if he hates witches. Most vampires do. They come to you because it's taboo and *exciting*. A witch freely offering her body and blood to vampires is unheard of. They can't resist having a taste of the forbidden."

"I know, but—"

"No excuses," she snapped, gripping my chin hard enough to leave a bruise. "Losing a client is dangerous for our business, as you well know, and therefore unacceptable. If you ever see that male in our club again, you will inform us immediately. He must be dealt with swiftly and silently. At least he only thinks you're a blood whore. The practice isn't illegal in our kingdom, so it's not enough to raise suspicion."

My throat tightened even more, but I managed to whisper, "Yes, Mistress. I take full responsibility for what happened tonight."

With a curt nod, she dropped my chin and stepped back. "Good. You will pay for this loss by working an extra hour tonight and forfeiting another day of pay."

My heart sank.

"Yes, Mistress."

"And the ruined duvet will also come out of your pay. Now, hurry up and finish eating. Your next client will arrive in fifteen minutes. Heath, see to her face and neck, please."

With that, she swept from the room and left me alone with her business partner. Remembering his earlier visit to my room, I tried not to stiffen as Heath invaded my space to inspect my wounds. My failed client hadn't bothered to heal the bite marks he'd left behind, and when he'd pushed me away, the punctures had torn.

I'd barely felt the pain, though. He'd given me enough venom to make me feel euphoric. I still felt high, which helped dull the ache in my cheek.

As Heath eyed the blood on my face and neck, I saw the hunger in his gaze. He'd never fed on me, but I'd seen him pull aside plenty of humans in his club. The man had a ravenous appetite, and he wasn't gentle with his conquests. If it wasn't for the healing properties in vampire blood, he probably would have killed several of his customers by now.

"You know, Star," he said, reaching out to touch my injured cheek. I didn't even flinch, the venom in my veins chasing the pain away. "Madame Faircroft has every right to be angry with you, as do I. We've worked hard to get where we are and made countless sacrifices to build names for ourselves. Venturi are coming to *our* nightclub. We serve respected drothen, nobles, and even council members. We've built *connections* with them. Invaluable ones. You know why this business is so vital, and I thought you wanted to help us."

"I do," I replied, hoping to stay in his good graces with my compliance. The sooner he was appeased, the sooner I could eat the rest of my sandwich. "I'm grateful you entrusted me to help. You're not the only one who wants revenge."

He tilted his head to study me, his doubt clear. "I'm starting to think you don't want it enough. I'm thinking your main goal has shifted to paying off your indenture so you can get far, far away from here."

His words snatched some of my high away, and I sat up straighter.

"I do want to pay off my father's blood debt, but I haven't forgotten what they did to him. I want justice just as much as you and Mistress do."

He studied me a moment longer, then dropped his hand. "Prove it then." Flipping his hand over, he dug a black claw into his palm. As blood began to pool, he dipped a finger into it and smeared the blood across my cheek. I immediately felt the tingling burn of my cut sealing shut.

"How?" I asked, watching as he dipped his finger into the blood again and pressed it to the bite marks on my neck.

"Secure us more clients. Make them *happy*, Star. So deliriously happy that they keep coming back for more."

I suddenly had the urge to throw up. When the little bit of sandwich I'd eaten threatened to come up my throat, I swallowed, careful to keep my expression blank.

He was asking me to prove my loyalty by giving up more of myself. By bringing in more and more vampires who would strip me of all that I was.

A small price to pay, right?

Struggling to breathe, I dipped my head in a small nod. "Okay. I won't fail again."

A big grin stole across his face. "That's my Star. Now get yourself cleaned up. Viscount Le Blanc is eager to have another session with you. Give him a blow job before letting him feed on you. He's one of our most important clients and deserves to feel like a king."

As Heath stood to leave, the last of my appetite vanished. The minute he closed the door behind him, I raced to the bathroom and threw up my meager meal.

I had the dream again. I was dancing for the masked man with amethyst green eyes. The man who'd escaped my intricate web of seduction.

Just like last time, I enjoyed having his gaze on me. Which was odd, especially considering how he'd treated me.

He saw me as a disgusting blood whore? Well, I'd show him just how disgusting I could be. Let's see him escape *this* time.

My dance turned erotic, and I slowly began to strip for him. His intense gaze remained locked on me as I removed my top, giving him an unobstructed view of my breasts. When hunger flashed in his eyes, I smirked in satisfaction.

He might think I was disgusting, but he still wanted me.

Rolling my hips seductively, I ran my hands down my body and hooked my thumbs into my tiny bottoms. Teasingly, I inched the material downward, smirking wider when his eyes followed the movement.

"Remove your mask," I said to him in dulcet tones, continuing to roll my hips.

At first, he hesitated, but when I flashed him a little pussy, he reached up to tug on the black strings. Victory sang in my blood. Only a few more seconds, and I'd know who he was. Once I did, I'd pay him back for his insults. He'd rue the day he ever laid eyes on me.

As the mask started to slip, so did my bottoms. Lower and lower.

Rewarding him. I was almost fully stripped now, but so was his face. Heavy dark brows shadowed his pale eyes, eyes ringed by thick black lashes. His nose was strong and straight, his cheekbones sharp, but not overly so.

The more of his face he revealed, the more I liked it. His features were severe yet handsome, as if chiseled from stone.

I tugged my bottoms lower, fully revealing what he wanted to see. In return, he pulled off his mask.

The second he did, the dream dispelled in swirling black smoke.

I awoke with a groan, punching my pillow in frustration.

So close. I'd been *so close* to discovering who he was.

You were moaning in your sleep.

"Ack!" I yelped, rolling over to peer at Pepper on my nightstand. "What? I wasn't moaning."

Her large pink ears twitched with amusement. *You were definitely moaning. Have a nice dream?*

Uh.

Instead of answering, I reached for my phone to check the time. *Gotta go, Pep. I can't afford to be late today.*

She squeaked in protest as I threw back the covers and jumped from the bed. My usual "hangover" from all the venom I'd received the night before barely slowed me down. Today, I needed to prove myself. To show how *committed* I was to my caretakers' cause. Only then would Mistress pay me the money I'd earned.

Quickly dressing and splashing my face with ice-cold water, I hurried up the basement stairs two at a time.

Be careful, my familiar called to me in parting, clearly perturbed with my hasty exit.

Always am, I threw back, reminding myself to apologize later. I'd returned so late last night that I'd passed out the minute I'd gotten back. I'd only slept two hours, but I'd take a long nap after my chores were done this afternoon.

Fatigue chased me all the way up the stairs, yet I didn't let it slow me down. I had to be on my A game today. Nothing short of perfection would do.

So long as *he* didn't show up tonight and ruin everything again. Admittedly, being rejected had shaken my confidence a bit. It was one thing to conjure up a dream of the green-eyed vampire falling under my spell, but quite another to actually make him do it.

He wasn't like the other Venturi I'd charmed into my bed. He was stronger. Just how powerful, I didn't know. If he'd swallowed my blood, I would have known everything about him. The mask he wore would no longer be able to hide his identity from me. *I* would be the strong one.

I hated that my perfect track record was now tarnished. If I ever saw him again, I would pull out all the stops. He couldn't resist me forever.

I flew through my errands and chores in record time, falling back into bed early enough to get a decent nap for once. I'd even managed to grab a quick bite to eat, which Pepper was super pleased about. Today was shaping up nicely. I just needed to get through tonight, and Mistress would surely start paying me again.

By the time evening rolled around, I was in high spirits, all things considered. I was cage dancing tonight, my least favorite, but even that couldn't dampen my mood. Nothing was going to stand in my way today. I was a force to be reckoned with.

As I prepared to leave my room at the club and dance for the next two hours, I paused at the decorative mirror beside the door to put on my mask. My *shield*. It hid who I was, allowing me to become someone I wasn't. With this mask on, I could pretend the world couldn't touch me.

Not the *real* me, anyway.

My brown and gold eyes shined back at me, filled with a renewed light. Determination. This world wasn't going to kill me. I wouldn't let it. I just needed to keep my head held high for a little while longer.

With confidence thrumming in my veins, I left the room and made for the catwalk suspended high above the dance floor. My appearing and vanishing acts every night were only smoke and mirrors, courtesy of a fog machine and fast pulley system. I wasn't allowed to use *real* magic for my performances. That would give me too much control.

Not that I could use magic to escape, even if the opportunity arose.

I was tied up in knots, ones that grew tighter and tighter with each passing day. There was no way out of my blood debt other than paying my dues. Mistress had made sure of that.

Right at ten o'clock sharp, I entered my silver cage and prepared for the pulley system to lower me. As much as I didn't like being cooped up in this contraption while I danced, at least I didn't have to worry about anyone touching me. I could tune out the world for the next two hours and lose myself to the music and dancing.

Except that Heath had told me to secure more clients, which meant that I needed to keep an eye out for prospects. Stifling a groan, I pulled myself onto the bar suspended in the cage right as it began to lower. So much for pretending this hellhole didn't exist. No matter. I'd keep a sharp eye out and hopefully score another client or two.

Today was my day.

Nothing was going to get me down.

But, as the cage and music stopped, leaving me suspended several feet above the crowd, I made the mistake of looking toward the booth in the darkest corner of the club.

My stomach bottomed out.

Him. It was him.

He'd come back.

And he was looking right at me.

CHAPTER 5

EVERETT

Every inch of me balked at being here again.

Coming back felt all sorts of wrong, but I'd spent the past twenty-four hours thinking about the time I'd had with the silver-haired witch. I couldn't get her out of my head. Couldn't stop analyzing the moment we'd shared, rehashing every detail.

She was a blood whore, no doubt about it. I'd been with countless of them, especially in my earlier years, but none of them had been a witch.

Blood whore *witches* didn't exist. Or, at least, they shouldn't. My brothers and I had made certain of that. So it didn't make sense for Star to be at this club.

Something wasn't right. I'd felt it last night when she'd stiffened at my touch, and I felt it now as I observed the goings-on around me with fresh eyes. My father might be right after all. Dreamscape Lounge appeared to be a harmless nightclub from the outside, but something dark was brewing on the inside.

And the witch was somehow involved.

No one bothered me as I claimed my usual booth in the darkest corner of the club. After what happened last night, though, I wondered if sitting here was wise. The owners might not realize who I was yet, but they knew that I'd visited Star's room. She would have told them. Maybe even given them a loose description of me. The witch was probably too young to figure out who I was, but her employers weren't.

No matter. By the time they figured it out, I would have this place cracked wide open.

My phone buzzed with an incoming text.

Father's wondering if he needs to bring on a couple new maids. He noticed that you didn't seem all that interested in the ones he sent you last night. His words, not mine.

At Loch's lame attempt to stay neutral in all of this, I quietly snorted and texted back, *Tell Father that I'm perfectly capable of finding females all on my own. My sex life is none of his business. And tell him to start texting me himself. It's about time he joined the twenty-first century.*

Will do, my brother replied. *Not that it'll do any good. You know how he's been lately.*

I sure did. Our father had been so focused on the welfare of his second child for the past century that I didn't know how to cope with this sudden shift. Now *I* bore most of his attention, and he seemed hellbent on finding me a love match.

Probably because Loch was so happy with his wife and two children. He wanted his eldest son to experience that same joy.

But I wouldn't force something that wasn't there. I'd never cared about the females I'd been with more than a passing interest.

Maybe I wasn't capable of that kind of love.

When Father had asked me to check out Dreamscape, I'd jumped at the chance to get away from the castle for a little while. He rarely left our home these days and often used me as his proxy. I was the crown prince, after all, and would someday take his place as king. Something he'd been reminding me of more and more lately.

Sighing, I checked the time. Ten o'clock. Unbidden, anticipation swirled in my gut. I curled my lip, disgusted with myself, but the feeling wouldn't go away. The witch had enchanted me somehow. That was the only logical explanation. Never in a million years would I *willingly* be attracted to her kind. She'd bewitched me, and I could only hope the spell would wear off soon.

I couldn't afford to be distracted again. My father was relying on me to keep the kingdom safe, and I didn't take that lightly. Protecting my family always came first, and this insane infatuation with a witch couldn't get in the way of that.

But, as I caught the slightest movement above the crowded dance floor, my gaze was pulled to her once more. She was in a large silver cage this time, perched on a swing. As if sensing my attention, she looked my way. Our eyes locked, even as the music stopped and a spotlight flooded her cage.

Time ceased to exist for a moment. It was only me and her, our gazes saying what words couldn't.

I'm onto you, my narrowed eyes openly conveyed.

Her bright golden eyes widened a fraction, before narrowing as well and replying back, *I don't know what you're talking about.*

I curled my lips in a wicked smirk, hoping to rattle her.

She took in the smirk, then matched it with one of her own.

Oh, she wanted to play? Well, little did she know that the *hunt* was my favorite part.

As she began to gracefully swing on the bar, expertly flipping and twirling, I tracked her every move. She could hide behind her silver masks and pretty little smirks all she wanted. I would unearth her secrets soon enough. Maybe not *too* soon, though. I wanted to have a little fun with her first. A little payback for blindsiding me last night.

She wasn't the only one who excelled at luring in prey.

Maybe an hour passed before her movements changed, becoming more erotic. I sat up straighter, realizing what was happening. She was on the hunt. Not for me, though. Following her line of sight, I spotted her unwitting target in the crowd below, staring up at her in rapture.

Had *I* looked like that? Like a drunken fool missing all of his brain cells?

I snorted, disgusted once more.

Not surprisingly, she crooked her finger at him minutes later, pulling a card from her top as she dangled upside down from the bar to give it to him. I shook my head, glancing down to see my hand tightly fisted on my thigh. Relaxing my hold, I watched her for several more minutes, not missing the way her diamond navel piercing flashed in the light. My mind suddenly pictured her dancing in that cage completely naked.

I quietly swore and banned the image, but my pants tightened all the same. She still had a hold on me. Maybe I should leave and come back tomorrow night. The spell should have worn off by then. But before I could get up, she crooked her finger a second time, choosing a new target. My gaze shot back into the crowd and found the male. He was masked like everyone else, but as he reached up and eagerly accepted the card, recognition shivered through me. There was no mistaking the intricate clock tattoo on his forearm.

Benjamin Osborne was a Venturi noble. An earl. Centuries old, even if he only looked to be in his early twenties, same as me.

He used to be a close friend of mine, up until recently. We'd attended our fair share of feeding dens and orgies together, but that felt like a lifetime ago.

Knowing what I knew about him, a sudden wave of protectiveness surged through me. Not for him. For *her*. For a split second, I considered leaving her to her fate. She'd chosen this life. Chosen to allow males like Benjamin into her bed night after night. I banished the cruel thought before it could finish forming. Despite my personal grievances against her, she didn't deserve to spend a night with the likes of Ben Osborne.

I was out of my seat in a flash. But as I rushed forward, the spotlight winked out and she vanished.

Cursing under my breath, I sought Ben out in the crowd. When my search came up empty, I made for the exit that led to the elevators. The same two bouncers were standing guard there, but Ben was nowhere to be found.

"Did you let someone go up a few minutes ago?" I questioned them, not bothering to keep my voice down. "A male about six feet tall with black hair similar to mine."

They just stared at me. After a moment, the bigger one held out his hand palm up.

I shook my head, irritation bleeding into my tone. "No, I'm not here for that."

"Clients only," the bouncer droned, lowering his arm.

Grinding my teeth together, I jerked a hand through my short hair before growling, "I'll buy her out tonight. Double the asking price. Send her clients away."

Both bouncers raised their eyebrows, but otherwise, didn't react.

"I want the whole night with her. Call your boss and have it arranged, if need be. Do it now, and I'll *triple* the price, plus pay you each a thousand for the trouble."

That put a fire under them.

The burlier one wandered off a short distance to make a phone call, while the other studied me with renewed interest. Instead of staring him down like instinct demanded, I gave him my profile. Keeping my identity hidden was going to be nearly impossible now.

A whole *night* with her? I'd officially lost all common sense.

The bouncer returned before I could change my mind, extending his hand once more. "One hundred and twenty grand, and she's yours for the night."

"I'll need to wire transfer the money over," I said and pulled out my phone. Using an untraceable offshore account, of course. I wasn't going to let a little money exchange expose my identity. Unfazed, the bouncer just nodded. Within minutes, the transfer was complete.

Pocketing my phone, I gave them each a grand in cash, as promised.

Moments later, Ben and the other male Star had given a keycard to emerged from the elevator, escorted by another pair of bouncers.

"I demand an explanation," Ben snarled at them, his voice filled with fury. "She chose *me*."

"I already told you," one of the bouncers replied, stopping him from reentering the elevator. "She's not feeling well tonight. Come back tomorrow."

Ben stormed past with a growl, and I averted my gaze. He was too angry to even notice me, though. The other male left more slowly, looking like a kicked puppy. I wanted to sneer at how pathetic they were both acting, but if I'd been turned away last night, I probably would have responded the same.

As the bouncers gestured for me to enter the elevator, reason finally punched me in the gut. What was I doing? I couldn't return to the lioness's den. This was *insane*.

Lowering my voice, I said to them, "On second thought, I want her to remain alone tonight. No one is to disturb her."

But, as I turned to leave, a bouncer replied, "It doesn't work like that. She's here to serve clients. If you don't go up, someone else will."

Bristling, I bit back a frustrated retort and simply nodded. "Fine."

I entered the elevator and punched the button for the third floor, already knowing that this night would be pure hell. If I didn't end up falling under her seductive spell again, I was going to strangle her for putting me in this terrible position.

Maybe she would have been safer with Benjamin after all.

CHAPTER 6

ADALYN

I'd barely settled against the satin pillows when I heard a knock at the door.

"Come in," I called, situating my robe so that only teasing hints of flesh were visible. It was my routine with new clients. They focused so hard on catching glimpses of my naked body that they gave me all the control—at least long enough for me to make the first move. I couldn't always predict what happened after that, but the sooner I got them to feed on me, the better.

Two new clients tonight. Mistress was definitely going to be pleased.

I'd been disappointed that the green-eyed vampire had kept his distance while I danced, but I'd done everything I could to lure him in. Instead of focusing on him, I'd ignored him completely, setting my sights on other males. Guess he wasn't the jealous type after all. I thought for sure he would be.

Oh well. He'd watched me the entire time, which had to mean something. Maybe he wasn't a complete lost cause yet. I'd have to beg Mistress to let me have another chance at him.

Something told me that he would make an invaluable client, even more than Viscount Le Blanc. My mouth puckered in disgust when I recalled the oral job I'd given him last night. He'd left happy as a clam, promising to return soon, but I'd spent the next fifteen minutes gargling mouthwash.

As I heard the door of my suite open, I adjusted my mask and replaced the disgusted look with a small smirk.

You're Star, not Adalyn, I reminded myself while I listened to the approaching footsteps. *They can't touch you. Not the real you.*

The footsteps stopped at the open bedroom door, and I lifted my gaze to greet the new client. When I saw who it was, the words died on my tongue.

Recovering swiftly, I masked my shock and purred, "Well, well, well. Look who the cat dragged in. I knew you couldn't stay away."

I lifted a hand to touch my collarbone, gratified when his gaze followed the movement. Slipping my fingers beneath the edge of my robe, I shifted the material to reveal more of my breasts. Heat flared in his pale green eyes.

Smirking wider, I crooned, "Come in. We can pick up where we left off. You never got to finish last night, poor thing."

His nostrils flared as I slowly dropped my gaze to his pants where a noticeable bulge already strained against the dark material. I straightened from my relaxed position, allowing my robe to flutter open. His eyes hungrily devoured my flesh, just like I wanted them to. Rising onto my knees, I exposed the rest of myself to him, pleased when he greedily took in every inch.

You're mine now, I thought to myself, giddy that I'd managed to right the wrongs from last night. I wouldn't fail again. All I had to do was seduce him into drinking my blood. One glance at the starved look on his face, and I knew I could do it.

As I crawled to him on my knees, I decided to go all out and give him the full show. With a little shrug, the robe slipped from my shoulders and fell to the mattress, leaving me completely nude before him. I heard the air rush from his lungs. Brushing my hair back so there was nothing obstructing his view, I watched as his eyes began to darken. Within seconds, they were a deep red, the color of blood.

He was losing control. Good. This would be easier than I thought.

When I reached the foot of the bed, I slid off and slowly approached him. My hips swayed with each step, making his eyes practically go feral.

"It's okay," I whispered, shushing him softly. "I'm going to make you feel so good."

As I stopped just short of touching him, his hands balled into fists. Like last time, I boldly reached out to cup his manhood. Before I could make contact, he had me up against the nearest wall with a hand wrapped around my throat.

Startled, I flailed against his grip, which only made his hold tighten. "Let *go*," I croaked, hating how panicked I sounded. How *helpless*.

In a split second, he'd stolen all of my control.

There was nothing I could do against his superior strength. Not even my magic could help me.

He abruptly released my throat, and I slumped against the wall, gasping for breath.

"Get dressed," he said, the clipped words laced with venom. "You won't be touching me tonight."

When all I did was gape at him, he left the bedroom and slammed the door shut.

"Hey!" I protested, lunging for the door. I grabbed the handle and yanked, but it wouldn't budge. "Let me out of here!"

"Get dressed, and I will," he said through the door.

I continued to yank on the handle, but there was no way I could muscle it open. Knowing he was completely in control of the situation now, anger flushed through me. "What the hell is your problem anyway?"

"You," he muttered, but I managed to catch the word.

"*Me?* I'm the one being held prisoner in my own bedroom. I didn't force you to come up here. If you don't want my services, then leave."

"I *can't*," he hissed, clearly upset, which made no sense. Why was he even here?

I stopped pulling on the handle and stepped back to calm myself. After a moment, I quietly entreated, "Look, just let me out, okay?"

"Are you dressed?"

"No."

"Then you're going nowhere."

Biting back a frustrated scream, I stomped to the bed and grabbed my robe. "Fine, I'm *dressed*. Let me out."

As I jerked on the robe, I heard him release the handle. In a flash, I was at the door and yanking it open. Expecting him to be gone, I was surprised to find him sitting on the couch in the living room.

At the sight of me in my open robe, his lips pulled back in a silent snarl. "*Close* it."

I grabbed the belt and tied it with a snort. "Since when did you become a prude?"

"Since I discovered you were a witch."

I openly scoffed, not bothering to hide my irritation. What was *with* this guy? "You didn't have any complaints a minute ago while you watched me strip."

"A momentary lapse in judgment."

"I'll say. Make up your mind already."

"I already have."

"Oh?" I mockingly raised an eyebrow. "So if I strip right now, you won't watch?"

Even from across the candle-lit room, I could see his eyes darken with lust behind his mask. "Don't."

I flirted with the idea of doing it anyway, just to see what he would do. This scenario was playing out just like my dream this morning. A little strip tease in return for revealing his identity. If I couldn't get him to drink my blood, I'd have to get creative.

Instead, I waved a hand dismissively and turned toward the kitchen. "Fine. If you're not interested in me, I'm going to eat my dinner. I have a whole hour to kill."

"Four."

Confused, I peered at him over my shoulder. "Huh?"

"Four hours. I paid to spend the whole night with you."

I blinked at him, trying to mask my shock. He'd done *what*? "Why would you do that?"

He leaned forward and rested his elbows on his knees before answering. "I recognized one of the males you chose tonight. His name is Benjamin Osborne, and he's very possessive with females. His impulse control is weak, and most of the females he feeds on wind up dead. Not *clean* deaths either."

I tried to suppress a shiver, but couldn't quite manage it. To hide my reaction, I turned and opened the fridge to grab the sandwich I'd ordered earlier. "I know how to handle possessive males. It's part of my job. You shouldn't have stopped him from coming up here. I need new clients."

"I paid triple. You'll be compensated for the loss."

I froze, staring blankly into the open fridge as I quickly did the math. He'd paid over a hundred thousand dollars to spend the night with me? Who *was* this vampire?

Straightening, I carefully closed the fridge and made sure to wipe all emotion from my face before turning toward him. He probably thought he'd done me a huge favor by buying me out for the night.

Maybe even thought he'd *saved* me. Not that my safety should matter to him. He'd made it abundantly clear that he loathed my kind.

Knowing that I'd never see a single cent of that money nearly brought tears to my eyes. I could barely hold them back, desperately wishing I could release them in a torrent and scream at the misguided vampire for ruining another day. Not only was that money out of my reach, but I'd probably lost two more clients as well.

I'd tried so hard today. *So hard.* But I'd failed again.

It was all I could do to keep a straight face while my world came crashing down. I was suddenly exhausted. My bones felt encased in lead, and I quickly sat at the table before I could collapse.

The vampire studied me for a moment, then said, "You don't seem thrilled with the news."

My lips tilted into a sardonic smile. "On the contrary. You're my knight in shining armor, my lord." I bit into my sandwich, chewing thoughtfully before adding, "Or is that title too informal? How about earl? Duke, maybe?"

No reaction.

Hmm . . .

"My employers won't be pleased with this little arrangement," I went on, gesturing between the two of us. "I'm not being paid to sit on my butt all night long. My *back*, maybe, but—"

"Get to the point," he interrupted, clearly annoyed with my little joke. Jeez. The guy needed to release some of that pent-up frustration. Not that he would let *me* help him.

"The point is, they're expecting us to be intimate."

"Not happening."

I set my sandwich down with a huff. "You didn't let me finish."

"Don't need to. You're not coming anywhere near me."

"Now hold on. You're here for a reason, right? Something to do with me?"

No reaction. He had a good poker face, I'd give him that. Almost as good as mine.

"Well, here's the deal," I went on, undeterred by his silence. "If we don't get cozy soon, they'll become suspicious. And when they get suspicious, they'll ban you from their club. We're talking forever. So if you don't want to end up on their blacklist, then I suggest you let me join you on that couch."

The faintest of sneers twisted his lips. I tried not to be offended.

After a long moment, he said, "How many are there?" At my confused look, he sighed impatiently and added, "Cameras."

I licked my lips, trying not to look nervous. He knew we had cameras in here? They were well hidden. Like *really* well hidden.

Deciding to throw him a bone, I replied, "Three. Two in the bedroom, and one out here. The one out here is video only, though."

He snorted in disgust, probably remembering the *moment* we'd shared last night. Yep. We hadn't been alone.

He was silent for another long beat, probably wishing he'd never tried to "save" me. That made two of us. Still, I was going to make the best out of this situation. He just had to take the bait.

Finally, he blew out a sigh and said, "So, if you join me on this couch, they'll leave us alone?"

"Yep." Hopefully. We'd have to make it look convincing, though, which wouldn't be easy.

"Fine. But keep your hands to yourself."

At the long-suffering look he gave me, I nearly rolled my eyes. What a baby. Before he could change his mind, I rose from my chair and sauntered into the living room.

A scowl pulled at his full lips. "What are you doing?"

This time, I *did* roll my eyes. "Joining you on the couch. Did you already forget?"

"No, but why can't you walk normally?"

"Normally?" I glanced down at my legs. "I'm just walking."

"No, you're sashaying."

A laugh burst from me. "Sashaying? Is *that* what this is?"

I gave him a mocking little twirl, then froze when I saw his face. He looked like lightning had just struck him.

"What?" I asked, making sure all my bits were still concealed by the robe.

He cleared his throat and sat up straight. "Nothing. Just hurry up and get over here."

I shrugged. "Your wish is my command." Picking up the pace, I beelined for the spot next to him. Before I could take a seat, though, he snagged my waist and deposited me on his lap. *Horsey* style, with my front facing his and my legs straddling his waist.

My body immediately tensed, unprepared for the move. Every instinct demanded I pull away, but I forced myself to remain where I was. "What are you doing?" I asked, struggling to keep my voice even.

"You said we needed to get cozy."

My heart beat a little too fast, panicking at how close he was. His hands were still on my waist, and I could feel their heat through my thin robe. Swallowing roughly, I replied, "Yeah, but I thought you didn't want me to touch you."

"I don't. But if you keep your hands off my cock, we'll be fine."

I choked back a nervous laugh, caught off guard by the blunt statement. "Fair enough. Where do you want them then?"

"My shoulders will do."

"Okay." I raised my hands to his shoulders and lightly rested them on top, then airily exclaimed, "Oh, wow. What broad shoulders you have, my lord."

He really did. He was built like a tank, every inch of him hard muscle.

He looked at me like I'd lost my mind. Sure enough, he grunted and said, "No witch in their right mind would work in a place like this."

"You're right," I glibly replied with a smirk. "I'm not in my right mind."

He shook his head, but I didn't fail to notice how his gaze rested on my mouth a little too long.

Hmm . . .

"Tell you what," I said, keeping my tone casual. "I'll make sure my employers aren't suspicious of you if you tell me who you are."

He lightly scoffed as if I'd said something funny. "I have a better idea. Tell me about the secret operation you're running here, and I'll tell you who I am."

I nearly swallowed my tongue.

Before I could compose myself, he said, "You flinched again."

"Flinched? I didn't flinch. I just didn't expect you to say that. If that's why you came back, I hate to disappoint you. My employers work very hard to keep everything at Dreamscape legal. You could even check the cameras."

Please don't check the cameras, please don't check the cameras.

I didn't think it was possible for me to get embarrassed anymore, but the thought of him seeing footage of me being intimate with countless other males was mortifying.

He abruptly reached up to touch my cheek, and I definitely *did* flinch this time. Silently cursing, I commanded my body to hold still. But it was too late.

"Your pupils are dilated. You're scared."

"Scared?" Breaking into a cold sweat, I desperately tried to steer the conversation to safer waters. "How do you know I'm not just turned on? I'm straddling your lap, after all."

He slowly cocked his head to the side, the predatorial move rattling me more than I wanted to admit. "I can find out easily enough."

He let go of my waist, only to place both hands on my upper thighs. I stiffened all over, unable to stop my reaction. A wicked gleam entered his eyes, all challenge and no mercy. Before I could prepare, his hands began to move. Inch by inch, they trailed up my widely spread thighs. I knew exactly where they were headed, and there was absolutely nothing blocking their way. My robe easily parted, allowing him to carve a path toward my quivering center.

"Does this turn you on?" he said in hushed tones, watching me closely with those piercing amethyst eyes.

"Mmm," was all I managed to say, gripping his shoulders a little too tightly.

"You pleasured me last night," he went on, torturing me with a slow smirk. "Maybe it's time I repay the favor."

Spirits save me. There was no way out of this one. He meant business, and I had no choice but to play his game.

"I'm a witch," I reminded him, hating how nervous I sounded. "You think I'm disgusting."

"True, but I've done far more terrible things than have sex with a witch."

The confession should have terrified me, but it somehow spoke to my own darkness. I'd done some pretty terrible things too.

Still, I needed to deter him. The farther up his hands went, the more my body trembled.

"Maybe you should let me finish what I started first," I said, struggling to breathe. His thumbs were skating up my inner thighs now, inches away from their goal.

His smirk grew, the tilt of his mouth decidedly bitter. "No. Ladies first. It's the gentlemanly thing to do, even though I'm anything but a gentleman."

My heart jackknifed inside my chest.

"Well, I'm not a lady, so—"

His thumbs found my center and pressed on the bundle of sensitive nerves, stealing the words from my mouth. My hips bucked, and he gripped my thighs to keep me in place. I squirmed against the hold, squeezing my eyes shut as he began to rub my clit with both thumbs. While he did, a feeling stirred low in my belly, one that I tried hard to deny.

Pleasure.

I was experiencing pleasure at the hands of a *vampire*.

Shocked by how unexpected and good it felt, I arched my spine and breathlessly cried out like a brazen hussy. Which was what I was, I supposed.

His mouth was suddenly on my neck, nuzzling the throbbing vein there as if dying for a taste. This was my chance. I arched my neck back even more, encouraging him to bite me. He groaned against my skin, massaging my clit harder. I bucked against his thumbs again, quivering as a familiar sensation rushed through me.

Euphoria.

I'd only ever experienced it through venom, not touch. This was . . . this was bad. Really bad. I should *not* be feeling like this right now.

"Please," I whimpered, trying to pull away, even as I dug my fingers into his shoulders.

Misunderstanding my plea, he stopped rubbing to slide a finger into my entrance. As he pulled it out, now wet with my arousal, I gasped. There was no denying it now. I was turned on. *Majorly* turned on. My body had never reacted this way to a client before. Not once.

At the discovery of how wet I was, he bit out a curse and fumbled to undo his pants. My normal instinct to recoil didn't come as he pulled out his hard erection and positioned himself at my entrance. In one smooth thrust, he was deep inside me. We both moaned at the same time, struggling to breathe as we adjusted to the intimate position. He filled me up completely, stretching my walls to capacity.

I usually hated the feeling. Hated knowing that something was invading my body against my wishes.

But this. This almost felt better than venom in my veins.

As he began to thrust in and out of me, though, I swiftly changed my mind. This was *better* than venom. I had no idea sex could feel like this. Like my very essence was being merged with another's. It was terrifying. Utterly terrifying, yet thrilling. For once, I didn't want to fight the feeling of being intimate with a stranger.

He didn't feel like a stranger at all right now. He felt . . . he felt like a part of me. Like a missing piece of my identity.

I suddenly needed to know more. Know everything about him. It was essential. Life or death. I couldn't go another second without knowing.

"Please," I gasped, pulling his head down to my neck once more. "Bite me. Please bite me."

He hissed, as if disgusted by my plea. But the hiss ended in a groan, one that sounded a lot like defeat. Still thrusting inside me, he gripped my hair and tilted my head to the perfect angle. He struck fast and true, burying his fangs deeply into my flesh.

I stiffened at the pain but was already anticipating the sweet rush of . . .

With a sigh, I melted like butter against him, the hit of venom turning my world to rapture. My mind blanked for an endless moment as the high spread throughout my system, leaving me wholly compliant in the vampire's arms. But as I felt him begin to feed, I struggled to regain some sense. Some *control*.

At the first taste of my blood, he blissfully groaned into my neck. I allowed him to fully swallow it, then made my move. It was only a suggestion, really. A faint thought. I didn't push too hard, gently coaxing him into giving me what I wanted. Whispering into his mind the words that would be his undoing.

Reveal to me all that you are.

Your secrets are mine, willingly so.

What you have hidden shall now be unveiled.

Like a winding river, your secrets shall flow.

I cringed at my poor rhyming attempt, but the spell sank into the vampire's consciousness all the same. Barely reacting to the spell, too fixated on consuming my blood, he unwittingly began to spill his secrets. Just as my thighs tensed, the need to orgasm whipping through me, he gave up his name.

Everett D'angelo.

The name didn't register at first, but as pleasure exploded through me, a torrent of information flooded my system.

I rode the endorphin high, a victorious smirk stretching my lips.

Well, hello there, prince. Nice to meet you at long last.

CHAPTER 7

EVERETT

"You were out late last night."

The question was directed at me, as most of them were these days. I barely glanced up from the gold goblet I was toying with to answer, "I decided to stay until the club closed. See if I could learn anything new."

My father was unfazed by my cryptic reply, pressing, "And did you?"

Supple olive skin flashed before me. The smell of lavender and incense. The feel of silky hair clenched in my fist. The cloying scent of arousal. The explosive taste of exotic floral blood.

Sudden hunger burned my throat, and I raised the cup of blood to my lips. Taking a sip, I nearly spat it out. Wrong. The taste was all wrong. I set the goblet on the table before replying, "Possibly. But I'm still working on it."

The king leaned back in his velvet-cushioned chair, placing both elbows on the wood armrests to steeple his fingers. I knew that pose well. My evasive responses had only made him more curious.

Sure enough, he said, "You've barely touched your breakfast. You're usually on your fifth or sixth glass by now."

I shrugged. "I ate at the club last night."

"Oh, really? Did you have sex as well?"

At the probing question, tension lined my body. It wasn't unusual for us to have conversations like this, but I felt a sudden need to protect my secret rendezvous with Star. I wasn't ready to share with my family what had happened. Not today. Maybe not ever. Which wasn't like me at all. I'd never been the secretive type. My brothers, on the other hand . . .

I glanced across the table at Loch, expecting to see a teasing gleam in his dark eyes. Normally the center of father's questions, he'd been enjoying his anonymity at my expense lately. It was currently just the three of us at the table. I'd missed the first half of breakfast when his mate Kenna and their two children had been present. The twin toddlers had recently learned to walk and didn't like to stay in one spot for too long. Their mother was probably chasing them around the castle right now, doing her best to keep them out of trouble.

Loch stared back at me, his expression surprisingly solemn. Guilt tightened my chest. I knew what he was thinking. That I'd fallen back into my old ways.

It was on the tip of my tongue to reassure him, but I quickly swallowed the words. They would be a lie. I hadn't spent the evening carousing in a feeding den drunk out of my mind on blood and sex, but my actions hadn't been innocent either. Far from it. I was just *paying* for blood and sex now. An exorbitant amount too.

After I'd given in to my baser instincts last night—instincts that had screamed at me so loudly that I couldn't think of anything else— I'd been struggling to wake up. The four hours I'd spent with Star had passed in a blur. I could remember bits and pieces, but when I'd finally succumbed to my need to have her, a shroud had blanketed my mind.

Being with her had been like swimming in ecstasy. I'd been wholly wrapped up in her essence, experiencing things I'd never felt before. I'd felt calm. Content. *Close* in a way I'd never felt with another being. I could have stayed there forever, blissfully lost in her body. It was warm and comforting, the only place I wanted to be. But when I'd woken up this morning in my own bed, I'd felt . . . untethered. The feeling still haunted me, leaving me more than a little unsettled.

Even during the times when I'd been blood drunk out of my mind, I'd never felt this disorientated.

"Yes," I finally answered my father, looking away from Loch's disappointed expression. "But it's not what you think."

It was worse. So much worse.

"I don't know *what* to think, Everett," the king replied, his garnet gaze studying me thoughtfully. "You're almost two hundred years old and can bed whoever you wish, but lately, you've seemed a bit aimless. Lost, even. You'll be king someday, and a king can't get drunk or have sex with every wanton strumpet who'll spread her legs for him. Not in this kingdom, anyway."

A spark of anger heated my insides, but I clenched my jaw to keep a retort at bay.

Noticing my stiffness, my father's expression softened. "I know it hasn't been easy for you. For either of you." He encompassed Loch in the look before focusing on me again. "I'm still coping with the death of your younger brother and my own frail state."

"You're not frail, Father," I replied. "And Troy's death isn't your fault."

"But I should have done *more*," he said, his eyes suspiciously bright. "I haven't done enough to protect my sons."

I shook my head. "Troy and Loch were *my* responsibility the day everything went to hell. I'm the one who failed to protect them, not you. But I promise you I'm not making those same mistakes again." The words sat like ash on my tongue. I meant them, but they still felt like a lie.

"Good," he said after a lengthy beat, dropping his hands to place them on the armrests. "You're my heir apparent, son, and I need you to be ready to take the throne. I won't be king for much longer."

Once again, I bit my tongue. He'd been saying that more and more lately, as if he planned to abdicate the throne any day now. He was five hundred years old, and his strength wasn't what it used to be, but I still couldn't imagine myself taking his place. He was larger than life, *born* to be king. His magnetic charm made him the perfect ruler. I, on the other hand, was cold, bordering on cruel. I didn't know how I was supposed to measure up to him.

As if sensing my confliction, he changed the subject, but not to one I wanted to discuss. "I noticed you turned away the new maids last night. One of them is a virgin. She'd make a great first wife. Young, healthy, beautiful, and very fertile. I'm certain she would produce you an heir in no time."

I'd barely noticed her. When I'd returned home, I'd dismissed the two maids without a thought. I'd only wanted one pair of hands on me and had fallen asleep with her image firmly planted in my mind.

Sighing at my father's blatant attempt at matchmaking, I shook my head and replied, "I don't think I'm interested in having a harem of human wives like you, Father. I know you love and care for each of them equally, but I wouldn't be able to do that. And don't even bother mentioning a soulmate. That's not in the cards for me."

He shared a glance with Loch. Noticing the sympathetic look they exchanged, I pushed back from the table and stood.

"I think I'm going to spend some time with my niece and nephew this morning. They can barely talk, but at least they won't meddle in my love life. Or lack thereof."

My father raised his hands in surrender, chuckling quietly. "I get it. I'll back off. At least for a little while. But consider what I've said, Everett. It's important for you to settle down. Finding that special someone to share your life with could be just what you need."

I acknowledged his words with a nod, but I couldn't promise him anything. In fact, I was pretty sure a special someone didn't exist for me. And if they did, they should probably run far, far away before I ended up hurting them. Or worse.

CHAPTER 8

ADALYN

Last night had been the most thrilling experience of my entire life.

And also one of the most awful.

Why was the crown vampire prince, second only in power to the king himself, seeking *me* out? Now that I knew who he was, I struggled to make sense of everything that had happened. Despite my young age, I knew all about Everett D'angelo and the Demonic Trinity. He and his two younger brothers had spent the past several decades terrorizing my kind, simply because one witch had dared to cross paths with them.

Everett had been the worst, though. He'd hunted down and killed hundreds of innocent witches and warlocks without mercy, all to appease his bloodlust for revenge. His mindless killing spree had taken place over a century ago, but he was still known for his cruelty and hatred of witches.

Knowing who he was changed everything. My own need for revenge thrummed hotly in my veins. I hadn't seen the vampire who'd killed my father six years ago, but I knew they'd been a Venturi. A *powerful* one. Nothing less could have killed a powerful Oracle elder. He'd been training me to follow in his footsteps when the battle against the Venturi had taken place.

The vampire kingdom had been divided, on the brink of destruction. The elders should have just let them kill each other. My dad would still be alive if they hadn't gotten involved, if they hadn't made the fight theirs. Now, because of the choices they'd made, I was forced to deal with the aftermath.

I'd been stupid to follow him that night. By the time I'd arrived, it was too late. My father was gone, and I'd been thrown into servitude to repay a debt that wasn't mine.

At least I understood now why Everett had seemed so familiar to me. I'd seen him that night. Not up close, but I remembered his eyes. They'd met mine, albeit briefly. Their depths had been hard and cold. I remembered that much.

I shivered, recalling how it had felt to be intimate with him. What if I'd had sex with my father's killer?

Rubbing my arms, I readied for another night of dancing. Tonight's entertainment would be up close and personal. *Intimate.* But if the vampire prince showed up again, I was going to avoid him like the plague.

The thrall I was under demanded that I give up his identity to Mistress, but for the very first time, I'd lied to her. The moment she'd confronted me about the night I'd shared with him, I'd looked her straight in the eye and given her a false name.

Benjamin Osborne.

The name had popped into my head and spilled from my lips before I could think better of it. How I'd managed to get away with a lie was still a mystery to me. The thrall forced me to tell the truth. There was no way around it. So how did I manage to keep Everett's name to myself? And *why?*

I should *want* to give him up. Mistress would be ecstatic if she knew that I'd lured in a royal. This was the moment we'd been waiting for. With Everett under my spell, we could push forward with our plans.

But I hadn't. I'd hesitated, and I didn't know why.

As the music changed, I set aside my conflicted thoughts for later and focused on my job. Hopefully the *real* Benjamin Osborne didn't show up tonight. Heath and Mistress would know I was hiding something if I secured two clients with the same name.

My cue to dance came, and I hurried into position. The second I climbed on top of the low table, a spotlight struck me. Immediately, the people at the round table stopped what they were doing to take me in. Despite being on a glass tabletop, I wore six-inch silver stilettos. The rest of my outfit was a holographic silver made up of straps and little else. I'd worn my hair up for a change tonight, pulling it into a high chic ponytail.

When the music started again, I whipped my ponytail forward, then snapped my head back. As my hair arced through the air, I struck a provocative pose to the delight of my audience. They hooted and hollered, and I threw them an amused smirk. They thought that was impressive? I was just getting started.

Table dancing was fun, actually. Without anything to hold onto, I could freestyle, using my body however I wished. My hands and hair were my greatest assets, moving and twisting in ways that kept my audience captive. They especially loved it when I sensually touched myself. Flashing a bit of forbidden skin also got them going. As I cupped my breasts, throwing my head back as if in ecstasy, they went wild.

Money fluttered through the air, and I rewarded them by running my hands over my stomach. Snapping straight again, I made eye contact and slipped my hands lower, teasing the straps of my bottoms.

"Take it off!" several of them screamed, cheering when one of the straps "accidentally" came undone. I teased them for several minutes, but my job wasn't to strip. My employers didn't believe in giving away the goods that easily.

I moved on to the next table soon after, knowing that I had several more to go. As I danced, my gaze kept wandering to the farthest booth in the darkest corner. It was empty.

The prince hadn't shown up tonight, which shouldn't have surprised me. He'd gotten what he wanted, after all.

Well, good riddance. This way, I wouldn't have to reveal his identity. More importantly, I could stop *thinking* about him. I'd barely been able to sleep this morning after work. My body had felt too charged. Too *alive*. Despite what I now knew about him, my libido was off the charts. It was like he'd awakened something inside me. Something I'd thought was dead.

And that was dangerous. It gave him control over me, and not being in control while I was with a client could get me killed. *Especially* when that someone was him. If he knew the full extent of what I did here, he wouldn't hesitate to kill me.

Minutes before midnight, I approached my last table. There was only one person sitting at the booth, and I immediately recognized him. It was the second male I'd chosen last night. He wore a gold mask, the same one he'd worn before. As I stepped onto the table, his eyes devoured every inch of me. Used to the attention, I didn't flinch, but something in his gaze made me uneasy.

Was this the Benjamin Osborne that Everett had told me about? Remembering what he'd said about him, sudden nerves fluttered in my stomach. Maybe I shouldn't invite him to my room tonight. If he was *that* violent with women, securing him as a client might not be worth it. Still, I had a job to do, and that included dancing for him.

As I did, the hunger in his gaze intensified. He was as still as a statue, but his eyes tracked my every move. A minute away from calling it a night, I laid on my back on the table and spread my thighs wide in a provocative pose. His eyes practically went feral, but I held the pose, reaching down to touch myself through my bottoms.

I was almost finished with my table routine when I suddenly heard him say over the pumping music, "So are you gonna invite me up again or should we get started right here, sweet thing?"

I froze. My hesitation cost me.

Faster than I could blink, he had me in his lap. "On second thought, why wait? I'm already nice and hard for you," he purred, pressing me down until I felt just how aroused he was.

Panicking, I tried to put space between us. He only laughed and started to rock me against him.

"Mmmm, I've been thinking about you nonstop since last night, sweetheart. There are so many things I plan to do to you." In a flash, he reached down and unzipped his pants, letting his dick spring free. So fast that I didn't have time to react.

But when he hooked a finger into my bottoms and pushed them aside so he could thrust inside me, I cried out, sounding like a frightened rabbit. The second the sound left my lips, the world exploded around me. The booth and table went flying. Screams rent the air as the objects struck anyone standing in the way.

I started to fall, but something picked me up and set me aside. I teetered on my stilettos, trying to follow what was happening as I caught my balance. A dark shape blurred past, heading straight for Benjamin Osborne—or who I assumed was Benjamin Osborne. His pants were still unzipped, his dick wagging in the air as the form rushed him. Before he could get out of the way, the blur struck him square in the chest. He went flying back. Back, back, back. So far that I lost sight of him and his dick. All I heard was a huge *boom* as he hit the club's cement wall.

A second later, I was being led away from the scene.

Still in shock, I stumbled forward, but the hand gripping my elbow steadied me. My senses slowly came back to me, and I prepared to pull away. Before I could, I realized who was leading me. Shocked once more, I simply followed in his wake, watching as everyone who stood in his way scattered like ants.

In no time, we reached the elevators. The bouncers stationed there immediately recognized me, their eyes going wide when they saw Everett. His skin was *black*. Jet black, the same color as his short hair. I could only imagine that his eyes were blood red, his lips peeled back to reveal a pair of lethal fangs.

He was *livid*. I could practically feel his anger pounding in my chest alongside my racing heart.

The fact that he'd just revealed his true form spoke volumes. Any number of humans could have seen, but he didn't seem to care.

"Let us pass," he ordered the bouncers in a guttural tone. "I'll wire over the same amount of money as last night."

They stepped aside without a word, and Everett paused only long enough to hand them each a wad of cash. Once we were in the elevator, everything went dead silent. He didn't release his grip on me, but he didn't say a word. I glanced down, noting the way his black claws lightly dug into my flesh.

I should be terrified. *Terrified*. He could rip me to shreds in seconds. No one could stop him if he chose to attack me right now.

If he knew the truth about me, he definitely would.

And yet, the greatest emotion I felt right now was relief. He'd saved me from being publicly humiliated by that creep. He definitely would have had sex with me in front of everyone if Everett hadn't stopped him.

I opened my mouth, surprised when a soft "thank you" slipped free. For once, I actually meant the words.

"Don't thank me," he replied, his tone still guttural. "My motives for saving you from Ben are anything but pure."

I blinked. Oh.

He wanted a repeat of last night. Maybe Benjamin Osborne wasn't the only possessive male I should be worried about. What if Everett was even *worse?*

With that thought in mind, some of my nerves returned. As the elevator opened onto the third floor, I thought about calling for help. But I doubted anyone would come to my aid if I did. I'd been roughly handled by clients before. *Many* times, actually. No one had ever come to stop them.

By the time we reached my suite, I'd worked myself into a panic. Still, I pulled my keycard from my top and let us both in without complaint. All I needed to do was regain control. Once my blood was freshly flowing through his veins again, I could make him do whatever I wanted. The thought gave me a sick sense of satisfaction as it always did.

I could endure a little rough treatment if it meant being able to control the *crown prince* for a few hours.

So, when he secured the door behind us and led me into the bedroom, I didn't balk, slowing only when we approached the bed.

"Not here," he said, tugging me toward the bathroom. "I don't want an audience for this."

My panic flared once more. Was he just going to kill me then? Had he figured out that I'd played with his mind last night?

As we entered the bathroom, he shut the door and began to undress. A swallow lodged in my throat. I'd touched his dick and had sex with him, but I hadn't seen him naked yet. With how firmly muscled he was, though, I could imagine he had a nice body. I bet he even—

Oh.

Nope. My imagination hadn't done him justice.

As his shirt fell away, I couldn't help but admire his sculpted chest and abs. He wasn't overly bulky, but his build wasn't lean either. His skin was still black as pitch, and a light trail of dark hair disappeared into his pants, making me curious about the rest of him. I've never seen a vampire naked in their true form before. His hands fell to his belt buckle next, and I openly watched him undo it. Seconds later, he jerked his pants down and his dick sprung free. It was already hard and saluting the air, the skin stretched taut and slightly shiny.

Wow. Bigger than I thought it would be.

Sudden warmth pooled between my legs, and I quickly pressed them together.

"Not bad," I told him, hiking up my eyebrows in appreciation.

"Your turn," he brusquely said, clearly not in the mood for foreplay.

Reaching into the stand-up shower, he switched on the water, then impatiently crossed his arms. Okay, then. We were getting right down to it. The fact that he'd undressed told me he wasn't planning on drowning me in the shower. At least not right away.

Choosing to think positively, I reached for my top and undid the straps. They loosened one by one, and as they unraveled, I saw Everett's chest expand. His eyes were locked on my every move, but unease didn't fill my belly. Just like in the dreams I'd had of him, I enjoyed having his gaze on me. It made me feel . . . wanted. *Desired.* But not entirely in a sexual way.

It felt like he wanted more from me. More *of* me.

My hands began to tremble, but not from fear. I was anticipating what would happen next. *Wanted* it to happen. I didn't feel the need to pretend for once. The look in his eyes mirrored how I felt inside.

Quickly removing my top, I slid off my bottoms and slowly

approached him. I kept my stilettos on, though. The six inch heels made me feel less small compared to him, at least in height. But my body mass was a *toothpick* compared to his. He could easily snap me in half like one too.

As soon as I was close enough, he pulled me into the shower and backed me against the wall. My spine met the cold tiles, warm water soaking my hair and body within seconds. And then his body was flush against mine, the heat of it penetrating my skin and bones.

I gasped at the heady sensation, my chest pushing against his. In reply, he pressed his pelvis to mine. A moan slipped free as his hardened length rubbed against my core. He pressed me more firmly against the tiles and blew out a ragged sigh, shutting his eyes.

Intrigued by his reaction, I whispered, "Why did you come back?"

He inhaled several breaths before replying, "I need to cleanse you from my system."

A small smirk tugged at my mouth. "By having sex with me?"

His eyes reopened and met mine. "Exactly."

He rocked against me, and my lips parted in a small whimper.

His gaze dropped to my mouth, and he uttered a curse. Reaching up, he touched my bottom lip. The pressure was featherlight, but I felt it all the way down to my toes. When my lips parted wider in response, he hissed through his teeth, "I hate this."

So did I. Hated and loved the way he made me feel.

"Are you going to kiss me?" I breathed, blinking up at him.

His jaw hardened, and he dropped his hand. "No. I don't kiss my conquests."

In the next moment, he was positioning himself at my entrance and sliding inside. I grabbed onto his biceps and squeezed my eyes shut, wondering if it would feel as good as the first time. With the first thrust came my answer. *Yes*. Better, even. Because I was expecting it to feel good, my body readily charged awake, eager to experience more.

As we found a rhythm, it dawned on me that I hadn't tried to make him bite me first. I'd been too distracted by his dick and how it would make me feel. But as that feeling washed over me, I suddenly didn't care. Who needed control when having sex felt this *good?* I knew the feeling wouldn't last, though. Knew that this was probably the last time I'd ever feel it. But if this was the last time, then I was going to enjoy it to the fullest.

Throwing my head back against the tiles, I used my flexibility to wrap my legs around his waist. The new angle drove him deeper inside me, and I cried out in pleasure. His hands found my backside and squeezed, his claws pricking the sensitive flesh. The action drove him even deeper, so deep that he hit a nerve that made me see stars. I groaned loudly, opening my mouth in rapture.

He hit the spot again. Again and again until I was making all sorts of noises.

Responding to the erotic sounds, he jerked me up higher and lowered his head to my neck. With one swift bite, his fangs sank into my flesh.

"*Yes*," I moaned, my breaths coming in short spurts as his venom flooded my veins. My eyes rolled back, bliss filling me from head to toe.

He stayed in his true form the entire time we had sex, every inch of him revealing the powerful predator he was inside. The sight should make me fear him. Anyone in their right mind would be afraid. But I'd told the truth to him last night. I wasn't in my right mind. Hadn't been for quite some time. In order to survive this bloodthirsty world, I'd had to adapt. To give up who I used to be.

The girl I was today didn't shy away from danger. She embraced it, knowing that death was only a knock away. If I was going to die, I might as well stare it down with a smile.

So, as death gripped me tight, I gripped it back, riding it like there was no tomorrow.

As both our pleasures built, our movements became frantic. Everett greedily pulled from my neck, holding me impossibly close as he drove inside me like a madman. It almost hurt, but I embraced the pain and matched his tempo, panting loudly as my body stiffened from the pleasure.

Overwhelmed by the sensations flooding my system, I opened my mouth and screamed. My orgasm whipped through me, sending me so high that darkness pulled me under. I returned to the surface in time to hear Everett bellow, his head thrown back in ecstasy as he spilled his release inside me.

We both struggled to catch our breath, our movements gradually slowing as the high faded. When it was a languid buzz, he lowered his head again to lick the blood from my neck. Startled by the almost tender gesture, I sputtered out a laugh.

He lifted his head again, no longer in his true form. Through his mask, I could see his pale green irises staring at me.

When he cocked his head in question, I simply said, "I've never screamed during sex before."

He stared at me for another long moment, then huffed a small laugh of his own.

The pleasant sound startled me enough that I blurted, "I know who you are."

I froze. So did he.

Spirits save me, *why* had I told him that? I'd just experienced the most mind-blowing orgasm of my entire life. And now, because of my stupid mouth, I was going to die.

Well, at least I got to enjoy sex before I kicked the bucket. Gotta look at it with the glass half full.

His eyes flickered. With what, I wasn't sure. Anger? Relief? Both?

Making me wait an eternity, he finally said, "How?"

"I'm a witch. I know things."

Oh, that'll for sure stop him from killing me. Way to sell it.

"How do I know you're not bluffing?"

"Guess you'll just have to take my word for it, *Your Highness.*"

His brows pulled together, shifting his mask. "You're an Oracle."

"Yep." My lips made a popping sound, drawing his gaze to them once more. The dude *really* needed to be kissed. He was clearly pining for it.

"Did you have a premonition about me or something?" he asked, studying me closely.

I shrugged. "Or something. Look, I won't tell my employers who you are, but they're going to find out eventually if you keep coming back."

His expression shuttered. "I won't be coming back."

"So I'm out of your system then?"

Doubtful. His *dick* was still inside me.

Instead of answering, he lifted a hand to my face and touched my mask.

Panic flushed through me. I batted his hand away without thought, then froze again, certain he would punish me for my insolence. But all he did was search my face, then reach for my mask again.

"What are you doing?" I breathlessly asked, holding still this time.

"You know who I am. It's only fair that I know who you are as well."

Oh no. I was so not okay with that. If he took off my mask, I would be more than naked. I would be laid *bare*. All of me. The *real* me.

I couldn't let him see that part of myself. Not here. Not like this.

I would break. *Break*. Crumble into a thousand pieces. Pieces that I could never hope to recover.

He couldn't remove my shield. It was the only thing keeping me *alive*.

Desperation pounded through me as he grasped the edge of my mask and began to lift it. No, no, *no*. I couldn't. I couldn't let him do this.

The mask lifted higher. And *higher*.

Not knowing what else to do, I grabbed his head and dragged it down to mine, then kissed him. Full on the mouth. With all of the determination and strength I possessed.

He ripped his mouth from mine with a growl. Jerking back, he released my mask, including me. I brought my stilettos down and caught myself, reaching up to pull my mask back into place.

We stared at each other for a long moment, the tension between us palpable. He was furious. *Furious* that I'd kissed him. But it had been the only way. The only way to protect my real identity.

"You shouldn't have done that," he said through clenched teeth. He glared at me a moment longer, then stormed from the shower. In a flash, he grabbed his clothes and was gone.

CHAPTER 9

ADALYN

Rocky trailed me closely as I exited the back door and crossed the empty parking lot.

As far as vampire's went, the quiet club bouncer was a pretty decent guy. I didn't know if Rocky was his real name, considering how everyone at Dreamscape liked to conceal their identities, but he *looked* like a Rocky. Big and burly with a shock of curly black hair.

He was a Feltore, though, so he hurried me along, needing to get home himself before the sun rose. As much as I loathed his species, I didn't have anything against him personally and had no desire to see him burn to ash. So I picked up the pace, knowing how late it was— or early, depending on how you looked at it.

After the prince had stormed out of my room, I'd been forced to entertain three more clients. None of them were new, so at least they'd been easier to control. I'd worked extra hard on them, needing to focus on anything but Everett.

There was just something about him. Something I wanted more of. Which was twisted, considering who he was. I'd been smart to kiss him. To push him away. Hopefully that was the last I saw of him. He'd already caused too many problems for me, and I couldn't afford to be distracted. To *want* something that could never be mine.

I really was sick in the head. The only thing I should want from the vampire prince was his heart on a silver platter. He'd used me for sex. He'd killed hundreds of my kind. He might even be my *father's* killer.

So why didn't I hate him as much as I should?

Mistress had already left for home, but she would definitely give me the third degree when I got back. I'd managed to secure a new client, only to *lose* him again. She was going to be suspicious and would no doubt use thrall to pry answers from me. I didn't know if I could keep his identity from her a second time, but did it even matter now?

He said he wasn't coming back, and I believed him. That kiss had stolen any desire he might have had to return. I'd seen it in his eyes.

Suddenly more than a little tired, I approached the Aston Martin on autopilot. Hopefully this weird dejected feeling would go away with a few hours of sleep. My sole focus needed to be on securing as many clients as I could and paying off my indenture. A vampire prince didn't fit into that equation, no matter how good he made me feel.

Reaching the car, I turned to bid Rocky goodnight. I was no longer wearing stilettos and a mask, but I didn't need to. I wasn't Star anymore. I was Adalyn. Rocky was one of the few vampires entrusted to keep my real identity a secret. He'd seen my face hundreds of times.

"Goodni—" I started, then froze when I saw something blur toward him from behind. Before I could warn him, a pair of hands grabbed his head and savagely twisted. As a sickening *crack* slapped the air, I stumbled back against the car.

Rocky collapsed like a bag of bricks, hitting the asphalt with a meaty thud. I stared in horror at his oddly bent neck, then forced my gaze up to the man who'd broken it.

"Hello, Star," he purred, darkly grinning at me. "Recognize me?"

At the blank look I gave him, he reached up and fitted a gold mask over his face.

"How about now?"

My blood turned to ice. It was the vampire who'd tried to shove his dick inside me in front of everyone. The one Everett had attacked. Benjamin Osborne.

Fear shivered up my spine.

Despite how dark the parking lot was, I knew he could clearly see my face. Pushing the fear down, I straightened and said, "You must have me mistaken for someone else. My name isn't Star."

He tossed the gold mask aside, his grin widening. "I don't care *what* your name is, sweetheart. I've memorized your scent, and it led me here. So how about you stop playing games and give me what I came for. I've been *more* than patient."

I swallowed carefully, willing my voice not to tremble. "It doesn't work that way. You have to pay first, and then—"

He pulled a wad of cash from his pocket and tossed it at me. I jumped as the bills exploded in the air like confetti. That split second of distraction was all it took. He rushed me in a blur, sweeping me clean off my feet. The impact knocked the air from my lungs, leaving me stunned as he carried me into the woods behind the club parking lot.

When I finally had enough air in my lungs again, I opened my mouth to scream. Before I could, he abruptly let go of me, and I hit the ground. My head took the brunt of the fall. It bounced off the hard-packed earth, and the world went dark.

As I came to again, the first thing I saw was the sadistic grin on Benjamin's face. I blinked, forcing myself not to pass out once more.

Slowly, he crawled on top of me and pressed my body into the dirt with his. An excited moan left him as he positioned himself between my legs. I didn't fight, knowing it was pointless. He had to see me as helpless. As his captured prey. It was the only way out of this.

"I hope you taste as good as you feel, sweet thing," he breathed, reaching up to brush hair off my face. "It's been a long time since I've been with a witch, and none of them were as pretty as you. I'm going to take my time, and if you please me, I'll make sure you feel good too."

As he settled more fully on top of me, revealing just how turned on he was by my helpless state, I inched my hand toward my back jeans pocket. He tipped back my head and exposed my vulnerable throat, growling softly as he bent and inhaled my scent. I stiffened when he began to kiss and nip at my flesh, slowly grinding himself against me. Knowing what I had to do, I clenched my teeth and arched my neck back, encouraging him to bite me.

"Oh, so eager," he crooned, dragging his tongue up my throat. "Are you wet for me too, sweetheart?"

He slipped a hand between us and fumbled to undo my pants. As the button popped open, cold resolve filled me. Yanking the small knife from my back pocket, I plunged it into his side.

He jerked off me with a roar, staggering back to clutch his side. I stayed still long enough to see the feral rage on his face when he realized the weapon was made out of silver. And then I was up in a flash, running for my life.

"What have you done, you conniving *whore?*" he screamed after me, shouting obscenities while he tried to remove the knife without burning himself. It wouldn't kill him, but the injury would hopefully buy me enough time to reach my car.

But as I ran, I realized with a sinking heart that he'd carried me farther into the woods than I thought. I wasn't going to make it.

Sure enough, I hadn't even reached the treeline before he caught up with me. This time, there was no mercy in his movements. He plucked me up and slammed me against the nearest tree, punching the air from my lungs. I gaped like a fish out of water, pain streaking up and down my spine like lightning. Gripping my throat, he leered in my face, his mouth twisted in fury.

"You're going to pay for that, slut," he hissed, spittle hitting my cheek. "I'm going to make you feel so much pain, you'll wish you were dead."

I opened my mouth to scream, but he struck like an adder. As his fangs brutally ripped into my neck, no sound left me. The shock of the pain crashed into me all at once, freezing me in place. The usual hit of venom didn't come, his aim to *punish* and not pleasure.

His mouth rapidly jerked against my neck as he began to feed, inhaling great gulps of my blood at alarming speed. Panic pushed through the shock, making me tremble from head to toe. Too much. He was taking *too much*. I tried to calm myself so I could gain control of his mind, but he slammed me back against the tree again, leaving me stunned and disorientated.

By the time I cleared some of the fog from my brain, I knew I was in trouble. My arms and legs were already starting to go numb. He was consuming too much blood. *Draining* me. I only had seconds left before it was too late.

A scream built in my mind, one formed of desperation and fear. I didn't want to die. I thought I was prepared to face death, but I wasn't. There was still so much life in me. Still so much I wanted to do. I'd barely begun to *live*, and leaving the world like this filled me with fury.

I didn't deserve this fate. No matter what I'd done to survive, I didn't deserve to be killed and tossed aside like *trash*.

The scream grew and grew, invading my mind so completely that I let it explode. No sound left my frozen lips, but I was burning up inside, raging against the unfairness of it all.

Benjamin suddenly let go of me. His fangs tore open my neck even more as he jerked away. More like *he* was jerked away. My ears rang as a deafening roar lit up the night, the tree behind me trembling under the force of it. Shadows darker than the night streaked past and tangled with Benjamin, bringing him to the ground. They landed with a *boom*, shaking the tree once more. The impact tore up a path of pine needles and dirt before the pair came to a grinding halt.

I slowly blinked, trying to make sense of everything. The shadows looked a lot like a person. Like . . .

"Everett?" Benjamin stopped struggling as he recognized who'd tackled him to the ground. "Ever, it's me. Ben. Ben Osborne."

"I know," Everett growled, his voice far from human. The shadows whipped around him, so thick that I could barely see his face. He was staring so hard at Ben that I expected red lasers to shoot from his eyes at any moment. "You never should have touched her."

He gripped Ben's head with both hands.

"Everett? What are you doing? We're friends. *Ever!*"

With a sharp twist, Everett broke Ben's neck. I slowly blinked again, barely hearing the *crack*. The ringing in my ears had grown louder and louder, each ring matching the tempo of my heart. With each ring, the tempo slowed, along with my heart.

Another blink, and I saw Everett rip Ben's head clean off. As it fell to the ground, I lost the battle with gravity and hit the ground as well. I stared up at the night sky, watching as it slowly darkened.

This wasn't good. I was probably at death's door now.

A face suddenly took the night's place. A face I knew. A face that was no longer hidden by a mask.

He took one look at my neck and swore colorfully. Wow. It must be pretty bad. My eyes drifted shut.

"Star. *Star*. Don't do this to me. Open your eyes."

Oh. He knew who I was. Also not good.

But I couldn't seem to care. I couldn't feel much of anything anymore, and the beats of my heart had slowed to a crawl.

Everett swore again, louder this time. Hands jostled my body, as if he was picking me up, and then something pressed against my mouth. Something warm and wet. I immediately tried to pull away.

"You have to *drink*," I heard him say, the distant words laced with what sounded like panic. "*Drink*, Star."

Something leaked past my lips. Something that tasted a lot like

. . .

I jerked away again, whimpering, "No."

"You'll *die*," he growled, pressing more firmly on my mouth. My lips parted, and I couldn't stop it. Couldn't stop the blood from filling my mouth. *His* blood. "Come on, Star. I'm not letting you die."

I weakly thrashed against his grip, trying to spit out the blood. But he was relentless, sealing a hand over my nose and mouth until I had no choice but to allow the blood inside. Exhausted, I stopped fighting, my energy depleted.

The last thing I felt before the world disappeared was his blood trickling down my throat.

CHAPTER 10

ADALYN

The first thing I did when I woke up was stretch languidly like a cat, throwing my arms over my head with a yawn.

I felt good. *Really* good. Like I'd slept for several hours straight, which I hadn't done in years.

My fingers grazed the pillow beneath me, and I froze. This wasn't my pillow. My pillow was old and lumpy. *This* pillow was plump and soft. So was the bed I was lying on.

My eyes sprang open.

"Pepper?"

The usual comforting voice of my familiar didn't respond back.

Panic flooded me. Had that mangy tabby gotten inside last night? Why hadn't I seen him?

"Pep!" I cried, sitting up and throwing the covers back. Covers that were far too luxurious to belong on my bed.

"Who's Pepper?"

Startled by the unexpected voice, I whipped my gaze to the far corner of the room. It was so dark that all I could make out was a shadowed figure sitting in a chair.

"Who are you? What do you want? Where am—?"

An image of being drained flashed in my mind. I jerked a hand to my throat, gasping when all I felt was smooth skin.

A lamp switched on, and I recoiled at the brightness, shielding my eyes. I froze again, horror flitting through me.

My *mask*. It was gone.

I glanced in the far corner again and dread filled my stomach.

"You," I whispered.

When all he did was silently watch me, a feeling of vulnerability settled over me. Never in my life had I felt this naked. This *exposed*.

He could see me. The crown vampire prince could see *me*. Adalyn. The real me.

Forcing my hands to my sides, I willed my voice to remain even as I said, "Where am I?"

Everett watched me a moment more, then replied, "In my bedroom."

My spine went ramrod straight. "Excuse me? Your bedroom? As in, your bedroom in the royal family castle on *Sanctum Isle?*"

He dipped his chin in confirmation.

All the blood drained from my face. Mistress was going to *kill* me. Who knew how much time had passed since I'd been attacked. I felt in my pockets for my phone, but it was gone as well.

"I-I can't be here. I have to leave." Disoriented and completely out of my element, I scrambled from the bed and hurried to the door. At any moment, I expected Everett to stop me, but he didn't. He simply watched as I beelined across the huge room and yanked the door open.

When a wall of muscle greeted me on the other side, I flinched back with a small yelp. I was surrounded. Completely surrounded by powerful royal vampires. Huge and intimidating ones that were looking at me like I was a rabbit caught in their snare.

"Aww, she's frightened. I think she needs a hug," the biggest one with sunkissed skin and caramel-colored hair said. When he stepped forward with his arms spread wide, I stumbled back, right into a hard body.

Before I could jerk away, an arm curved around my waist, trapping me there.

"No hugs, Kade. That'll only frighten her more." The rumbling voice at my back was definitely Everett's, and my body's first instinct was to relax, which was the *last* thing it should be doing right now.

"Well, *you're* hugging her," the big vampire said, faintly smirking at Everett's arm around my waist.

Everett dropped his arm. "That wasn't a hug."

"Then what was it?"

The prince blew out a long-suffering sigh. "Can you call off your drothen, Loch? He's been extra annoying this morning."

Morning. My ears perked up at the word. Maybe I hadn't lost as much time as I'd originally thought.

"Kade. Behave," the other vampire quietly said. I did a double take at his face. He was definitely Everett's brother. The main difference between them was the color of their eyes and hairstyle. His brother wore his black hair longer. It fell across his brow in a stylishly messy way, further shadowing his dark eyes.

The vampire called Kade stuck out his bottom lip and retorted, "I *am* behaving. Your brother is just being extra *ornery* this morning."

At that, Everett's brother cracked a small smile.

"Don't encourage him, Loch," Everett lightly growled, yet there was no anger behind the words. In fact, his sharp tone held something that caught me entirely off guard.

Affection.

I'd always been told the royal family were merciless, cutthroat killers devoid of kindness or affection. Then again, hadn't I seen for myself that Everett could be kind? He'd just rescued me, after all. *Again.*

Yeah, because he wants inside your pants, I bitterly reminded myself.

A sudden thought struck me, and I whirled toward him with a gasp. "Rocky. Did you see him? Benjamin snapped his neck before he came after me. He can't be out in the sun. He'll burn to *ash*. I have to go. I have to make sure—"

I turned for the door again, my only thought on getting the bouncer to safety before he went up in smoke. Deep down, though, I already knew it was too late. Still, I needed to get out of here. There was no telling what Mistress would do when she found out I hadn't come home last night.

"Have you seen my phone? I have to make a call." I paused at the door, gesturing at the wall of muscle to move aside. There was no time for diplomacy and certainly no time for fear. If they intended to kill me, they would have already done so.

Then again, they might want me alive for *other* things. Maybe they liked to share their females like the Faircroft sisters liked to share men. I shoved the thought aside before panic could take hold. No matter what they planned to do, I couldn't reveal how unnerved I was to be here. The minute I showed even an ounce of fear, they'd attack like the predators they were.

When the two vampires stepped aside, allowing me to pass into the hallway, I struggled to mask my shock. Huh. That had been easy. *Too* easy. Deciding not to look the gift horse in the mouth, I kept going. A tall window at the far end of the hall cheerily revealed the time of day, which only made me cringe. Yep. Rocky was toast by now. There was probably nothing left of him. I sure hoped he didn't have a wife and kids waiting for him at home.

"Star."

I cringed again, hating the sound of that name on his lips. Knowing that I'd only embarrass myself by making a run for it, I stopped and slowly turned to face Everett. He was leaning casually against the doorway of his bedroom, his arms crossed over his chest. I couldn't help but notice that he was wearing the same dark outfit as last night. The only difference now was that he wore a gold and ruby ring on his pinky finger and didn't have a mask on. He looked . . . tired. Worn out. Like he hadn't slept for a day or two. A feeling I knew all too well.

Wait. Had he sat in that chair all morning and watched me sleep? The thought should disturb me, but instead, a warm feeling settled in my stomach. Yup. I most definitely was not in my right mind.

When I raised an eyebrow at him in question, he said, "Rocky is fine. I placed him on the shaded side of the building. His neck was already halfway healed when I left."

I stared at him for a long moment, trying to understand what he'd just said. As his words finally sank in, the warm feeling in my belly intensified. Giving my head a slight shake, I said, "I need to speak with His Highness alone, please."

"His Highness," the vampire called Kade repeated with a quiet chuckle. "I like her."

Everett shared a look with his brother, who nodded and turned to leave.

When Kade continued to stare at me with a big grin on his face, Loch called back, "Kade."

Kade winked at me, then took off after the prince.

Everett stepped back into his room, and I followed him, casting one last longing look down the hallway. I really needed to leave, but I couldn't just walk out of this place. The island was huge. I wouldn't make it to the mainland on my own—not in one piece anyway. Most of the kingdom's Venturi lived here, and with their ability to walk in the sun, they'd catch my scent for sure. One whiff and I'd be a goner.

At least the nightclub afforded me *some* protection. Out here, I was a sheep among wolves with very sharp teeth.

Everett shut the door behind me, sealing us inside his room once more. I tried to conjure up a healthy sense of fear but couldn't quite manage it. Probably because the shock of staring death in the face earlier this morning hadn't worn off yet. Resisting the urge to touch my throat again, I said without facing him, "Do they know what I am?"

"That you're a witch?"

"No. A . . . a blood whore."

I worried my lip, waiting for his answer. It came all too soon.

"Yes. They know I've been with you for the past few nights. I couldn't avoid telling them when I came home carrying your unconscious body."

Great. Just great. Nothing like bringing home your dirty little secret for the family to meet.

Feeling exposed again, I crossed my arms over my chest. "How did you find me anyway? I thought you'd be long gone."

He paused for a beat, then said, "I was in my car across the street. I was going to follow you home, but then I heard you scream."

My eyes widened. Screamed? But I hadn't screamed out loud. Or had I? Setting aside my confusion, I dropped my arms and turned to look at him. He really was a handsome devil. Even when he'd worn a mask, I'd enjoyed looking at his face. I wondered if he felt the same about me, or if seeing my entire face killed the mystery for him. He really had no reason to want me anymore. I wasn't anything special under all the makeup, sequins, and sultry looks.

Star was sexy and alluring. A pretty package that begged to be unwrapped. Adalyn, on the other hand, was simply tired. Tired and fighting to survive.

Suddenly unsure of myself, I covered my insecurity with a light scoff and said, "For a vampire who hates witches, you sure do rescue me a lot. I'm surprised you didn't turn me when you had the chance. I was almost drained, after all."

"I don't."

I blinked. "Don't what?"

"I don't hate you."

Something fluttered in my chest, and it wasn't panic. Confused, I blurted, "You might crave my body and blood, but I saw how angry you were when I kissed you." At that, his eyes flashed in warning. "See? I struck a nerve. I'm still just a disgusting witch to you."

He didn't respond, but his eyes were slowly peeling back my layers, seeing far more than I wanted him to.

Growing desperate, I said, "I've heard the stories about you. I know what you've done to my kind. How you went on a killing spree up and down the coast, all because of one witch's deeds."

His expression hardened, making the hairs on my arms slowly stand on end. I was definitely treading on dangerous ground now. "And yet you still had sex with me."

I swallowed carefully before replying, "Yes. It's my job."

His brows lowered. "Is it? You don't seem to like it when your clients touch you."

I opened my mouth, but no words came out.

He suddenly moved. *Prowled.* Like a predator on the hunt. As he approached me, I went poker straight. The need to run trembled through me, but I knew how dumb that would be. So I held still and let him invade my personal space, tilting my head back as he filled my vision. Once there, he stopped and stared down at me with so much intensity that my toes curled.

"I don't have to like it," I finally replied, needing to cut through some of the thick tension between us. "I just have to pretend to."

"Is that what you did with me? Pretend?"

A swallow got stuck in my throat. It almost hurt to maintain eye contact with him now, but I didn't dare look away. "I'm very good at pretending."

"Is that so?"

I was suddenly on my back in the middle of his gigantic bed. A sharp gasp escaped me as his body settled on top of mine, pressing me into the mattress. We lined up perfectly from chest to pelvis, and my core immediately lit on fire at the intimate contact.

To play off how strongly my body had just responded to his, I gave him a sardonic smirk and cooed, "Yes. I'm very good at my job."

"I agree," he rumbled, dipping his head to breathe in my ear. "But you're not pretending right now. I can smell how aroused you are."

As he paused to inhale my scent, more of that delicious heat unfurled in my belly. Silently cursing, I replied, "Fine, I admit that you make me feel things."

He chuckled quietly, reaching up to slide his fingers into my hair. I felt the contact all the way to my toes. "You make me feel things too. Naughty things. Things that I want to feel again right now."

At his confession, the heat spread to every inch of my body. My breaths grew shallow and a touch needy. "Do you plan to keep me here as your own personal whore, then?"

"Maybe I will." He brushed his nose up the column of my throat. "And would that be so awful? That way, no other males could touch you."

I immediately perked up at the idea, thrilled at the thought of being free of all the groping hands and leering gazes. But reality chose that moment to knock some sense into me, to remind me of why I'd accepted the job in the first place. Pursing my lips, I shook my head and forced out, "I like my job. It gives me purpose."

Undeterred, Everett inhaled my scent again and whispered, "I can give you the same purpose. And with me, you'll actually enjoy it."

My eyes fluttered shut as pleasure skated through me, making me grow wet.

Spirits save me, what was happening right now? It felt like he was seducing me, something I'd never experienced before. Even worse, I *liked* it. I should be offended that the crown vampire prince was offering to make me his little play thing, but my body was thoroughly enjoying the proposal.

His other hand cupped my cheek, the thumb stretching along my jaw toward my mouth. My *lips*. He really needed to put himself out of his misery and just kiss me already. Despite his distaste for it, I could sense he wanted to.

Before I could encourage him to do that very thing, he asked, "Why did you resist drinking my blood?"

My eyes popped back open. Oh, yeah. He'd forced me to drink his blood so I wouldn't die. I'd had no choice, despite the command in my head telling me to spit it out. I'd tried, but Everett was so much stronger than me. At the reminder that his blood was now flowing through my veins, the heat vanished. It was like a bucket of ice water had just been tossed over me.

Knowing I couldn't tell him the truth, I lamely said, "I'm not a vampire. My body doesn't naturally want to consume blood."

As if sensing the lie, he pulled back to search my face. "You were bleeding out. Would you rather I have let you?"

I didn't respond right away, and that told him far too much.

His gaze darkened, and he opened his mouth again. Before he could say anything, though, a knock came at the door.

"Father wants an audience with you, Everett."

Everett's body tensed over mine. "Now?"

"Yes. He wants to meet her."

Now it was *my* turn to tense. Everett felt it and focused back on me. "I won't let him harm you."

He was getting *way* too good at reading me. The sooner I left this place and put my mask back on, the better.

Before I could respond, he lifted off me and stood. "Come on. He doesn't like to be kept waiting."

As he adjusted his clothing, hiding how turned on he'd been moments before, I glanced down at my own clothing. Cringing, I scooted off the bed and hurried to the gold floor-length mirror in the corner.

One look and I turned to vehemently shake my head. "Nope. No way am I letting the vampire *king* see me like this. It's bad enough that you have."

He paused to lift an eyebrow. "None of that matters. He'll see right through any mask you put on anyway."

A nervous laugh burst from me. "Was that supposed to make me feel better? Because it didn't. I still have *blood* on my sweater." Not on my skin, though. Everett must have cleaned it off while I slept, which didn't fill me with revulsion like I thought it would. Not even a little. Something was definitely wrong with me.

"He just wants to meet you, Star. I'll find you fresh clothing afterward."

Afterward. There wasn't going to *be* an afterward. I was leaving the first chance I got. Now that Everett wasn't invading my personal space, I could think clearly again. Time was ticking, and I needed to get back to Faircroft Manor before something terrible happened.

With that in mind, I pushed aside my bout of insecurity and gestured for him to lead the way. The sooner I got this meeting over with, the better. I just hoped I survived it.

As Everett opened the door, his brother greeted us on the other side. They both waited for me to join them, then took off down the hallway. Kade was nowhere to be found, but I didn't have time to wonder where he was.

The brothers' long strides ate up the marble floor, leaving my average-length legs struggling to catch up. I was barely able to focus on my surroundings, but the glimpses I saw took my breath away. Faircroft Manor and even my room at Dreamscape Lounge were decorated with lavish, expensive things, but this place was the epitome of wealth. The furniture was gold and encrusted in jewels. The walls were adorned with dozens of paintings that I recognized. *Original* paintings, which meant that they were priceless.

The more I saw, the more I realized how out of place I was. I didn't belong in this world, and that fact had never been more glaringly clear. But there was nothing I could do other than hold my head high and hope the king didn't kill me on sight.

If he only knew what I knew, I'd be dead in a heartbeat.

Minutes later, we reached the throne room on the second floor. A legit *throne* room. How bizarre and archaic that sounded. The witch community never had fancy houses for their elders to reside in. My father had been well off, but we'd lived rather simply in order to blend in with the human populace. The community boasted several schools for learning magic, and that was it. I'd been attending one of those schools up in Canada when my dad had received the call to unite with the other elders.

I would never forget his final words to me as he'd portalled into my school dorm room that night and awakened me from sleep to say, *"You're my bright shining star, Ada darling. Whatever happens after tonight, don't let anyone dull that light. Shine brightly for all to see."*

Sudden sadness filled me. It had been six years since I lost him, but in some ways, it still felt like yesterday. If he could only see me now, surrounded by the creatures he'd so desperately tried to keep me safe from.

When Everett looked over his shoulder at me, I quickly wiped my expression clean. He frowned but faced forward without comment as we entered the throne room. I followed him and his brother, keeping my face free of emotion while I took in the massive room. It was mostly empty, with the opposite side sporting several tall windows. Light poured into the space, which wasn't normal for a vampire dwelling.

This place wasn't normal, though, and neither were the vampires who lived here. The sun couldn't hurt Venturi. Not much could, actually. Silver could harm them, but only a direct hit to the heart could kill them. That and decapitation. Only vampires were strong enough to pull each other's heads off, though.

Remembering how Everett had ripped his friend's head off, I struggled to stay focused. This was a violent world, and I was about to meet its leader. I spotted him at the far end, sitting on a regal throne perched on a dais. The first thing that struck me was how young he looked, barely older than his sons. Age hadn't lined his face, a face that looked strikingly similar to his children's.

He was sitting on his throne rather casually, with one long leg crossed over the other and an elbow propped on a golden armrest. He wore his medium-length hair loosely swept back, and his black suit looked tailor-made to fit his lean body.

"Ah, my sons. Come in, come in," he said, the smooth words rich with authority. He was used to being obeyed, that much was clear. "And what is it that you've brought me today? Step forward, young lady. Don't be shy."

Shy? Did he think I was *trying* to hide behind his sons? I couldn't help it if they were so huge.

Slightly annoyed by the label he'd so readily placed on me, I shouldered my way past the brothers. Everett immediately grabbed my arm to haul me back.

"*Stop.*"

The command sliced through the air like a whip. We all froze in our tracks to look up at the king.

"Let her go, son. Let her approach."

It was Loch who spoke next. "Father," he started, sliding forward a step as if to shield me.

The king waved a hand dismissively. "No. She had the guts to step forward, so let her."

Uh. Had I accidentally challenged him or something? My time with vampires hadn't exactly taught me proper royal etiquette.

Everett slowly released me, but I could practically feel his unease. Which didn't exactly boost my confidence. Still, I was used to facing vampires who saw me as nothing but a bug to be squashed. If the king wanted to rattle me, he'd have to try a little harder.

Straightening my spine, I pulled away from Everett to approach his father. By habit, I put a little sultry swagger in my step, and the king's eyes brightened with amusement. Interesting. I'd heard about his human harem. He collected wives like some men collected cars. I'd anticipated at least a *little* lust in his eyes.

When I was a handful of yards away, he uncrossed his legs and set both feet on the dais. I took that as my cue to stop, so I did, staring up at him expectantly. He met my stare with growing amusement, which annoyed me further. Did he want me to dance around his dais like a court jester? I would if he commanded me to, but that didn't mean I had to like it.

Not knowing what else to do, I dipped down in a graceful curtsy and murmured, "Your Majesty."

When I straightened once more, he was inches from my face, grinning like a fiend.

CHAPTER 11

ADALYN

Despite my resolve not to let him fluster me, having the vampire king inches from my face was terrifying.

He'd used his supernatural speed to catch me unaware, which had clearly been his intention. I flinched at his closeness but didn't jerk back. As much as I wanted to, retreating would be a sign of weakness, and I definitely couldn't afford to look weak right now.

"Well, hello there," he said, his voice almost a croon. "I'm King Ambrose, which I'm guessing you already know. And you are?"

I struggled to swallow as I stared into his garnet-colored eyes. Eyes that regarded me with open curiosity. "Star."

He tilted his head, those penetrating eyes slightly narrowing. "Just Star?"

"Yes, Your Majesty."

He studied me for an unbearable moment before saying, "Well, here's the thing, *Star.*" He said it as if all too aware that Star was my stage name. "I want to know what you've done to my son. He's never taken an interest in a witch before. Not sexually, anyway. Did you enchant him with a spell?"

Whoa. Not even *I* was ready for that one. My mouth opened, but nothing came out. When all I did was gape like a fish, he whipped a hand up and caught my chin.

"What. Have you done. To my son?" he slowly enunciated, his eyes boring into mine.

Fear spiked through my calm facade. I waited for the *pull* to suck the words from my mouth, but it never came. He couldn't thrall me. Not with his son's blood fresh in my system.

"Don't touch her!" Everett suddenly snapped. He was at my side in a flash, ripping me away from his father. His arms banded around me like a shield, trembling with barely-restrained fury.

Shocked senseless, I didn't even think about pulling away. And I wasn't the only shocked one. The king's mouth fell open as he took in his son's anger. He looked between the two of us for several moments, and then his expression filled with sudden understanding.

"Oh, I see."

"See *what?*" Everett hissed, holding me so tightly that my ribs ached.

The king watched his son for a moment longer, then quietly said, "She's your soulmate. It's why you brought her home instead of hiding her away."

Every line of Everett's body stretched taut. I didn't react, certain I'd heard wrong. Did he just say *soulmate?*

"No. That's impossible." Everett vehemently shook his head. "I've had sex with her. *Twice.*" I winced at how dirty he made it sound. "I would know by now if I shared a bond with her. I haven't felt her emotions and there's been no telepathic connection."

I didn't say anything, and yet, the king's attention abruptly swung to me. "You know something. What is it?"

I gawked at him, about to deny knowing anything, but a sudden memory came to me. I swallowed, certain I was going to be sick. "This morning when I was attacked, he said he heard me scream. It's how he knew I was in trouble. Only . . . I didn't scream. Not out loud anyway."

Everett jerked against me, like he'd just been shot. When his arms tightened painfully, I made a small sound. He let go of me and leapt back as if he'd just been burned.

"Lochlan, escort Miss Star to a room on the third floor," King Ambrose said. "Everett is in no condition to do so."

As Everett's brother moved forward, Everett whirled toward him with a growl. Loch slowed, holding his hands up. "It's okay, Ev. I won't touch her."

That didn't seem to appease him. He reached for me again, but I quickly evaded his hands, suddenly needing space. *Lots* of it. "Actually," I began, deciding to address the king, "I need to head home. My . . . my family will be worried that I didn't come back this morning, and I can't find my phone."

Everett reached for me again. "You're not going anywhere, Star—"

"*Everett.*"

The crown prince drew up short, just shy of touching me. Curling his hands into fists, he dropped them and faced his father.

"Miss Star will not be held prisoner in our home. We have no grounds to keep her here, and you heard what she said. Her family is worried. Now, let your brother take her home. We need to talk."

Everett's fists began to tremble. He looked ready to explode, and I braced myself for whatever violence was about to unfold. But, after a lengthy moment, his trembling ceased and he slowly unclenched his fists.

"Take her," he gruffly said, jerking his chin at his brother. "But don't—"

"Touch her. I know," Loch interrupted quietly. "You have my word."

As Loch gestured for me to follow him, I took a tentative step forward.

"Don't be afraid, Miss Star," King Ambrose said. "Everett won't try to stop you again."

I paused to glance back at the king and say, "I'm not afraid. I just don't want him to break all my ribs."

He stared at me for a moment, then burst out laughing. Clutching his stomach, he wagged a finger at me and said, "I'm starting to like you, young lady. I really hope you don't prove to be a disappointment."

He kept on laughing, but I felt the threat deep in my bones. He was going to keep an eye on me. And now that I was on his radar, I didn't know how much longer I could hide my true identity—not to mention the truth about my shady nightclub job.

Loch and I managed to leave the castle without incident, but I could practically *feel* Everett's restless energy as I left the building. What if it was true? What if we were really . . . soulmates?

I knew little about the soulmate bond, only that it was more powerful than a witch's bond with their familiar. I couldn't imagine feeling closer to someone than I did with Pepper. She was *literally* a part of me, a piece of her celestial spirit now mine. It was the price all spirits had to pay if they chose to inhabit the earthly plane, be they angel or demon. Many spirits that made the sacrifice chose not to seek out the mortal who now owned a sliver of their essence, but my familiar had found me when I was just a child. I didn't remember a time when she hadn't been in my life.

Besides my dad and the school for witches I'd attended, she'd helped me learn how to harness my Oracle magic. It had originally been hers, after all. I'd brought her with me that terrible night six years ago, another huge mistake I'd made. If I hadn't, she could have moved on to discover a better life for herself instead of being cooped up in a dank basement.

This world wasn't safe for a mouse familiar. Her celestial spirit was powerful, and so was her magic, but her tiny body wasn't. I'd never forgive myself if something happened to her.

An uncomfortable silence settled over us as Everett's brother drove me from the castle. I'd thought *Everett* was quiet, but his brother was even more so. Deciding that idle chit chat would just be a waste of energy, I sank into the seat of the expensive black Lexus and enjoyed the view. The six-story limestone castle was situated on the west side of the island, surrounded by thick forest and rocky coastline. The road we were on was smooth, lazily winding through pine trees and majestic oaks.

After a few minutes, I rolled down my window to enjoy the experience more fully, inhaling the salty air rich with flora and fauna. Loch looked over at me but didn't say a word, which I was slowly starting to appreciate. It almost felt like he understood how overwhelmed I was and that silence would help me process it all. When it became clear that he had no intention of touching me, I allowed myself to relax, if only a little.

We were nearing the gated bridge, the only entrance and exit to the island, when I finally broke the silence. "If you could drop me off at Dreamscape Lounge, that would be great. My car is still parked there, and I need to find my phone. My family is probably worried sick."

He nodded, easily accepting my explanation as truth. He had no reason to suspect otherwise.

Half an hour later, my stomach broke the silence again. As it loudly growled, I peeked at Everett's brother. A faint smirk tilted his lips, but he didn't say a word. When we neared Bangor, though, he veered off the main road. Realizing where he was going, I struggled to keep my jaw from dropping.

Never in my wildest dreams did I think a vampire prince would visit a fast food drive-thru.

He waited for me to order, then ordered a burger for himself.

"You eat food?" I blurted before I could think better of it. Apparently, the thought of filling my belly had loosened my tongue.

"Occasionally," he replied, speaking to me for the first time. "I only enjoy savory foods, though. Anything sweet tastes gross to me."

He handed me the large milkshake I'd ordered with a small grimace. I couldn't quite smother a laugh.

"Thank you for this. You didn't have to," I said, taking a large gulp of my drink. I swallowed a moan as the cold liquid deliciously slid down my throat.

"I wanted to," was all he said, pulling onto the highway again.

The greasy food more than hit the spot, and I gobbled it down faster than was appropriate. When I caught him side-eyeing me, I quickly wiped my mouth with a napkin and said, "Almost being drained makes you super hungry, I guess."

Something like sympathy flickered in his dark eyes, which made me feel all sorts of confused. Why was he being so *nice* to me? Of all the vampires in the world, he should hate witches the most. Even more than Everett.

As if he knew where my thoughts had strayed, he quietly said, "My wife is a witch. She would have loved to meet you today, but she's having a girls' weekend with her best friend Isla. Her husband, Kade, came over to help with the twins. He and Isla often reside in Rosewood because of her job. They have a lakehouse there, newly remodeled so Isla can enjoy seeing the sun without getting hurt. She's a Feltore, by the way."

Overwhelmed by the influx of information he'd just shared, I focused on the most surprising tidbit. "Your wife is a witch? I heard the stories about her many years ago from my dad. I thought she was turned."

"She was, but the bond she shares with me and her familiar transformed her into a half witch, half vampire hybrid."

My jaw did drop this time. "My dad didn't mention that part. I didn't know something like that was possible."

"Neither did I. But since meeting McKenna, I've learned to expect the unexpected. To embrace the impossible. I definitely didn't anticipate fate giving me a witch for a soulmate."

I blinked at him, certain I'd heard wrong. "You're soulmates?"

His mouth curved into a soft smile. "Yes. And it's the best thing that's ever happened to me."

Hearing how genuine he sounded, sudden pain squeezed my chest. I could tell that he loved her. *Truly* loved her. I couldn't imagine finding love like that. Wouldn't even dare dream that it was possible. I recalled the intimate moments I'd shared with Everett, and the pain increased tenfold.

That wasn't love. What we shared had been purely lust, nothing more.

Bitterness coated my next question. "Does your brother hate her?"

Loch flicked me another glance. "At first. He worried that McKenna would hurt me. He's been overprotective ever since . . ."

"I know," I said, not needing him to finish. "I've heard the stories about the Syphon witch who kept a vampire prince as her personal blood slave."

His hands tightened on the steering wheel. Shockingly, I felt a pang of empathy for him. My own situation wasn't much different, not that I could tell him that.

"And then your brother went on a killing spree, murdering hundreds of innocent witches and warlocks," I added, needing to remind myself who the *true* victims were. If it wasn't for Everett, my life would be very different. He'd ruined it even before I was born.

Remembering that I'd *slept* with him, even after knowing who he was, my stomach soured.

Surprisingly, Loch didn't immediately come to his brother's defense. I'd expected him to be angry at my accusing tone, but he only sighed and said, "What Everett did was wrong. We both made terrible mistakes after I was abducted, and we lost our younger brother in the process. Everett has changed since then, but he's still haunted by the past. It doesn't excuse his poor behavior, but maybe this will help you understand him a little better. If you two really are soulmates, I believe he'll come around, just like he did with McKenna. He might be bullheaded, but he's also fiercely protective of his family and will do whatever it takes to keep them safe."

I didn't respond, struggling to process all that he'd said. He wasn't supposed to sound *remorseful*. Wasn't supposed to be a decent person who admitted his mistakes and had changed for the better. How was I supposed to hate the royal family now? How was I supposed to hate *Everett?*

And, more importantly, how was I supposed to follow through with my plan for revenge?

CHAPTER 12

EVERETT

We were at a stalemate.

I paced the long length of the throne room, wishing I was anywhere but here. It didn't matter what I said. My father was adamant that Star was my soulmate.

Impossible. I didn't feel any different.

I was more agitated lately, and seeing Ben with his hands on her had filled me with blinding fury, but that didn't mean we were fated for one another. If anything, Father's first suspicion was correct.

I was under her enchantment.

"You're in denial, son. You don't feel any different because you haven't accepted the bond. Neither has she, I'm guessing. Sex alone can't complete the bond. You have to *want* it. To truly desire a soul connection with your mate."

"She's not my mate," I replied through clenched teeth, losing the last of my patience. At the same time, the memory of her bleeding out flashed in my mind. Without a second thought, I'd offered her my blood. When she'd refused it, terror had gripped me. Breathing had been impossible until color slowly flushed her cheeks once more. Unwilling to let her out of my sight, I'd done the worst thing possible and brought her home with me.

Now, I was paying dearly for that mistake.

"Everett, you need to accept this," my father pushed once more, making my anger spill over. "She's a blood whore at a feeding den.

You won't be able to tolerate the thought of other males touching her. If you don't sort this out soon, she could get hurt or worse."

I whirled toward him with fire in my eyes. "I *know* what she is. That's why I wasn't going to tell you about her. I won't deny that I desire her, but she doesn't want to give up her job. So what am I supposed to do? Command her to stop having sex with other males because she *might* be my soulmate?"

He shrugged. "Yes. You're the crown prince."

I shook my head with a scoff. "You don't know her the way I do, Father. She's independent. *Confident.* There isn't an ounce of fear in that fragile mortal body of hers. She won't give up her job simply because the crown prince tells her to."

He was silent for a long beat, slowly tapping the armrest of his throne. Then, "Sounds like she would make the perfect queen for you."

I bared my teeth at him, completely done with this conversation.

He wasn't done, though. Rising from his throne, he stepped toward me and said, "When I heard the rumors surrounding that nightclub, I had you check it out to give you a sense of *purpose* again, son. Ever since the curse broke, I've watched you flounder. You've spent over a century hunting down witches to protect this family. Most of your life has been a race to save this kingdom from ruin, and along the way, you completely lost yourself."

"I'm not lost."

"You *are.*" He approached me slowly, keeping me locked in his gaze. "You've lost sight of who you're supposed to be. You're the crown prince. My *heir.* The future king of this kingdom. You don't have to run anymore, son. This kingdom is safe now because of you. Accept who you are and embrace it. Find purpose in your role as our future king because you *will* be king and best be ready. I don't think it was an accident that I sent you to that nightclub. I think it was your destiny to go there, and I think Star is your fate."

When he paused before me, I could barely hold still. I wanted to lash out at him and anything else within distance. I felt trapped. Backed into a corner. Powerless as the Universe decided my future for me.

Unable to bear it a moment longer, I turned to leave the throne room, along with my father and his great expectations of me. Before I could, tiny squeals interrupted the tension-filled moment.

"Papa! Papa!"

"Unca Evy!"

We turned toward the side door as two fifteen-month-old toddlers rushed into the room, followed by a harried-looking Kade.

"Sorry," he said, stopping the black-haired boy from face-planting on the marble. "They escaped the second my back was turned. I can only imagine the Houdini acts they'll pull when their vampire speed kicks in."

The little boy beelined for his grandfather while the girl toddled toward me. She also had her father's dark coloring, but they both had their mother's silver gray eyes. As her adorable face split into a toothy grin, all of my anger faded. I bent and scooped her up, careful not to let our skin touch. The twins had become better at controlling their Syphon magic over the past few months, but when they were hyper like this, they easily forgot about their abilities.

"Did you feed them sweets again?" I directed at Kade, already knowing the answer as Zoey clapped her sticky hands together.

"Kenna had a cheesecake made for me before she left," Kade replied with a sheepish shrug. "I just want Zo-Bee and Nico to appreciate finer cuisine. You know Lochie won't care if their palates are stunted like his."

Grunting, I dodged one of Zoey's sticky hands before it could smack me in the face. "Fast!" she cried, bouncing in my arms. "Fast, fast!"

"Fast!" her brother parroted, his cheeks stained with strawberry juice.

My father chuckled and tossed his grandson high in the air. Definitely higher than Kenna would approve of. The boy squealed in delight the whole way down. "You want to go fast, Nico? How fast?"

"Fast, fast!" Nicolas replied, gleefully shrieking as his papa took off across the room at supernatural speed.

I followed suit, smiling when Zoey belly laughed the entire way. Their interruption had come at the perfect time. I'd needed this, more than I knew. As the twins continued to shriek, "Fast, fast, fast!" I felt the last of my tension unravel.

Almost two hours later, when we'd tired out Nico and Zoey enough to get them down for a nap, my phone buzzed. My senses immediately went on high alert, the tension returning once more. I strode down the hall toward my room, accepting the call without needing to check who it was.

"Is she okay?"

"She's fine," came Loch's reply. Relief flooded me, until he said, "I dropped her off at her car, then followed her from a safe distance. You were right, Ev. She's definitely hiding something. The information she gave me about her home was false. She went straight to her employer's house and parked in the garage as if she lives there. She even has a key for the back door."

At that, I changed course, zooming down five flights of stairs within seconds. "Give me the address. I'm heading your way."

Loch sighed through the phone, but he didn't argue. Seconds later, he texted me the address. I hung up soon after that, needing to concentrate. Needing to plan. I didn't know what I would do once I got there, but the thought of Star living with the vampires who sold her for sex night after night filled me with growing dread. The second she'd flinched at my touch, I'd known in my gut that something was wrong.

If I found out they were forcing her to have sex against her will, there would be hell to pay.

CHAPTER 13

ADALYN

Mistress was yelling. *Screaming.*

Despite my precarious position, I took comfort in knowing that nothing had happened to Pepper while I was away. I desperately wanted to see her, to scoop her little body into my hands and pour out my emotions to her, but Mistress had pounced on me the second I'd entered the house.

"Are you listening to me, Adalyn?" she shouted, grabbing my chin. As her fingers dug into my flesh, no doubt leaving bruises, I struggled to remain calm. "You were gone for *hours* after Rocky called and reported you missing. We thought you were *dead*. I demand to know what happened."

Georgina and Octavia shuffled into the kitchen, still in their pajamas and blinking sleepily. They definitely hadn't lost any sleep over my disappearance.

"What did she do this time?" Georgina muttered with a yawn, nudging her sister aside on the way to the fridge.

"She didn't come *home* last night," her mother spat, her brown eyes slowly bleeding red. Wow. She was *livid*. I didn't know if I would survive this conversation.

Georgina threw me a nasty look. "Bet she was meeting a *client* for a secret rendezvous. We all know how much she likes to spread her legs. Guess she's not getting enough sex at the club."

Heat burned my cheeks, but I firmly bit my tongue.

"Is that true, Adalyn? Were you secretly meeting with a client?"

It was purely a question, not a *command*. Mistress hadn't used thrall on me yet, and I couldn't let her. If she tried and found out it wasn't working, she'd know that I'd consumed vampire blood.

"I was attacked," I evenly replied, my gaze steady on hers. "Someone jumped Rocky in the parking lot and broke his neck, then went after me."

Mistress narrowed her eyes, searching for a lie. "And then what happened? You have blood on your sweater, but your neck bears no marks."

Georgina turned from the fridge with a blood bag in hand, ripping it open to drink straight from the bag. Octavia struggled to grab her own breakfast as her sister leaned against the open fridge and watched us with a bored expression.

"I can't remember everything. It all happened so quickly. He bit me and drank a lot of blood, I know that much."

"Why didn't you *stop* him? For heaven's sake, Adalyn. Why do I give you the ability to defend yourself if you're not going to use it?"

"I'm sorry, Mistress. I really did try, but I got disorientated when he hit my head against a tree. I passed out soon after that, then woke up in the woods hours later, my neck fully healed."

Almost the truth. Enough that she might not detect the lie.

She tilted her head, as if listening to my heartbeat. It remained steady.

After a long, uncomfortable moment, she released my chin with a huff. "Guess I can't *entirely* blame you for that. It was probably just an overeager client desperate for more of your blood. At least they did the proper thing and let you live." She huffed again, only looking mildly put out at the thought of someone almost draining me. "I wonder who it was. Rocky didn't see a thing. Did you get a good look at his face?"

I quickly shook my head. A little *too* quick. Her eyes narrowed again, so I hastily replied, "He was wearing a mask."

"What color?"

"Gold."

"Hmm . . ." She reached up to tap her chin. "One of the males you recently tried to secure was wearing a gold mask. Rocky told me he was furious when his session was canceled."

I nodded. "He grabbed me last night while I was table dancing."

Her expression turned thoughtful. "I heard about that too. And then our newest, extremely *generous* client, Benjamin Osborne, intervened. He's already become quite possessive of you, Adalyn, which is a good sign. He's an earl, making him our highest-ranked client yet. He's also close friends with Prince Everett. Your job will be to target that connection. Make him reveal anything that could help further our cause, you know the drill. But don't push him too hard. We want him *hungry*, so focus most of your effort on keeping him happy and wanting more."

"Yes, Mistress."

"Good. Heath and I will look into the male that attacked you and see if we can figure out who he is. We don't want him causing any more trouble. You said he carried you into the woods?"

I nodded again.

"We'll send Rocky out this evening to search for clues. Maybe your attacker dropped something while feeding on you."

At that, everything in me went cold.

My *knife*. I'd spent a lot of money on that weapon, a purchase that Mistress didn't know about. Since I could only partially access my magic—and only when I was with a client—having a weapon made me feel a little less helpless. I'd tried to find it earlier when Everett's brother had dropped me off, but all I'd been able to locate was my phone.

Well, and Benjamin Osborne's decapitated head and body. Since he'd been a Venturi, his remains hadn't burned up in the sun. If Mistress found him, she'd definitely use thrall to pry more information out of me.

"I could go now and look," I offered, trying not to sound too eager. How I would dispose of Benjamin's body, I didn't know. I just needed to get it out of the woods before the sun went down.

Mistress waved a jeweled hand dismissively. "There are a mountain of things that need to be done around the house, so that should be your priority. Besides, I don't want you wandering off into the woods after what happened. Maybe I should have Rocky drive you to and from the club from now on. At least until we figure out who attacked you."

"Really, Mother?" Georgina said with a toss of her messy curls. "The *troll* needs extra protection? I still think you should make her live at the club instead of letting her come back *here* every morning."

"Don't forget who cleans your room every day, dearest," her mother gently replied.

"Why can't we just keep human servants like we did before Daddy died?" Octavia spoke up, not noticing her sister's eye roll as she turned to pour her blood bag into a crystal glass.

"Sometimes I wonder if you live under a rock, Tavia," Georgina responded before her mother could. "Remember when the royal family made an alliance with the SCA six years ago?"

Octavia paused in her pouring to consider. "The Supernatural Containment Agency? Yes, I remember. I'm not stupid, Georgina."

"No one's saying you are, dear," Mistress cut in, throwing her eldest child a chastising look, one that she ignored. "Vampires are no longer allowed to keep humans as servants against their will. Doing so will earn you a one-way trip to an SCA holding facility. I hear the cells are lined in silver and they only feed their vampire prisoners blood every few days to keep them docile."

Octavia turned from the counter with a gasp, nearly spilling her drink. "That's barbaric! Why would King Ambrose agree to such a thing?"

Her mother's eyes hardened. "Because he doesn't care about our quality of life. Venturi can afford to pay for their blood however they wish, and now that the curse has been broken, it's even easier for them. But Feltore must continue to live in the shadows, scraping out an existence as best we can. Our suffering doesn't matter to him, his sons, or the other Venturi. Only his youngest son cared, and look where that got him."

"Daddy too," Octavia whispered, blinking back sudden tears.

"Yes. Daddy too." Mistress swung that hard look my way, and I wisely cast my eyes to the ground. "He died to give us a better future, and we will do everything we can to honor his sacrifice by continuing that noble cause. Isn't that right, Adalyn?"

"Yes, Mistress."

"Good. Now see to your chores, and no nap this evening. I want you to leave for the club early so you can show Rocky where you woke up in the woods."

I nodded without comment, dismissing myself so I could do her bidding. Maybe, just maybe, I could leave early enough to beat Rocky to the club. If I did, I could at least wrangle Benjamin's body into the trunk of my car before he saw it. And the head, of course. Couldn't forget that.

He'd smell the blood, though. Benjamin had no doubt bled all over the forest floor after being decapitated.

As I left the kitchen, I pulled out my phone to check the weather app. *Please, let there be rain. Please, let there be rain.* I perked up when I saw there was a thunderstorm forecasted for this evening. What if it didn't arrive in time, though?

Choosing to hope for the best, I tackled my chores with gusto. The sooner I finished, the sooner I could leave and cover up the evidence of my eventful morning. After an hour, though, it became clear that Georgina was leaving me messes on purpose.

"*Troll*," she called for the umpteenth time. "Come clean my rug. I spilled nail polish on it."

I sighed through my nose, fighting back several choice words. The sheepskin rug in her bedroom was *white*. Although she often wore neutral nail colors, she'd probably spilled hot pink polish just to spite me. Whenever I received too much attention, making my life hell was her signature move. At least she didn't have male company over today. I'd much rather deal with her pettiness than watch the Faircroft sisters have a threesome.

A few minutes later, though, the front doorbell rang. Guess I'd spoken too soon.

"Get the door!" Georgina shouted.

Great. She'd probably make me clean the rug while she and her sister had sex a few feet away with their newest escort. They always chose a human male and never the same one, hiring up to five per week. Neither of the sisters had shown an interest in finding more serious relationships, and their mother turned a blind eye to the sex workers traipsing in and out of her home.

Probably because she was too busy selling *me*.

Plastering a smile on my face, I set down my cleaning supplies and made for the front door. Greeting the escorts was always a bit weird. It made me uncomfortably aware of how awkward Rocky and the other bouncers must feel when they sent clients up to me. Did they secretly hate that part of their job the same way I hated opening the front door?

If they did, they'd never tell me, least of all show it. I'd learned my very best poker faces from them, after all. They excelled at hiding their emotions.

I took my cue from them now and buried my distaste, opening the door to politely greet the newest sex worker. "Come on in. They're—"

"Thanks."

A tall figure, one that I immediately recognized, stepped over the threshold. Shocked, I stumbled back with a small gasp, then said the very first thing that popped into my head. "What the hell are you doing here?"

Everett took me in from head to toe as if he hadn't seen me in days. I knew I must look awful. My hair was a mess, and I was still wearing the bloodied sweater from this morning. But, after thoroughly inspecting me, he seemed relieved more than anything. I could almost feel how relieved he was, like he'd been expecting to find me in a much worse state than this.

Ignoring my question, he said, "I've got this, Loch. Go wait in the car."

My eyes widened. "Your brother followed me here?"

When Everett nodded, panic tightened my chest. I should have known. I should have *known* he would follow me. Everett himself had confessed his plans to follow me this morning.

"You can't be here," I hurriedly said, lowering my voice. "They'll find out what really happened this morning. Please leave. I—"

"What's taking so long?" a shrill voice interrupted, making me flinch.

Everett's expression immediately darkened. "I'm not going

anywhere until I get some answers. This isn't your home, so why are you here?"

My mouth opened, but nothing came out. Even if I'd wanted to tell him, I couldn't.

"Of course this is her home," a new voice interjected, making all the hairs on my body stand on end. "Please shut the door, dearest. You know the sun doesn't agree with my complexion."

I quickly obeyed Mistress, pausing briefly when I spotted Loch in the front yard. We shared a look, and I could have sworn he sent me a silent apology. I closed the door without acknowledging it, my sole focus on the two vampires facing off with each other in the foyer.

"Your Majesty, it is *such* an honor to have you visit Faircroft Manor," Mistress gushed, pausing to deeply curtsy before the prince. Somehow, in the past few minutes, she'd managed to don a plum-colored dress and make her face and hair presentable. She even wore a heavy diamond necklace and matching earrings. "To what do we owe this unexpected pleasure?"

"I'm not here for pleasant reasons, Madame Faircroft," Everett curtly replied. As she straightened, he said point blank, "Are you forcing Star to have sex with her clients at Dreamscape?"

Her expression froze. Only for a moment, though. It quickly transformed to one of appalled shock. "Why, Your Highness, I would never. I'm hurt that you would even consider such a thing. Trafficking is against the new laws your esteemed father has set forth."

Everett was unfazed by her wounded tone. "Then why is she living here with you? Why isn't she with her own coven?"

Mistress didn't miss a beat. "Sadly, the girl doesn't have parents or a coven. Her father died the same night my dear husband did. I'm sure you recall the tragic losses we all suffered the day the curse was broken?"

The question sounded innocent but was heavy with accusation. Still, Mistress managed to perfectly play the part of a widow who'd magnanimously taken in an orphaned witch during her time of grief.

"I'm sorry for your loss," Everett replied, not sounding the least bit sorry, "but I still don't understand why you would take her in."

Mistress shrugged delicately. "I don't hold anything against witches personally, and she needed a home. My own two daughters have come to see her as their sister. All three of them were robbed of their fathers that day, after all. They share a bond."

Sister? Yeah, right. They would sooner walk into the sunlight than think of me as their sister.

When Everett's eyes narrowed suspiciously, Mistress turned her attention to me. "Tell him, dear. Tell the prince that we see you as part of our family."

As she looked at me fondly, I struggled to respond. She'd never looked at me that way before. It was strange and awful, a painful reminder that I'd never see my parents look at me that way again.

Swallowing roughly, I forced myself to say, "It's true. The Faircroft family took me in when my dad died six years ago. This has been my home ever since."

Not a lie. It was the best that I could do.

"See?" Mistress spoke a little too brightly. "She *loves* it here. But, forgive me, Sire. Might I inquire as to your sudden interest in Star?"

He was staring at me. *Hard.* Trying to read my expression. Trying to detect the lie. I didn't dare meet his gaze.

"Your Highness?" Mistress implored, a tiny piece of her own mask starting to crack. She fidgeted with the rings on her fingers, giving away her nervousness.

Finally, Everett returned his attention to her. "I'm sure you've heard about what happened to my brothers at a feeding den over a century ago."

"Yes, Your Majesty. Such a tragic story."

"Then you'll know that a witch hasn't been caught dead in a vampire-owned nightclub ever since."

"Yes, but the curse has been broken. Times have changed, and Star is *very* well protected."

My spine slowly stiffened. *Don't say it, don't say it, don't say it,* I silently pleaded with him.

"Is she now?" Everett said, the words dripping with condescension. "She's surrounded by dozens of hungry predators every night, very few of whom have ever tasted witch blood in their lifetime. You dangle her in front of them like an irresistible treat, then offer them the full meal if they're willing to pay the price. I personally know many of the males who frequent your club, and all I can say is, I'm surprised Star is still standing here in one piece."

Mistress arched a sculpted brow, staring at him with new eyes. Uh oh. She was putting the pieces together, but she was doing it all wrong. She thought he was Benjamin Osborne. Rather, she thought Everett was the mysterious male in the gold mask, the one who'd been turned away, who'd grabbed me off a table and had later attacked me in the woods.

Crossing her arms, she replied in a rather haughty tone, "Be that as it may, Star isn't being *forced* to perform at the club. She's there of her own volition. Ask her if she's being forced to have sex. *Thrall* her into giving you an honest answer. You have my blessing."

Everett didn't even glance my direction, knowing full well that he couldn't use thrall on me. Not with his blood still in my system.

Taking his silence as proof that he believed her, Mistress went on, "Star is our main attraction at Dreamscape Lounge, and we value her tremendously. She's paid handsomely for her work and is well taken care of. And, if I'm not mistaken, hiring blood whores isn't illegal in this kingdom. Correct me if I'm wrong."

A muscle jumped in Everett's jaw. "No," he said after a lengthy beat. "It's not illegal."

"Glad to hear it. Then I don't see what the problem is here. Did you wish to schedule a private session with Star this evening? I can have it arranged."

"No," Everett replied, looking far from pleased with how this conversation had turned out. "Apologies for the intrusion. I'll see myself out."

Mistress curtsied as he left, holding the pose until he firmly shut the door behind him. Slowly straightening, she tilted her head and listened to him leave, hearing far more than I ever could. After a few minutes, the congenial expression on her face twisted into a fierce scowl.

"The *gall* of that male," she spat, her eyes flaring red. "Storming in here and demanding answers like that. *Accusing* me of sex trafficking you."

"Was that Prince Everett?" Octavia called in a distressed wail, scurrying toward us in nothing but a bathrobe. "Why didn't you tell me, Mother? I could have hurried up with my shower."

Mistress wrestled her anger under control before calmly responding to her daughter, "It wasn't a social call, dear. The prince still has no idea you exist and probably never will."

Octavia stuck her bottom lip out.

"But he knows who *Star* is," Georgina said, sauntering into the foyer at a more sedate pace. She was also wearing a robe, clearly still waiting for their escort to arrive. "Sounds to me like he has an unhealthy *obsession* with her."

She looked me up and down with distaste.

"You are not to go anywhere near him, Adalyn. Do you understand?" Mistress said, reaching out to roughly grab my chin. "If he's the male in the gold mask who attacked you this morning, then we must all be on our guard. He could ruin *everything* we've worked so hard to build."

Surprised that she wasn't trying to capitalize on the situation, I dared to say, "But what if he demands a private session with me? I could trap him like all the rest. Imagine the possibilities if we secured him as a client."

Excitement sparked in her eyes, yet she replied, "Tempting, but trapping a Venturi that powerful is too dangerous. He's clearly obsessed with you and feeding that obsession could quickly backfire on us. If we let him get too close, he could uncover our entire operation before we're ready, which would leave us vulnerable. Tell me you understand."

"I understand."

"Good." Appeased, she dropped my chin. "It's unfortunate that the crown prince has taken an interest in you, but he has no legal grounds to stop you from seeing your clients. We'll have to be extra careful, though. He might try to attack again when you're alone, so we'll need to adjust your schedule for added security."

My stomach dropped. Was she going to forbid me from driving anywhere by myself? It was my only reprieve. My one tiny slice of freedom. The walls suddenly seemed to close in around me, trapping me more than they already were. *Caging* me. Desperation clawed at my throat, but I carefully swallowed it back down.

Things felt extra dark right now, but I was used to living in the dark. Somehow, I'd survive this. I had no other choice.

CHAPTER 14

ADALYN

It started to rain just as I left the house.

Sighing in relief, I swiftly locked the kitchen door and hurried toward the garage. The Faircrofts had left only minutes before, staying longer than usual to make sure no one was lurking about the property. Mistress decided not to have Rocky pick me up, but he would be at the club waiting for me when I arrived. Which meant that I had to beat him there before he found Benjamin's body.

With not a spare second to waste, I jogged to the garage and hurriedly unlocked it, impatiently waiting for the garage door to rise as I scrambled to start the Aston Martin. I punched the accelerator the moment it was clear, and the car lurched forward. Barely out of the garage, though, the car made an awful clicking noise, then rolled to a dead stop.

"No," I whimpered, jumping out into the rain once more. As I popped open the hood, the rain picked up, dumping buckets on my head. "Great. Just great!"

I paused for a moment to yell at the sky, then forced myself to focus on something I could control. Peering inside the car, I began searching for what needed to be fixed. But seconds later, all the hair on my body stood on end, my senses going on high alert.

Someone was watching me.

I whirled around, gasping when I spotted a tall figure only a few yards away. Not recognizing who it was through all the pouring rain and gloom, my fight or flight instinct kicked in. I reached into my back pocket, but it was empty.

Before I could come up with a plan B, a familiar deep voice called, "It's just me."

I sagged against the car with relief, willing my racing heart to slow. "You scared the crap out of me."

When Everett didn't respond, I turned to resume my task.

"Back with more questions? I hate to disappoint, but I really was telling the truth earlier."

He stayed silent for so long that I snuck a glance at him over my shoulder. When I found him inches away, peering down at what I was doing, a startled yelp left me. "Don't *do* that," I scolded, pushing him back a step without thought. He glanced down at my hand on his chest, then slowly let me inch him backward. With a harumph, I added, "If you're just going to be in the way, please leave. I'm in a hurry and have no time for whatever this is."

Still no response.

Sighing impatiently, I strode toward the still-open garage, muttering to myself, "Probably just a loose bolt. I still have time. Now where did I leave my—?"

A body materialized before me, and I jerked back with a curse. "I told you to—" Everett held out the wrench I needed. "Oh. Thanks." I took it and hurried back to the car. "Look, I don't need your help. I have to get to the club before Rocky does, or I won't be able to hide Benjamin's body. If someone finds it, I—"

"Loch contacted the SCA. It's taken care of."

I whirled around to gape at him. "Really? The body is gone? Including the head?"

He nodded, then held out his hand again. "And this must be yours. Loch found it in the woods this afternoon, covered in Ben's blood."

When I saw what he held, my jaw dropped. It was my knife, carefully positioned on a scrap of fabric to protect his skin.

Still recovering from my shock, I stupidly blurted, "I'm surprised you're giving it back to me. Aren't you worried I'll stab you with it?"

His mouth twitched with what looked like amusement. "Do you *want* to stab me with it?"

I shrugged. "Not right now."

"Then I'm not worried."

My own lips twitched with silent amusement. As I reached for the knife, he carefully wrapped it in the fabric and handed it to me.

"I . . . thank you."

I tucked the knife into my pocket. As I did, a great weight lifted off my shoulders. Noticing that he was as soaked as me, all of Mistress's warnings about staying away from him came back to me. But I suddenly didn't care. He'd covered up the attack. He'd returned my *knife*. That meant more to me than he could ever know.

But after I'd all but thrown in his face that I'd rather be a blood whore than exclusively be with him, he shouldn't want anything to do with me. Even after what the king had said about us, who would want a whore for a soulmate?

That awful feeling of being *exposed* slid over me once more. Flustered, I turned to the car with my wrench in hand.

"Sorry about your friend," I said, peering under the hood once more.

"I'm not."

At his candid reply, a laugh burst from me. "Well, he *was* a sleazebag. I would have stuck him in the heart, but he was kind of on top of me at the time, so I didn't have a clear shot."

Not wanting to dwell on the memory, I reached inside the car and began searching for loose bolts.

After a moment, Everett quietly growled, "I hope he rots in hell."

I laughed again. "That's dark."

"Why didn't you use magic to stop him?"

I froze, suddenly terrified that he'd figured out what I could do. What I'd done to *him*. Forcing my tone to remain light, I quickly tossed back, "Guess I was too freaked out to remember."

"You're an Oracle, Star. Probably a powerful one if your father was at the battle six years ago. Defending yourself with magic should be instinctual for you. Unless you didn't really *want* to defend yourself."

A retort quickly sprang to my tongue. "Of *course* I did. Do you think I like being attacked in the woods and drained to within an inch of my life?" Annoyed, I savagely twisted the wrench to tighten a bolt. "If you must know, I *tried* to use my magic. Benjamin just happened to get the best of me."

When he fell silent again, panic flared in my chest. Was my response too flippant? Would he ask me questions about my dad and that *night* next?

Needing to distract him, I said, "They think you're the vampire in the gold mask who attacked me this morning, by the way. They also think you're obsessed with me."

"I don't care who they think I am," he replied. "And I'm not obsessed with you."

I smirked at him over my shoulder. "Whatever you say, solemae."

Before the word could finish leaving my mouth, I knew that I'd made a huge mistake.

Lightning flashed through the sky, illuminating his shocked face. Spirits save me, why the hell had I said that?

"What did you just say?" he asked, his voice deathly soft as thunder shook the ground.

Calling myself every bad name I could think of, I straightened from under the hood and said, "That should do it. Can you see if the car will start up?"

"Star."

I slammed the hood shut and rounded the car to the driver's door.

"*Star.*"

"Stop *calling* me that," I snapped, suddenly needing to be anywhere but here. Jumping inside the car, I placed the key in the ignition and begged for it to start. The engine turned over, only to sputter out. Once. Twice. Then rumbled to life on the third try.

Before I could celebrate, something blurred past me. So fast that I didn't realize what it was—rather, *who* it was—until the car died again. I glanced up just in time to see Everett pocket my keys.

"Hey!" I scrambled from the car to confront him. "Those aren't yours. Give them back."

"First, tell me what you said earlier and why I shouldn't call you by your *name*," he replied, staring down at me so intensely that I had no choice but to look away.

"It was a *joke*, okay? Forget I said anything. I have to go, so if you could please give me back my keys."

When I held out my hand and he didn't move a muscle, I considered turning my knife on him. A quick poke in the arm should get my message across nicely. But as soon as the thought formed, I banned it, disliking the idea of harming him. A *lot*. Which was incredibly frustrating.

"Why?"

I blinked up at him, caught off guard by his soft, imploring tone. "Why what?"

"Why did you choose to become a blood whore?"

At that, all the air left me in a rush. It felt like he'd just

135

suckerpunched me, even though the question had been delivered gently. I couldn't detect any judgment behind the words, but I still felt . . . dirty.

Forcing myself not to look away in shame, I replied, "You should leave. And I don't think you should come back this time."

Lightning forked through the sky, illuminating his expression once more. I could have sworn I saw hurt there, but it vanished in a blink.

As we stood there, refusing to voice out loud the many things between us, sudden emotion tightened my throat. Before I could think better of it, I pushed onto my toes and kissed his cheek. "Goodbye, Your Highness."

The words were final. Permanent.

Whatever this was between us had to end, for both our sakes. We'd shared a moment in time. A confusing, chaotic, *electrifying* moment. One that had left me disorientated, like a ship lost at sea. Problem was, I didn't want to be found again when I was with him. Being lost with Everett made me feel things. *Incredible* things. Things I'd never expected to feel, least of all with a vampire.

A vampire that had turned my life upside down six years ago, and was doing it now all over again.

I stepped away from him before I could change my mind. Before I could beg him to stay. Before I could *plead* with him to take me away from this life. It would only be a dream anyway, one that wouldn't last.

This was reality. I couldn't run from it. Couldn't hide.

My future—my *fate*—wasn't with him. It was here.

But before I could make it two steps, he grabbed my arm and spun me around. My eyes flew wide. "What are you doing?"

"Giving you something to remember me by," he gruffly said.

"Something *real*."

And then his mouth was on mine. I froze solid, shocked to my very core. He was kissing me. Everett D'angelo was kissing *me*, a disgusting witch.

But when he pulled back a moment later, disgust wasn't what I found.

"I shouldn't have done that," he said, his voice raw with emotion. "I really, *really* shouldn't have done that."

And then he did it again, grabbing my face with both hands so he could deepen the kiss. Rain slid between our mouths, making me ache for more. When I parted my lips, he didn't hesitate to sweep his tongue inside and seek out mine. As they touched, a whirlwind of emotion erupted inside me.

Lust. Pleasure. Longing. *Need.*

He kissed me until I was lost. Until I was drowning in a sea of ecstasy. I gripped his arms and held on tightly, my only liferaft in a storm of riotous feeling. His mouth and tongue explored me thoroughly, licking and nipping and sucking. My legs trembled, on the verge of collapsing.

Everett was turning my world upside down again. I had no idea that being kissed could feel like this. Like venom coursing through my veins. Like honey warming my insides. Like life-giving *oxygen*.

When he finally pulled back, his breathing was ragged. My breaths were equally erratic, my heart tripping like a snare drum. He suddenly reached down to grab the hem of my sweater. In one swift move, it was over my head. My heart nearly leapt from my chest as he slowly backed me against the car and removed my bra.

Closely watching me, he placed my soaked clothing on top of the car before saying, "I want you to experience what it feels like to be pleasured. Just you, with no thought of giving pleasure in return."

My lips parted in surprise. No one had ever offered to pleasure me without expecting something in return before. I'd never wanted them to. But Everett was different. Intimacy with him felt good. *Amazing,* even. I wasn't just a tool for someone else's pleasure with him. I was something *more*, and I desperately wanted to feel that one last time.

So I nodded. Just once. Giving him permission to touch me. To pleasure me. To make me *feel*.

At my consent, he kissed me again, so deeply that my toes curled. Soon, those lips began to explore other parts of my body. First my jaw, then my neck. I struggled to breathe as they traveled lower. And lower. Brushing across my collarbone, then the tops of my bare breasts.

As they found one of my nipples, I shuddered and slid my fingers through his wet hair. He didn't roughly bite me like I expected him to, choosing instead to lick the rain off before sucking on the sensitive flesh. I moaned at how good it felt, gasping softly when he gently nipped at the hard peak.

He explored my skin for several minutes, using his mouth in ways that left me breathless. When he reached my stomach, he darted his tongue out to play with my belly button piercing. I giggled but immediately froze as he began to undo my pants. Memories of groping hands, rough kisses, and savage bites invaded my mind.

Sensing my sudden unease, he pulled back again. "What is it?"

"I . . . I don't think I can."

The words slapped the air like a lightning bolt. I'd never, *ever* admitted those words out loud before. Never would have dared. The countless clients I'd slept with over the past few years would have eaten me alive if I'd shown them this kind of vulnerability.

But Everett . . . he looked at me with *understanding* and released my jeans without protest. Just like that. No threats. No manipulation or coercion. He simply . . . listened.

And it was that understanding, that willingness to respect my wishes, that made me change my mind. Reaching out, I grasped his hand and encouraged him to continue.

"Are you sure?" he murmured, searching my face.

I nodded. "I'm sure."

His pupils dilated, filling with heat. He clearly wanted to devour me, but instead of rushing the process, he resumed his task slowly, each movement carefully controlled. As he unzipped my jeans and tugged them down, my breathing sped up. The reaction was pure anticipation, and when he placed the rest of my clothing on top of the car, it was all I could do not to jump him.

"Just you," Everett reminded me, noticing the way I eyed him hungrily. I opened my mouth to complain, but I was suddenly splayed across the hood of the car with his head between my thighs.

When his tongue made contact with my clit, my eyes rolled back and I groaned out his name. His *real* name. Whoops. No taking that back now. He seemed to like it, though, rewarding me by swirling his tongue around my aching center several times. *Fast.* So fast that I arched against the hood and cried out like a hussy.

"Again," he rumbled against my clit, nipping at it gently. Pleasurable bolts of electricity zipped through me. "Say my name again."

"Everett," I panted, melting against the car like butter as he began to pleasure me in earnest.

Spirits above, what was he doing to me? I would never be the same after this.

Every time I said his name, he rewarded me with more pleasure. It didn't even faze me that we were *outside* where anyone could see, not hidden away in a bedroom. I was lying naked on top of a car while a vampire prince ate me out, and I'd never felt more alive. The experience was entirely new and erotic. It was venom and lightning and magic, all rolled into a powerful concoction that left me writhing and gasping, desperate for release.

Sensing how close I was, he spread my thighs wider and ate me like a man starved. Unable to bear the assault a moment longer, I threw back my head and screamed. Euphoria shot through every inch of my body, allowing me to leave the world behind for an endless moment of time. I stayed in that moment for as long as I could, greedily riding the exquisite high.

Just when reality started to coax me down, Everett swirled his tongue over my clit again, making me come a second time. I moaned loudly, too breathless to scream. He continued to pleasure me, prolonging the high as if he knew how much I craved it. How much I *needed* it.

He did it again and again, shooting me sky high every time reality tried to bring me down. After the fifth time, I lost count of how many orgasms he gave me. By the time he was finished, I didn't know up from down, let alone what planet I was on. I was swimming in a sea of utter bliss, every inch of me buzzing with contentment.

When he finally straightened, his expression one of pure satisfaction, I shakily whispered, "You've forever ruined me."

His mouth curved into a slow grin. "Good," was all he said.

He reached into his pocket to hand me my keys, then disappeared into the pouring rain, leaving me to deal with the devastation he'd just unleashed.

CHAPTER 15

EVERETT

The sounds she made while I pleasured her. The rapture on her face when she orgasmed.

It was all I could think about as the clock ticked ever closer to midnight.

I never should have kissed her. She wasn't the only one forever ruined by what had happened between us this evening.

I was that much closer to destroying her world now. *Both* our worlds.

Tick-tock. Tick-tock.

I couldn't stand much more of this. She'd told me not to come back, but that was before I'd claimed her body with my mouth. Before I'd thrown everything out the window and given in to what I most desired.

She was all I could think about. The cloying scent of her soft warm skin. Her exotic taste on my eager tongue. I was entirely addicted to her, and like hell would I allow another male to indulge in what I'd just experienced.

Tick-tock. Tick-tock.

It was nearly midnight now. I'd almost left my mask behind tonight. Had almost shown my face and demanded they let me in. They couldn't refuse the crown prince. I was tired of this deceptive dance. This sadistic game of cat and mouse.

They couldn't have her. Not tonight. Not tomorrow. Not ever. She wasn't theirs.

Everything had changed the moment I'd lowered my defenses and allowed myself to kiss her. She was in my head now. In my body. In parts of me I didn't know existed.

As I'd walked away from her hours earlier, her taste still dancing on my tongue, a feeling had settled deeply into my core. A feeling that I couldn't shake. That had only grown stronger the more I tried to resist it. It pounded through me now like a heartbeat, steady and undeniable.

There was nothing I could do about it. Nothing but heed its call. So I'd come back to the club. I'd hidden in the shadows once more, making sure she couldn't see me as she danced for the crowd below her.

Tick-tock. Tick-tock.

The clock struck midnight, and the spotlight winked out.

As she vanished, I made my move.

CHAPTER 16

ADALYN

I hadn't secured any new clients tonight. Every time I'd tried, I froze, unable to do it.

He'd done something to me. That cruel prince truly had ruined me. I couldn't focus properly. Even when I'd danced for the crowd, my movements had been stilted. Clumsy. I'd nearly lost my grip on the aerial hoop more than once, my concentration torn between dancing and looking for him.

He hadn't come back, though. I'd told him not to, so I shouldn't be surprised. Still, the empty feeling in my chest wouldn't go away. Even now, as I readied for my first client of the evening, I couldn't shake the feeling. It made me feel nauseous. Unsettled. *Lost.* And not the good kind.

Someone knocked on my suite door, and the feeling intensified, nearly swallowing me whole. I inhaled a few calming breaths and tried to settle my nerves before calling out, "Come in."

My voice trembled. It hadn't trembled like this in *years*.

What was wrong with me?

My client was definitely going to notice if I didn't pull myself together. He was one of my regulars and knew me quite well. In fact, he'd been my first. First client. First to steal my innocence. I'd trembled then. Trembled and cried. He'd been rough, taking sadistic pleasure in being the one to claim my virginity.

It had taken days for the aches and bruises to heal, but I was *still* recovering from the emotional damage.

I barely flinched anymore, though. Barely showed my distaste. But I was off my game tonight, and with him, that was dangerous. Remembering how it felt to have Everett's mouth and tongue on me, some of my trembling faded. Maybe if I just pictured *him* touching me and not the male who'd brutally destroyed a vital part of me, I could survive the next hour. And the following one. And the one after that.

At the sound of approaching footsteps, I adjusted my mask, struggling to wipe the emotions from my face. Confidence. *Charm.* Those were the emotions that allowed me a semblance of control. Without control, I couldn't fend them off when their hunger took over.

Just in the nick of time, I managed to tilt my lips in an alluring smile, greeting my guest with a sultry look. "Welcome," I said, holding still so the male filling the bedroom doorway could take me in.

I was stark naked, per his orders. Councilman Torres didn't like anything getting in the way of his time with me. He was over two hundred years old, but since he was a Venturi, he had the looks and stamina of a twenty-year-old. As usual, he got right down to business and started feverishly undressing.

"I've missed you, my Star," he said, greedily eyeing my breasts while he tore off his shirt. "I've been in meetings all week and couldn't get away."

"Sounds stressful," I cooed, hating that I couldn't quite hide a slight tremor. "Maybe you should lay back and let me do all the work tonight."

"Not tonight, Star baby. Daddy is too hungry. I need all of you."

My blood ran cold as he yanked off his pants, revealing how *hungry* he was. At the sight, another piece of me shriveled up and died. I tried to speak again. Tried to take back control. But he was on the bed in a flash, his eyes blazing with lust. Despite my years of training, I tensed, desperately trying to find a way out of this.

He would eventually feed on me as all my clients did, but he had something else on his mind right now. Something that had me inwardly recoiling. It was nearly impossible for me to stop him in this near-feral state. Without a fresh blood link, his will overpowered my influence.

So I did the only thing I could do and tightly sealed my thighs shut.

Annoyance immediately flashed in his eyes. "I thought you were over this, Star. Now stop testing my patience and open those pretty thighs."

"I'm still sore from a previous client," I quickly said, trying to sound apologetic. "If you could just feed on me first and share your venom, I'll gladly spread my legs for you."

That seemed to appease him. When he licked his lips and hungrily eyed my neck, I forced myself to tilt my head back, encouraging him to bite me. More than happy to oblige, he crawled on top of me, his fangs already descended. But as I felt the sharp tips graze my throat, I flinched.

Horror filled me.

Desperate to cover up my slip, I reached for his stiff erection. He grabbed my wrist, hard enough that I cried out in pain. His other hand gripped my jaw and forced my gaze to his. I stared at him with wide eyes, knowing that I'd screwed up big time. I was going to be in a world of pain very, very soon.

"Why is my pretty little Star acting like a frightened rabbit tonight?" he said, digging his fingers into my jaw so hard that tears filled my eyes. "You haven't been this jumpy in years." Before I could respond, a feral gleam entered his gaze. "Doesn't matter. Your resistance is only making me more hungry. Fight this all you want, Star baby. I'm eager to play the predator tonight."

In a flash, he savagely bit into my neck and crushed me to him. I gasped from the pain, a pain I knew wasn't going away anytime soon. He had no intention of sharing his venom with me tonight, not after I'd pulled away from him. There was only one thing I had left to protect myself.

As I struggled to gain control of his mind, he started to grope me. Each touch was a punishing bruise, a reminder of how mortal, how *weak* I was. My body couldn't handle the rough treatment without breaking, and that's exactly what Councilman Torres seemed intent on doing.

"Please," I whimpered, cringing away from his hands. I needed to focus. *Focus.* But I was too scared. Too *terrified.* So terrified that a scream built in my head, just like the last time I'd been attacked. But this time, I directed it toward something. Toward *someone.* Toward the male who'd invaded my world and saved me when I'd needed it most. Who'd proved himself to be so much more than a cruel, witch-hating prince.

As the desperate scream exploded through my mind, I heard an *actual* explosion, one that rang in my ears and rattled the bed. Startled by the noise, Torres jerked his fangs free to lift his head. In the next instant, he bared his bloody fangs at something I couldn't see.

"I'm not done yet. She's *mine*," he growled, clutching me to him so hard that I couldn't breathe.

"No, she isn't." The intruder's voice was dark and dangerous, promising untold violence. "And you'll pay with your life for touching what isn't yours."

"We'll see about that!" Torres roared, then shoved me aside so forcefully that I tumbled off the bed and hit the floor. As the two males collided in a blur of fangs, claws, and fury, I crawled to the corner of the room and curled into a ball.

Within seconds, the room was a warzone. It looked like a *bomb* had gone off. Glass and wood exploded through the air, and I covered my head as something sliced into my arm. The two males raged across the room, destroying everything they touched.

As quickly as the fight started, it ended with Torres on the ground, a huge chunk of the bed's frame protruding from his stomach. He bellowed in agony, reaching up to pull it out, but the other male shoved it farther in and savagely twisted. At the awful wet sounds Torres made, I uncovered my head to morbidly watch him.

He'd tortured me so many times. He'd stolen something *priceless* from me. Seeing him so miserable spoke to that dark part of me, the part that *he* had helped create. It took pleasure in his anguish, basking in the glow of sweet revenge. And when the other male punched a hole straight through Torres' chest, grabbing his heart so he could rip it out, the darkness all but sighed in contentment.

As the light left Torres' eyes, I continued to watch, wanting to make sure that he was good and dead. That he would never, *ever* touch me again. When his heart hit the floor with a wet *thump*, I finally focused on the other male. On my rescuer. My savior. My . . .

"Everett?" Disbelief coated the word. It couldn't be him. This was only a dream, my imagination *wishing* it was him. I'd pushed him away. I'd told him not to come back.

He had no earthly reason to be here.

But he moved toward me anyway. He crossed the room in great strides and knelt before me. And then he reached for me. Hesitantly. As if afraid to touch me. To *hurt* me. Not caring if this was only a dream, I uncurled from my protective ball and threw myself at him.

He gently caught me, and I tightly wrapped my arms around his neck.

He might not be real, but I was going to hold on to this dream for as long as I could.

"You're safe now," he said, the earlier violence in his voice replaced by soft reassurance. "He can't touch you anymore."

Hearing the words out loud, I finally broke.

The dam on my emotions burst wide open, and a wretched sob tore from my lungs. Everett lifted me into his arms, cradling me close as I cried. He was covered in blood and gore, but I didn't care.

Because I suddenly felt *safe*. Safer than I could ever remember feeling.

Unable to speak, unable to do anything but cling to him and cry my eyes out, I barely noticed when he carefully wrapped me in a robe.

"I'm getting you out of here," he said, lifting me once more. The words didn't register at first, not until he adjusted his hold to make a phone call. "Loch, I'm taking her to the lakehouse. Meet me there."

I immediately stiffened in his arms. "E-Everett. I c-can't."

"You almost got *raped*," he said, so forcefully that my heart stopped. "There's no way I'm letting that happen to you ever again."

Shocked, I didn't respond until he was storming through the suite toward the exit.

"Everett, I can't leave. *Everett.*"

He halted inches from the door he'd just violently destroyed. "You told me you weren't being forced to work here against your will. Then *prove* it. Let me take you away from here."

"It's not that simple."

"Well, I'm *making* it that simple. You aren't staying here."

Before I could protest some more, he marched through the exit and into the hallway.

"Everett, please. I really can't," I insisted, squirming to be let down. His arms tightened, causing me to suck in a sharp breath.

"You're *hurt*," he growled, slightly loosening his grip.

"Not much. I've had worse."

Realizing my mistake, I savagely bit my tongue, but it was too late. Fury whipped through me, so intensely that it stole my breath away.

"Everett," I gasped out, shocked to my core.

"I can't do it. I can't let you stay here. You're coming with me whether you like it or not."

"But, *Everett*—"

"No. I won't budge on this. Nothing you say will change my mind."

As the fury continued to whip through me, my shock turned into panic.

The emotion. The fury. It was him. It was *Everett*.

I could *feel* him.

Before I could completely freak out, he came to a dead stop.

"Your Highness, this is a surprise. I didn't expect to see you here. Is something wrong?"

My heart started to pound. Turning my head, I spotted Mistress standing directly in front of the elevators, along with Heath, Rocky, and the other bouncers.

Belatedly realizing that Everett wasn't wearing a mask, I broke into a cold sweat. He must have lost it in the fight with Torres.

"I'm in no mood to speak with you right now, Madame Faircroft," Everett replied, that dangerous edge to his voice returning. "Now get out of my way before I make you."

Spirits save us all, he was *furious*. I could feel it in my chest like an angry swarm of hornets.

Instead of arguing with him, Mistress turned her attention to me.

"Remember your promises, Star. You can't run away from this life."

Swallowing, I nodded, knowing she was right. But I wasn't running. I was literally being carried out of here whether I wanted to or not. Surely, she understood that. She *had* to.

With one last pointed look, she stepped aside and said, "Let them through."

"What?" Heath hissed, gaping at her like she'd lost her mind. "You can't do that. She's half *mine*."

A growl rumbled in Everett's chest, vibrating my insides.

"Heath, we'll talk about this later," Mistress firmly said, staring him down. "Star isn't a blood slave, and if the prince wants to take her, he has every right."

Heath's lips pulled back in a silent snarl, but after a tense moment, he stepped aside and motioned for the bouncers to do the same.

The second they did, Everett resumed his course. Even when Heath openly glared at him, he didn't falter. He had no reason to. Even this outnumbered, he was one of the most powerful vampires in existence. Going up against him was certain death.

Benjamin Osborne and Councilman Torres could attest to that.

When the elevator doors finally closed, I didn't say a word. I couldn't. I could barely *breathe*. Nothing like this had ever happened to me before. No one had *ever* tried to rescue me from this life. I'd never asked them to, convinced that no one could. I still wasn't convinced, but it felt nice, *really* nice to have someone take me away from it—if only for a moment.

There would be hell to pay when I returned, though.

Still, with each second that passed, the tension in my body eased. This was happening. This was *really* happening. It wasn't a dream. The vampire I should hate was carrying me away from my nightmares. What's more, I could feel his tension ease too.

When we finally left Dreamscape behind, relief hit me so hard that I knew the feeling wasn't solely mine. He carried me all the way to his car, then gently placed me in the passenger seat. At how attentive he was being, my throat closed. It had been *years* since I'd felt such tender touches. Since I'd been treated with such care.

Overwhelmed, I lapsed into silence as he drove. My exhausted mind was spinning, trying to sort through all that had happened. But eventually, there was only one thing I could truly focus on.

"I felt you," I said, pulling my robe shut as the admission left me feeling more than a little exposed.

"I felt you too," he quietly replied.

My heart skipped several beats.

"So what does that mean?" I asked. Deep down, I already knew the answer. I could feel the truth of it settling into my bones, leaving an undeniable mark that couldn't be erased.

But I needed to hear him say the words anyway. Needed to know that he had come to the same conclusion.

And he did. He slowly released a breath and said with finality, "It means that we're soulmates."

CHAPTER 17

ADALYN

I tried to walk on my own, but he wouldn't let me.

The drive had only taken half an hour, but each mile had sucked more and more of my energy away. By the time we pulled up to a secluded house in the woods, I could barely keep my eyes open. I needed the comfort of my familiar, but I didn't dare mention her. No one knew she existed but me, and it needed to stay that way.

As Everett scooped me into his arms and made for the house, I felt a presence in the darkness, right before a voice said, "Is she okay?"

"I don't know," Everett responded.

"Is she in shock?"

"Maybe. Probably."

"What happened?"

"I'll tell you later. I need to make sure she's not injured first."

Loch lapsed into silence, following closely in his brother's wake. I tried to respond and tell him I was fine, but I was too tired. It was like something in my brain had short circuited, and I was now running on an old backup generator.

When we entered the house, I barely caught a glimpse of the interior before Everett whisked me up the stairs. There were only a few lights on, but I saw warm hardwoods and a massive wrought iron chandelier dangling from three stories above. He took me all the way up to the third floor, pausing only when Loch quietly called his name.

Turning to face his brother who'd followed us up the stairs, he said, "She's safe with me, Loch. Father was right."

Shock lit his brother's face. Without another word, Everett turned into a bedroom. As he shouldered the door shut, we were immediately plunged into darkness. He easily maneuvered the room, though, his night vision similar to a cat's. When he set me down on what felt like a bed, I finally spoke. "Can I have a light on, please?"

A lamp immediately switched on, confirming that there was no one in the room but us. My relief was instant. With a small sigh, I gathered my robe around me and started to curl up on the bed, already half asleep.

"I need to check you first," Everett said.

"Can it wait until morning?" I mumbled, shutting my eyes.

"No. I need to know you're okay. I can't think straight until I do."

My eyes fluttered back open and met his. Oh. He was seriously worried. Struggling into an upright position again, I dutifully perched on the bed's edge and waited for his exam. He didn't waste any time.

Crouching before me, he lifted a hand and brushed back my hair to reveal the damage Torres had caused. Based on how sticky my neck was, I assumed the puncture wounds from his bite were pretty bad. Everett touched my throat with such gentleness that I didn't even flinch.

As he examined the weeping wound, his jaw hardened. "Do they always treat you like this?"

I blinked, wondering how honest I should be. Finally, I settled on admitting, "Not all of them. Torres is one of the rougher ones. *Was.*" I still couldn't believe he was dead.

"Torres," Everett bit out, trailing his hand up to my jaw. When his finger pressed on a particularly sore spot, I couldn't hold back a small wince. "Did he do this too?"

I nodded.

His touch became featherlight, but sparks practically shot from his eyes. "I would kill him all over again if I could and make sure he suffered even more. Father won't be pleased that one of his most trusted council members was involved in this."

A swallow got stuck in my throat. Trying to play it cool, I casually asked, "Involved in what? Having sex with a blood whore? Because even the crown prince does that."

He stilled. Uh oh. Maybe I'd pushed a bit too far.

As he lifted his eyes to mine, I struggled to keep calm. He couldn't know how close I was to panicking right now. When he wouldn't stop staring, I blurted, "What are you doing?"

His stare intensified. "Trying to read your thoughts."

"Read my *thoughts?*" Horrified, I adjusted the mask still covering my face out of habit. "No way. Fate might have thrown us together, but you are *not* reading my thoughts."

"It doesn't work that way. Now that you've started to accept the soulmate bond, our connection will only grow stronger. We won't be able to hide our thoughts and feelings from each other."

"Um, I didn't accept the bond. Did *you?*"

He shrugged. "I must have, or this wouldn't be happening."

"But we only learned about it this morning. When would we have—?"

Oh no. The intimate moment we'd shared in the rain.

I'd felt *different* afterward, like he'd ruined me for all other males. Like he'd claimed a piece of me. Not just a piece. *All* of me. And I'd liked it. *Wanted* it. And, dare I say it . . .

Accepted it.

I swore. *Loudly.*

Everett snorted. "My thoughts exactly."

How was this possible? Fate must have a sick sense of humor. We didn't even *like* each other. Well, we liked each other's bodies. A *lot*. But a bond shouldn't be based solely on sex. I would know.

"So, what now?" I asked, suddenly unsure of myself. It felt like my body had betrayed me somehow, forcing me to make a decision I hadn't intended to make. This soulmate thing wasn't going to work between us. There had to be a way to break it.

"I don't know," Everett replied, picking up my arm to examine the nasty cut I'd received during the fight. "But you need to drink my blood again. I can feel your pain, and it's messing with my head."

I pulled my arm free a bit too quickly. "It's really not that bad. I'd rather heal naturally."

He frowned, and I inwardly squirmed. "One drop of my blood will heal you in seconds. Why won't you take it?"

"I just . . . I can't, okay? I'm a . . . a vegan." Spirits save me, that was pathetic.

Apparently, he thought so too. "Bull. You're hiding something, and I want to know what it is."

Sighing, I said, "Look, I'm extremely overwhelmed right now. Can I just clean up in the bathroom and go to bed, please? We can discuss this more in the morning."

Or not.

I needed to leave at the crack of dawn and not a second later. I couldn't risk Mistress's wrath, and Pepper needed me. Without me there, she had no protection.

Everett stared at me far too intensely, but eventually, all he said was, "Fine, but this conversation isn't over. I need to know what's going on."

"Why, because you're the prince or because you're my soulmate?" I snarkily replied.

"Both."

Frustrated, I threw my hands in the air, then winced as my battered body complained.

"That's it." Before I could protest, Everett scooped me up and strode to the adjoining bathroom. "If you won't drink my blood, then you're going to at least let me patch you up."

I rolled my eyes but let him set me on the bathroom counter, watching as he pulled a first aid kit from a drawer. Still, I couldn't help but mutter, "Whatever you say, bossy pants."

Lifting an eyebrow, he turned on the faucet to wet a towel. "Did you just call me 'bossy pants'?"

"If the shoe fits. Or pants."

He wrung out the towel. "And what should I call you?"

"Huh?"

"Your name. I want to know your real name." When I stiffened, he threw me a knowing look. "I know it isn't Star."

Out of habit, I reached up to touch my mask, then paused. He'd already seen the real me, so what was the point in pretending? I was still alive. Still in one piece. He hadn't ripped the real me to shreds. He'd saved me more than once now. He'd come *back* for me, although I still couldn't understand why.

There were still secrets between us, secrets that could get us both killed, but he'd seen me. He'd seen the real me, and he was still here. Still trying to *help* me. And that was enough to make me lower my guard. Not all the way, but I pulled off my mask and set it on the counter, then opened my mouth to say, "My name is Adalyn. Adalyn Elise Starr."

A sudden emotion warmed my chest, an emotion that wasn't mine.

Pleased. He was *pleased*.

"Adalyn," he slowly said, testing the name out. The way it rolled off his tongue in a quiet rumble melted my insides. I stopped breathing as he reached up to touch my hair, running the sleek strands through his fingers. "It suits you."

A shiver worked its way up my spine. A good one.

My gaze fell to his mouth, and I shivered again.

"That's not a good idea."

My eyes returned to his. "What?"

"Kissing me. It'll lead to other things, and I don't feel right doing that so soon after what you've been through."

"*Kiss* you? I wasn't thinking about kissing you," I quickly replied, frantically trying to shield my mind from him. It was one thing to peer inside someone else's mind, but quite another to have them peer into *yours*. I was not okay with this. Not even a little.

"Maybe not," he said, slipping his hand to the nape of my neck and raising the towel. As he gently wiped the blood from my throat, I held perfectly still so I wouldn't do something stupid like kiss him. "But you *want* to kiss me. I can feel it."

"So? I enjoy kissing you. Is that a crime?"

That insufferable mouth of his curved into a faint smirk. "Not at all. I enjoy kissing you too."

Butterflies erupted in my stomach. We really needed to stop talking about kissing, because kissing was all I could think about now.

Desperate for a subject change, I blurted, "Do you still think I'm disgusting?"

He froze, and I immediately flogged myself for asking such a vulnerable question. What if he said yes? What if he hated that fate had chosen a *witch* to be his soulmate? A *blood whore*?

He was destined to become king of the entire vampire kingdom. He could have anyone he wanted. Did he secretly wish he'd never met me? If he hadn't, our soulmate bond would still be dormant. He wouldn't feel *obligated* to be with me.

The question left me feeling naked. I felt *self conscious* in a way I hadn't felt in a long time. I wanted to take it back, but before I could, he quietly replied, "No, Adalyn. I don't think you're disgusting. I never should have said that."

Tears of relief pricked my eyes. Quickly blinking them away, I said, "Well, I know why you did. You still blame witches for what happened to your brothers—and to the entire vampire kingdom, I suppose. I'm just a reminder of that."

With a short sigh, he set down the towel and met my eyes. "You do remind me of what happened, but it's not fair of me to put that burden on you. I put that burden on my brother's mate once, and I almost lost him because of it. Even Loch knew that persecuting an entire race for what one witch did to him was wrong. But he and our younger brother Troy went along with my need for revenge, which led to the entire kingdom being cursed for a century and ultimately Troy's death.

"*I'm* the one who should be blamed for that, not witches. They were just trying to protect their own the same way I was. Still, I've despised them all these years, unable to shake the rage I feel every time I remember how my brothers were tortured. Their innocence was stolen right under my very nose. They suffered because I failed in my responsibility to protect them, and I hate myself for that."

Stunned that he'd opened himself up so completely to me, I struggled to respond. Loch had been right about him. He was still haunted by the past, carrying the weight of it like his personal cross to bear. He'd done some terrible things in the name of justice, but I could feel his confliction. His *remorse.*

He was no longer the monster he thought himself to be.

The realization took my breath away, and I impulsively leaned forward to kiss him. He tensed for a moment, then whispered my name like a prayer and kissed me back. In a matter of seconds, the kiss turned passionate, our tongues eagerly seeking each other out. Warmth unfurled in my belly, and I urged him closer by opening my legs. With a quiet groan, he stepped between them.

The second his hard erection brushed against my inner thigh, though, he pulled back with a hiss. "Adalyn, I can't. I don't want to hurt you."

A protest sprang to my lips, my body aching for his attention. I could sense that he wanted this as much as I did, his desire making mine that much more intense. It would be so easy to reel him back in. One touch, one *thought*, and he wouldn't be able to resist me.

But I suddenly hesitated, remembering how he'd respected my wishes yesterday in the rain. How he'd *listened*, sacrificing his own wants in favor of mine.

The tables were turned now. I had a chance to respect him in return, to honor his request despite how badly I wanted to tear off his clothes.

He didn't want to hurt me, and that spoke volumes about who he was. It made me want to kiss him all over again, but instead, I nodded and quietly replied, "I understand."

The abject relief on his face almost made me laugh.

Shaking my head, I waited for my lady bits to cool off before saying, "It's for the best anyway. I'd probably fall asleep halfway through."

A smirk tilted his mouth. "Not possible with me."

"So cocky."

"If the shoe fits."

"Or pants," I added, making the mistake of glancing at his groin. When I saw how hard he still was, my lady bits burst into flames once more.

Groaning, Everett stepped away so he could gently draw my legs together.

"You should, um," I said, slightly out of breath. "You should finish patching me up now."

"Yeah," he replied, his voice strained.

Neither of us moved for a moment, as if afraid that we wouldn't be able to control ourselves. Then we were both lunging for the first aid kit at the same time.

"Sorry." I jerked my hands back as they made contact with his. "You . . . you do it."

He didn't comment, probably because he couldn't. The air between us was still charged with electricity, and it was almost impossible not to react to it. Somehow, we managed to behave ourselves though, and he finished dressing my wounds in minutes.

When it was time for us to leave the bathroom, I was still slightly horny. He'd briefly entered an attached closet to replace his blood-soaked clothing with a pair of gray sweatpants and black t-shirt. Seeing him dressed so casually did funny things to my insides. *Delicious* things. I allowed my eyes to wander a bit, noticing the way his dick looked extra big in sweatpants.

Catching my stare, he rolled his eyes and muttered, "Okay, time for bed."

Before I could hop off the counter, he scooped me up again and carried me to the bed. Still in nothing but a thin robe, I let him pull back the covers and tuck me in. The second my head touched the plush feather pillow, exhaustion finally caught up to me. My eyes slammed shut, and I started to drift off.

But as he left my side, I jerked my eyes back open and blurted, "Where are you going?"

He paused. "To the chair in the corner. I don't think I can sleep in a separate room from you tonight."

That made two of us.

"Sleep here," I said before I could think better of it, patting the mattress beside me. As uncertainty crossed his face, I quickly added, "It would make me feel better. Please?"

Nothing like guilt-tripping a guy into your bed, right? It felt strange wanting him beside me. I'd never actually *slept* with any of my clients before. They had me for an hour and that was it. But Everett didn't feel like a client anymore, and I didn't want to fall asleep in a strange house without him next to me.

When he continued to hesitate, I added with a smirk, "I'll keep my hands to myself. And lips. And other things. Promise."

He squeezed his eyes shut and groaned out, "You're killing me, Adalyn."

My stomach went crazy with butterflies again.

"I like when you say my name," I openly confessed.

He slowly reopened his eyes. "It's a beautiful name."

At the intense way he looked at me, my toes curled. "Thanks. I've always liked it. Now, are you going to get into this bed, or do I have to make you?"

He huffed out a laugh. "No female has ever spoken to me the way you do."

"Hmm. Probably because your scowl scares them into silence."

He frowned. "What scowl?"

I pointed at him. "That one."

He scoffed but didn't argue. Suddenly losing the battle with sleep, I shut my eyes and sank into the mattress. Just as I was drifting off, I felt the mattress dip behind me. A moment later, Everett's scent surrounded me. He still smelled of blood and violence, but also warmth and safety. When he reached out and tucked my body against his, I sighed in contentment.

This was the best thing I'd felt in *years*. Maybe ever.

Snuggling against him, I murmured, "Thank you."

"For what?" he asked.

"For coming back."

I was almost asleep when I felt him whisper against my hair, "Always."

CHAPTER 18

ADALYN

> *The room was alive with music and dancing.*
>
> *Everywhere I looked, there was a face hidden by a mask.*
>
> *Gold glittered. Skirts swished. Bodies twirled in sync to a haunting strain.*
>
> *At the center of it all stood Prince Everett. Even with a dark mask on, I knew it was him.*
>
> *He suddenly reached up and removed the mask, then gestured for his dance partner to do the same.*
>
> *Her back was turned to me, but I saw her remove a silver mask.*
>
> *The prince smiled as she revealed her true identity.*
>
> *But as she did, I saw what she hid in her other hand.*
>
> *It caught the light, its silver surface flashing wickedly.*
>
> *She abruptly swung her hand in an arc, thrusting it toward the prince's chest.*
>
> *The knife sank deeply into his heart.*
>
> *He stared at her in shock. In disbelief.*
>
> *As the light started to fade from his eyes, she turned and ran.*

I jerked awake, my heart thundering wildly. As the dream replayed in my head, I tried to shrug it off. It was just a dream. A *dream*. But deep down, I knew better.

It wasn't a dream at all, but a premonition.

Out of the five kinds of witches that existed, Oracles were the only ones with the natural ability to foretell the future. I used to have visions all the time while in magic school, but most of them had been vague. For the past six years, though, Mistress controlled what my magic could or couldn't do. I hadn't dreamt in *years*, let alone had a premonition.

Until the day I'd met Everett.

Something was changing in me. The invisible leash Mistress kept on me at all times didn't feel as tight. She was still in control of my magic, but it was starting to act out. To break *free*, if only a little. The premonition still swirling through my mind was definitely the clearest one I'd ever received. There was no mistaking Everett's presence. Or mine.

Or the knife I'd plunged into his heart.

My knife.

But I wouldn't do that to him. I *couldn't*. Not since I'd stopped seeing him as a cruel, bloodthirsty vampire. The premonition had come too late. My need for revenge didn't involve him anymore—or his family, for that matter.

Which ruined *everything*.

He really had ruined me, in more ways than one. Nothing made sense anymore. My feelings. My job. My *life*.

Feeling lost again and desperately needing a liferaft, I reached for Everett on the bed beside me. Alarmed when I found the space empty, I sat up straight and searched the room for him. The bedside lamp was still on, revealing that I was alone. With the heavy curtains drawn, I had no idea what time it was, but it still felt early.

The premonition reared its ugly head again, and I struggled to breathe. It was too late. Too *late*. My magic must be on the fritz after so many years of repression. Still, all I could think about was making sure Everett was okay, so I ignored my protesting body and scrambled from the bed. As I hurried to the door, I heard a noise and paused to listen. Some of my panic instantly faded. Changing direction, I headed for the bathroom.

The door was closed, so I silently tested the handle. When it easily gave way, I opened it without knocking. If he'd wanted privacy, he should have locked it. Stepping through the door, I immediately found him in the shower. His back was turned to me, and as I entered, he visibly tensed.

"Sorry if I woke you," he said, his voice extra gruff. When I shut the door behind me, he tensed even more.

"Couldn't sleep?" I asked, letting my gaze travel the length of him. The semi-frosted glass obscured his lower half, but I gobbled up what little I could see. He was made of pure muscle, and I had a sudden urge to touch him. Every single inch.

"Please don't do that," he quietly groaned.

I frowned. "Do what?"

"Whatever it is you're doing."

"I'm not doing anything."

"You're feeling *aroused*. Which is making this ten times worse."

"This?"

"I've had a raging hard on ever since last night, and waking up beside a gorgeous female only made it harder," he said, not the least bit embarrassed to admit it.

I snickered.

"This isn't funny, Adalyn," he growled, still not turning around. At least I knew why he was so tense now, poor guy.

"Let me guess. I came in before you had a chance to jerk off?"

"Yes," he curtly replied.

Ooh, cranky. A smirk slid onto my lips.

"Well, I'm awake now. No need to be quiet about it. Go right ahead."

He scoffed. "I'm not giving myself a hand job while you watch."

"Why not? Too shy?"

"I think you and I both know that shyness isn't something either of us suffer from."

"True. Maybe you're just hoping I'll offer to do it for you."

Sudden desire spiked through me. *His* desire. My smirk widened. Maybe this soulmate oversharing thing wasn't so bad after all.

Untying my robe, I let it fall to the floor.

As I stepped forward, he tensed even more. Every muscle on his back stood out in stark relief.

"You don't have to," he said. Yet I could hear the plea, the *hope* in his voice.

"I know," I replied, opening the shower door to slip in behind him. "But I want to."

He stopped breathing.

"Let me prove it to you," I softly said, reaching up to touch his back. At the contact, he violently shuddered. Encouraged when he didn't pull away, I placed my other hand on his back, marveling at the way his muscles rippled beneath my fingertips.

I began to explore him, touching him in a way I'd never touched a male before. I was curious and intrigued, wanting to know him more fully. He held perfectly still while I ran my hands over his muscled back, even though I could tell this was torture for him. I could only imagine how painful his stiff erection was, made all the worse by my presence and touch.

Finally taking pity on him, I stepped closer and slid my hands to his front. As they slowly trailed down the ridges of his hard stomach, his breathing grew labored. "I want to make you feel good, Everett," I whispered, my lips caressing his warm spine. "Not because it's my job. Not even because fate destined us for each other. But because I *want* to."

To prove it, I slipped a hand down to grip his shaft. It was rigid as stone and swollen to the max, as if he was already moments away from release. The second my fingers closed around him, he groaned. So loudly that I instantly grew wet.

Well, that was new. I'd never become aroused by a male's pleasure before. It was exciting, and I quickly lost myself to the feel of him beneath my fingertips.

Unlike the first time I'd pleasured him, I wasn't pretending to enjoy myself. I *was* enjoying myself. I was enjoying his reaction to my touch. I was enjoying how it felt to touch him. I was enjoying how my body reacted to *his* reaction.

It was incredible, and for once, I didn't want the moment to end. I wanted to relish it, to *milk* it. So I milked him slowly, taking the time to appreciate his body. I'd thought all dicks were the same, but I'd been wrong. Everett's was a masterpiece. It was somehow rock hard and silky soft, the girth and length beyond impressive.

If I wasn't so busy enjoying the feel of his cock in my hand, I would have eagerly dropped to my knees and tasted it. *Sucked* on it. Which shocked the hell out of me. I'd never liked using my mouth in that way, but with Everett, everything felt different. *I* felt different. I didn't feel the need to be someone else when I was with him.

I wasn't Star in this moment. I wasn't a blood whore pleasuring her client to completion. I was simply me. I was Adalyn.

Stunned by the realization that *I* wanted to do this of my own free will, I pressed even closer to him. To the male that I no longer saw as a client. He was something else now, something I couldn't quite define. That should terrify me, but it only made me want to be closer. To lower my guard even more so he could see the real me.

He suddenly braced himself against the tiles and choked out my name. My *real* name. The sound was so raw, so *vulnerable* that I felt utterly exposed to him. And, for once, I didn't hate the feeling. I basked in it, allowing myself to fully share this intimate moment with someone I *wanted* to share it with.

"Almost there," I crooned against his back, tightening my grip so I could stroke him faster. He tensed all over, his chest heaving as I brought him closer and closer to orgasm. Knowing he was about to come, my stroking turned feverish.

At the last second, just as he was about to spill his release, I squeezed him. *Hard.* A muffled shout left him. He violently jerked against my hand, shooting out an impressive stream of cum. Pleased with myself for giving him such a good orgasm, I continued to stroke his cock. Even when he was fully finished, I held on to him, enjoying the feel of his afterglow.

Still breathing heavily, he finally turned and drew me into his arms. His body was warm and slick against mine, filling me with contentment. When he tucked me against his chest as if I belonged there, I closed my eyes with a self-satisfied smile.

"Like it?" I whispered, even though I knew he had.

"It was amazing," he said, pressing his mouth to my hair. "*You're* amazing."

My smile widened.

I didn't know how long we stood there in each other's arms, but Everett suddenly said, "You're still in pain."

My eyes fluttered back open. "What?"

"You're in pain," he repeated, sliding his hands over my back as if to search for injury. When he started to pull away, I tightened my arms around him.

"I'm fine, Everett. It's only a few bruises. There's no need to worry."

"No, that's not it. There's a deeper ache." When he pulled away again to look at me, I swallowed a disappointed whimper. "Something that's causing you to shake."

"I'm not shaking," I started, then stopped when he grabbed one of my hands and lifted it. Sure enough, it was shaking.

I quickly snatched it away.

"Adalyn."

"It's nothing. I'm just hungry. Low blood sugar gives me the shakes."

He caught my chin, so gently that he managed not to disturb my bruises. "Look at me, Adalyn."

Knowing I couldn't hide this from him, I met his gaze with a sigh. As he searched my face, I saw the moment he figured it out.

"You're addicted to venom."

With another sigh, I pulled my chin from his grasp. "I'm not proud of it, but in my line of work, it can't be helped."

He didn't say a word for several moments. Then, "I didn't see the signs."

"I'm good at pretending, remember?" I gave him a bitter smile. "Revealing an addiction makes me look weak, and I'm already weak enough as it is."

"You're not weak."

I laughed, but the sound held no humor. "Yet here I am, battered, bruised, and shaking from withdrawals. Not to mention *hiding* from my responsibilities. That doesn't scream weak to you?"

"No. All I see is a survivor, a rather brave and resilient one. And you're not hiding. I took you away from a dangerous situation, one that I hope you won't return to."

I looked away, but not quickly enough.

He swore. "How could you think about going *back* after what you just went through?"

As his voice raised, I stiffened, wiping all traces of emotion from my face.

"Wait, what just happened?" he pressed, reaching for my arm. I forced myself not to flinch away. Feeling how rigid I was, he swore again and let go. "You just disappeared on me, Adalyn. Why? Tell me what you're hiding."

When all I did was stare at him, he squeezed his eyes shut with another curse. After a long moment, a sigh fled him and he slowly reopened his eyes.

"I could thrall you into telling me," he quietly said, but the words didn't sound like a threat. More like a plea.

"You could," I replied, knowing that I couldn't stop him if he tried. It had been twenty-four hours since he'd fed me his blood, long enough that it should be out of my system by now.

When his jaw hardened, I braced myself for the inevitable. But a moment later, his expression fell, and he roughly said, "Problem is, I don't want to. The very thought of forcing you to do *anything* makes my blood run cold."

At his heartfelt admission, the mask I'd erected to protect myself crumbled.

"I'm sorry," I said, unable to keep the tremor from my voice. "I've made promises that I can't break. But I need you to know that I don't . . . I don't *enjoy* what I do."

It was on the tip of my tongue to tell him more, but I knew the words wouldn't form, no matter how hard I tried to say them.

No doubt seeing the turmoil on my face, Everett sighed and whispered, "Come here."

I readily went to him, immediately feeling better the second his arms were around me again.

"When do you leave?" he asked after a moment, surprising me.

Was he really letting me go, just like that?

Worrying my lip, I finally answered, "As soon as I can."

Something hit me in the chest then, an emotion that wasn't mine. Hurt. He was *hurt*.

Wanting to reassure him, I opened my mouth, but nothing came out. There was nothing I could say anyway. Nothing he wanted to hear.

"Then I guess we should get this over with," he said, sliding a hand to the nape of my neck.

My eyes widened. "Get *what* over with?"

Was he going to thrall me after all?

He angled my head back so that I had to look at him. "You need venom. I'm going to give it to you, but you should know how dangerous venom addiction is."

"I know," I replied, all too aware of how powerful it was.

I *hated* myself for this weakness, but I still craved venom. Still needed the high it gave me in order to survive this world. Without venom, I would have fallen apart a long time ago. Would have succumbed to my darkness and allowed the remaining pieces of myself to be torn to shreds.

The false promises it offered kept me from losing my mind entirely. If I held out until the next hit, I'd eventually make it to the other side. To *freedom*.

It was a lie. All of it. But I'd embraced the lie to stay alive.

I hadn't had venom for over a day now, the longest I'd gone without it in three years. Need pounded through my body, making my head spin.

"Please," I whispered, unable to stop the desperation from entering my voice. I trembled harder, already anticipating the high his venom could give me. Lifting my chin, I exposed my throat to him.

"Oh, baby girl," he sadly said, leaning down to press a featherlight kiss to my neck. "What have they done to you?"

"Please. It hurts," I begged, struggling to breathe. The anticipation. The *need*. It was too much. I needed venom *now*.

Responding to my pain, he opened his mouth and sank his fangs deeply into my neck. I jerked against him, the burning agony of his bite a shock to my system. Only for a moment, though. On the heels of his bite came a flood of venom. It poured into my veins and chased the pain away, filling me with indescribable bliss.

I went boneless in his arms, uttering a breathless moan as every corner of my body filled with euphoria.

He clutched me tightly to him and released a groan of his own, pulling deeply from my neck. My eyes rolled back as I gave in to the pleasure of being fed on. Normally, I needed to remain lucid enough to control my client while he fed, but I had no desire to control Everett right now. He'd refused to thrall me. The least I could do was respect him the same way.

As he fed, I completely gave myself over to the moment, not even worrying about how much blood he was taking. I felt safe and blissfully warm, something I'd never experienced with a pair of sharp fangs in my flesh before.

This wasn't a simple high. This was rapture. *Heaven*. And I wanted to stay here for as long as I could.

The venom made every pore in my body sing with pleasure, and I reached between my legs to relieve the ache. With a growl, Everett backed me against the cold tiles and wedged his thigh between mine. I reached for my aching center again, but he suddenly had my arms locked above my head, one large hand firmly gripping both my wrists.

"Everett," I whimpered, starting to squirm in desperation. "I need—AH!"

I cried out, the sound embarrassingly loud as his other hand dove between my legs and found my clit. The contact was overwhelming, deliciously heightened by his venom. Each stroke of his fingers sent jolts of electricity through me, making me see stars. I trembled and writhed, viciously biting my lip as more embarrassing sounds left me. He stroked me harder. *Faster.* Making me deaf and blind to everything but him.

Too much. Too *much.*

The pleasure was all-consuming, filling me up so completely that my body could no longer contain it. A scream belted from my lungs, my orgasm exploding through me. Wave after wave of ecstasy left my body in a powerful rush. I dug my nails into my palms to keep from unraveling completely. He continued to rub my clit, his firm grip on my wrists anchoring me in place. I shook like a leaf and groaned as another orgasm jolted through me.

Again and again, he encouraged me to orgasm, not letting my poor body rest. I'd never been this high before. My world was mind-blowing ecstasy, and Everett seemed determined to keep it that way. His fangs were still embedded in my neck, his venom thrumming hotly through my veins. His fingers continued to work my clit, making my body scream with endless pleasure.

I knew he was ruining me again. But this time, I knew he was doing it on purpose. He *wanted* to ruin me. With his touch. With his venom. Making me think of nothing else.

He might not be forcing me to stay here, but he sure as hell was making it impossible to leave. I couldn't pull away, even if I wanted to. Which I didn't. I wanted to stay like this with him forever.

But eventually, I went limp against the tiles, exhausted from the orgasms and powerful venom flooding my mortal body. I couldn't take it anymore, despite wishing that I could.

Everett released my wrists and caught me before I could melt into a puddle on the floor. As he carefully withdrew his fangs from my neck, he bit into the pad of his thumb and murmured, "May I?"

I didn't even flinch at the sight of his blood. I was only prohibited from *drinking* vampire blood, and he wasn't asking me to drink it this time.

When I nodded my consent, he gently smeared his blood over the fresh bite marks, then patiently waited for me to come down.

It was going to take awhile. I was somewhere deep in another galaxy at the moment.

"Like it?" he asked after several minutes, even though he knew *exactly* how I was feeling.

"Duh," I slurred out, sounding more than a little drunk.

A heavy dose of satisfaction pulsed through our bond. He chuckled quietly and murmured, "I knew you would."

"Cocky bastard," I mumbled and closed my eyes, ready for a nap.

"No time for rest, unfortunately. The others are waiting for us."

My eyes fluttered back open. "Huh?"

"Someone prepared breakfast for you."

I struggled to understand, still trying to clear the haze from my brain. "How do you know?"

"I can smell it."

"From all the way up *here?*"

He shrugged. "I can hear them in the kitchen too."

Filled with sudden realization, I pulled back from Everett's chest to gawk at him. "That means they could hear *us.*"

"Yes."

"You *knew?*"

A wicked smile tilted his mouth. "Did you think the walls were soundproofed?"

"No, but I didn't think anyone could hear me *orgasming*. Wait, who are 'they'? I thought only your brother was here."

"Loch's mate and her best friend, Isla, are here too."

"Seriously? We *crashed* their girls' weekend?"

He shrugged again. "They won't mind. They've been wanting to meet you anyway."

Oh, he was *definitely* trying to make me stay.

Seeing my suspicion, he added, "Just stay for breakfast, and then you can leave. Okay?"

I narrowed my eyes. "This feels like a trap."

"It's not a trap. Promise. I just want to feed you and introduce you to the rest of my family."

I tried not to let his words affect me but couldn't quite hide my excitement. He wanted to *feed* me. That was almost better than venom and orgasms.

I kind of adore you right now, I inwardly thought, smiling a little.

A stunned look crossed his face, and my smile faded.

Can you hear me?

I held my breath, praying to the spirits that no one would answer.

Yes, came his reply, loud and clear. Inside my *head*.

Panicking, I jerked away from him, only for my legs to give out. Everett caught me before I could hit the tiled floor.

"I'm fine," I said, trying to pull away again as the need to run overwhelmed my senses.

Ignoring my protests, he scooped me up and carried me from the shower. Only when I was tightly wrapped in a towel and sitting on the bed did he finally let go.

"Stay," was all he said, then left the room.

As soon as he was gone, I beelined for the exit. There was no way I could stay here now that he had access to my thoughts. This little vacation from reality had just turned into a nightmare.

I'd barely made it two steps before I was scooped up and deposited on the bed again.

"I said *stay*," Everett said, ignoring the way I gawked at him. He was fast. Like *really* fast. I hadn't even seen him come back in. "Here, put these on."

He dropped a pile of clothing on the bed beside me.

At my confused look, he explained, "They're Kenna's. She's a bit taller than you, but you're close to the same size."

I slowly dropped my gaze to the rest of him. "Did you just go out there in the nude?"

He shrugged. "I was quick. No one saw."

"Mmhmm. Sure. Good thing I'm not the jealous type." Or was I? I suddenly didn't like the thought of another female seeing his dick.

"Well, *I* am," he said, crossing his arms over his chest. "And I'm not letting you leave this room until you're properly dressed."

Oh my. This was going to be a problem.

I straightened from the bed and let the towel drop. His gaze immediately dipped to my breasts. "So, let me get this straight," I purred, sauntering toward him. "If I continue to strip naked in front of men every night, you're going to be jealous?"

A possessive growl vibrated his chest. Lightning quick, he darted a hand out and dragged me against him. "Yes, Adalyn, I'll be very jealous. *Murderous*, even."

Anger darkened his eyes, and I shivered. This was *definitely* going to be a problem. Pushing at his chest for him to release me, I soothingly said, "Forget I said that. Of course you would be jealous. I'm your—"

As his hold on me loosened, I stepped away without finishing the sentence and quickly began to dress.

"You're my what?" he pressed, still sounding angry. "My solemae? You can say it, Adalyn, because it's true. You're *mine*."

Now it was *my* turn to be angry. Whirling to face him, I snapped, "I'm not yours. I'm not *anyones*. I'm my own person, okay? No one *owns* me, not even you."

When surprise chased the anger from his eyes, I turned and resumed dressing.

"Adalyn," he softly murmured after a moment, making me feel all sorts of vulnerable. "I didn't mean it like that. I would never think of you as a possession."

My throat closed. He sounded so genuine that I couldn't help but believe him. Still, he needed to know why I'd reacted so strongly. Why this soulmate thing freaked me out so much. "It's just that males have treated me like an object for years," I began. "My head is pretty messed up because of it, which makes this soulmate stuff sort of terrifying. I want to show you who I really am, but I'm still afraid of what that will do to me. What *you* will do."

Wow. I sure hoped that confession didn't end up biting me in the butt. I'd seriously just stripped myself bare, emotionally speaking.

"God, Adalyn. I've been such a selfish bastard," he said with a sigh. "You must hate me."

Smiling a little, I finished buttoning up my borrowed jeans before facing him again. "I don't hate you, Everett. I probably *should*, but I can't make myself do it. Now get dressed. I'm starving and want to apologize to Kenna for stealing her clothing."

When he just stared at me, still processing all that I'd said, I swept past him and crooned, "Better hurry. If I make it downstairs before you do, I might tell your family how we met. And not the PG version."

"Adalyn," he growled.

I laughed and hurried from the room.

CHAPTER 19

ADALYN

Everett found me frozen at the bottom of the stairs.

Voices came from the room just around the corner. *Several* of them. Loud and carefree and . . . happy. I could hear laughter, teasing, and even giggling from little children. I didn't know what I was expecting, but not this.

I was used to shouts and criticism and barked orders. Would the carefree mood change the moment I entered the room?

"What's wrong?" Everett quietly asked, stopping on the stair beside me.

At his close proximity, some of my nerves faded, but I couldn't help feeling like I was about to intrude on something special. Once again, it was painfully clear that I didn't belong in this world.

"You didn't tell me there would be this many people," I replied, careful to keep my tone light.

He descended the final stair to fully face me. "I heard Kade arrive with the twins a few minutes ago. Why? Are you feeling shy?"

When his mouth curved into a teasing smirk, I gave him a flat look. Normally, I'd tease him right back, but I was feeling too much like a fish out of water at the moment.

Noticing how tense I was, his expression softened. "Just be yourself, Adalyn. You don't have to pretend with them. They'll accept you just as you are."

He might as well have ordered me to dance naked in front of his whole family. Without a mask on, without a *shield*, he had no idea how hard it was for me to survive this world.

Seeing the doubt on my face, he reached out and threaded his fingers through mine. "Come on," he said, giving my hand a little squeeze. "They won't bite. I promise."

I completely ignored his lame joke, too focused on his warm palm pressed against mine. He'd seemed to take my hand almost without thinking, like comforting me through touch was something he did all the time. Shocked at how good it felt to have my hand in his, I let him guide me past the foyer and into the room beyond without protest.

The massive living room was decorated in earth tones, with floor-to-ceiling windows that allowed the early morning light to filter in—minus harmful UV rays. The window treatment must be for Kade's wife, since Loch had said she was a Feltore. Now that it wasn't dark, I could see a peaceful blue lake surrounded by thick woods just outside. We were miles from everything, secluded in a little oasis.

Which meant that I was a sitting duck if the rest of the royal family decided they didn't like me.

Everett didn't give me a chance to change my mind, though. As soon as we turned the corner and saw a kitchen-full of people— correction, *vampires*—he said, "Everyone, this is Adalyn."

The happy sounds immediately switched off. Even the two children sitting in highchairs stopped what they were doing to stare. It felt like I'd been thrust into a spotlight, the crowd eagerly waiting for me to start my performance. The need to hide, to slip on a mask and pretend I was someone else, trembled through me.

Everett suddenly drew me in front of him and slipped an arm around my waist. With his solid presence behind me and his arm acting as a shield, I felt protected. *Safe.* It gave me the confidence to stand up straight and say, "Hi, everyone."

No one spoke. It was like the sight of me and Everett together had short-circuited their brains. Even the chatty golden vampire, Kade, was staring at us with his mouth wide open.

Okay, this was all sorts of uncomfortable. Maybe I could convince Everett to let me take breakfast on the go.

Before I could speak, though, a feminine voice exclaimed, "Good goddess, you're *gorgeous*. Kade failed to mention that part."

A short and curvy girl with blonde hair dyed pink at the ends suddenly beelined toward me, a huge grin on her pretty heart-shaped face. Everett's arm tightened around me, but when she swooped in for a hug, he didn't stop her.

"I'm so happy to finally meet you, Star—"

"Adalyn," Everett interrupted. "Her name is Adalyn."

"Adalyn? Oh, that's such a pretty name!" the female sang, squeezing me tightly. When a few of my bruises protested, Everett growled quietly. She didn't seem to hear it, though, pulling back to beam at me. "I'm Isla, Kade's wife. He told me all about your visit to the castle yesterday, and I was so jealous to have missed out. I can't believe Everett has a *soulmate*. We were starting to think he would never find someone. He sure didn't waste any time claiming you, though. And *deeply*. But I can't blame him. You smell absolutely divine, and your hair is like spun silver. It looks stunning on you, but I'm too pale to get away with that color. And don't get me started on your skin. It has that ageless look Asian people are so lucky to inherit. Sorry I'm talking so much. I'm just so *excited*."

I stopped listening halfway through, a word she'd said stuck on repeat in my mind.

Her expression abruptly fell. "Oh, no. Did I say something wrong?"

When she glanced up at Everett, I spun and forcefully shoved him in the chest. "You *claimed* me? Is that why you were so okay with me leaving? Because you knew your scent would deter other males from *touching* me? You have no idea what kind of *damage* you've just caused."

Isla gasped, but I was too furious to care that I'd just made the worst possible first impression in history.

"*Answer* me," I snapped, shoving Everett again.

He stumbled back a step, but only because he'd *let* me push him. Knowing this made me even angrier, and I prepared to shove him again. Before I could, he caught both of my wrists.

I fought to break free, shouting, "Let *go* of me, you bastard. I *hate* you."

The second the words were out, I realized my terrible mistake. Terrified that he'd retaliate, I stopped fighting and waited for the inevitable. I'd *never* spoken to a vampire like that before. If I had, I'd be long dead.

Casting my eyes to the floor, I braced for the punishment to come. He was more than capable of violence, and it wouldn't take much effort for him to crush the delicate bones in my wrists to dust.

I waited and waited, but the pain never came.

Unable to bear the silence a moment longer, I blurted, "I'm sorry. I don't hate you, okay? I was just surprised to hear that you'd claimed me."

"Don't be sorry," he quietly replied. "You have every right to be angry with me. You can even hate me if you wish. But I won't apologize for claiming you. I had to. I didn't feel like I had any other choice."

More angry words sprang to my tongue, but I shoved them back down. He could still punish me when we didn't have an audience. Still, I wanted to *scream* at him for betraying me this way. He'd said that he didn't think of me as a possession, and I'd *believed* him.

Had everything he'd said to me been a lie? Had it just been a way for him to *control* me?

My anger abruptly gave way to another emotion. Hurt. I was *hurt*. More hurt than I could ever remember feeling.

"Adalyn," Everett softly implored. I could hear the remorse in his voice, but I wasn't ready to acknowledge it. When I didn't respond, he let go of my wrists with a sigh.

Needing to be anywhere but here, I dredged up the courage to say, "I should leave. Sorry about the scene, everyone."

But before I could take a single step, I heard Loch say, "Not until you've had breakfast."

Surprised, I turned to face him. He was standing behind the kitchen island with his arms crossed over his chest. I expected to receive a stern look for yelling at his brother, but he wasn't even looking at me. His eyes were on Everett, and there was more than a little disapproval flashing in their dark depths.

"Yes, Adalyn. Please stay," a new voice spoke, drawing my attention to the far side of the island. A beautiful brunette with a kind smile on her face stood there. Right away, I felt a little less out of place. This must be Kenna, Loch's wife, the vampire witch hybrid who'd broken the century-long curse six years ago.

Like me, fate had thrust her into a dangerous world where she didn't belong. Yet, here she was, happily mated to a vampire prince and the mother of twins. I glanced at her adorable children and wondered if they shared their mother's special abilities.

Seeing where my attention had strayed, Kenna said, "This is Nico and Zoey. They have a tendency to forget about their Syphon abilities when they're excited, so be mindful of their skin."

Out of nowhere, Zoey launched some of her breakfast at her

twin. Nico made a startled noise, then gleefully reached into his bowl of oatmeal, prepared to escalate the food fight.

Kade, who'd been surprisingly quiet until now, lunged off his stool toward them. "Quit it, you little goobers." He tried to stop Nico from lobbing the oatmeal at his sister, but the goo ended up hitting him instead. The twins shrieked with laughter. As the big vampire got pelted a second time by Zoey, I couldn't help but smile a little.

Just like that, the tension in the room vanished.

While Kenna helped Kade break up the fight, Loch looked on with amusement dancing in his eyes.

"They *never* listen to me," Kade grumbled, setting Nico's bowl of oatmeal a safe distance away.

"You just have to be more firm with them," Kenna said and grabbed some paper towels to wipe up the mess. "And don't give them sweets first thing in the morning."

"I didn't this time, I *swear*," he replied, pausing to give me an apologetic look. "We're not usually this chaotic. The twins are just going through a throwing phase."

"And a 'test their pushover uncle' phase," Isla muttered under her breath.

"I heard that, shortcake," Kade growled at his wife. When she tossed him an impish grin, he winked at her.

Overwhelmed by all the back and forth, I kept silent, until I caught a flash of silver from the corner of my eye. Following it, I gasped at the sight of a *fox* in the living room.

"Is that a . . . ?"

"Kenna's familiar. Her name is Silver."

I still didn't acknowledge Everett, choosing to ignore my hurt by ignoring him. As the fox turned to face me, I was struck by her beauty. Pale blue eyes were set in a silver and white face. Her neck ruff and legs were pure white, but the rest of her fluffy body was silver, similar to my hair color. Her large, black-tipped ears swiveled forward as she in turn assessed me.

Knowing she was only part animal, I dipped my head respectfully before saying, "Hello, Silver. It's nice to meet you."

Good thing Pepper wasn't here. Although the creature before me housed a celestial spirit, she still possessed animal instincts. Foxes *loved* to eat mice.

Silver dipped her head in return, and I smiled. She was friendly. Not all familiars were.

"She senses the angelic magic within you," Kenna said, moving from the kitchen to join me. As she did, Silver hurried over and pressed herself against Kenna's legs. "Do you possess a familiar of your own?"

A lie instinctively sprang to my lips, born from the necessity to protect my tiny familiar. But I didn't feel the need to hide her for once. A fellow *witch* stood before me. Maybe not a full witch anymore, but she understood how important the bond between witch and familiar was. I could trust her.

I just didn't know if I felt the same about the male standing behind me.

Still, I decided to lower my guard once more and admit, "Yes. Her name is Pepper. She's a . . . she's a mouse, actually."

"A mouse? That's adorable!" Kade exclaimed, joining our ever-growing circle. "Is she here? Can I hold her? Silver never lets me hold her."

"That's because you squeeze the daylights out of her," Isla commented with an eye roll. When Kade came up from behind to wrap her in a tight bear hug, she squealed and playfully slapped his arm. "Like *that*, you big oaf."

In reply, he bent down to nuzzle her neck and squeeze her even more, which she didn't seem to mind in the least.

When I fished for a reply but came up empty, Loch saved me by saying, "I think that's enough questions for now. We should let Adalyn eat."

"Yes. Adalyn, we made several different things, not knowing what you liked," Kenna said, gesturing for me to follow her into the kitchen. Suddenly more comfortable with *them* than the male I'd come in here with, I obediently trailed after her. As she pointed to the impressive spread on the kitchen island, my focus went solely to the food.

There was so *much* of it. Pancakes, scrambled eggs, fruit, bacon, and toast with jelly. There was a carton of orange juice, and I could smell fresh coffee brewing. I hadn't seen this much food in *ages*.

Barely able to contain my excitement, I waited impatiently for Kenna to finish speaking so I could dive in. The second she stopped, I was off like a shot, piling as much food as I could onto the plate she'd offered me. When someone handed me a fork, I plopped onto a stool and got to work.

Only when my plate was half-cleared did I finally realize how quiet it had become. With my mouth still full of food, I lifted my head to find the entire room staring at me.

Great. My social skills were apparently a bit rusty.

Noticing that Everett was now across the island from me, I made the mistake of glancing at his face. He looked . . . troubled. Feeling uncomfortable all over again, I quickly swallowed my food and said to no one in particular, "This is really good, thank you. It's been awhile since I've had breakfast." Alarm trickled through me, the emotion decidedly Everett's. Cursing my slip, I hastily amended, "A breakfast this *big*, I mean. I usually eat pretty light the first half of the day."

And the second half.

Belatedly realizing that I was the only one eating, heat crept into my cheeks. Not much embarrassed me anymore, but I felt like a strange creature in a circus show at the moment. I swirled my fork in the air, trying to keep the unease from my voice as I asked, "Do you all only drink blood for breakfast?"

Way to be the odd man out.

When Kade barked a laugh, Isla quickly elbowed him in the side. "Shush! We're making her uncomfortable. To answer your question, Kenna and the twins usually eat food once a day, but the rest of us don't need it like they do. And *definitely* not like you. Wow, girl, you sure can wolf down food. How do you keep your figure? If I ate like that during my time as a human, it would go straight to my thighs and butt."

"More to grab on to," Kade purred, reaching behind her to do just that.

She yelped and batted his hand away. "*Behave.* We have a guest."

He looked over at me with a wink. "Adalyn isn't a guest. She's family now."

I suddenly found it hard to breathe. Did he really mean that, or was I not supposed to take it seriously? Either way, I hadn't been part of a family in *years*. The thought of being included in this one made my heart ache, but not in a bad way.

I snuck a glance at Everett again and found him closely watching me. *Too* closely. The bastard was trying to read my *mind* again.

Needing a distraction, I answered Isla's earlier question. "I do a lot of dancing, which definitely helps keep me in shape."

"Oh!" Her eyes lit up. "Kade told me you were a dancer. So what made you choose that profession?"

I inwardly grimaced, wondering what *else* he'd told his wife. Isla seemed genuinely interested, though, so I decided to answer her honestly.

"It's sort of in my blood, actually. My mom was originally a prima ballerina from Japan. She and my dad met and fell in love while she was at an international ballet competition here in the states, so she decided to relocate here after they got married. She started to teach me how to dance when I was only two, but she died in a car crash a couple years later."

Isla's expression flooded with sympathy. "I'm so sorry. I lost my mom too. I bet she'd be so proud of you for following in her footsteps."

I huffed a wry laugh. "Thanks, but I doubt she would approve of my type of dancing."

Um, yeah, my social skills were definitely stunted. Who admitted that kind of stuff to perfect strangers? Now I'd just made everything awkward again.

"Your dancing is beautiful," a voice smoothly cut through the awkwardness, and my eyes jumped back to Everett's.

He was still watching me closely but not like before. His expression was soft now and *open*. So open that I knew he'd meant what he said. He truly thought my dancing was beautiful. Overwhelmed by how that made me feel, I dropped my gaze to my plate.

"Thank you," I managed to whisper.

He really needed to stop coming to my rescue and saying stuff like that. Stuff that made me feel things. *Confusing* things. Things that flipped my world upside down and had me questioning everything.

Like how I could possibly return to my old life after this. Like how I could keep pretending that he wasn't worming his way under my skin.

The insufferable bastard had claimed me without my permission, but I could no longer deny my feelings. I cared about him. *Cared.*

And that was bad. Really, really bad.

I might as well stick my knife into my own chest. Nothing good would come of these feelings. For *either* of us.

CHAPTER 20

EVERETT

As we left the lakehouse, I was still reeling from all that I'd learned about Adalyn this morning.

She had a mouse familiar named Pepper, and her social skills were adorably awkward. She *fit* into the family. Rather seamlessly, actually, like a glove. If I wasn't so pleased by that fact, I'd almost be jealous.

But I was also troubled by her addiction to venom and the way she devoured food. Her build was naturally petite, but I could see it in her eyes now. The hunger. The desperation.

She was in survival mode.

She was good at hiding it, but our bond was growing stronger. I could feel her conflicted emotions more. Hear more of her chaotic thoughts. They were everywhere, bobbing and weaving as if in a boxing match. As if the match was between *us*, and she was doing everything in her power to avoid me.

I couldn't blame her, though. I knew that claiming her had been a huge breach of trust. Our bond was still so fragile, so *breakable*, and I'd recklessly put it in jeopardy.

But when I'd bitten her, all I could think about was the countless males who'd tasted her. Who would *continue* to taste her. A wild and feral need had coursed through me, one that *demanded* I protect her from them. She wasn't theirs. They didn't deserve her.

She was mine. *MINE.*

Mine to keep safe from the cruel world she lived in.

I still couldn't regret claiming her. Knowing that my scent was buried deep within her, so deep that any male who came near her would recoil in disgust, had calmed some of my frenzy. But the need to protect her continued to simmer in my veins. Each step we took from the lakehouse was an awful reminder that she was *choosing* to go back. To allow males into her bed that weren't *me*.

This feeling was new for me. This feeling of wanting someone for myself. Hundreds of females had entered my life over the years, none of them staying long enough for me to care if they left. But none of them had been *her*. Even before I'd accepted that Adalyn was my soulmate, I'd wanted her. And now, she was *all* I wanted.

Which was why I'd practically begged Loch and Kade to join us on the drive to Faircroft Manor. They were the only two things stopping me from throwing Adalyn over my shoulder and locking her inside the lakehouse. When she chose to sit in the backseat, though, I nearly ordered them both to leave so she would be forced to sit up front with me.

Seeing my agitated state, Loch shot me a warning look from the passenger seat. I peeled my lips back in a silent snarl but eventually wrestled my instincts under control and started the car. No one spoke while I maneuvered down the long private drive, but when I turned onto the main road, I couldn't help saying, "You can still change your mind, you know."

I glanced in the rearview mirror in time to see Adalyn smirk, but there was no humor behind the action.

"No, I can't. I have unfinished business."

My grip on the steering wheel tightened. "And what's that? Securing new clients?"

Her gaze shot to mine in the mirror. "Really? You want to have this conversation right *now* in front of your family?"

"They already know what you do."

She scoffed. "Thanks for reminding me."

"We're kind of used to awkward family conversations," Kade butted in from his spot directly behind me. "Just pretend we're not here."

She rolled her eyes. "Yeah, no problem. I'll just openly admit to a car full of males I barely know that I have sex with strangers for a living."

Kade made a choking noise but didn't respond. Good thing too, or I'd probably bash his teeth in.

"Is it the money?" I pressed, ignoring Loch's warning look this time. "If you need money, just say so. Do you owe someone a debt?"

A panicked look crossed her face. She quickly wiped her expression clean, but it was too late.

Heat surged through me, a growl threatening to tear from my throat. Barely able to focus on driving, I pushed, "A debt? Is that it? To *whom?*"

She clenched her jaw, refusing to say a word.

"*Adalyn.*"

She jumped at my raised voice.

"Everett," Loch warned, staring daggers at the side of my face. "You're scaring her."

"I don't care," I growled back, the heat whipping into a wild frenzy. "She *needs* to tell me."

"She doesn't have to tell you *anything.*"

"Yes, she—"

"She's being thralled," Kade interrupted.

I jerked the car onto the shoulder and slammed on the brakes. Setting it in park, I twisted around to face Adalyn. She was pale, paler than I'd ever seen her. She stared at Kade in disbelief, like he'd just betrayed her.

"What do you mean she's being thralled?" As the words left me in a deadly hiss, Adalyn visibly winced.

Kade threw her an apologetic look before saying, "I remember how Isla acted when she was being controlled by the sire bond and allure. Adalyn's acting the same way. She's not telling you because she *can't* tell you."

The heat turned to blinding rage. I focused on Adalyn again, but she was already scrambling out of the car.

"*Adalyn.*"

I jumped out after her, prepared to chase her if she ran. She didn't, though. She simply marched down the road at a fast walk as if she intended to reach Faircroft Manor on foot. I surged after her, only for Loch to block me.

"Get the hell out of my way, Lochlan," I snarled inches from his face, baring my fangs at him.

He didn't even blink. "Calm down, or I'm not letting you anywhere near her. She doesn't deserve your wrath."

"Of *course* she doesn't," I barked, trembling as the heat threatened to explode from me. "But whoever did this to her is going to suffer. I won't rest until I know who that someone is."

He stared me in the eye, realizing all too quickly what I intended to do. "*Don't*, Everett. You've already claimed her against her wishes. Abusing your soulmate bond will only lead to heartbreak and misery."

I stubbornly clenched my jaw. "I need to know, Loch. It's *killing* me. I need to know who did this to her."

Surprise flickered in his gaze. "You truly care about her."

"Of *course* I care about her," I said without thought. Without hesitation. There was no use denying how I felt about her.

Seeing the truth of it in my eyes, he slowly relaxed his stance. "You might care about her, Everett, but you could end up destroying the soulmate bond if you push her too hard. For both your sakes, tread carefully."

Recalling how I'd almost destroyed our brotherly bond, I reached out and gripped his shoulder. "I'm trying, Loch. I'm really trying."

"I know you are," he said, then pulled me into a tight embrace. "But she needs *space*, Ev. Trust me. The choice has to be hers."

Leaning into his support, I blew out a pent-up sigh before confessing, "I don't know if I can do this. I did everything wrong with her."

"I made my own fair share of mistakes with McKenna."

"Not like I have. I treated Adalyn like a whore. Like she was nothing more than an object for my selfish pleasure. I've screwed up so badly."

He pulled back to look me in the eye again. "Maybe you have, but you can still make things right. You forget how far you've come, Everett. You spent the better part of a century being cold and cruel to anyone outside our family. You barely even tolerated Kade, despite the fact that you chose him to be my drothen. But you've started to let others in again, first McKenna, now Adalyn. If you truly care about your soulmate, let your heart guide your actions."

I nodded, allowing the last of my rage to fade. "Thank you, brother. I will."

He let me go then. Let me hurry to catch up with the female who'd entirely taken over my world. Kade had been following her from a distance, but he easily stepped aside at the sound of my approach.

"Thanks," I told him, actually meaning it. I didn't often give him the credit he deserved. He'd been nothing but steadfast and loyal to my family for over a century, and I could already sense his desire to include Adalyn in that circle.

He turned to stare at me as if startled that I'd acknowledge him. "No problem, man."

"And thanks for being there for my brother when I couldn't," I added before I lost the nerve. "You've been a good drothen to him."

His mouth fell open as I swept past. Still, I heard him mutter under his breath, "I like this new Everett."

A smirk crept onto my lips. Pretty sure I agreed with him. A newfound purpose had filled me since meeting Adalyn, and I had every intention of holding onto it. But Loch was right. I needed to tread carefully where Adalyn was concerned. She might come across as confident and fearless, but she felt lost right now. Lost and terrified.

"Adalyn," I finally called, my long strides quickly eating up the ground between us.

She visibly stiffened before calling back, "Glassport isn't too far away from here. I'll just walk back. I need time to think anyway."

"About what?"

She threw her hands in the air. "About *everything*. Things are really screwed up right now."

"They are, but that's nothing new for you, right? How long have you been under thrall?"

She barked a laugh. "You know I can't answer that. I am *literally* tongue tied."

"Fine. Then let me guess. Six years ago when you went to live with the Faircrofts?"

She was silent for a long beat. Then, "That's a good guess."

Hope and anger swelled in my chest, but I chose to focus on the hope. She was speaking to me. Not in definite terms, but I could work with this. "Okay, next question. Did the Faircrofts thrall you to stay with them?"

A pause. Then, "Not such a good guess."

Frustrated, I racked my brain for more clues. "But you owe them a debt?"

I watched as her spine went poker straight.

"I'll take that as a yes. What kind of debt?"

"I can't tell you."

Uttering a curse, I fought to remain calm. We were making progress, albeit slowly. At least she was *trying*. Something finally came to me, and I said, "Your father died in the battle six years ago. Were you there too?"

She stayed silent for so long that I didn't think she would answer. Then she slowly nodded.

"Oh, baby girl." She would have been young. *Too* young. The horrors she must have witnessed. Had she seen *me* that night? So much happened that I couldn't remember if I'd seen her. Everything had been chaos. "How old were you?"

"Fourteen."

Sadness pierced me. "I'm so sorry, Adalyn."

She suddenly whirled to face me. Tears glittered in her eyes as she forcefully said, "You can't keep *saying* stuff like that. Every time you apologize or make me feel better about myself or stand up for me, I get *confused*. You're supposed to be my enemy, Everett. I should hate you for everything I've lost, but I don't, and I *hate* that I don't. My dad never should have been there that night, and I shouldn't have either. Everything changed after that, and I've been paying for it ever since. If only he hadn't ki—" She paused to grip her throat as if it had seized up. "I . . . I can't . . ."

She gasped for breath, and I realized that it *had*.

"Adalyn!" I lunged and caught her as she started to collapse. "Don't try to speak. The thrall is forcing you into silence. Just breathe, baby girl. Good. That's really good. Breathe and focus on my voice."

The words were soft, but they shook, my rage returning tenfold. Whoever had done this to her was going to die slowly. *Painfully.* They'd rue the day they chose to mess with my soulmate.

As her breathing slowly returned to normal, I said, "I can fix this, Adalyn. If my thrall is more powerful than theirs, then I can break its hold on you. Just look into my eyes, and I'll have you freed in no time."

But when I tilted her face up toward mine, she struggled to pull away and cried, "No, *don't.*"

An ache built in my chest when I saw how hard she fought. She was desperate. *Terrified.*

"It's only the thrall. Whoever did this probably told you to resist having it removed," I tried to reassure her.

I reached for her again, but she shoved my hand away and shouted, "No!"

Surprised by her vehemence, I didn't stop her from wrenching free of my arms and stumbling back.

"No," she firmly repeated, her eyes wide with fear. "It's more than that. Any attempt to break . . . You *can't*, okay? Pepper needs me. I won't leave her all alone like this."

As I struggled to understand what she couldn't say, she clenched and unclenched her fist. But only her right one, like she was unconsciously sending me a message.

A thought struck me, a terrible one that immediately filled my stomach with dread.

"A pactum. You're bound by a pactum."

A lone tear slipped down her cheek, and I knew I was right.

"Oh, Adalyn. Come here, precious."

When she came to me with a sob, I gathered her tightly in my arms, offering her my strength and comfort. She shook against me, crying into my chest without restraint.

"It's okay," I whispered. "We're going to figure this out. You're not alone anymore."

She only cried harder.

CHAPTER 21

ADALYN

"I bet it's Deloris Faircroft. She and her late husband spent the past several decades trying to claw their way up the social ladder. She also admitted that her husband died the day the curse was broken."

"What's your point, Loch?" Everett asked his brother.

"Her husband might have been a rogue. If so, she might have been one too—or at least a sympathizer. The rogues may have gone into hiding, but we know many of them still exist and aren't happy with how this kingdom is run, especially now that we've allied with the SCA. Therefore, it makes sense that someone like Deloris would bend our new laws to get ahead. She runs a highly profitable nightclub, and I bet Adalyn is the key to that success. No other vampire-owned nightclub has a witch in their employment, and that's what makes Adalyn so valuable. Of course Deloris would find a way to keep her from leaving. If she proposed a pactum to ensure Adalyn worked off her debt, then that's technically not illegal. Neither is using thrall to keep the details of their agreement private."

Everett's knuckles bled white on the steering wheel. "She *forced* that pactum on Adalyn. There's no other explanation. Why would a fourteen-year-old witch willingly agree to stay with a vampire family? It doesn't make sense and neither does this supposed *debt* she has to work off. What could she have possibly done that would require her to throw away her life like this?"

Loch grunted. "I agree it doesn't add up, but pactums aren't always formed on truths. If both parties *believe* the oaths they swear, then it's enough to bind them. The important question is, what consequences will Adalyn face if she tries to break the pactum?"

"By how terrified she sounded earlier, I'm guessing death."

Everett glanced at me in the rearview mirror. I didn't look away, silently confirming his guess. Cursing, he gripped the steering wheel so hard that it cracked.

As the miles flew by, bringing me ever closer to Faircroft Manor, I quietly listened to Everett and Loch work out the missing pieces. They were doing a pretty good job, except that they thought I was the helpless victim and entirely innocent in all this. If they only knew the full story, they wouldn't be trying to help me so much.

More confused and conflicted than ever, I kept silent. Nothing I said could fix this anyway. Layers of thrall had ensured I couldn't spill any secrets, and the pactum kept me from fighting the thrall. As much as I yearned to be rescued from this messed up situation, I didn't think even Everett could save me from it.

I was in too deep, my bindings too tight. The only way out was to see it through.

"My wife has been thralled a few times. And also allured by an ancient."

I turned to Kade in surprise. "An *ancient*? I thought they were a myth."

"So did I until a year ago."

"Is that how she was turned?"

Some of the light left his twinkling blue eyes. "No. I turned her."

Wow. He seemed like the *last* person who would turn a human. Despite his intimidating size, he was a big huggable teddy bear at heart. "What happened?"

"Six years ago, she was kidnapped by rogues and used as bait.

Before we could save her, one of them drained and killed her. I didn't want to turn her, but . . . I'm glad I did. She's the joy of my life."

A lump formed in my throat. The more I learned about the royal family, the more my sympathy for them grew. They definitely weren't the bad guys I'd been taught to believe. It made me wonder what else I'd been taught that was a lie. Maybe I had this all wrong. And if I did, how on earth was I going to fix it?

As if sensing my inner turmoil, Kade said, "Everett is right, you know. You're not alone anymore."

The second he reached between us to squeeze my hand, Everett growled, "Hands off, Feltore."

"Feltore? And here I thought we were becoming friends," Kade drawled. Still, he promptly withdrew his hand and added, "I'm happily mated, man. I'm not a threat to you."

"I don't care. Keep your hands off Adalyn, or I'll rip them off."

Kade threw back his head and roared with laughter. "Now there's the Everett we all know and adore. I was wondering where he'd wandered off to. What do you think, Lochie? Is your brother just being his usual jolly self, or is he suffering from the mating frenzy?"

"Definitely the mating frenzy," Loch replied.

Kade roared with laughter again and slapped his thigh. "I can't," he wheezed. "I just can't. This is too good."

Failing to see what was so funny, I asked, "What's the mating frenzy?" When all three males turned to me with stunned looks, I wrinkled my nose at them. "What?"

"Looks like we have another *innocent* on our hands, boys," Kade said with a fiendish grin.

I snorted, muttering, "I'm far from innocent."

Everett stared at me in the mirror, for so long that I worried we would crash.

201

"On the contrary, sweet Adalyn," Kade spoke again. "You're far more innocent than you think."

"Oh, really? I've had sex hundreds of times with dozens of strange males. Still think I'm innocent?"

I'd meant to remind them of who I was, to make them see that I wasn't this virtuous little girl with a clean slate. I was a blood whore. I'd let countless males violate my body. I was tainted. Tarnished. The exact *opposite* of innocent.

Then why did they suddenly look sad, like they felt sorry for me?

Feeling all sorts of uncomfortable, I looked out my window and lapsed into silence.

After a long moment, Everett said, "Yes, Adalyn, we think you're innocent. You didn't choose this life. You were forced into it."

A retort sprang to my tongue, but I chose not to voice it. I was tired of trying to convince him that no one had forced me into becoming a sex worker.

Thankfully, Loch chose that moment to change the subject. "What are we going to do when we reach Faircroft Manor?"

"Demand Madame Faircroft release Adalyn from her debt," Everett matter-of-factly replied.

"But what if she decides to enforce the pactum? Adalyn could get hurt or worse."

"Then I'll just have to kill her," Everett said, so dangerously soft that goosebumps erupted over my flesh.

"I know how you're feeling right now, Ev, I really do. But if we kill her without proper cause, then we could have a political nightmare on our hands. You already killed two Venturi, and their deaths won't go unnoticed for much longer."

"They deserved it. I would kill them all over again if I could."

"Regardless, we're supposed to be restoring order and peace to the kingdom after what happened with the rogues. Who knows how many people saw you walk out of the club with Adalyn last night. There will be talk. Rumors. It's only a matter of time before they link the Venturi deaths to you and begin to panic. And if you kill Deloris simply for employing a witch, it could incite another revolution."

"But she isn't just *employing* Adalyn. She's whoring her out to slimy rich bastards who want a taste of the forbidden. It's sick and twisted, and I won't stand for it in my kingdom!"

He was shouting now, flooding our bond with his rage.

Unable to keep silent a moment longer, I blurted, "I'm not helpless, you know."

"Sweet, sweet Adalyn," Kade smoothly said, cutting through some of the tension. "You're tough as nails for surviving this long in our world, but you're also mortal, not to mention a hundred pounds soaking wet."

"I'm also a *witch*. My dad was a powerful Oracle elder, and he taught me many things before he died."

Everett and Loch exchanged looks. Too late, I realized my slip. Telling them that my dad had been an elder was the same as shouting, *"Hey! My dad fought against you in the battle six years ago. That makes us enemies."*

But all Everett said was, "Let me guess. You've been thralled not to use your magic?"

I almost said yes, but that would have been a lie. I could still access my magic, just not the way I wanted to. I couldn't tell them that though without revealing what I could do. And if they knew that, I might as well jump out of the car and kill myself now.

"Look, I'm not as powerless as you think," I finally settled on saying. "I've been taking care of myself for a long time and will continue to do so. I got myself into this mess, so it's my job to get out of it. I just need a little time."

"Does that time involve being with clients?"

At Everett's blunt question, a swallow got stuck in my throat.

"Everett," Loch rumbled in warning. "Remember what we talked about."

Everett looked about ready to argue, so I quickly said, "I'll call for help if I need it. I promise."

"How?" Everett asked.

"Through our bond."

His eyes met mine in the mirror. "What if the bond isn't strong enough? What if . . . what if you can't reach me?"

At the uncertainty, at the open *vulnerability* in his voice, I gave him a soft smile. "It's strong enough, Everett. You've helped *make* it strong enough."

But as we neared Faircroft Manor, his uncertainty only grew. I thought for sure he would drive right past the house and keep on going, if it wasn't for Loch reminding him of the pactum.

Deep down, Everett knew that letting me go was the only way to save me. A pactum was a sacred blood oath that couldn't be undone unless both parties willed it. If broken, the consequences were often catastrophic. I'd been so distraught over my father's death at the time that I'd easily agreed to the pactum with Mistress, even when Pepper had begged me not to. I owed the Faircroft family a blood debt, and I'd wanted to prove that I could honor it.

But I realized now how naive I'd been.

A pactum with Mistress was forever—unless she *chose* to let me go free. It didn't matter how hard I worked to pay off my father's blood debt. Didn't matter if I gave up my virtue and self worth and dignity. Didn't matter if I did everything right to please her.

Until she deemed it time to release me, I was hers.

I knew it, and so did Everett. I'd lied to him earlier. I *wasn't* my own person. As long as Mistress held the leash to my fate, she owned me. So unless I found a way to incriminate her, I wasn't going anywhere and there was nothing Everett could do about it.

Still, I was barely able to convince him to let me walk inside the house on my own. If I was going to find a way out of this mess, he needed to give me the space to do it. He couldn't save me this time. I had to deal with this alone like I had been for the past six years.

Only this time, I wasn't truly alone. I might be the only one entering the house, but I knew Everett was waiting nearby. It was the only way I'd been able to convince him to let me go. As soon as possible, I was to let him know how I fared via our soulmate bond. Until then, he wasn't going anywhere.

Knowing he wasn't far away gave me the strength I needed to push forward and enter the house. The second I closed the kitchen door, something rushed toward me. So fast that I didn't have time to react. In a flash, a hand clamped over my mouth and pinned me against the door.

"Shhh!" a familiar voice hissed, the cold metal of several rings digging into my face.

Quickly adjusting to the house's gloomy interior, I focused on Mistress, who was no doubt listening for Everett. She wouldn't hear anything. He'd parked the car a solid mile down the road. She wouldn't be able to detect any heartbeats from here.

Ada!

The sound of my familiar's voice threatened to break my concentration, but I didn't let my relief show through the invisible mask I'd carefully constructed.

I'm fine, Pep, I quickly responded. *No need to worry.*

Worry? Are you kidding me? I've been going crazy out of my mind!

This is the second day in a row that something happened to you. Mistress Evil has been in a temper all day, threatening to enforce the pactum if you didn't return soon. Is it true that the crown prince stormed into Dreamscape and stole you away?

I'm sorry, Pepper. I really am. I would have contacted you if our bond had allowed it. Speaking of, I have a lot to tell you. Everett didn't steal me away; he rescued me. And . . . he's my soulmate.

Soulmate? she loudly squeaked.

As I started to tell her more, Mistress grabbed my chin and forced me to look deeply into her blazing eyes.

"Did you tell the prince anything you're not supposed to?"

Her thrall invaded my mind like a parasite and pulled words out of my mouth, words that I had no choice but to give her. "Only that my dad was an elder."

It was the truth. I hadn't *told* Everett anything. He'd guessed it.

Still, Mistress was far from appeased. Her grip tightened, painfully pressing on my bruises. "Why did he take you?"

"He . . . he wanted me for himself. But I told him I couldn't stay."

Her eyes narrowed suspiciously. "He didn't *force* you to stay?"

"No, Mistress."

"Did you convince him to let you go with your magic?"

"No, Mistress."

She released my chin with a disgusted huff. "He got bored of you, then. Typical Venturi, taking whatever he wants, then throwing it away. I hear he's slept with every maid in his castle." She leaned forward to sniff me, then recoiled with another disgusted huff. "Of course he claimed you, like a spoiled child with a new toy. See, this is why our mission is so important, Adalyn. The Venturi only think about themselves, not caring how their actions affect others."

Grumbling to herself, she stormed to the fridge and practically ripped the door off. She grabbed a blood bag and quickly poured its contents into a glass.

"You have no idea how stressful it was for me to watch him take you away, Adalyn," she said, downing half the glass in one huge gulp. "I haven't drank this much since my poor Richard died, God rest his soul. The thought of you in that monster's clutches . . ." She tipped back the glass and finished off the blood. "I've been beside myself for *hours*, thinking the worst. He didn't hurt you, did he?"

Recalling how he'd carefully taken care of me, fed me, and treated me like a part of his family, my throat tightened. Unable to speak, I just shook my head.

She shrewdly glanced at the bandages still on my neck and arm from last night. "And he didn't feed you his blood, I see. Good. Maybe I won't have to punish you too severely after all."

Aaand there it was. The moment I'd been waiting for. I braced myself for whatever punishment she had in store for me.

"Because of the *claim* the prince put on you, working at the club isn't an option. Dominant males are babies like that, turned off when something has been claimed by another male. They don't care if you've had sex with hundreds of other males, so long as they're not *reminded* of that fact. Their egos are so fragile. Anyway, you'll stay here until the claim fades, understood?"

I bobbed my head. "Yes, Mistress."

"But you'll continue to do your chores. Without pay, of course, to help compensate for the days you're not working at the club. This is a huge setback for us when we're *so* close to reaching our goal, Adalyn. Your clients aren't going to handle your absence very well. And we lost Councilman Torres, one of our best. Such a shame. He would have done just about anything for us."

At the reminder that he was dead, I struggled to keep a smile off my face.

"Oh, and I had the Aston Martin brought back, along with the clothing you left in your room."

She set down her glass and reached inside the pocket of her robe. As she pulled out a small object wrapped in fabric, my blood ran cold.

"I assume this is yours," she went on, carefully lifting a corner of the fabric to reveal my silver knife. "*Answer* me."

As her voice snapped through the air like a whip, my lungs seized. "Yes, Mistress."

"Oh, Adalyn, you disappoint me." She tucked the knife back inside her pocket. "Letting you own a weapon that can kill vampires is dangerous, not to mention how expensive it must have cost. I'm hurt that you didn't tell me about it. If you were feeling unsafe, you should have told me." She lightly clucked her tongue in disapproval before adding, "Until further notice, your phone and car privileges are revoked. Understood?"

I clasped my hands together to keep them from shaking. "Yes, Mistress."

"And you aren't to step foot outside this house until I say so."

"Yes, Mistress."

Her face relaxed. A second later, she was inches away, our noses practically touching. Her brown eyes bored holes into mine as she hissed, "*Swear* it."

I barely managed not to flinch. "I swear."

"You'll do well to remember the blood debt you owe this family, Adalyn. Any attempt to run away or break the promises you've sworn will trigger our pactum. You don't want to die, do you? After all the hard work you've put in?"

"No, Mistress."

"Good. Now run along and see to your chores. I've got an extra long list for you today. That should keep you busy until this evening, maybe longer. Tick-tock, Adalyn. Time does not reward a lazy spirit."

"Yes, Mistress."

I accepted the written list she handed me and hurried from the kitchen like my tail was on fire.

CHAPTER 22

ADALYN

Mistress hadn't been exaggerating. She'd ordered a *deep clean* of the house from top to bottom.

Several times throughout the day, either she, Georgina, or Octavia came to check on my progress. At one point, Georgina tossed a toothbrush at me and demanded I scrub her entire bathroom with it—even the toilet. I worked without complaint, my mind elsewhere while my body slaved away.

It had taken an hour of laser focus, but I'd finally managed to reach Everett through our bond. Hearing the relief in his voice lifted my spirits, and I'd spent the past several hours sending him little updates on my wellbeing. I was safe, all things considered. His claim on me had frozen time, allowing me to brainstorm and *think* for once. I didn't know how I could break the pactum's hold on me without dying in the process, but I was going to turn over every possible idea.

As the Faircrofts prepared to leave for the evening, I finished telling Pepper all about the time I'd spent with Everett and his family.

Sounds like your soulmate isn't the villain we believed him to be, she mused. *Not anymore, at least. Which is a hard thing to admit, considering all the terrible things he did to witches in his lifetime.*

I smiled a little. *He's no Prince Charming, but I can't blame him for being a bit rough around the edges after all he went through with his brothers and the curse. At least he's learning from his mistakes and attempting to fix them.*

Wow, Pepper said in an amused tone. *I think you might like him.*

I mean, I'm starting to respect him, I evasively replied.

She snorted. *You've spent too much time pretending, Ada. You don't have to hide how you really feel.*

Oh, yes, I did. Because the truth was too dangerous to face. Keeping my feelings about Everett carefully locked away was my only option right now. There was too much at stake, too many things that could go wrong. I couldn't get distracted by feelings when my very survival was in question, not to mention his.

Mistress's voice suddenly rang through the house. "We're leaving, Adalyn. Remember your promises and don't stop working until you've completed the list."

I paused in my task, waiting for the sound I'd been longing to hear all day. When the front door snapped shut and silence finally descended over the house, I jumped up and started to dance. Not like I'd been trained to, but however I wished. I leapt and twirled, oddly excited to be stuck in the house all night. It meant that for the first time in three years, I didn't have to work at the *club.*

Racing down the stairs, I turned on every lightswitch I passed, pausing only to shimmy out of my jeans and toss them on the floor. Wow, that felt *amazing.* I was wasting electricity *and* making a mess.

"We have the whole house to ourselves, Pepper!" I belted out. "My wicked taskmasters have left the building!"

She cackled in my mind. *What should we do first? Jump on all their beds? Paint each other's toenails with Georgina's pink polish? It's been ages since we've had a girls' night!*

I know, Pep, I'm so sorry. But I'm going to make it up to you. I'll rummage in the pantry and see if I can find us a snack, then we can lounge around and be lazy. Let's watch a movie or something. Mistress would have a fit if she knew.

Pepper cackled again. *Forget her. The night is ours. I just wish I could leave a nasty little present in her bed. Hearing her disgusted shriek would be the perfect end to the evening.*

I laughed as I headed for the kitchen, still turning on lights and shedding clothing. My shirt hit the floor with a satisfactory plop. *I agree, but if she knew a* mouse *was in the house . . .*

I know, I know. She'd probably hunt me down herself and eat me raw. Well, she could try, *but she'd never catch me.*

Still, you know I can't risk it, Pep. I'm sorry you've been stuck in the basement for so long, but—

No need to apologize, Ada. You're innocent in all this.

"Ha!" I said aloud, nearing the basement door. "You're the second person—no, *third*—to call me innocent today." Dramatically throwing a hand to my forehead, I twittered, "Oh, to be an innocent *virgin* again."

"I'm all for pretending you're a virgin, so long as I get to pop your cherry."

Startled by the male voice, I whirled toward the kitchen door and screamed like a banshee. Spotting the hulking form in the doorway, instinct took over. I grabbed the nearest object and threw it at the intruder, realizing too late who it was.

Everett whipped a hand up and easily caught the object, then said with a soft tsk, "Did you really think this would stop a vampire, Adalyn? And not that I don't appreciate the view, but why are you half naked?"

I blinked down at my bra and panties. "Um, I have the night off. Guess I like to relax without my clothes on."

"Good to know."

At the amusement in his voice, I threw him a smirk. "As for the glass paperweight, it was all I had. Mistress confiscated my only weapon. By the way, what are you doing here?"

"Is that what she makes you call her? Your *mistress?*"

"I guess. But seriously. Why are you—?"

Everett abruptly squeezed the paperweight, so hard that it exploded in a poof of sparkly dust.

Listening to the tiny shards ping off the kitchen tiles, I groaned, "Great. Another mess for me to clean up."

As I stepped forward to do just that, Everett said, "Don't. Show me where the broom and dustpan are, and I'll do it."

I stopped dead in my tracks to gape at him. "*You?* The crown vampire prince is going to clean up a mess in the kitchen? Now *this* I gotta see."

In a flash, I grabbed the broom and dustpan, then thrust them at him, grinning like a fiend.

Ten bucks says he doesn't know how to use a broom, Pepper said, clearly eavesdropping on our conversation.

Everett gave me an odd look as I replied out loud, "You're on. But if you win, don't you dare turn that money into a new nest."

No promises, she sang back.

When he continued to stare at me like I'd lost my mind, I waved a hand and explained, "It's just Pepper. She thinks you don't know how to use a broom."

Because he's a spoiled little prince who lives in a pretty castle run by human servants, she chortled. *I bet he's never washed a dish or folded laundry in his life.*

When I snickered, Everett's green eyes narrowed. "Oh, really? What *else* does she think?"

I blinked at him innocently. "Nothing interesting."

"Mmm," he grunted, then became a whirlwind. Literally. My hair flew every which way as he moved at lightning speed. A second later, he was standing before me again.

"Done," he said, handing me the broom and dustpan. A dustpan that was now filled with little shards of glass.

My mouth fell open. As I wordlessly took the tools, Everett slowly smirked.

"So, when do I get to meet your familiar?"

"Uh . . ."

Now, Pepper excitedly said. *I want to meet the magical, broom-wielding prince you have the hots for.*

"Pepper," I hissed, giving Everett a nervous little smile when he raised a brow in question. "Look, this really isn't a good idea. Mistress will know you were here if you come inside."

"Then we'll go outside."

"I can't. She forbade me from stepping foot outside this house."

His jaw hardened. "What does she expect you to do, then?"

I shrugged. "Mostly clean."

Anger sparked in his eyes. "So you're her servant."

I didn't respond, choosing to empty the dustpan and put the cleaning tools away instead. When I returned with a shirt on, he barely seemed to notice. He was too busy being angry, so angry that I wouldn't be surprised if he started tearing down the house with his own two hands. He probably would too, which made me nervous.

To distract him, I said, "Look, Everett. It was nice of you to check on me, but I'm perfectly safe here. I think you should—"

A soft scratching noise suddenly came from the basement door.

Let me up, Ada. If you're going outside with the hunky prince, then so am I.

I hurried to the door and opened it, bending to scoop Pepper into my hands. "You shouldn't have come up here," I quietly scolded her, trapping her between my palms when she tried to race up my arm.

Don't make me bite you, Adalyn, she warned with a perturbed squeak. *I'm super hangry, and witch tartare sounds mighty tasty right about now.*

Knowing that she wasn't bluffing, I opened up my hands. "Fine, but be careful."

Why? Do you think your boy toy will swallow me whole?

Before I could scold her again, Everett asked, "What's she saying?"

I whirled to face him. "Um . . . you probably don't want to know."

Chicken, Pepper goaded me.

I poked her little side.

She squeaked in protest and lunged for my finger, but I pulled it out of reach in the nick of time.

"Pepper, this is Everett. Everett, this is Pepper," I quickly said, needing this introduction to be over with so I could shoo Everett away. I had no idea why he was here, but conversing with him like this was dangerous on so many levels. At least he was still in the doorway. Mistress might not be able to detect his scent later on, so long as he stayed where he was.

Ooo, he's handsome. For a bloodsucker, I mean, Pepper said, boldly checking him out. *I can see why you're attracted to him.*

Denial sprang to my tongue, but I didn't voice it. I'd be lying to say I wasn't attracted to him.

Everett took her in, then said the *last* thing I expected him to say. "Can I pet her?"

Oh ho ho! Pepper chortled, practically preening in my hands. *Sorry, Ada. I can't help it if this body is irresistibly adorable.*

"Sure," I answered, stifling an eye roll. As I stepped forward, though, I couldn't resist the instinct to tuck her close to my body. "Just . . . be careful, okay? She's really small. And delicate."

Everett's expression noticeably softened. "Like you?"

Aww, he likes you too, Pepper sighed in a dreamy voice.

My heart gave a weird little flutter. Did he?

Girl, don't be daft. He's making googly eyes at you right now, Pepper said with a snort.

That stupid vulnerable feeling stole over me again. I could barely look him in the eye, too afraid of what I'd find.

"I won't hurt her, Adalyn. I promise," he said, making my heart flutter again.

Good enough for me, Pepper said. *Let the petting commence.*

I shook my head with a small laugh. "Fine. If you're okay with it, Pep, then so am I. I'm going to let the big scary vampire pet you now."

"Scary?" Everett said with an amused tilt of his mouth.

"*Very* scary. To all the people who upset you and wind up dead."

A laugh rolled from him, one that made me forget how to breathe. Spirits save me, he had the sexiest laugh. Too bad he didn't whip it out more.

He laughed again, louder this time. "Whip it out? Interesting choice of words."

I groaned, feeling the beginnings of a blush stain my cheeks. "Well, *that* was embarrassing."

"You? Embarrassed?"

"I know, right? Apparently, the thought of you reading my deepest darkest thoughts does that to me."

He laughed again.

This is the cutest thing ever, Pepper interrupted. *Wish I had some popcorn for this little romcom moment.*

"Seriously, Pepper? Knock it off already, would you? Here. Everett's going to pet you now."

Oh, goodie. It's my turn to get a piece of him. You've been hogging him all to yourself, you greedy girl.

Ignoring her, I held my hands out toward Everett. As he reached up to pet my tiny familiar, some of my nerves vanished.

"What?" Everett asked, seeing the little smirk on my face.

"You just don't seem like the mouse-petting type, is all."

"Then what type am I?"

"The squish-mice-for-fun type." When he frowned and Pepper squeaked in protest, my smirk grew. "Just saying."

"Well, maybe I have a soft side for small creatures," he replied, keeping his gaze on me as he gently stroked Pepper's back with his index finger.

I swallowed hard, pretty certain he wasn't referring to Pepper.

He abruptly jerked his hand back with a hiss.

I looked down and saw that his finger was now bleeding. "Pepper, how could you?" I scolded, mortified that she'd bitten him.

Just wanted to see how he'd react. Don't worry. He passed the test.

"Oh, Pepper," I sighed, shaking my head.

"What did she say?" Everett asked before popping the finger into his mouth to lick the wound clean.

"Apparently, she wanted to test you. Good thing he didn't *squish* you for that, Pep."

She twitched her whiskers, not the least bit apologetic.

"So, did I pass?"

"Yep. You're all clear. Whatever *that* means."

I suddenly felt something through our bond, making my eyes widen. He was *pleased.*

"You're both crazy," I muttered.

He huffed a laugh. "Come on. Let's go outside."

My nerves returned tenfold. "I really shouldn't. What if the Faircrofts come back early?"

"I'll hear if they come back. I can have you inside the house in seconds, and my car is parked a mile down the road. They won't even know I was here."

Still not convinced, I blurted, "But I'm not wearing pants."

He lifted an eyebrow. "I've seen you outside in far less."

Oh my. Now I was remembering our time in the rain with me naked on the car and his head between my thighs. My resistance started to melt, along with my panties.

Squeezing my legs together, I made one last weak attempt at an excuse. "I still can't step foot outside this house."

Faster than I could blink, Everett scooped me into his arms. "Then I'll just have to carry you."

Spirits save me, he'd totally won. As he stepped out the door and into the dusky evening, I cradled Pepper close and allowed my resistance to fade.

Fresh air! Pepper sang, her little nose happily twitching. *It's been so long since I went outside. I'm officially a fan of your vampire prince.*

He's not my vampire prince, I scolded her, hoping Everett wasn't trying to read my thoughts. *And don't even think about taking off while we're out here. That tabby is probably still around, not to mention the owls and coyotes and—*

I get it, Ada, she groaned. *Everyone wants to eat me. Except your dashing prince, who only wants to eat you.*

I started to choke.

"You okay?" Everett asked when my coughing subsided.

"Yeah, fine," I quickly said, frantically fishing for a subject change. "Are Loch and Kade nearby?"

"No. Kenna picked them up. They're on standby at the lakehouse until further notice."

"Standby?"

"In case I need them."

"And what about you? Why are you still here?"

He glanced down at me. "Because I can't stay away from you. I meant it when I said you aren't alone anymore. I'm not going anywhere."

My heart did that weird little flutter-thingy again. Blinking up at him, I whispered, "Ever?"

"So long as you want me here, I'll stay."

So romantic, Pepper said with a dreamy sigh.

Overwhelmed, I didn't say anything. As I struggled to process his words and my emotions, I looked out into the night to see where he was taking us. We were approaching the shore of the Atlantic, but before we could hit the rocks, he veered left.

"Where are we—?" I started, then sucked in a quiet gasp as I spotted something up ahead. "Is that a picnic?"

"Yes. Loch and Kade helped me set it up before they left."

You were totally wrong, Pepper said with a delighted squeak. *He is Prince Charming.*

Biting my lip, I took in the unexpected scene before me. Tucked beneath a huge red maple tree was a blanket spread out on the grass. A single lantern warmed the space, revealing a large picnic basket, along with plates and silverware set for two.

"Wow. This is . . ." I said, at a loss for words. When he stopped at the edge of the blanket, I looked up at him and blurted, "Is this a date?"

A soft smile curved his lips. "I'm hoping it will be. I didn't do things right with you, but I want to fix that—if you'll let me."

At the open honesty on his face, I couldn't help but smile back. There were a million reasons why this shouldn't happen. A million reasons why I should demand he take me back to the house and leave. But, instead, all I said was, "I'd like that."

CHAPTER 23

EVERETT

She had no idea how nervous I was. In the one-hundred-eighty-eight years of my existence, I'd never once been on a date.

If it hadn't been for Loch and Kade, I never would have thought to bring her out here for a picnic dinner. Thoughtful gestures weren't exactly my forte. I'd been focused so long on protecting my brothers and breaking the kingdom's curse that something as simple as a picnic seemed foreign to me now. It was almost awkward when I set her down and waited for her to claim a spot on the blanket.

I shouldn't have worried, though.

The second she sat down, she loudly moaned, "Yummm. Do I smell chicken? I'm *starved.*"

A smile twitched my mouth, but that wasn't the only thing twitching. I was enchanted by her every move. Bewitched. Despite the literal darkness she lived in, she continued to brightly shine like a star. I couldn't stop watching her. Couldn't stop *wanting* her.

To hide the growing bulge in my pants, I sat across from her and replied, "Loch found a little restaurant not too far from here. I think it's called Chicken and . . ."

"Chicken n' Things? Yes! I've always wanted to go there."

She hungrily eyed the picnic basket, nearly shaking in her eagerness. Sudden emotion surged through me, and I couldn't help but say, "Do the Faircrofts not feed you?"

She glanced up at me, then quickly looked away, but not fast enough. "I know what you're thinking, but they don't *starve* me. They're just not used to feeding a mortal. Besides, I'm perfectly capable of feeding myself."

"Adalyn, I'm not judging you. I just want to know if you're being taken care of."

At the softness in my voice, she sighed and looked up again. "I really do get paid for the work I do, if that's what you're asking. I just get busy and forget to eat sometimes."

Her little mouse familiar scampered onto her thigh and loudly squeaked, sounding very much like she was scolding Adalyn.

"Well, I can't tell him that," she replied to whatever Pepper said. "And I *do* eat. Just not as much as I want to."

As they bickered, I opened the basket and started pulling out food. Fried chicken, mashed potatoes, caesar salad, and buttery biscuits. I tried not to sneer at it all, but couldn't quite manage it.

When the bickering abruptly stopped, I looked up to see Adalyn's gaze glued to the food. So was Pepper's. I might as well no longer exist. Smirking, I said, "Help yourself."

Adalyn dove right in, dumping a bit of everything onto her plate. "Oh man, Pep. This is gonna be so good." Grabbing a chicken leg, she took a huge bite before adding, "I can't believe I get to have two huge meals in one day. A girl could get used to this."

Once again, emotion heated my insides. The more I learned about her abysmal living conditions, the angrier I became. I wanted nothing more than to wrap her in my arms and carry her far away from here.

If it wasn't for that bloody pactum, I'd have her out of here in a heartbeat.

As she ate, making sure to set aside tiny pieces of biscuit for Pepper, she failed to notice me watching her. Her entire focus was on rapidly consuming the food, as if afraid it would be taken from her at any moment. I wondered for the umpteenth time today if the Faircrofts punished her. If they withheld food when she displeased them. Or worse . . . if they physically beat her.

Just the thought of them touching her small breakable body made me see red.

"You okay?"

I quickly blinked the red away and saw that Adalyn had finally noticed me. Clearing my throat, I gruffly replied, "Yes."

"Hmm," she said, studying me thoughtfully. "You don't like food much, do you?"

I smiled a little at her rhetorical question. "The longer a vampire lives, the less they enjoy food. My father doesn't even eat food anymore."

"Oh. So you're not enjoying the picnic?"

"Quite the opposite. I might not be enjoying the food, but I'm enjoying the company just fine."

My smile grew as I felt through our bond how pleased she was. And flustered. *Very* flustered.

"Uh," she said, reaching up to fiddle with her hair. "So I don't know what the proper etiquette is for a picnic date with a vampire. Am I supposed to offer you my blood?"

My cock twitched again, the thought of feeding on her instantly arousing me. "Only if you're offering it to me of your own volition. No strings attached."

I heard her pulse quicken. So did mine.

"I mean, you know that I crave venom, so I'm not opposed to it. If you're hungry, I can feed you."

My cock hardened into a full-blown erection. I didn't respond, the sudden lack of blood flow to my brain robbing me of speech.

"By the way, you never told me what the mating frenzy is," she said, effectively adding fuel to the flames.

I swallowed a groan, fairly certain I was in the midst of the frenzy right now.

"I'm guessing it has something to do with mating," she went on, making it hard for me to breathe. "And frenzy."

"The mating frenzy happens shortly after a soulmate pair completes their bond through intercourse," I ground out, hoping to quickly explain and direct the conversation to safer waters. "They feel a constant need to be close and to mate."

She stared at me for a moment, then hesitantly said, "Oh. Is that . . . is that what you're feeling right now? Do you need to have sex?"

I squeezed my eyes shut, ignoring my raging hard on to calmly reply, "Your job isn't to pleasure me, Adalyn. That's not what I came here for."

She was silent for a beat. Then quietly said, "I don't mind, Everett. Yes, you claimed me without my permission. Yes, I was hurt. But I no longer think you did it to control me. I don't feel used when I'm with you. I feel safe. I feel *seen*. I've shown you the real me, and you're still here. You still . . . you still want me."

"Of course I want you," I groaned, reopening my eyes to look at her. "But I don't just want you for your body. My father was right. It wasn't a coincidence that he sent me to Dreamscape. Fate brought me to you because you're my purpose. My *light*. And I crave that light more than anything. I don't care if you're a witch or a blood whore, Adalyn. I just want you. You're *all* I want."

I didn't know where the words had come from. They'd just spilled out of me, rolling off my tongue before I could stop them. I wouldn't take them back, though. I'd meant every word and could only hope she felt a fraction of what I felt for her.

"Adalyn," I said, worried that I'd terrified her. She was still as stone, her golden eyes frozen wide in shock.

I was about to change the subject when she suddenly moved. In a breath, she was in my lap and claiming my mouth. Elated, I fisted her hair and returned the kiss with equal passion.

When her lips parted, I slipped my tongue inside to curl it around hers. With a breathless moan, she hitched her bare legs around my waist and sank onto my throbbing cock. I returned the moan and cupped her backside to rock her against me. She rocked back, thrusting her hips in time to the thrusts of my tongue.

In no time, we were both desperate for more. I removed her top, and she removed mine, all without breaking the kiss. We continued to feverishly kiss as I leaned forward to lay her on the blanket, shoving aside plates and food containers in the process. I assumed Adalyn would tell me if Pepper was in danger of being squished, so I didn't hesitate to cover her body with mine.

Not even caring if the little mouse familiar was watching, I rocked against Adalyn again, pleased when she arched up for more. I reached between us to undo my pants, but she broke the kiss to pant, "Wait. You pleasured me the last time you were here. I want to return the favor."

I started to protest, but the words ended in a groan as she reached down and gripped me through my pants. Pleasure shot through me, robbing me of air. When she rolled us so that I was on my back instead, all I could do was surrender. Her skilled little hands made quick work of undoing my buckle and unzipping my pants, allowing my erection to spring free.

"Adalyn," I said, breathing her name like a prayer. I looked up at her, just as she lowered her head and took me into her mouth. At the beautiful sight of her lips around my cock, I groaned without restraint.

Pleased by my reaction, she curled her tongue around me and began to suck. Euphoria rocked my body, and I jerked against her mouth, the need to thrust overwhelming.

"Adalyn, baby," I moaned, reaching up to slide my fingers into her hair. "Your mouth feels so damned good."

As she continued to suck, she cupped my balls, making me see stars.

God, her mouth and hands were magic. Every time she touched me, I was blown away by how good it felt. She was wrecking me in the best way possible, making me forget all others before her. Nothing before her mattered. She was the only one I desired and craved. The only one I wanted to touch me. To pleasure me. To fill my world with indescribable bliss.

Needing more friction, needing more *her*, I gripped her hair and started to thrust. She let me, answering my need by swallowing more of my shaft. Unable to keep my eyes open a moment longer, I let them roll back and focused on the growing tension in my body. The *delicious* tension that her hands and lips and tongue were creating.

She added a second hand, squeezing the base of my shaft until I jerked again, barely able to hold off my orgasm. She kept squeezing and sucking and pumping until my entire body was a riot of sensation, screaming for release. My thighs quivered, the orgasm building and building.

She squeezed once more, and I lost it. With a roar, I surrendered to the ecstasy pounding through me and spilled my release. But she didn't pull away. She continued to suck on me, taking all of me into her mouth. Tasting me. *Swallowing* me.

I peeled open my eyes to watch her. She was beautiful. The most beautiful creature I'd ever seen and ever would see. When she finally released me, tilting her swollen lips into that captivating smirk I couldn't get enough of, a feeling flooded my body. One that stole my breath and left me stunned to my very core.

I was falling for her.

I was falling for my soulmate.

CHAPTER 24

ADALYN

It was day three of being stuck inside the Faircroft home. Arguably, the best three days of my life.

Despite how busy Mistress kept me during the day, I was full of energy the moment she and her daughters left each evening. When the coast was clear, Everett would arrive, immediately making the hard hours of work fade away. Every time he came, he brought with him more food than I could possibly eat in one sitting. I mourned the fact that I couldn't store the leftovers in the fridge, but I ate as much of the food as I could before we were forced to part ways.

Tonight, he'd brought lobster, shrimp, and cod, and Pepper received a selection of cheeses, nuts, and berries. We sat down in our usual spot beneath the red maple, contentedly listening to the waves crashing against the rocks as we stuffed our faces. When I couldn't eat another bite, I laid down on the blanket with a groan, using Everett's lap as a pillow.

Something had shifted between us these past few days. We'd both stopped resisting the soulmate bond and had embraced it, which had allowed the connection to deepen. I was growing more and more comfortable with him having access to my emotions and thoughts, but not all of them. Not the parts that were tightly locked under thrall. Every day, I'd try to tell him about my mistress's evil plans, and every time, I'd fail.

The clock was ticking as Everett's claim on me faded. It wouldn't be much longer before I had to return to Dreamscape and give up these forbidden magical evenings with him. I was no closer to figuring out how to break the pactum, and I could sense that Everett's patience was wearing thin.

I couldn't blame him, though. He didn't want me to work at the nightclub any more than I did, and as our bond had grown stronger, so had our need for each other. Being apart was becoming more and more difficult. We spoke to each other telepathically, sometimes for hours at a time, but it wasn't enough.

We craved each other's presence. Each other's *touch*.

Every evening after I ate my fill, Pepper would wander off to give us some privacy while we gave in to the mating frenzy. We had sex for *hours*, only coming up for air when time forced us to. Each night, he would feed on me, making sure to only give me enough venom to chase away the pain. I still woke up with headaches. Still craved the high that venom gave me. But it was getting easier to survive without it.

Riding the high that was Everett satiated me in ways that venom never had. Being with him made me feel less and less like frightened prey desperate to survive and more and more like *me*. Like who I used to be before my life had been turned upside down.

I finally broke the comfortable silence to say, "The stars are beautiful tonight."

"Very beautiful," he murmured, watching me instead of the night sky.

My heart fluttered, a feeling I'd been experiencing more and more lately. A feeling I was beginning to enjoy. Smiling softly, I reached up and touched his lips. He kissed my fingers, then leaned down and claimed my mouth. I slid my hand into his hair and parted my lips, eager for more of him. As our tongues tangled, I sighed blissfully into his mouth.

Aaand that's my cue to leave. Have fun, kids, Pepper said.

I didn't hear her leave, my need for Everett rising up to eclipse everything else. Fumbling to undo my pants, I awkwardly shimmied them down while simultaneously removing my top. Everett continued to shower me with kisses, but I wanted more. Sitting up, I wrestled off his shirt, then pushed him back onto the grass.

"Pants off," I breathlessly said, already buzzing with need.

He smirked, but when I growled at him, he removed his pants with a small laugh. The second he was naked, I climbed on top of him and sank onto his erection. We both moaned at the feeling of becoming one, a feeling that was entirely my new addiction. The more he was inside me, the stronger my need for him became. I couldn't get enough. It was like his dick had awakened an animal inside of me. A hungry one. *Starving.*

Every time we merged our bodies into one, it felt like our souls danced. The feeling took my breath away, filling me with pure delight. It was the best feeling in the world, a feeling I wanted to experience again and again.

When we were together like this, everything else ceased to exist. I was wholly immersed in him. He filled me up, lifting me higher than venom or dancing ever could.

We were one entity, our hearts beating in sync. One soul, dancing beneath a starry sky.

He grabbed my hips, watching my breasts bounce while I greedily rode his cock. I was on the edge of orgasm in no time, seconds away from falling over.

I was suddenly beneath him, blinking up into his pale amethyst eyes. He slowed the pace, effectively robbing me of my orgasm. I gave him my best death glare. "What are you trying to pull, you bastard?"

"You've been insatiable lately, baby girl. It's my job to keep you in check," he lazily purred.

He continued to slowly thrust in and out of me, driving me wild with need. "Not fair," I pouted. "Sex isn't the same as venom. It's not like I can become addicted to your penis."

"I disagree," he said, pulling out so his swollen tip could tease my entrance. When I whimpered pathetically, he grinned like a fiend. "See? You would do anything to have me back inside you, wouldn't you."

It wasn't a question, the cocky bastard.

"Yes," I admitted, batting my eyes at him. When his grin broadened, I used the distraction to hitch my legs up and around his waist. With one thrust, I had his dick inside me balls deep. Now it was my turn to grin.

He buried his face in my neck with a laugh, not the least bit mad that I'd taken charge. "You want it fast, baby girl?"

"Yes," I breathed, trembling with excitement.

He smiled against my skin. "Then you'd better hold on tight."

Lightning quick, he grabbed my hips again and started to thrust. So fast that my mouth fell open in a silent scream. He was using his *vampire* speed, pumping inside me so swiftly that my poor body went into shock. Within seconds, I shot skyhigh, pleasure blasting through every inch of me. The friction was unlike anything I'd ever felt before, constant and all-consuming. My back bowed off the ground, the silent scream building and building inside my head.

I suddenly exploded, shattering into a million pieces. The scream tore from my lungs and rang through the night as orgasm after orgasm whipped through me. They were never-ending, one on top of the other, mercilessly pounding through my body as Everett continued to thrust inside me at vampire speed.

Time lost meaning. My world was one big orgasm, filling me with so much pleasure that all I could do was hold on for dear life and scream.

When I started to black out from sheer ecstacy, Everett threw back his head to bellow at the stars. His dick jerked inside me, spilling his release in a violent stream.

Struggling to catch our breaths, we stayed in each other's arms for several minutes as we came down from our highs.

Eventually, Everett murmured, "Was that fast enough for you, baby girl?"

"Uh-huh," I breathlessly replied. "Do it again."

He laughed, so loudly that I grinned a mile wide, basking in the beautiful sound. Placing a kiss just below my ear, he said, "Your poor mortal heart would give out if I did it again so soon."

"Then I'll die happy," I sighed, still grinning.

Until he said in a dead serious voice, "But I wouldn't."

My high faded as the reality of our situation crowded in. My days on this earth were numbered. Knowing that a billion different things could kill me in an instant was pretty sobering.

"Sorry. Lame joke," I said. "I know I'm fragile compared to you."

"You are, and I don't take that lightly."

"I don't either. I'd just rather laugh at my situation than cry all the time. Staying positive is the only reason I've survived this long."

He paused. Then said, "Will you go back? To Dreamscape?"

"I don't want to," I admitted.

"Do you have a choice?"

"I was never forced, Everett. I *chose* to work there because—" My throat sealed shut before I could get the words out.

"It's okay. Don't try to fight it," he said, kissing me again.

Sighing my frustration, I stopped trying to speak.

When my body relaxed once more, he added, "I'm guessing you agreed to work at Dreamscape because of the debt you owe the Faircrofts. But I don't think that's the only reason. My father heard rumors that some of the Venturi have been complaining about his leadership. Not to his face, but he has a few trusted sources among the Venturi who spy for him.

"Since the curse broke, many have been discontent with the newly-enforced rules. The kingdom's laws are stricter now because of our SCA alliance, and not everyone is on board with these changes. We expected this, but not from the Venturi. They've always been afforded privileges, so it came as a shock to learn that some might be secretly meeting at Dreamscape Lounge and discussing ways to dethrone the king. My father has been challenged many times, but now that he has two young grandchildren, he's determined not to let the problem escalate beyond what we can handle.

"After meeting you and learning about what you're dealing with, I think these rumors have merit. I think Dreamscape is being used for darker purposes than blood and sex. You were the first clue that something wasn't right, and I think you're tied to whatever secrets the club is hiding. I know you can't tell me, but I think you're well aware of what's going on. Problem is, I don't have evidence to back up my suspicions. And since you can't tell me what you know, I can't confront anyone at the club. They need to all be in the same place at the same time where I can better control the outcome. So I've decided to host an event at the castle. A Masquerade Ball. It'll take place in two days' time."

Everything in me went cold. My mind screamed at me to tell him what a terrible idea that was, but no words came out.

When the silence stretched, Everett said, "You don't approve. I can feel how opposed you are to the idea. But I can't just sit back and do nothing anymore, Adalyn. I've felt useless these past few days. *Powerless* to help you. And I can't feel that way anymore. My job is to protect my family, and that includes you. As your soulmate, I have little power, but as the crown prince who will someday be king, no one would dare ignore my summons. It's too late anyway. I've already had the invitations sent out."

I lifted my head to look at him. At the hard resolve I found in his gaze, my heart sank. "You invited the Faircrofts."

"The entire household, to be precise."

"Me? You invited *me*?"

"Yes. I left explicit instructions to include you in the festivities. They think I'm obsessed with you, right? Well, let them think I'm still obsessed. It's the truth, anyway."

I could tell he was trying to lighten the mood, but I frowned and said, "This is dangerous, Everett. More dangerous than you can know. Trust me on this."

His eyes glittered with determination. "I do trust you, but I'd rather face danger head on than allow it to stab me in the back. This isn't the first time my family and I have dealt with disgruntled vampires, nor will it be the last. We need to turn the tables in our favor, and I need you at the ball to make that happen. And if Deloris Faircroft knows that I'll be expecting you there, she wouldn't dare harm you. This is our best chance to address the court's malcontent and free you from the pactum."

My bottom lip quivered. When he reached up to touch it, I almost broke. Shaking my head, I whispered, "You're a fool, Everett D'angelo. But you're going to make a wonderful king someday."

I only hoped he survived long enough to become one, and I was alive to see it happen.

I knew he was pleased by my words, but I couldn't share in

the emotion. So many things could go wrong at that ball. So many terrible things. I was surprised by how much he'd learned, but he'd only discovered the tip of the iceberg and I was helpless to tell him more.

He trusted me. *Me.* And that's what terrified me the most.

He was inviting vipers into his nest, but the viper with the deadliest bite . . .

Was me.

CHAPTER 25

ADALYN

"A ball, a ball, we're invited to a ball!" Octavia shrieked, bouncing up and down in the foyer. "I'm so excited that I could *puke!*"

I grimaced, certain she wasn't exaggerating for once. She was definitely blood drunk, and if she vomited, I would be the one to clean up the mess.

"Yes, but what am I going to *wear?*" Georgina huffed. "How am I supposed to have a new dress made in *one* day?"

The only one not in a tizzy was Mistress. She continued to stare at the invitation that had arrived just before sunset, reading the words over and over again. I pretended disinterest, my focus on dusting the foyer.

As her two daughters dramatically twittered, she slowly set the gold-embossed invitation on the foyer's round table and said, "Georgina. Octavia. Go on ahead without me. I need to have a word with Adalyn."

I froze, the duster poised over a Tiffany lamp. My hand began to shake, and I quickly lowered the duster to the table.

Still twittering about the ball and what they would wear, neither of the sisters noticed how tense their mother had become. When the door shut behind them and their voices faded, the silence that settled over the house was deafening.

I tried not to show my nerves, but I knew my heart was beating faster than it should.

"Come here, Adalyn," Mistress said.

I did as instructed, clasping my hands together to hide their trembling.

When I stood before her, she whipped up a hand and grabbed my chin. "Did you have something to do with this?"

"No, Mistress."

"The Faircrofts have never once been invited to attend a function hosted by the royal family. Even when my dear Richard was alive, the king and his sons never acknowledged our efforts to be included in the aristocratic class. The timing of this invitation can't be a coincidence, especially since they want *you* to attend. What did you say to the prince when he took you? What does he *know?*"

"I didn't tell him anything, I swear. I *can't* tell him anything."

She gave my head a little shake, spitting out, "Don't play me for a fool, Adalyn. Did you feed him information while he *claimed* you?"

"I didn't! I promise."

"Well, you must have done *something*," she hissed, releasing my chin with a frustrated huff. "We'll have to discuss this later. The past three days at the club have been hell, and we can't afford for you to miss another shift. You still reek of the prince's claim, but we'll just have to hope your clients missed you badly enough not to care. Come. You're riding with me tonight. I'm not letting you out of my sight, especially now that we know Prince Everett still has an interest in you."

She grabbed my arm and hauled me toward the front door, not giving me a chance to protest. Despite how hard I tried not to panic, my heart started to pound like a runaway horse. She was taking me back to Dreamscape. To the place that had stolen my identity. My *soul*.

Somehow, I'd managed to survive that hellhole for the past three years, but now that Everett was in my life, everything had changed. My perspective. My will to live. My *dreams*.

I didn't think I could return to the place that had taken so much from me. Didn't think I could pretend to be someone else anymore.

Everett wanted me. Not Star. *Adalyn*. And he was doing everything in his power to save me from this life.

He wouldn't understand if I returned. If I slept with my clients again, I knew he wouldn't be able to forgive me.

I was his *soulmate*.

Our bond was sacred, and to willingly defile it was worse than stabbing him in the heart with a silver blade.

He wouldn't understand.

He wouldn't understand.

As Mistress shoved me into her car and peeled away from the house, my mind was a riot of thoughts. How could I get myself out of this without making her suspicious? If she sensed that I no longer agreed with her mission, she'd thrall me so hard that I'd have no choice but to reveal everything I knew. She'd figure out that Everett was on to her scheming, that he and I were soulmates, and realize that I was too much of a liability. That it was better to cut her losses and *kill* me so I couldn't be used against her.

It would be so easy to kill me. She wouldn't even have to do it herself. But I couldn't help thinking that everyone would be better off if I died. If I no longer existed, Mistress couldn't use me anymore. Everett and his family would be *safe*.

So distracted by my dark thoughts, I forgot to contact Everett about my current situation. We were halfway to Dreamscape when I heard his voice in my head say, *Where are you? You're not in the house.*

Struggling to remain calm, I replied, *I'm on my way to Dreamscape with Mistress.*

You're WHAT? he shouted, so loudly that I almost flinched.

I'm sorry, but she was really upset about your invitation. She thinks I told you something, and if I refuse to perform tonight, she'll get even more suspicious. I really am sorry, Everett. I was hoping she'd keep me in the house until the ball so we could avoid all this.

Anger dripped from every word as he replied, *If you're going there tonight, then so am I.*

Everett, please don't. You'll only be torturing yourself.

I don't care. If you're being forced to degrade yourself, then I won't let you do it alone.

Blinking back tears, I let silence settle between us, even more sick to my stomach now. I knew he was just trying to show his support, but I didn't want him to be there while hungry males watched me dance. While they encouraged me to reveal more skin and lusted after my body.

I especially didn't want him to be there when the clock struck midnight and the lights went out, signaling me that it was time to perform my duties as a blood whore.

He couldn't be there for that. Even if he somehow survived it, *I* wouldn't. I couldn't bear the humiliation, shame, and *pain*. Not anymore. Not when those feelings were no longer just mine. They were his now too.

We pulled into the Dreamscape parking lot an hour earlier than I usually arrived. Mistress marched me up to the third floor, slowing only when Heath hurried down the hallway toward us.

"Her new room is all ready," he said, wrinkling his nose when he came within sniffing distance. "She still stinks."

"I know," Mistress replied with a huff. "We'll have her soak in a heavily perfumed bath for the next two hours. That should help. See to it that the bath is set up properly, then meet me in the hallway.

There's been a new development."

"But of course, Madame Faircroft," he smoothly replied, taking my arm as she handed me off.

His fingers tightened possessively, and I almost begged Mistress not to leave me alone with him. But he was already whisking me away at a fast clip, forcing me to lightly jog so I wouldn't be dragged. We passed by my usual room in a blur and stopped at the very last one. Heath slid the keycard in, and the door unlocked, allowing us entrance.

The room was identical to my old one, and Heath quickly marched me past the kitchen and living room to enter the bedroom.

Once there, he let go of me and ordered, "Strip. I'll fill up your bath."

As he headed for the bathroom, I blurted, "I can do it myself."

He froze in his tracks, then slowly turned to face me. "I don't think you realize how stressed we've been this past week, Star. How *close* we came to having all of our hard work ruined. You've been attacked, stolen, and now you're drenched in the crown prince's scent, making it nearly impossible for us to use you. I have the right to ensure nothing like this ever happens again, so get undressed and meet me in the bathroom. Defy me, and I'll have no choice but to use force."

He smiled a little, as if the thought of stripping me bare and bathing me excited him.

I quickly started to undress, relieved when he turned and disappeared into the bathroom. The bath started to run, and I waited as long as I could before joining him. At the sound of my arrival, Heath stopped pouring lavender-scented oil into the water to glance over his shoulder. Seeing me naked, lust immediately dilated his pupils. He set the oil on the cart and slowly approached me, boldly raking his eyes down my body.

"You really are an exquisite creature, Star," he purred, reaching out to touch my hair. I held perfectly still while he slid his fingers through the strands. As his knuckles bumped my left breast, a growl of need rumbled from him. Quick as an adder, he gripped my neck and jerked me against him. "What I wouldn't give to spend an hour alone with you. To taste you, to feel your hands on me, to seek pleasure in your gorgeous body. Maybe after we've fulfilled our mission, you and I can come to an arrangement."

Disgust roiled in my gut, but instead of shoving him away like my instincts screamed at me to do, I gave him one of my secretive little smirks and cooed, "Maybe we can."

His face split into a pleased grin. I almost gagged as his groin brushed against my thigh, revealing how hard he was. Years of pretending kept me from fighting tooth and nail to get away.

"Go ahead and wash up," he said, his voice creepily soft as he released my neck. "I'll be in the bedroom to give you a little privacy."

And probably so he could jerk off to the image of my naked body.

When I stepped around him, his hand came down and smacked my butt. I almost whirled and clawed his eyes out. Instead, I threw him a sultry wink and sauntered toward the tub, pretending for all the world like I enjoyed his attention.

But inside, I was tightly curled in the fetal position, praying that Everett couldn't feel how miserable I was.

Two hours later, I was primped to perfection and sliding onto my aerial hoop for another night of dancing. As I waited to be lowered, I searched the undulating crowd below for Everett. He hadn't contacted me again, but I knew, just *knew* that he was here somewhere. I touched my mask, reminding myself that I was no longer Adalyn. No longer Everett's *soulmate*. But the more I reminded myself, the louder my mind shouted that it was a lie.

You're not Star, you're not Star, you're not Star.

The shouts were so loud that I couldn't hear anything else. Not the pounding sensual music. Not the crowd's raucous laughter. Not their moans and cries of pleasure. I was deaf to it all, drowning in my mind's frantic insistence that I was no longer Star.

You're not Star, you're not Star . . .

The hoop started to lower, and I desperately tried to clear my thoughts. To focus. I couldn't let them see me without my mask. My *shield.* I needed to be the confident, alluring witch that everyone came here to see.

But when the hoop stopped and the fog began to clear, I still wasn't her. Light blinded me, and I had nowhere to run. Nowhere to hide.

They could see me. The real me. They could see *Adalyn.*

The crowd below froze at the sight of me, and I froze as well, utterly terrified. Everything I'd been taught, everything I'd done to survive this place, completely fled my mind. I was prey dangled before bloodthirsty predators, exposed and scared witless.

The music started again, my cue to dance. But as the crowd continued to gape at me expectantly, a dull roar filled my ears. My breath came in short spurts, my heart thundering out of control.

Realizing what was happening, I ordered myself to breathe. To calm down. Darkness crowded my vision anyway.

You're having a panic attack, baby girl, I dimly heard a voice say. *You need to breathe. Adalyn? Adalyn!*

The room precariously tilted. My hold on the hoop slipped.

As I started to fall, everything went black.

CHAPTER 26

ADALYN

I fell like a rock toward the unforgiving ground, the darkness lifting just enough for me to realize that I was screwed. The silk I normally wound around my leg to slow my descent was nowhere to be found. The crowd parted, believing the fall was an act. A part of my routine. I braced for the pain, wondering if this was how I would die. Broken by the place that had shattered my innocence, this time beyond repair.

It would be a terribly tragic ending.

I tried to will magic to my fingertips, one last pathetic attempt to save myself, but it wouldn't obey me. I was helpless. *Hopeless.* Utterly alone in a dangerous world bent on destroying me.

But just as I was about to hit the ground, dark shadows embraced me. Shielded me. *Saved* me from my terrible fate.

In a blur, the shadows swept me away from the crowd. Familiar strong arms held me close, and I instinctively clung to them, to *him* as he carried me away from the crowd at vampire speed. Several startled gasps followed in our wake, Everett's movements too fast for the humans to track. If we were lucky, they'd simply think I pulled off a miraculous disappearing act.

I didn't know where he was taking me, but I didn't care at the moment. All I cared about was being in his arms. In his presence. The only place that made me feel safe. The longer he held me, the more I felt like myself again. Like Adalyn.

Within seconds, Everett closed us inside a room. A storage closet, by the smell of it. The space was pitch black, but I didn't ask him to turn on a light. I didn't need it. He was here with me, and that's all that mattered.

When he carefully set me on my feet and ran his hands down my arms as if to check for injury, I held still. I couldn't see him, but I could feel him. He was upset. Angry. *Afraid*.

"You fell. You *fell*, Adalyn. Do you have any idea what it would do to me if you died? Do you have any idea how *terrified* I was?"

I didn't respond, too overwhelmed by the fear pumping through our bond. He continued to run his hands over me, his touch firm yet achingly gentle. Tears came unbidden to my eyes.

"I thought I could let you do this, but I can't," he said, his voice noticeably trembling.

"Everett," I whispered.

"No," he fiercely said, reaching up to cup my face. "I have to protect you. Every cell in my body is *demanding* I take you away from this place. It's going to kill you, Adalyn. This place will *kill* you."

"Everett," I tried again. "I can't leave. You *know* I can't. I have to see this through."

He pressed his forehead to mine, the movement shifting our masks. As his scent surrounded me, I gripped his forearms and closed my eyes.

"I hate this," he breathed, skating his thumb across my bottom lip. "Every molecule of my being hates that you're in this place."

"I hate it too," I whispered back.

As our breath mingled, he kissed me. Softly at first, then with more urgency, clearly needing comfort as much as I did. I stood on tiptoe and kissed him back, knowing that this beautiful moment would have to end all too soon. He backed me against the door, and a thrill went through me as our bodies perfectly aligned.

The kiss became heated. Tongues and teeth clashed, our need for each other growing like a wildfire. I lifted up even more so I could suck his bottom lip into my mouth and thoroughly taste him, then greedily bit into the soft flesh.

When he violently shuddered against me, I did it again. He lowered his hands to grab my backside and grind me against him. Feeling how hard he was, I purred through our bond, *Do you like it when I bite you?*

As I continued to nibble on the flesh like he was my personal chew toy, he quietly groaned, *I'm going to come in my pants if you keep doing that.*

I was tempted to make him, but I'd already been away for too long. Heath and Mistress would have heard about my disappearance by now and had no doubt ordered the bouncers to search for me.

With a resigned sigh, I ended our blissful moment and forced myself to pull away.

"Everett," I started.

"I know," he replied, not needing me to finish.

We paused to catch our breaths and allow the arousal between us to settle.

And then he said, "I'll let you go, but I'm not leaving. If I think you're in danger, I'm coming for you again. And if anyone stands in my way, they're dead."

"Everett," I began, but I didn't know what to say. I hated that he was here, but I hated the thought of him leaving even more.

"You're more important to me than anything, Adalyn. I'll allow you to do your job, but I won't tolerate you getting hurt. That's all I can promise you."

My heart fluttered, his words warming me like a blanket. A sudden need to protect him hit me, and I blurted before I could think better of it, "I'll tell Mistress that I'm not feeling well tonight. If she thinks I'm too weak to perform, she'll let me go home."

His relief flooded our bond so swiftly that my knees almost buckled. "Oh, thank God," he breathed and gathered me into his arms. He held me so tightly that it was nearly impossible to pull away.

But I did. I forced myself to leave our little closet bubble and face whatever came next. It wouldn't be pretty, but I felt lighter, certain I'd made the right decision—for *both* of us.

Rocky found me a minute later. As he checked me over for injuries, he looked worried but didn't say anything. A quick phone call had Mistress joining us soon after.

"What happened?" she demanded. "I received several reports that you fell and then disappeared."

"I don't know," I replied, trying my best to appear dazed. "I must have passed out. When I came to, I was in a closet."

Her gaze hardened as if she didn't quite believe me. I tensed, certain she'd try to thrall me. Instead, she turned to Rocky and said, "Did you see any sign of Prince Everett tonight?"

My throat closed.

He opened his mouth, then slowly closed it and replied, "No, ma'am."

"Well, keep a lookout. If you have even the slightest suspicion that he's here, inform me immediately." She whirled back to me and grabbed my arm. "Come. You need to get back out there."

As she swept down the hallway with me in tow, I allowed myself to stumble a little. To show *weakness*. "I'm not . . . I'm not feeling very well, Mistress."

"*Enough* of this, Adalyn," she snapped. "You have a job to do."

When she continued to drag me forward, I tripped again, nearly falling to my knees.

Growling, she whipped around and yanked me upright by my hair. "You're useless. *Useless!*" she screamed in my face.

Pain shot through my scalp, and Everett's voice immediately filled my head. *Adalyn, what's wrong? I can feel your pain. Adalyn! Screw this, I'm coming to get you.*

No! I inwardly cried, struggling to keep my composure in the face of Mistress's wrath. *I can handle this. Please don't let her see you.*

He didn't respond, but his silence said far more than words ever could. If I didn't get this situation under control soon, he would make good on his earlier promise.

"I don't know *why* I put up with you," Mistress continued to rail at me, giving my head a shake. "Mortals are so weak and pathetic, always needing to be taken care of. You're more trouble than you're worth these days, Adalyn."

"I'm sorry, Mistress," I started, then had the balls to add, "I just need a little food and rest. Then I can—"

"Rocky!" she barked, releasing my hair with a disgusted curl of her lip. When the bouncer joined us once more, she shoved me toward him. "Return Star to her room. And make sure she gets some *food.*"

Tossing me one last glare, as if my body's needs had just ruined her life, she angrily stormed down the hallway.

Rocky watched her go, then inclined his head for me to follow him. I quickly assured Everett that all was well, but I could still feel how upset he was. If my employers continued to manhandle me, I doubted he would stay away much longer.

When Rocky and I reached my new room, he wordlessly held the door open for me. Expecting him to leave just as silently, I was shocked when he paused to say, "My wife is mortal."

I turned to face him. "She's human?"

He nodded. "I wanted to have children. We're still trying."

"Oh." I understood enough about vampires to know that their females were barren. The king himself had chosen to marry humans instead of a Venturi female, his desire for heirs more important to him than having a queen by his side. Still, it took years, sometimes decades for a vampire to conceive a child. I gave Rocky a small smile. "Best of luck to you."

He opened his mouth, then closed it. Nodding, he simply replied, "I'll get you some food."

"Thanks," I said. He really was nice for a bouncer. Too bad he worked for Mistress.

As he shut the door, I turned and started to pace. I'd just bought myself some time, but for how long? Mistress hadn't sent me home, which meant that she still wanted me to work tonight. To entertain *clients*. They knew I was here, and a handful of them were already prepared to spend an hour with me this evening. Mistress would be livid if I forced her to turn them away again, but forcing myself to have sex with them was even worse. *Much* worse. The thought made me want to hurl my guts out.

I'd never enjoyed being a blood whore, but now that my feelings for Everett were growing, I downright hated the thought of being touched by any other male but him.

There was only one thing I could do. One thing I could live with. But doing it could ruin everything.

When Rocky returned with food, my stomach was tied into so many knots that I couldn't eat. Even when I'd lost my virginity to Councilman Torres, I hadn't felt this ill. I'd always managed to endure what needed to be done in order to survive this life, but things were different now. *I* was different.

The more time I spent with Everett, the more Adalyn came out from hiding. Star was cracking. *Breaking.* Even a mask couldn't hide the real me anymore. And the real me couldn't endure this place. She *refused* to.

It didn't matter that I still owed the Faircrofts an insurmountable blood debt. It didn't matter that I'd *agreed* to this job, that I'd accepted it in order to work off my indenture and seek revenge on the vampires responsible for my father's death.

It didn't matter, because this body wasn't for sale anymore. This body was *mine*, and I would no longer give it to anyone undeserving.

As a new sense of resolve filled me, I stopped pacing to laugh. I laughed like a person unhinged, like someone who'd just discovered that their world was about to implode. Because it was. This dangerous world I lived in was about to shatter into a billion pieces. I could only hope that I didn't shatter with it.

That moment came an hour later.

Mistress stormed back inside my room, and I slowly rose from the living room couch to face her. She took one look at me and froze. "What do you think you're doing? You should be *naked* right now. And where's your mask? Your first client will be here in ten minutes."

I glanced down at my baggy jeans and threadbare sweater, then looked back up at her with a shrug. "Send them in. But this is all they're going to see."

Her eyes practically bugged out of her head. "This isn't funny, Adalyn. Remove your clothes and get into the bedroom *now.*"

"Is that an order?" I dared to ask. "Are you *forcing* me to have sex?"

Her face turned beet red. "Of *course* not. You *agreed* to this job. You jumped at the chance when I offered it to you."

I shrugged again. "Well, I've changed my mind. I can't handle it anymore, so I've decided to quit."

Quit.

Quit.

Quit.

The word danced through the air, taunting her and damning me.

I'd done it. I'd finally uttered the words I should have said the moment my innocence had been stripped from me. The moment I'd realized that giving up my soul wasn't worth surviving this life.

I felt intoxicated. *Empowered.* I was nowhere near free, but I was in complete control of this moment. I didn't know how long Mistress stared at me, but I didn't look away once. My normal submissiveness was nowhere to be found, and I refused to take back my condemning words.

This was it. My life or death moment. The moment I'd hidden from for the past six years.

But I was done hiding. I was finally ready to face it. Finally ready to put my foot down. Finally *demanding* I be treated as more than a slave. I might still be bound by a pactum to serve out my indenture, but I was *done* allowing vampires to abuse me.

From now on, I would fight back. I would no longer take it lying down.

The desperation that had driven me to accept this mistreatment was nowhere to be found. In its place was a strange sense of peace. A *knowing* that I'd done the right thing.

Mistress must have seen the change in me, because the anger in her eyes suddenly vanished. Sighing dejectedly, she said, "You've been through a lot this past week, Adalyn. I should have seen that you were reaching your breaking point. Mortals really *are* fragile things. I'm sure you'll feel better after a little rest, then we can discuss your return to Dreamscape."

As she turned to leave, I replied, "I won't change my mind." She froze in her tracks. "I won't break the promises I made to you six years ago, but I can't work off my debt this way anymore. You gave me a choice to become an exotic dancer and blood whore, and I'm choosing now to reject them."

"Reject." She spoke the word as if she'd never heard it before. "You *choose* to reject them. Are you also choosing to *reject* our mission?"

When I didn't respond, she swept from the room without a word.

The door shut, sealing me inside with my chosen fate.

CHAPTER 27

ADALYN

The ride home with Mistress was spent in tense silence.

Well, mostly.

When we left at midnight, hours earlier than usual, Everett's voice had immediately filled my head.

Everything okay? Does she think you're sick?

I'd debated what to tell him, then finally decided on honesty. *No. I quit the club.*

Quit? For good? He didn't bother to mask the relief, the *excitement* in his voice.

Yep. I'm never going back.

And you're okay with that?

I am.

I was more than okay. Until now, I hadn't realized the toll working at Dreamscape had taken on me. How I'd ever adopted an "end justifies the means" attitude was beyond me now. Freedom wasn't worth giving up who I was. I'd find another way out of this pactum, one that didn't involve losing my identity.

Are you safe? Everett asked next, his concern clear.

For now. But, Everett? You should keep your distance until the ball. She suspects it was you who stopped me from falling tonight.

I don't care. She needs to know that I expect you to be alive and at that Masquerade Ball tomorrow night.

Yes, but desperation makes us do stupid things. She needs space. I need space. Please, Everett. Go home. It'll be safer for both of us.

I waited for him to argue. Instead, he said, *If that's what you wish.*

It is, I replied, worried that I'd upset him.

Then I'll wait. I'll wait for you to come to me.

I bit my lip to hide a smile.

I spent the rest of the silent ride to Faircroft Manor on cloud nine. I wasn't free by any means, but I *felt* free. The darkness I'd lived in for so long was receding, and hope was blooming in my chest. *Real* hope. I just needed to get through the next day. One more day.

I'd stood up for myself and quit the job that had been sucking the life out of me. I had a soulmate, one who treated me with respect and was doing everything in his power to support me. With each passing day, it was getting easier and easier to genuinely smile. To be *myself.*

One more day.

One more day of enduring my mistress. She might be angry with me right now, but what could she possibly do to me in one day?

Everett was right. If she harmed me before the ball, she knew her life would be forfeit. She had no desire to become a martyr, even for her precious cause. That much I knew. So I was safe, at least until the ball.

But as we neared the house, something didn't feel right. The front door was wide open, and I felt a sudden spike of fear. The fear didn't belong to me, though. It belonged to . . .

Pepper! I inwardly cried. Before the car could finish rolling to a stop, I was out the door and racing for the house. As I barged inside, the most terrifying scene greeted me.

Georgina had my mouse familiar by the tail and was dangling her in front of the stray tabby. Octavia stood behind her like a spectator at a game, her brown eyes wide as Pepper angrily squeaked and thrashed, trying to bite anything that came too close.

When the cat rose onto his hind legs to bat at Pepper, my heart leapt into my throat. But when Georgina cruelly laughed and shook Pepper like a *toy*, I lost it.

"You freaking *psycho!*" With a battle cry, I launched myself at her.

She looked up, but I was already on her, slapping and punching and clawing and kicking. As I raked my nails down her cheek and drew blood, she shrieked and stumbled back into Octavia. Pepper twisted free and dropped to the floor, but I didn't stop. Six years' worth of righteous anger was exploding from me, and I used it to inflict as much damage as I could.

"Run, Pepper!" I shouted, grabbing fistfuls of Georgina's long golden hair. When I yanked a huge chunk out, she finally reacted, shoving me with a roar. I flew through the air like a ragdoll. My head struck the foyer wall, and everything went dark.

I awoke seconds later, crumpled on the floor with a splitting headache. Georgina was screeching at the top of her lungs, but I ignored her and frantically searched for Pepper.

A shadow fell over me, and I paused to look up at Mistress. My heart plummeted when I saw what she held.

"Is *this* what you're looking for?" she said, a sneer pulling at her lips. Pepper squirmed in her grasp, and she slowly tightened her fist, drawing a pained squeak from the mouse.

"Please!" I begged, terror climbing my throat. "Please, don't hurt her!"

"*Kill* it, Mother!" Georgina screeched again. "She ripped out my *hair.*"

The chunk of hair was still locked in my fist, but I felt no satisfaction, only fear as I helplessly stared at my tiny familiar clenched in Mistress's hand.

I'm so sorry, Pepper, I whispered to her, unable to stop my tears from falling. *I'm so so sorry.*

It's okay, Ada, she weakly replied. *It's going to be . . .*

Her little eyes fluttered shut.

"She can't breathe!" I cried, scrambling to my feet.

"Don't move, or I'll feed her to the cat," Mistress threatened. I slowly sank back to the floor. "Good. Now that I have your full attention, it's time we cleared the air. Did you think I didn't know about your little pet? I've known about your *familiar* from the very beginning, Adalyn. For years, I've heard her in the walls, foraging around like disease-ridden vermin. I let you keep her so long as you cooperated. But that's not the case anymore, is it?"

"I'm sorry," I told her, desperation paralyzing me once more. "I'll cooperate. I'll do *anything*. But please don't hurt her."

Mistress arched a manicured brow. "Anything?"

"Yes," I said, meaning it. She had Pepper, and that's all I could think about. Nothing mattered but ensuring my familiar's safety. It was my job, my sacred *duty* to protect her.

Satisfied that she was in control once more, Mistress said, "Octavia, put this *thing* in a cage. Your job is to keep it alive until I say otherwise."

"Me? But, Mother, I'm *terrified* of mice. Their little claws and teeth are so—"

"*Now*, Octavia."

Her youngest daughter rushed forward and flat out blubbered like a baby as she thrust Pepper into her hands.

"Do *not* let it escape. I'm counting on you, Octavia."

"I-I won't, Mother," she sobbed, then dashed away with my familiar.

I kept my gaze on Mistress, consoling myself with the fact that Pepper was still alive.

"Well, now that we have that unpleasantness behind us," she said, brushing off her hands with another lip curl, "we can direct the conversation to more important matters. I know Prince Everett has been coming here the past few days. I had a camera installed. Not only that, I can *smell* him on you, and I'm not referring to the claim. You two have been having sex. *Lots* of it. Why? Why does he want you so badly?"

All the blood drained from my face.

When I didn't respond, she crouched before me in a flash and roughly grabbed my chin. "Tell me what I want to know, or your familiar is dead," she hissed in my face. "*Why* does Prince Everett want you?"

As I felt the pull of thrall loosen my tongue, another tear slid down my cheek. "Because . . ." I choked out, unable to keep my voice from breaking. "Because I'm his soulmate."

"That's *disgusting*," Georgina shrilly said. "What a terrible thing to say. She has to be lying, Mother. The crown prince couldn't possibly be fated to someone like *her*."

Mistress was silent. *Deathly* silent. She searched my face, confirming for herself that I spoke the truth. A sudden spark entered her eyes, making me shiver with dread. I knew that look. She was thinking. *Planning* something.

"Does he know about our pactum?" she finally asked.

The word slipped free before I could catch it. "Yes."

"Does he know about our mission?"

"He . . . he suspects."

"Does he know what *you* can do?"

"No."

Her mouth curved into a cruel smile. "Of course he doesn't. He's *blind* like so many males are, too drunk on lust to think with anything but his dick. He would never believe that his fated *mate* could do something so heinous. Is that what the Masquerade Ball is for? To expose us? To *demand* I release you from our pactum?"

I desperately tried not to answer, but her thrall forced the word from me. "Yes."

She hissed, baring her fangs at me.

I didn't say more, already knowing that I was doomed. She was the cat, and I was the mouse helplessly caught in her razor sharp claws. She was unraveling me, ripping out secret after secret. I couldn't hide from her. Couldn't *fight* her. Not when she had Pepper at her mercy.

There was only one thing I could do. One thing that could possibly save us both.

But before I could cry out to my soulmate, Mistress stared deeply into my eyes and demanded, "Can you communicate telepathically with him?"

A scream built in my head. "Yes."

"Good. Then from now on, you're going to put on a show for him. Convince him that all is going according to plan. That I am blissfully unaware and you're perfectly fine. You know all about pretending, don't you, *Star*? It shouldn't be hard. Nod that you understand."

The command sank into my mind with all the rest, tightening around my free will like a noose, *thralling* me into being her obedient servant. The scream faded, and I woodenly nodded.

"Good. Then get some sleep. We have a big day ahead of us tomorrow."

As she dropped my chin and stood, she almost sounded chipper. *Victorious*, even.

She was definitely planning something. Something terrible.

And there was nothing. Absolutely *nothing* I could do about it.

CHAPTER 28

EVERETT

"Do you really think this'll turn into a bloodbath?"

The question came from Isla's brother, Noah Andrews. He and his father, Bill, had arrived at the castle early this morning, shortly after I'd called in a meeting. A top secret one that had required them to come by portal. Although I didn't have concrete evidence of a coup attempt, I wasn't going to take any unnecessary risks when it came to my family's safety. Having a few of our SCA allies on standby in case things went south made sense.

From my spot at the end of the table directly across from my father, I acknowledged the field agent's question by saying, "I think we should be prepared for anything. If the Venturi are planning something behind our backs, they probably won't respond well when I confront them about it."

"But why the *Venturi*? It doesn't make sense," Bill said, crossing his beefy arms.

The Rosewood sheriff and his twenty-seven-year-old son were almost identical in looks. The main difference was their hair. Noah still preferred his blond hair long, usually keeping it in a messy bun. Not a look I would ever adopt for myself, but the Cosmic warlock was the exact opposite of me in appearance and personality. Easygoing and often sarcastic, he had a penchant for breaking hearts wherever he went. He was always on the move, too focused on taking any job the SCA threw his way to settle down.

I tolerated him more than anything. His stern father, on the other hand, wasn't half bad. His mere presence commanded respect, and he'd earned mine many years ago by helping us during the battle against the rogues and elders. Since then, he, Noah, and many other SCA operatives had helped us defeat various enemies.

It was the SCA's job to keep a close eye on the supernatural world, and as one of their leaders, Bill often knew things before we did. But apparently even he was baffled by this latest turn of events with the Venturi.

"I think we've allowed them too much free rein," I slowly answered him. "Before the alliance, rules barely applied to them. Now that we're enforcing our new laws, they must want to challenge the system. For vampires, that usually means killing whatever is standing in their way."

I met my father's gaze, and he acknowledged my words with a small nod.

"And you think these Venturi are collaborating with rogues and their sympathizers?" Isla asked, sitting on the edge of her seat. As a private investigator for the SCA, she'd gobbled up the news of a possible coup and had demanded we include her in the secret meeting held in my father's soundproofed study. Knowing what she'd endured at the hand of rogues, no one would even think of denying her.

"That's a definite possibility," I replied. There were too many tie-ins to think otherwise.

"What if the rogues are trying to emerge again? What if they attack?" she said, sharing a worried look with her husband. Kade reached between them and gave her hand a comforting squeeze.

"That's why we need to be prepared. Anything could happen when I start interrogating the Venturi."

"Should we ask our werewolf friends for help?" Kenna suggested.

"I could make some calls."

"Not yet. My suspicions could be for nothing. I only called in Bill and Noah as a precaution, and they can easily cast an invisibility spell to hide their presence unless we need them. If the Venturi *are* planning a coup, we don't want to tip them off that we're aware of it."

"Regardless, we should have the twins stay at your parents' place tonight," Loch murmured to his mate. When her eyes widened, he reached over and wordlessly pulled her into his lap.

I knew exactly how he was feeling for once. His soulmate had been caught in the middle of a vampire war six years ago, but now it was *my* soulmate in trouble. Who knew how deeply she was entwined in this possible coup. Not knowing was eating me alive.

Needing to reassure myself for the umpteenth time that she was safe, I reached out to Adalyn through our bond. I'd been worried at first that the physical distance between us would make it hard to communicate, but it was like speaking to her through a phone—well, without the need to move my lips. The only thing we couldn't do was feel each other's emotions. Loch told me that the bond would continue to strengthen with time, allowing our senses to span greater distances. We'd even be able to *find* each other, like a built-in GPS system.

You okay? I asked her, sending the question down the invisible thread that bound us together.

Yep, came her immediate reply. *Right as rain. Looking forward to tonight.*

Some of my tension eased, her positive outlook lifting my spirits. I didn't know how she always managed to remain upbeat, but I greatly admired her for it.

"Is she okay?" Loch asked, correctly guessing the reason for my silence.

"Yes," I replied, all too aware of the sudden shift in the air. The piqued interest. Every eye went to me, expectation written on each of their faces. I shook my head with a quiet snort. "She's *fine*. She knows how to take care of herself."

"Yeah, but she quit her job," Kade spoke up, looking uncharacteristically solemn. "I don't think she's as fine as she says she is."

My tension returned tenfold.

"That doesn't mean you should rush over there and cause her even more problems, Ev," Loch quickly said as I fisted my hand on the mahogany table. "Remember the pactum."

"The effects of a broken pactum are lifelong, son," my father joined in. "I know you're worried for your mate's safety, but your brother is right. Visiting her at this point could cause more harm than good. Wait until tonight. We'll deal with the situation then. Together."

Nodding, I forced my fist to unclench.

"Did you send the dress?" Kenna asked, clearly sensing the need for a subject change. Loch turned his face to nuzzle her neck, and she instinctually leaned into his affection.

Sudden pain tightened my chest. What I wouldn't give to have Adalyn in my lap right now. To openly shower her with my affection. To show the world that she was mine.

Glancing at the gold and ruby ring on my pinky finger, I replied, "Yes. It should arrive at Faircroft Manor within the hour."

"Good. That'll leave no question in the Faircroft's minds that you expect Adalyn to be there. She'll be fine, Everett. You'll see. Now, how about you start preparing for the speech you're going to give when she arrives?"

I blinked up at her. "Speech?"

"The *proposal*, man," Noah drawled in that annoyingly sarcastic way of his.

When I scowled at him, Kade burst out laughing. "The poor sod doesn't even know, and it's *his* party! This is way too good."

He let out an *oof!* as Isla elbowed him in the side and hissed, "*Behave.*"

"I *am* behaving."

Sighing impatiently, I said to no one in particular, "Can someone *mature* tell me what the hell is going on?"

Loch and Bill exchanged smirks but frustratingly kept quiet.

Rolling my eyes, I focused on my only remaining hope. "Well?" I questioned him, knowing by the look on his face that he was in on it as well. Whatever "*it*" was.

Thankfully, he didn't keep me waiting long.

"The ball, my son. Possible coup aside, it's the perfect occasion."

"For what?"

My father grinned at me a mile wide. "To publicly announce your intention to marry your soulmate."

CHAPTER 29

ADALYN

I couldn't stop shaking, and not only because of my nerves.

Everett hadn't been able to give me any venom last night. It had been two whole days since my last dose, and although my cravings had lessened this past week with his help, I desperately needed a fix.

I'd been naive and incredibly stupid to think that Mistress wouldn't find out about our secret nightly rendezvous or about Pepper. She had me exactly where she wanted me, and I'd never felt so small. So *helpless*. Pepper was locked away in Octavia's room, and I was currently locked in the basement. I'd reached out through our bond countless times to make sure she was safe, but knowing hadn't made me feel any better.

This was all my fault. I never should have quit the club. Never should have allowed a grumpy, green-eyed prince into my life. Never should have dared to wish I could be anything but an indentured blood whore.

Because of my rash behavior, everyone I cared about was in danger. If anything happened to them, I wouldn't survive. I wouldn't want to.

Quit it, Adalyn. You're not to blame for any of this. And if you keep thinking so loudly, your mate is going to overhear and start asking questions.

At Pepper's scolding, I clasped my trembling hands in my lap with a sigh. *He's going to hate me after this. I'm about to ruin everything.*

Pepper snorted. *That boy is head over heels for you. And if I'm not mistaken, you feel the same way about him.*

I do care about him. A lot. But that's the problem. He's trying to save me, and I'm about to betray him.

That premonition isn't set in stone, Ada. It will only happen if you allow it to, if you don't fight to change your fate.

I'd woken up drenched in sweat this morning, the same dream of me stabbing Everett in the heart racing through my mind. Pepper had felt my panic, and I'd finally told her about the premonition. She knew how my magic worked even more than I did. On the spirit plane, she'd spent centuries honing her skills, using magic in ways I couldn't even fathom. I'd only been allowed a few short years to practice my Oracle magic before Mistress had forced me to lock it all away, save for one ability.

An ability that had been twisted into something ugly, all in the name of survival.

You're stronger than you think, Adalyn, Pepper gently continued. *You had a premonition, and that's an encouraging sign. It means you've taken back some of your control. Tonight is your night to change your fate. You might not believe it, but I do. Now go get your prince charming and stop worrying about me.*

But—

I mean it, Ada. I might be small, but I'm a survivor like you. Trust me to look after myself.

I started to protest again, but the basement door suddenly rattled as someone turned the lock. I shot off my bed and quickly smoothed my skirt, hoping I hadn't wrinkled it. The blue satin fabric was thin and delicate, yet surprisingly strong. It had a high slit in front, allowing the light fabric to billow behind me in waves. The top was simple, held up by thin straps that criss-crossed behind, the back so low that my entire spine was on display.

A dancer's dream dress. It allowed for free movement, the only adornment a simple bow tied around my waist. The dress had arrived several hours ago, along with a silver mask and simple note.

"For Star."

I immediately knew who had sent it and so had Mistress.

"Be ready promptly at ten," was all she'd said, then shoved the box into my arms and ordered me down to the basement.

I'd decided to keep my hair down for the occasion, the silvery strands falling neatly to my waist. Most of my makeup and accessories were in my room at Dreamscape, but I'd managed to find a pair of silver stilettos and do a decent job on my face. Fake sapphire earrings and sapphire-studded cuff bracelets completed the ensemble. My silver mask was already in place, transforming me into the person Mistress wanted me to be.

Mysterious. Charming. Alluring.

Star.

I waited for her to call me up, but as the basement door swung open, I heard the sound of high-heeled shoes on the stairs. A cold sweat broke out on my forehead. She *never* came down here. To say I was freaking out would be an understatement.

When she reached the bottom and turned to face me, I forced myself to hold still. Had she changed her mind? Had she decided that killing me was the best solution? Despite how terrified I was, I lifted my chin as she inspected me from head to toe. She was wearing a black dress that hugged her curves and showed off ample cleavage. Diamonds dripped from her neck, wrists, and fingers. They were even woven into her elaborate updo. Her mask was black shot through with gold, making her look mysterious, but in a creepy villain sort of way.

She took a few more steps and thrust something at me. "Put this on."

I reached out with trembling fingers as if the object was a venomous snake. It might as well be. The second it was in my hand, I realized what it was.

My knife.

I almost dropped it. Almost *hurled* it across the room.

This couldn't be happening. This couldn't—

"*Do* it, Adalyn," Mistress snapped.

Trembling even harder, I slipped the garter onto my right leg and made sure the attached knife was situated on my outer thigh. The dress barely managed to conceal it, but the high slit made it all too easy for me to reach down and pull the weapon free.

Unable to keep silent a moment longer, I blurted, "Why?"

"Because you're going to start a revolution tonight," she replied, stepping back to eye me with a satisfied smile. "You'll call on the blood bonds you've nurtured over the past few years, telling every single noble, drothen, and council member that the time has come to rise up. When the battle is imminent, you will then turn to the crown prince and stab him in the heart."

Dread sucked all the air from my lungs. "No," I whispered, my heart starting to break.

"*Yes*," she said, piercing me with her eyes. "When the clock strikes midnight, Prince Everett will be dead and the revolution will be reborn. A Masquerade Ball at the castle is the perfect opportunity to make our move. The Venturi will start eliminating each other, and in the chaos, the royals won't realize that rogues have invaded their precious island and joined the fight until it's too late. With the help of our weak-minded Venturi clients, we'll finally be able to seek change. No more begging the royal family to hear us. To *see* us. Once they've been overthrown, we'll create a new government for this kingdom, one where Feltore have the same privileges as the Venturi."

Even though I'd known about her plan for years, my mind reeled at the news. When I'd first agreed to help her ensnare clients by planting false dreams inside their minds, I'd only wanted two things. To pay off my father's debt as quickly as possible, and to seek revenge on the vampires who'd killed him. Helping my enemies go to war with each other was just icing on the cake. Both sides would suffer losses, and that was fine by me.

Was fine by me. But not anymore. Not since I'd met Everett. He was heavily flawed, but he was everything I needed. Everything I craved. My heart *danced* when he was near. He made me feel alive and safe, and the thought of hurting him was more than I could bear.

"I can't kill Everett."

The words were out before I could stop them. Mistress didn't react for a painfully long moment. Then, she threw her head back and laughed. "Oh, you stupid, *stupid* girl. You've fallen in *love* with the brute."

My mouth fell open, but nothing came out.

Seeing the shock on my face, she stopped laughing to cluck her tongue disapprovingly. "Oh, Adalyn, you disappoint me. I thought you were smarter than this. It doesn't matter that he saved you a time or two. It doesn't even matter that fate mistakenly made him your soulmate. He's the *enemy*. You've always known this. You should have gotten inside his head when you had the chance. Instead, you allowed him to get inside yours. Pathetic."

Recovering from my shock, I shook my head and repeated, "I can't kill him. I'll call on the blood bonds. I'll become your blood whore again. I'll do anything you want me to do. But *please*, Mistress. Don't ask me to kill Everett."

Her expression flattened. In a blur, she was in my face, viciously gripping my chin. "I wasn't asking, Adalyn," she hissed. "I was *telling* you. Who do you think you are making *demands* when you're completely at my mercy? Did you think I would *sympathize* with you? Well, guess again. Everett D'angelo needs to die for this revolution to begin, and you're the perfect person to kill him. The bastard trusts you and won't expect your treachery until it's too late.

"But I'm not completely heartless," she continued, her sneering mouth inches from mine. "Once you've completed this task, your blood debt to the Faircroft family will be forgiven. I'll release you from our pactum, and you and your *mouse* can go free. How is that for sympathy? Pretend one last time for me, Star. Put on your greatest performance, and your reward will be your freedom. Promise me you will do this. *Promise.*"

When my only response was to glare at her in open defiance, her eyes slowly turned red.

"Octavia!" she yelled, so loudly that I flinched. Her nails bit into my skin, anchoring me in place. "Bring me the mouse!"

My heart leapt into my throat. "Please, no. Don't hurt her. *Please*, Mistress."

"Then *promise* me," she barked, her eyes fully red now. "Better yet, swear on a new pactum that you'll complete this task for me."

Letting go of my chin, she willed her dagger-like claws to emerge and dragged one across her palm. As blood rose from the cut, true terror filled me.

"I can't. I *can't!*" I wailed.

"Then I'll kill your familiar!"

"No!" I cried, feeling my legs buckle beneath me.

She grabbed my arm to keep me upright, screaming, "*Promise me, Adalyn!*"

I heard the sound of feet rushing down the stairs. Heard Octavia excitedly say, "I've got it, Mother. I've got the disgusting mouse. Should I kill it?"

"Yes, Octavia. *Kill* it."

At her command, I broke. *Shattered* into a billion pieces.

Darkness crashed into me, dragging me down, down, down.

"O-okay," I whispered.

No, Ada! Pepper shouted, but it was too late. My mind was made up.

"What?" Mistress demanded. "Speak up, Adalyn."

"Okay. I'll . . . I'll swear on a pactum."

Pepper continued to shout at me, but I was deaf to her pleas. Reaching down with trembling fingers, I drew my knife from its hiding place. Mistress's eyes gleamed expectantly as I lifted it and slowly cut into my palm. The second the skin split, she whipped her hand forward and tightly clasped mine, sealing our blood together.

"Say the words, Adalyn. Say that you promise."

My voice shook. My entire *body* shook as I forced myself to say, "I . . . I promise to complete this task for you."

"And?" she urged, the gleam turning wicked.

"And should I intentionally break that promise, may I die a slow, painful death."

The words sank deeply into my blackened soul, condemning me to the darkest pit of hell.

Oh, Adalyn. What have you done? Pepper mournfully whispered.

Victory flared in Mistress's blood-red eyes. Releasing me, she stepped back with a faint smirk. "Now, was that so hard? Honestly, Adalyn. You can be so dramatic sometimes. Be sure to wash your hands and knife before we leave. The prince must not know about the new deal we've struck."

Feeling numb all over, I looked down at my hand and watched the cut slowly seal shut from Mistress's blood.

"Hurry up now," she cheerily said and swept toward the stairs. "We don't want to be late for the ball. And make sure to leave that vermin here where Adalyn can find it, Octavia. She can collect her things and be on her way once the job is done."

CHAPTER 30

ADALYN

It was just like in my dreams.

Everywhere I looked, jewels sparkled and skirts swished. Stringed music softly played, allowing the roomful of guests to chat and mingle. Each face was hidden by a mask of varying color, concealing their identity. Several couples twirled about the room, their movements unnaturally graceful as they danced.

The ballroom itself was massive, made entirely of gold. Even the ceiling was elaborately sculpted in burnished golden hues. Chandeliers, columns, and candelabras made the space appear to have been fashioned from a fairy tale. Human maids flitted about the guests along the edges of the dance floor, holding trays of golden goblets. Since every guest here but me was a vampire, I knew the goblets were no doubt filled with blood. I watched more than one vampire reach for a drink, even as they hungrily eyed the maids—vampires that I *recognized*.

It didn't matter that they wore masks. The intimate moments I'd spent with them were etched into my brain. I would know them anywhere.

As I stood at the top of the grand staircase overlooking the room below, stuck between Mistress and her two daughters, an intricate grandfather clock tucked in the far corner caught my eye.

"Tick-tock, Adalyn," Mistress murmured for my ears alone, noting where my attention had gone. "One hour until midnight."

My throat closed.

Before I could start panicking, though, I finally spotted him. He was off to the side, speaking to the king and a few males I didn't recognize. As my gaze landed on him, he abruptly stopped speaking to search the room. To search for *me*.

My heart beat wildly in my chest.

Cruel nails bit into my arm as Mistress leaned close to hiss in my ear, "Fulfill your promises, Adalyn. Do this one final job for me, and you will be free."

Free.

Free.

Free.

The word had never felt so empty.

She released me when Everett's gaze swung our way, climbing the stairs to rest on me. The moment our eyes met, the room and everyone in it disappeared. For a moment, a wondrous moment I never wanted to end, it was simply him and me. A vampire prince and the witch fated to be his mate.

I quickly took him in from head to toe, noticing the way his black three-piece suit fit him to perfection. As usual, his short black hair was neatly in place, his chiseled jaw and chin closely shaven. A black mask hid the rest of his features, but I already had them memorized. Already knew how devastatingly handsome he was. How *perfect*.

Everything about him was perfect. Perfect for *me*.

I started to tremble again, feeling lightheaded.

I couldn't do this, couldn't do this, couldn't do this.

He checked me over as well, his appreciation at what he found obvious. I could feel it. Feel *him*. Even though my heart raced and my head pounded, his emotions came through loud and clear. They flooded the bond, filling me with relief and happiness.

He was happy. Happy to *see* me.

My eyes started to burn.

Before I could do something terrible, like cry in front of a room full of bloodthirsty predators, he headed my way. The crowd parted at his approach, naturally deferring to his superiority and power. Without a word, he commanded their attention. Their *respect*. Even the Venturi under my control stepped aside, their eyes following him as he strode with purpose across the room.

The desperate need to run shivered through me, both *to* him and away. I was torn. Shredded into a million pieces. *Frozen.*

Faces from around the room started to turn our way, tracking his progress. I suddenly wanted to shout. Wanted to scream at Everett to run. To take his family and flee before the vipers in his house could strike. I glanced at the clock again.

Tick-tock. Tick-tock.

Time bore down on me, reminding me of the job I was destined to do. Less than an hour to go. Less than an hour until I betrayed the man who'd tried to save me. The man who'd somehow burrowed his way into my heart.

A heart made of twisted lies. Of wicked deceit.

"You're my bright shining star, Ada darling. Whatever happens after tonight, don't let anyone dull that light. Shine brightly for all to see."

My father's words chose that moment to cruelly taunt me. To remind me of how dark I'd allowed myself to become. I didn't know how to shine anymore. The only thing the crowd would see tonight was a fallen blood whore named Star.

As Everett started to ascend the stairs toward me, that's *exactly* what they saw. I could tell that several of my clients had spotted me. Spotted and *recognized* me. There was no hiding who I was to them.

If my silver mask and hair didn't give me away, then the blood bond we shared surely would.

They could sense me the same way I could sense them. It was a whisper. A mere impression of thought. A delicate web that linked us together, one they didn't realize they were caught in.

I see you, the bond softly breathed, caressing the air between us. *The time has come. Wait for the right moment. Just wait . . .*

Almost without thought, the magic trickled from me and into them. Awakening our bonds. *Flaring* them to life.

I'd been doing it for so long that it came instinctively. The magic was strongest when we were touching, when my blood was fresh in their veins, but I'd formed a strong enough connection with them to wield my control from a distance.

Their minds were wide open right now, ripe for the taking. I could make them do just about anything. I'd learned the hard way that I couldn't bend their minds to my will while they were in a frenzy. Influencing them took finesse and patience. But once I was in control, I could sway even their most stubborn thoughts. I'd spent years encouraging them to drink my blood, knowing that the more they fed, the less I had to endure their touch. Once they started to feed, I simply made them *believe* they were having sex with me.

To them, I was the blood whore who made all their dark, twisted fantasies come true. In reality, I was the witch who planted lies deep inside their minds.

The royals only care about each other.

They would rather listen to outsiders than their most loyal subjects.

The king is weak.

The princes are cruel and have rejected their own kind, including their own brother.

They see the Venturi as useless figureheads.

Feltore are nothing to them, and they kill them without cause.

The royals must be stopped.

Must be stopped.

Must be stopped.

The lies went on and on, painting the royal family as heartless monsters. Feeding my client's doubts and insecurities. Even the strongest of them eventually broke, allowing me to pollute their minds with thoughts they didn't actually believe. Truthfully, most of them were deeply loyal to the royal family, which was the most twisted thing of all.

I'd ruined them as they had ruined me. I'd done it *gladly*, tainting their minds while they had tainted my body. They'd deserved it for treating me like a lowly blood whore. Like I was nothing more than an object for their pleasure.

I'd justified my actions, condemning them when *I* had been the one to lure them in.

If anyone was a heartless monster here, it was me.

But it was too late. There was no undoing the damage I'd done. If I didn't finish what I'd started, the pactum would kill me. Even worse, Mistress would kill Pepper.

I was tied up in knots tighter than ever, and I didn't know how to escape. I *couldn't* escape. Mistress had made certain of that.

She was the first to speak as Everett paused a few steps below us. "Your Highness," she demurred, curtsying deeply. "It is such an honor to be invited to your beautiful home. We can't thank you enough."

Georgina and Octavia curtsied as well, the latter stumbling a bit. She wasn't even blood drunk, but the youngest Faircroft had all the grace of a giraffe. Which was quite the feat considering how naturally graceful vampires were.

"Madame Faircroft. Ladies. Thank you for coming tonight,"

Everett acknowledged, yet his tone was formal. Clipped. Anger trickled through our bond, but he kept the emotion firmly in check.

When his gaze rested on me again, I started to curtsy. Before I could finish, he stretched up his hand and said, "Dance with me?"

I froze, my eyes flying wide. The entire *room* froze, every masked face turning toward us in shock. Not everyone here knew who I was, but it was clear that I wasn't one of them. And if I accepted Everett's request, they would know all too soon what I was.

A *witch*.

The very thing that had cast them into darkness a century ago. The thing they had hunted and killed. That *Everett* had killed.

I could only imagine what they were thinking. Could only imagine how horrified they would be if they knew what I was capable of.

Whispers swept through the crowd as I hesitated. Every eye was on me now. Waiting. Waiting for me to *perform*.

Years of training kicked in. I straightened and placed my hand in his.

Everett's fingers tightened around mine, and I desperately sought comfort from their warmth. Their *strength*. He could feel me trembling now, but there was no hiding it. Without a word, he guided me down the stairs and onto the dance floor. The crowd parted for him as easily as before, but they were staring at *me* now. They audibly inhaled when I passed by, gasping when they realized what I was.

Everett ignored them all, his strides strong and steady. When he reached the center of the room, he turned and reeled me in. I swallowed a gasp as his hand on my lower back pulled me flush against him.

Spirits save me, he wasn't even *trying* to keep his distance. Not even a little.

He splayed his fingers wide over my bare skin and breathed in my ear, "You look mouthwatering in that dress, but I can't wait to take it off you later."

My cheeks flushed scarlet.

Not from embarrassment, but from how *reckless* he was being. I didn't respond, wholly unprepared for his behavior. We were less than an hour away from all hell breaking loose, and he was *flirting* with me.

Before I was ready, the music started up again and we were dancing. Muscle memory saved me from stepping on Everett's toes as he led us into a waltz, his movements sure and confident.

Surprised, I finally found my voice to say, "I didn't know you could dance."

"I'm a one-hundred-eighty-eight-year-old prince. Of course I can dance."

I didn't even bat an eye at his age. I was used to being around ancient creatures who looked like gorgeous supermodels in their early twenties.

After a moment more of silent dancing, he murmured, "You're in pain."

"Just a slight headache. Nothing I can't handle."

His fingers tightened around my trembling ones. "And nervous."

I forced myself to lightly laugh. "I've never been to a fancy ball before."

"You're also scared."

"I'm the only mortal in a room full of vampires. Of course I'm scared."

"But that isn't anything new for you."

I tipped my head back to smirk at him. "Dancing with their crown prince is."

His eyes dipped to my mouth. "You're pretending. You don't have to pretend with me. Ever."

My smirk faded, and I looked away, but not fast enough.

"Something's troubling you. What happened?"

I quickly glanced around to see if anyone had overheard. A couple dancing nearby turned toward us, and I blinked in surprise. Kenna gave me a friendly smile while Loch nodded in silent greeting. Another couple I recognized swept toward us, forming what felt like a protective circle.

As Isla waved and Kade threw me a wink, Everett said through our bond, *We won't let anything happen to you. You're safe.*

But you're not safe! my mind screamed, so loudly that I felt him tense. Only for a second, but long enough that I knew he'd heard it.

We've taken precautions, he tried to reassure me. *If anyone is planning to attack us tonight, we're ready. My father's wives are safely hidden, and the twins have been sent away. Before this night is over, everything will be revealed. No more masks. No more secrets. We'll get to the bottom of this once and for all. Every debt, pactum, and coup attempt will be addressed publicly. Anyone who refuses to see reason will be put in their place. Forcefully, if need be.*

I opened my mouth to warn him, but thrall silenced the words.

He abruptly dipped his head to ghost his lips over my jaw.

Tensing, I whispered, "What are you doing?"

"Staking my claim," he rumbled back, aligning his mouth with my ear so he could nibble on the lobe and earring. "Showing every sick bastard in this room who's touched you that they'll never touch you again. The only male allowed to touch you from this moment on is me."

I couldn't help but melt at his words. Couldn't help but desperately cling to them, wishing with all of my heart that they were true.

But maybe they *could* be true. Maybe I could stop pretending, if only for a moment. If this was to be my last moment with the man who made me feel things I hadn't dreamt were possible, then I was going to make each second count.

Besides, what could they do? What could *anyone* do? It wasn't midnight yet. This time was mine. Mine and Everett's. This was our happily ever after, however short it ended up being. And like hell would I let anyone, including Mistress, take that time away from me.

So I did the unthinkable. I grabbed Everett's face and kissed him full on the mouth. In front of *everyone*. Staking my claim. Making one last defiant stand.

Screw you. Screw you all! the kiss shouted, echoing across a room that had suddenly gone deathly quiet. Even the music had stopped. I didn't care. I kissed Everett harder. More urgently. Pouring into it the fear, desperation, and helplessness I felt. The need and desire I had for him. The hopes and dreams that were rapidly slipping through my fingers.

Tick-tock. Tick-tock.

Destiny clawed at me, threatening to tear us apart. I clung to him with all of my might, whimpering when he crushed me against him and returned the kiss with equal force. Time drifted away, our passion eclipsing everything else. Nothing mattered but *this*. This kiss and my feelings for him. Feelings that flooded our bond, feelings I no longer tried to hide. I wanted him to know how I felt. He *deserved* to know.

It was the only thing I could freely give him, and no one could stop me.

I gave him everything, holding nothing back. I gave and gave, allowing him to know without a shadow of doubt my feelings for him.

Tears slid down my cheeks, but I didn't wipe them away. Showing weakness didn't matter anymore. I was at the end of my rope, and this was all I had left.

This final moment with the man who held my heart.

This perfect moment with the man that I *loved*.

CHAPTER 31

EVERETT

I couldn't breathe.

Her kiss was destroying me. Tearing apart everything I once was. Everything I'd believed in order to protect myself. To keep me and my family safe.

The person I used to be was unraveling by the second, disintegrating to ash as she poured her entire being into the kiss. A kiss that rocked me to my core, leaving me stunned and shaken.

She didn't say a word, but she didn't have to. I felt everything, each emotion more potent than any word she could utter. All I could do was hold on and return the kiss that was drowning me. That was wreaking havoc on my senses. That filled up my heart so completely I thought it would burst.

I had no idea that it could be like this. That I could share a connection with someone so deeply that our emotions were one and the same.

We *were* one. One being. One heart. One soul.

What she felt in this moment, I felt as well. I didn't have the courage to tell her before. To even *face* it. But I did now. I opened up the floodgates of our bond and sent back a deluge of my own emotions. I didn't even have a name for them all, but I made sure she felt every single one. Everything I'd been feeling from the moment I'd seen her dangling from that silver hoop above the dance floor.

As salt from her tears slid onto my tongue, I cupped her face and gently wiped them away. A sob caught in her throat, but she didn't pull away. The kiss slowed, each press of our lips a soft caress. We'd stopped dancing, but our emotions continued to dance around each other. Twirling and swaying, coming together again and again until I couldn't tell them apart.

Her emotions were mine, and mine were hers.

They were one, our hearts and minds wholly in sync.

This was magic. Perfection. *Right.*

Needing to voice out loud what I felt in every fiber of my being, I broke the kiss to breathe, "I'm in love with you."

Several gasps filtered around us, but I paid them no heed. Neither did she.

The most beautiful, radiant smile bloomed on her lips, and she whispered back, "I'm in love with you too."

My heart swelled, and I thought for sure it would explode. I kissed her again, our masks shifting as I rested my forehead against hers. Still trying to catch my breath, I said in hushed tones, "I want you to marry me."

She huffed a quiet laugh. "Are you asking me or telling me?"

I grinned, so wide that it hurt. "Asking. Definitely asking. I wouldn't dream of telling you what to do."

Her smile softened. "Well, in that case—"

"Adalyn, *enough* of this!" a voice shouted, dispelling the magical moment. "How *dare* you say such things to the prince."

Adalyn's fear spiked through our bond.

It's not time yet. It's too soon! she inwardly whimpered, clearly not intending for me to overhear.

Protectiveness surged through me, and I pulled her close before turning to face an angry Madame Faircroft. As she stormed toward us, I threw her a warning look, and she halted several feet away.

"You're calling her Adalyn now?" I calmly said, making sure to keep my growing rage in check. "Why not Star? That's what her clients at your nightclub know her by."

Her eyes widened a fraction, but she recovered remarkably fast. "Star is her stage name, yes. I won't pretend otherwise. But as a blood whore, she has no business making professions of love to you. It's a bald-faced lie anyway. I'll take her off your hands before she can spout any more nonsense. Come, Adalyn. I think you need some fresh air to clear your head."

When she stepped forward to grab Adalyn, Kade smoothly blocked her path. "Yeah, I don't think so."

Looking up at the wall of muscle, she sternly ordered, "Step aside, drothen. You don't have the authority to keep me from collecting my employee."

As she tried to veer around him, Loch cut her off. "What about a prince?"

"Forgive me, Prince Lochlan," she said with a quick curtsy. "But Adalyn is my responsibility and is currently making a *fool* of me. She's here as a guest and is disrespecting Prince Everett by pretending to—"

"*You* are the one pretending, Deloris," I interrupted, gratified when her mouth snapped shut. "You and about half the people in this room. You've been pretending for years, bowing and scraping before the royal family while whispering behind our backs about how much you despise us. Isn't that right?"

Her only movement was a slight lip quiver, like she was trying really hard not to sneer.

"Isn't that *right?*" I roared. She flinched, along with several others in my line of sight. My eyes connected with my father's, and he gave me an encouraging nod. Leaving Adalyn in my family's protective circle, I strode toward the nearest nobleman and ripped off his mask.

"What about you, Lord Farley? Have *you* been pretending?"

His face turned ashen as I openly challenged him to defy me. When he submissively dropped his gaze, I whirled toward my next target.

"What about you, Councilman Singh?" His mask hit the ground with a clatter. "Do you secretly wish to depose the royal family? To *kill* us?"

"N-no, Your Majesty. *Never.*" He sank to his knees before me and lowered his head.

Clenching my teeth, I slowly made my way around the room, confronting every face I came upon. Some of the faces couldn't hide their guilt. Their *loathing.* My father had been right. Many in his court were secretly discontent. Each time I revealed a new face, I wrestled with my surprise. I'd known most of these males for decades and thought they'd been loyal to the crown.

How had this happened? How had we not noticed *sooner?*

"I'm disappointed. I'm disappointed in *all* of you," I said, tossing another mask to the ground. "You're privileged enough to have the ear of the king, yet you secretly complain behind his back like *cowards.*"

"King Ambrose has barely spoken to us in six years," a voice behind me said. I pivoted to face Viscount Le Blanc, and he paled. But when a few more voices around the room grumbled their agreement, he stood taller and added, "I've heard rumors that something happened to him. That he's been weakened, both in mind and body."

Before I could speak for my father, he blurred past me to confront the male himself. "Would you like to test that theory, old *friend?*" he purred, casually reaching out to brush invisible lint from Le Blanc's suit. "You've known me for almost two centuries and have personally seen me execute subjects for less accusations. Perhaps you'd like to serve as my latest example?"

As Le Blanc tensed, so did I, prepared to intervene if he attacked. Despite the unflappable confidence my father exuded, he *had* been weakened. A pactum gone awry had stolen much of his power from him, and although he was still stronger than most Venturi, a fight would reveal what we'd carefully kept hidden for six years now.

That King Ambrose was no longer the most powerful vampire in his kingdom.

But if I intervened on his behalf, there would be no undoing the damage. The vampires in this room were the strongest of our kind. They'd immediately sense their king's weakness and seek to flush it out. To *eradicate* it. Despite our fancy clothes and diplomatic words, we were animals at our core. *Predators* whose instincts were to prey on the weak.

They wouldn't hesitate to savagely rip their king to shreds if they knew just how far he'd fallen. And as Viscount Le Blanc continued to stare at my father, I realized with dread that he had no intention of backing down. The longer he held the king's gaze, the more confident he grew. And the more confident he grew, the more the others took note, seeing far more than I wanted them to.

There was only one thing I could do. One thing that would ensure my father got out of this situation unscathed.

The fear and doubt I'd harbored for years vanished as I stepped forward to protect him, speaking loudly for all to hear, "If you wish to challenge the king, then you'll have to challenge *me*. King Ambrose has abdicated the throne, and I, Prince Everett D'angelo, will become this kingdom's newest ruler."

Shock rippled through the crowd, including mine. That didn't stop me from taking another step and drawing Le Blanc's gaze to me. At the menacing look I gave him, some of his confidence faded. I continued to hold eye contact until he clenched his jaw and finally looked away.

"Anyone else?" I said, slowly searching the faces around me. "Anyone else want to challenge the *king?*"

My father passed by me, pausing to clasp my shoulder and murmur, "I always knew you could do it."

I stood taller, bolstered by his confidence in me. Confidence I hadn't allowed myself to feel until a small, albeit courageous, witch had danced into my life. I returned to her side and drew her close as I faced the crowd again, noting how restless it had become. Not everyone was happy with my surprise announcement. In fact, many of them looked downright livid.

I was losing them. If I didn't find a way to turn things around soon, someone was going to step out of line. And when that happened, I wouldn't hesitate to protect my family. Even if I had to fight every last Venturi in this room, I would keep them from hurting those I loved.

At the reminder of what I'd just confessed to Adalyn, I glanced down at her. She was visibly trembling, her brow beaded with sweat as she vacantly stared at the crowd.

Alarmed, I quickly said through our bond, *You okay?*

"I'm so sorry," she whispered, still staring at the crowd. "I have to. I *have* to. I'm so very sorry."

The crowd grew even more restless, whispering amongst each other, throwing more and more scathing looks my way. Not just at me, but at the rest of my family. At *Adalyn.*

My patience snapped.

"Do you know the real reason why you're all here today?" I thundered, letting my anger boil over. "Because of *her.*" I gestured at Adalyn, who was growing paler and paler by the second. "This woman is *proof* of why this kingdom needs to change. She's been abused by vampires since the day we were liberated from the curse.

If not for her, I wouldn't have realized how *corrupt* this kingdom still is. I've made some terrible choices in my lifetime, but over this past week, I'm *sickened* by what I've seen vampires do to those they consider inferior or weaker than them. We're predators, but we don't have to act like *monsters*."

"You killed your brother! *You're* a monster," someone from the crowd shouted.

"Troy *lost* himself!" I shouted back, allowing emotion to fill my voice. "He didn't just betray his family the day he unleashed the rogues on the world. He betrayed our entire *race* by recklessly exposing us. If he'd been successful, we'd all be dead right now. I should have seen how lost he'd become and stopped him sooner, but I was lost too. For most of my life, I've allowed myself to do monstrous things, believing I was justified in doing so. But those actions cost me. They cost us *all*. For that, I deeply apologize. I've set a poor example, and I've foolishly put this kingdom in danger more than once."

Slowly exhaling, I continued more calmly, "But my father has always sought to protect this kingdom from the rest of the world, and the recent changes he's made are only meant to protect it more. World domination isn't the answer, and neither is enslaving those we consider *weak*. As your future king, I won't stand back and allow this kingdom to fall into darkness again. We are better than that. We can peacefully coexist with the rest of the world."

I looked down at Adalyn again. "To prove it, my first act as king will be to marry this woman. Many of you saw her as an object, as something to conquer and control. She is none of those things. Fate has chosen this courageous witch to be my soulmate, and I in turn have chosen her to be my wife. To be our future *queen*."

Shouts of outrage erupted from the crowd. Not exactly the reaction I was hoping for, but I wasn't all that surprised either. I'd just proposed something that had never happened before. We'd never had a queen, the laws stating that only a Venturi female could fill that role. But we'd already changed so many of the kingdom's rules in the name of progress. What was one more?

If I was to be this kingdom's king, then I desperately needed a strong queen by my side. I didn't care that she was a witch who'd once been a blood whore to my people. I only cared that it was *her*.

Adalyn didn't even flinch at the growing hostility surrounding us. Her lips silently moved, the bright golden hue of her eyes dulling as they glazed over.

"It's time, baby girl," I spoke to her over the shouting and reached up to touch her chin. She flinched this time, her glazed eyes flaring wide.

"No. No, please, no. It can't be time. I'm not ready!"

At how terrified she sounded, worry filled me. Something was wrong, but I didn't have time to figure out what.

"Look at me," I gently encouraged her, tipping her chin up. As those glazed eyes met mine, I slipped off my mask. "It's time for them to see who you really are, Adalyn. It's time for them to see what *I* see."

"Oh, Everett," she sobbed, violently trembling as she reached up to undo her own mask. "I'm so sorry."

I smiled softly as she bravely revealed her face to the crowd for the very first time. Tears tracked down her smooth cheeks, and I gently wiped them away.

"It's going to be okay, Adalyn," I said. "We're going to release you from your debt and pactum now. You'll finally be free. I won't let them hurt—"

"Everett, watch out!"

Loch's roar filled my ears just as Adalyn whipped her arm forward, clutching what looked like a silver knife in her hand.

A knife headed directly for my heart.

CHAPTER 32

ADALYN

When the clock struck midnight, everything froze.

It was like the entire Universe paused, curious to see what would happen next. To see if I'd fulfill my destiny. As Everett spoke, valiantly trying to reason with the Venturi, I'd slowly tightened my web, robbing them of their free will.

Every time their voices rose in anger, another piece of me shriveled up and died. Their anger was my fault. They were only reacting this way because of *me*. Because of the lies I'd woven into their minds. They were deaf to Everett's words. Blinded by the enchantment I'd cast over them.

It was only a matter of time now. The second I attacked, they would too. Like mindless animals, they would follow my lead and destroy each other. Destroy the family who'd shown me nothing but kindness.

My time was up. I had no choice but to initiate the revolution Mistress had planned in the shadows ever since the last one had failed. Once it began, the Venturi would fight to the death. The ones under my control would attack their friends, family, and the royals I'd fashioned into their enemies. They had a mission the same way I did. A mission they couldn't run away from.

It would be a bloodbath. And when the rogues arrived, very few Venturi would survive, if any. They'd been waiting six years for this moment. Six years of silently hating the royal family and Venturi for turning against them. For protecting a *witch* instead of their own kind.

And so they'd used a witch to destroy their own. To tear down the government they so despised.

Me. They'd used *me*. And I'd let them. I'd given them my body and soul. I'd let them abuse my magic. I'd done everything they asked of me. *Everything*.

I'd single-handedly ignited a revolution, seeking my revenge on the creatures who'd stolen my father and life from me in the process.

I'd become a monster. *Their* monster.

All to survive. To *save* myself.

But in order to save myself, I'd given up my light. Bit by bit, I'd fallen into darkness. My brightness had faded. Dulled. I'd thought it was gone completely until I'd met Everett. Until he'd slowly pulled me from that sucking darkness and reminded me of who I was.

Until he'd saved me. *Truly* saved me. Bringing the light back into my life.

And this was how I repaid him. By destroying his kingdom. By *betraying* him. By throwing away something beautiful. Something that a monster like me could never hope to deserve.

He loved me. *Loved* me. And I was about to stab him in the heart.

A silent scream started to build in my mind. A scream of sorrow and despair and hopelessness. A scream of injustice and frustration and *rage*.

It couldn't end like this. I'd been allowed to experience my happily ever after for a single moment in time. To be that bright shining star again. To be *free*.

It had only been a moment, a brief moment of pure perfection, but I would cherish it forever. Even if my forever ended tonight.

So I let the scream continue to build, encouraging it to grow louder and louder. Stronger and stronger. Giving it my fear and desperation. My helplessness. Even my will to survive. To *live*.

Because I couldn't save myself this way. If I followed through with this premonition, I would lose myself. Adalyn would be gone forever, and I couldn't live with that.

I couldn't live without *him*. Couldn't live in a dark world where Everett D'angelo didn't exist. *He* made me bright. He encouraged me to shine, to show the world the real me. And someone like that deserved to be protected. To be *saved*.

So I let that scream consume me. Let it build until I could no longer contain it. Until the need to fulfill my mission began to crack. To break apart. To *shatter*.

I was splintering. Fracturing. Pouring every last desperate thought into tearing myself free from six years of oppression. From every last thralled command. From every last promise.

I won't do it anymore, I won't do it anymore! I screamed and screamed inside my head, not caring that I was breaking. That I was sentencing myself to death.

He deserved it. Everett deserved it. I had to *save* him.

So when my premonition began to unravel—when I slipped my knife free and prepared to kill the man I loved—I fought. I fought with everything I had, consequences be damned. The knife arced through the air, aiming straight for his heart. Mistress had been right. He wouldn't suspect me of treachery until it was too late. Until the deadly blade was buried hilt deep in his vulnerable organ.

Recalling in my dream how that beautiful light had left his eyes, I threw back my head and let the scream explode from me.

"NOOOOOO!"

It was a detonation of pain. A wave of anguish. A tsunami of *rage*.

I felt myself shatter into a million pieces. Felt the invisible ropes tying me into knots burn to ash. Felt my magic return in full force.

I was free. *FREE.*

The knife slipped through my fingers as the scream continued to belt from my lungs. It went on and on, destroying the last of my invisible prison. Freeing my magic from its cage. Relieved beyond measure to feel it freely flowing through my veins for the first time in six long years, I let it burst from me. My feet left the ground as magic exploded from my hands, from every pore in my body.

Suppressed for so long, I could barely contain it. The magic twirled and leapt, spinning me higher and higher, catapulting me into the air like a mighty creature stretching its wings. Light burst behind my closed eyelids, and I squinted them open to see that I was bathed in bright cerulean magic. Everywhere I looked, the magic spun and danced, happy to be free at last.

Free. I was truly *free.*

Mistress no longer controlled me. I could see her down below, a dark insignificant speck. I'd feared her for so long. Feared what she could do to me. But all that fear started to fade away like a bad dream.

I was free now. She couldn't hurt me anymore. Couldn't use me.

I'd just destroyed everything that had bound us together.

At the realization, the magic holding me aloft suddenly vanished, and I fell.

Too shocked to react, I let myself plummet to the ground. Down, down, down I went, succumbing to reality. To my chosen fate. The faces of my cruel past surrounded me from all sides, forcing me down to the cold, unforgiving ground.

But, at the last second, strong arms stopped my descent. Saved me from falling once more into the darkness's waiting embrace.

Only this time, it was too late.

Darkness had already claimed me. He just didn't realize it yet.

"Adalyn."

As Everett's voice washed over me, I waited to hear his disbelief, his *anger* at my betrayal. But it never came. Instead, he sounded worried. Worried for *me*.

Pain suddenly splintered my vision. So powerful and abrupt that I curled against his chest with a strangled cry.

"Adalyn, what's wrong?" he said over the pounding in my ears. Over the agony threatening to tear me apart. "Adalyn!"

"I'm so sorry," I whimpered, forcing my lids open so I could see his beautiful amethyst eyes one last time. "I'm so sorry about everything. It's not their f-fault."

"Um, Everett?" Kade called from nearby. "We might need you in a second here. They're looking mighty pissed."

Everett ignored him, his concerned gaze still locked on me. "Tell me what's wrong, baby girl. Let me help you."

"Everett!" Loch snapped. "They're going to—"

The room suddenly exploded into chaos.

Several vampires rushed toward us en masse. Loch and Kade met them head on, their bodies a blur as they used their supernatural speed to hold them back. Isla and Kenna hurried forward to help them, the latter sending a bolt of fiery red magic at the charging crowd. Even King Ambrose joined the fray, grappling with a member of his council.

As a vampire broke through the line and streaked toward us, Everett set me down and met the male with a bellowing roar. They clashed in a powerful display of brutality, their movements a blur as they fought each other.

His opponent was Viscount Le Blanc, one of the clients under my control. Scrambling to focus on our blood connection, I tried to stop him. Tried to reverse the damage I had caused.

"Kill them! Kill them all!" a voice shrieked, breaking my concentration.

I paused to search the restless Venturi that hadn't yet joined the fight. Most of their faces were lined with confusion, and hope thundered in my chest. Maybe I'd broken some of the blood bonds when I'd freed myself. Maybe some of my clients were coming back to themselves, remembering how they *really* felt about the royal family.

Out of nowhere, two blond males emerged from behind the crowd, their hands encased in bright magic. I froze, caught off guard by the sight. I hadn't seen warlocks in *years*, not since the night my dad had died. What shocked me the most was that I recognized the younger one. Instructor Noah Andrews had been a teacher at the magic school I used to attend.

"Kill them!" the same voice shrieked again, and I finally spotted her.

Mistress still stood at the top of the grand staircase, her eyes gleaming wickedly as she surveyed the growing carnage below. Her two daughters cowered behind her, their expressions more excited than afraid.

Six years of pent-up emotion suddenly erupted from me.

With a feral battle cry, I flung a bolt of blue magic at them. Then another and another. One singed Mistress's dress. Another hit Georgina in the arm, while the third exploded at Octavia's feet. As they scattered like frightened ants, pain warped my vision once more. I curled forward, all the air leaving me in a rush. When I managed to blink away the darkness, red splotches dotted the floor.

Blood. *My* blood.

Ignoring it, I quickly focused on the stairs again, but the Faircrofts were gone. A sickening *crack* rent the air, and I turned just as Everett broke Viscount Le Blanc's neck. When he grabbed the head to rip it off, I stumbled forward and croaked, "Don't kill him."

Everett whipped his gaze to me, the blood red of his eyes filled with bloodlust. "Why not? He *attacked* us," he said, his voice little more than a growl. "He's probably one of your clients and, therefore, doesn't deserve to live."

"He's *enchanted*," I cried, then doubled over in a coughing fit. I covered my mouth, but not fast enough. Blood sprayed onto the floor once more.

"Adalyn!" Everett shouted. As I teetered sideways, he dropped Le Blanc to catch me. "Where are you hurt?"

"It doesn't . . . doesn't matter."

"What? Of *course* it matters. Here, take my blood."

He swiftly bit into his wrist and held it out to me, but I turned my head away and rasped, "They're all enchanted. You have to . . . you have to spare them. They don't . . . they don't mean it. They're *loyal*." I coughed again, so forcefully that my lungs screamed in agony.

Sudden dread filled our bond. Struggling to breathe, I looked up again and caught the devastation on Everett's face. The *horror*.

"You broke the pactum," he whispered, the words barely audible.

"I'm sorry," I whispered back, then forced myself to push away and stand on my own. "I can tell you the truth now. The Venturi aren't your enemies. I've spent the past three years poisoning their minds against you, but that's not how they really feel. Don't kill them. Please. It's the rogues you need to worry about. They've been orchestrating this attack from the very beginning. Call on your allies, because they're coming. They—"

"Too late," Everett said, his red eyes flaring bright. "They're already here."

My insides turned to ice as the human maids started to scream. I looked toward the stairs just as dozens of rogues poured into the ballroom.

"You heard her!" Everett shouted to his family and warlocks still valiantly fighting. "Spare the Venturi. Give the rogues no quarter. Now is the time to rid this kingdom of their deception once and for all!"

Battle cries rose into the air.

"Heads up!" Noah hollered and muscled his way into our circle. He tossed a silver sword with the hilt carefully wrapped in leather, and Kade whirled to catch it.

"Thanks, man!" Kade hollered back, ducking as his Venturi opponent swiped a clawed hand at him. With one smooth stroke, he sliced the hand off, and the Venturi grabbed his spurting arm with a scream. "You'll thank me later," Kade grunted, then lunged toward his next opponent.

Not far away, Loch tore off his jacket to reveal a twin pair of silver pistols strapped to his sides. Whipping the pistols free with gloved hands, he faced the approaching horde of rogues and lit them up.

"Yeah, baby!" Noah crowed, lighting up the horde as well with his Cosmic magic. The other warlock went back-to-back with him, focusing his efforts on the Venturi still under my enchantment. Every time one of them attacked, he used a spell to freeze them in place. Then Everett or King Ambrose would race forward and snap their necks.

Kenna and Isla had also teamed up in a similar manner, one using magic to stun their opponent while the other rushed in and knocked them out.

We were outnumbered by far, but everyone in the tight circle worked as a unit. They were a well-oiled machine, feeding off each other's strengths and protecting their weaknesses. If I wasn't feeling so helpless, I would have taken a moment to admire the beautiful way they danced together.

After several minutes of fighting, the tide started to shift in our favor. Venturi were submitting everywhere, backing off from the fight as my influence on their minds faded. And despite the rogues' numbers, they didn't stand a chance against the royal family's power.

I coughed again, blood filling my mouth as I desperately tried to stay out of the way. In too much pain to help, all I could do was fight to remain conscious so Everett wouldn't get distracted.

Never had I been more aware of time. Each second that ticked by reminded me that it could be my last. I was living on borrowed time now. The moment I'd broken both pactums, the lease on my life had expired. The pain was growing more and more unbearable, and I was losing way too much blood.

I wanted to stay. With everything in me, I wanted to stay and help. To see the Venturi fully freed of my enchantment and the rogues defeated.

But I couldn't. There was one more thing I needed to do. Time was relentless, and if I didn't leave now, I wouldn't make it.

So I forced my aching body to pick up my knife from the blood-flecked floor. Forced myself to turn away from the love of my life and accept that I wouldn't be able to say goodbye. And when the opportunity came, I forced myself to leave the protective circle. To dart through a gap in the fighting and slip through the crowd.

To *vanish*.

CHAPTER 33

ADALYN

More than once, a rogue almost got the better of me.

I used my knife and weakening magic to ward them off, and they soon moved on, clearly interested in bigger game. I'd barely left the ballroom behind when an earth-shattering roar pounded my eardrums.

Pure devastation flooded the soulmate bond, and I nearly fell to my knees.

He knew. Everett knew that I'd run away.

ADALYN! he roared again, this time through our bond.

I didn't respond. Couldn't. He needed to focus on protecting his family, and so did I. Even the slightest distraction could spell our doom.

So I ignored the growing ache in my chest, an ache that had nothing to do with the broken pactum and everything to do with Everett. With the hurt he felt that I'd left him. Apologizing wouldn't help anyway. No apology could fix what I'd broken. What I'd destroyed.

This was the fate I'd chosen, but I wouldn't allow it to become my familiar's fate. I might be dying, but that didn't mean she had to. I just had to get back to the house before my body gave out. If my last act was freeing Pepper from this life, then I could die knowing that I'd done at least one thing right.

I might have screwed everything up with my soulmate, but he still had his family. Pepper had no one. No one to protect her. I was her one and only hope.

I used that knowledge to fuel me onward, to stop myself from looking back. From returning to Everett. Pepper needed me more, and I was going to save her.

As I continued to stumble toward the exit, the sounds of fighting started to fade. A few human maids scurried past, but the halls were otherwise empty. Still, I kept my guard up, not knowing where the Faircrofts had scuttled off to. Maybe they were already claiming their spot on Sanctum Isle, prematurely celebrating their victory by picking which house they wanted to settle down in. I knew Mistress had always coveted the Venturi mansions on the island. Or maybe she planned to make the *castle* her new home.

Either way, I kept a sharp eye out as I reached the grand foyer that would lead me outside. The double doors were wide open, and when I neared, I caught sight of the guards splayed across the floor. Dead. Fresh pangs of guilt racked my body, further adding to my misery. If only I'd broken the pactum earlier, I could have prevented their deaths. I could have stopped this *all* from happening.

But I'd been selfish. I hadn't wanted to sacrifice my happily ever after. I'd wanted to *live*.

Doubling over, I threw up what little remained in my stomach. Weakness stole over me, and I grabbed on to the doorframe to keep from collapsing.

Give up, my failing body urged me. *Lie down and succumb to your fate.*

No! I shouted back. *I'm done lying down. I will fight. I will fight for however long I have left!*

Gritting my teeth, I forced myself upright and stumbled out into the night. It had begun to rain, and my hair and dress were soaked through within seconds. The added weight threatened to pull me down, but I trudged onward, barely able to see through the deluge. I was almost to the stone stairs that led to the packed roundabout when I staggered to a halt. No way would I reach Pepper in time if I used a car.

There was only one way I could reach her, and now that my powers were fully restored, I had the ability to do it.

The thought of reuniting with Pepper in a matter of seconds filled me with fresh resolve, and I willed magic to my fingertips. When it quickly sputtered out, I dredged up the last of my strength and threw my arms wide with a determined cry.

A circular portal sprung into existence before me, the edges glowing bright blue. Sighing in relief, I swayed toward it. I would make it in time. I couldn't say goodbye to Everett, but at least I could to Pepper.

But when I stepped forward, something small darted in front of me. I recognized Kenna's fox familiar as she lunged for my legs and latched onto my dress, frantically yanking on the delicate material. It started to rip, but she only pulled harder. Not toward the portal, but *away*.

"Silver, *no*. I can't go back," I firmly told her. "I have to save my familiar."

The portal began to flicker. Desperate to enter it before the last of my magic faded, I surged forward. As I did, something barrelled into me from behind. Something *huge*.

The force of the hit sent me flying into the air. I shot past my dying portal and down the steep stairs. When I struck the unforgiving stone, a sickening *crack* filled my ears. I struck again and again, uncontrollably tumbling down the stairs. Several more cracks rent the air, my frail body breaking under the fall's impact.

When I reached the bottom, I rolled to a stop, unable to breathe.

Pain consumed every inch of my body. Pain that stole the last of my strength. I tried to move, but agony locked me in place.

My time was up. I was done. I had nothing left to give.

Silent tears coursed down my already wet face. Tears of defeat.

I was suddenly flipped onto my back. My injuries screamed at me, so loudly that darkness edged my vision. I squinted through the rain, struggling to focus on the face peering down at me.

"Leaving so soon, *Star*?" a familiar voice said, one that filled me with dread.

I openly glared up at Heath, letting him see how much I despised him.

He chuckled, as if he found my reaction to him amusing. "You always did think you were too good for me," he drawled, crouching beside me so I could clearly see his face.

When he swept the hair off my neck, I ignored the pain shooting up my arm and slowly reached for my thigh. Noticing the movement, he clucked his tongue and yanked the garter off my leg, along with my knife. The violent action sent fresh agony streaking through my body. As I cried out, I succumbed to a coughing fit, each movement like a jagged knife cutting into my flesh.

Blood spilled from my mouth, and Heath cocked his head to the side. "Oh, I get it now. You're dying. What, you didn't think I knew about the pactum? Shame you had to break it. I was looking forward to making you my personal blood whore. Well, at least I can taste you before you die. Waste not, want not, and all that."

Before I could fully process his words, he lunged for my vulnerable throat and sank his fangs in deep. I weakly flinched, opening my mouth in a silent scream as fresh pain flooded me. I tried to move, but my body was done. All I could do was stare blankly at the night sky and wait for him to drain the last of my life away.

Perhaps it was better this way. Quicker. My suffering would come to an end all too soon.

He didn't dull my pain, though. Didn't feed me his venom. He *wanted* me to suffer. He always had. He took sadistic pleasure from it, using pain to remind me of how weak I was compared to him.

That reminder hit me full force now, filling me with indescribable agony. But something else was filling me too. *Rage.* The emotion whipped through me so forcefully that I knew it wasn't just mine.

It was Everett's too.

It pounded through me like a wardrum, infusing my body with sudden strength. Even as Heath ravenously drained the blood from my body, I felt strong. Strong enough to say, "You forgot one important thing, Heath. Something that will be your downfall." A small smile stretched my lips. "I can control your mind now."

He stiffened, realizing his terrible mistake too late.

I struck like a python, coiling my magic around his mind, then *squeezed.* Just like that, he froze, his will now *mine.* With a single thought, I commanded him to release me. He did, sliding his fangs from my neck.

I felt the rage grow stronger.

He was coming. Everett was *coming* for me.

Struggling to stay focused, I told Heath in a shaky voice, "Now stand up. Stand up and face the fury of your future king. Face your fate, Heath Clancy, and know that *I* control it."

He obeyed my command. Like a puppet, he woodenly stood to face the stairs. I squinted through the rain just as a dark figure appeared at the very top. I could barely make out his features, but it didn't matter. My heart weakly fluttered inside my chest, recognizing its mate.

As he took in the scene below, shadows erupted from him. He

released a furious roar, then streaked toward us like a torpedo.

Wanting him to fully feel Everett's wrath, I let go of Heath's mind. At the last second, he realized the danger he was in. Realized what I'd done.

But it was too late.

Too late.

Too late.

He didn't even have time to scream.

With one violent sweep of his arm, Everett knocked Heath's head clean off. It flew through the air like a soccer ball and vanished into the night. Before the headless body could finish crumpling to the ground, Everett was kneeling by my side. He softly touched me, wincing when he saw how broken I was.

"What can I do?" he croaked, looking so lost that fresh tears squeezed from my eyes. "Tell me what to do, Adalyn. Tell me how to help you."

"You came," I whispered, struggling to keep my eyes open.

"Always. I will always come for you, baby girl." He gently touched my cheek, his face lined in agony. "Tell me how to fix this, Adalyn. *Please.*"

He couldn't fix this. The broken pactum was calling for me. Calling for my death. It grew louder and louder by the second, and there was nothing Everett could do to stop it.

I tried to smile at him, but my lips suddenly felt cold. Numb. My entire body did, the pain slowly melting away. "It was a dream. A beautiful dream. I'll cherish it forever." My eyes fluttered shut.

"No. No! Adalyn, open your eyes. Open your eyes for me, baby girl. Don't leave me like this. I *need* you!"

My heartbeats slowed. I tried to open my eyes, to see him one last time, but they were too heavy. Everything pulled me down, down,

down. Darkness dragged me into its waiting embrace. Before it could fully claim me, I managed to whisper one last thing.

"Save Pepper."

CHAPTER 34

EVERETT

I felt the moment she slipped from me.

Her breaths and heart slowed. Slowed and slowed until they stopped. Just stopped. Like a clock that ran out of time.

When they did, the soulmate bond I'd stubbornly resisted but now desperately needed *snapped*.

I immediately plunged into darkness, not knowing up from down. I was utterly lost, free-falling into nothingness. I'd felt lost before, but not like this. This felt permanent, like I'd never see the light of day again. This felt *hopeless*, like I'd never find myself again.

Not without her. An existence without Adalyn just felt . . . empty. Not worth living.

I stared at her still form, now free of pain. She looked so peaceful. So serene. So . . . so *untouchable*. She was an ethereal goddess just beyond my reach, slipping farther and farther away. The longer I stared at her, the more she vanished.

And I couldn't go after her. I couldn't *save* her.

At the realization, I broke. I broke into a billion wretched pieces. Pieces I would never put together again. There was no point. Without her, I had no purpose. She *was* my purpose. She made me better in every way. And now that she was gone, I was nothing. Nothing worth holding on to.

Too afraid to touch her, I simply watched her. Watched as the rain washed the blood from her mouth and neck. Watched as she grew paler and paler. Colder and colder.

She made death look beautiful.

Laying down on the wet ground beside her lifeless form, I whispered, "Take me with you, baby girl. Don't go where I can't find you."

She didn't respond.

There wasn't even a flicker from the bond. All was still. Deathly silent. She was gone. Truly gone. There was nothing left for me but memories. Memories that threatened to drown me.

"Everett."

I heard the voice, but it sounded far away. On a distant plane. In a separate world. I was cut off from it. Indifferent to it.

Still, I flatly replied, "Touch her, and I'll kill you."

"Everett, there's still time," the voice persisted. "Snap out of it. You can still save her."

The words were cruel. Unfair. I closed my eyes, praying they would disappear. That *I* would disappear.

"Everett James D'angelo!" the voice barked. "Your soulmate died, but she's not *gone*. If you won't turn her, then I will."

I struggled to comprehend the words, but one thing registered loud and clear. "If I force her to become a vampire, she'll hate me forever."

"No, she won't. She deserves a new beginning, Ev. You can give that to her. A new life. A *better* one. Don't throw this opportunity away."

"I can't," I whispered, my voice breaking. "I'm too empty, Loch. The bond is gone. I can't . . . I can't find her."

My brother knelt beside me and rested a hand on my shoulder, forcing me back to reality. To a world where Adalyn didn't exist.

"I know, Ev," he said. "I've been where you are. It's unbearable.

The worst feeling you'll ever feel. But you have to be strong for her like you've always been strong for us. Even when things seemed absolutely hopeless, you've never given up. You've always protected us, always *saved* us, doing whatever it takes to keep this family from falling apart. You're our backbone, brother, and it's time for you to rise once more. So get up. Get up and rescue your mate. She *needs* you."

Somehow, his words managed to penetrate my world of nothingness, giving me fresh purpose.

She needed me. My soulmate *needed* me.

My movements were sluggish, but I forced my limbs to gather beneath me, to push me into a sitting position. Every action hurt, sending shards of agony through my bones. Reminding me of the terrible pain Adalyn had been in before her death. I looked down at her still face again and suddenly couldn't breathe. Everything she'd been through rushed at me all at once, locking my limbs once more.

"I don't know if I can do this," I rasped. "I don't know if I can turn her into a vampire."

What if she didn't *want* this? What if she forever despised me for turning her into one of the creatures that had ruined her life? I'd told her I would never force her to do anything against her will. After all she'd been through, this felt like the worst betrayal.

"Maybe she won't have to become one entirely," a new voice spoke. I peered up through the rain to see that Kenna and her fox familiar had joined us.

"What do you mean?" I questioned Kenna, still too distraught to connect the dots.

"When Lochlan turned me, the combination of our soulmate bond and my bond with Silver allowed me to become a hybrid. I might be a vampire now, but I'm still a witch too. Adalyn needs her familiar for this to work, Everett. She needs Pepper."

Pepper.

Pepper.

"*Save Pepper.*"

Those had been Adalyn's final words to me. Her one last request. Her cry for *help*.

Some of that lost feeling vanished, replaced by another feeling. Hope. Wild, desperate *hope*.

Pepper. I had to find *Pepper*.

My gaze shot to Loch's. "There's not enough time."

Determination lined his face. "Then we'll *make* time."

In a flash, he disappeared back up the stairs. Seconds later, he returned carrying a terrified-looking Noah.

When he set him down, Noah sputtered out, "Dude! *Never* do that again! I was in the middle of— Oh." His expression fell as he caught sight of Adalyn's broken body.

"We need you to portal her and Everett to Faircroft Manor right away. Can you manage it?" Loch urgently asked him.

"Faircroft . . . Yeah, I can manage. I know where it is. Why? What's at Faircroft Manor?"

"Adalyn's familiar."

His eyes went to me. "You're planning to turn her into a hybrid?"

"Yes," I replied without hesitation. Without apology. The thought of turning her into something that didn't completely take away who she was had renewed my hope. But I'd already wasted precious minutes in my frozen moments of grief. Time was ticking away, and the small window available to turn her was swiftly flying by.

Focusing on Adalyn's body, I carefully slid my arms beneath her. When I felt how slight she was, how *broken*, pain squeezed my heart and cut off my air. I moved even slower, afraid she would fall apart.

Only when her head was safely tucked against my chest, the rest of her gently cradled in my arms, did I allow myself to breathe again.

When I stood, Noah cautiously approached. Good thing too. Now that my hope had returned, so had my need to protect what was mine. One false move from the warlock, and I would probably lose it.

"Are you sure her familiar is at the manor?" Noah questioned me. "I only have enough juice for one trip."

Before I could respond, another voice replied, "She's there."

Loch whirled toward the stairs with a growl, nudging Kenna behind him. "You should have run, *rogue*," he shouted to the figure standing at the top.

I squinted through the rain, surprised when I recognized the hulky Feltore. "*Wait.* I know who you are." With one word, I could command his execution. He deserved it. *All* of the rogues did. But instead, I allowed a few more precious seconds to tick by and called, "Why shouldn't I have you killed where you stand?"

"You should," Rocky replied back in that deep, quiet voice of his. "But I know who you are too. I know that you tried to protect Adalyn in the club. I know that you saved me from burning to ash. You aren't who I thought you were. The rogues are wrong about you. *I* was wrong. And for that, I know I deserve death."

A few more precious seconds ticked by as we stared at each other through the downpour.

Finally, I said, "For your honesty, I will spare you. It's what Adalyn would have wanted."

He bowed deeply, murmuring, "For that, I owe you my undying loyalty. I pray she survives the transition."

I acknowledged his words with a nod, praying for the same thing. She'd survived so much in her short lifetime. I could only hope her spirit hadn't broken along with the pactum. Could only hope she still *wanted* to survive.

"Ready?" Noah asked, coming alongside me.

When I nodded again, he fashioned a bright portal into existence. Sudden fear gripped me. Fear that I'd mess up. That I'd destroy the last of her instead of saving her.

"Trust in your heart, Everett," Loch said over the pounding rain and humming portal. "Trust in your love for her. Now *go*. Save your mate. We've got your back."

I knew they did. Knew they could handle the mess the rogues had made of our home. Knew they would protect each other while I tended to the woman who held my heart, even in death.

With renewed purpose, I accepted Noah's help and stepped into the swirling portal. The world immediately blurred around us, passing by even faster than a vampire at full speed. I cradled Adalyn close, trying to shield her from the screaming wind. But as quickly as the gale erupted around us, it ended. I blinked and the world righted once more, the Faircroft's mansion only yards away.

Impressed by the warlock's accuracy, I decided he wasn't half bad after all. "Thanks," I told him, then took off for the house.

"No problem, E-Man," he called after me, and I wasn't even annoyed at the nickname.

Nearing the front entrance, I spotted a mangy cat prowling by the door. At my approach, it whirled around and hissed. I bared my fangs and hissed right back, sending it scurrying into the night. Not bothering with the door handle, I kicked the door in and rushed inside with a bellow. "*Pepper!*"

I paused to listen. For an unbearable moment, the only thing I could hear was my pounding heart. And then I heard it. The tiniest of squeaks. I raced toward the kitchen and kicked down the basement door as well, my feet barely touching the stairs as I descended at vampire speed.

Swiftly taking in the damp, dingy space, I spotted the mouse trapped in a cage on the bedside table. The sight broke my heart. When she saw me, Pepper grew frantic. She clawed and screeched, throwing herself at the walls of her cage.

"I know, I know," I told her, hurrying forward. "I'm coming."

Treating Adalyn's body like a porcelain doll, I gently placed her on the bed, then quickly released Pepper from her cage. The moment she was free, she leapt onto the mattress and scurried toward Adalyn. When she butted her little head against Adalyn's neck as if to wake her, my heart broke even more.

"I'm so sorry, Pepper," I croaked, lowering myself to sit on the bed beside them. "I failed to protect her. She was all alone, and I didn't see it. But I'm going to bring her back. I don't want to change a single thing about her, but if we bring her back together, she won't have to give up everything. Not completely. She'll still be the Adalyn we both know and love."

Pepper looked up at me. At the tears glittering in her round black eyes, my own eyes started to burn.

"Yes, I'm in love with her," I told the little mouse. "But our time together was so short, and I need more of it. I need Adalyn, Pepper. I need my *soulmate*. I can't see my way forward without her. She's my direction. My light through the darkness. So, please. Please, help me bring her back."

I held my hand out toward her, praying she understood my heartfelt plea. Praying she accepted this new fate for the witch under her care. She had every right to walk away, to reject my proposal. She was free now. Free to leave this dangerous world behind. Free to live the life she'd chosen when she'd joined the earthly plane.

Beneath her tiny exterior, she was a celestial being, immortal and powerful. Who was I to make demands on her? To cheat death of its latest victim? In the grand scheme of things, I was no one. A vampire prince was nothing compared to the Universe.

Maybe fate didn't *want* me to bring Adalyn back. Maybe this had been her destiny all along. To bring me back to myself. To fill me with purpose once more. To make me better.

Grief threatened to snatch my hope away, and I bowed my head in defeat. Just when I started to lose all hope, a tiny body settled onto my palm. Raising my head, I looked at Pepper perched in my hand, and hope burgeoned in my chest once more.

"Thank you, Pepper. We're going to save her. We'll save her together."

I never thought I'd feel a connection with such a small, insignificant-looking creature, but I knew now that I'd been wrong. Not just about her, but about many things. My eyes were wide open, and I could see clearly now. This world was vast, and every living creature deserved a place in it. It didn't matter who was stronger. Didn't matter what their race or rank was.

We were equal.

A little mouse familiar and a powerful Venturi prince were the same, and I made sure she could see that realization in my eyes.

I knew in my heart that things were going to change after this. I might not be half the king my father was, but I was no longer cold and cruel. I cared, truly cared about what happened to my kingdom. To *every* creature that fate chose to bring into my life. Things were going to change, and I knew deep down that Adalyn would be by my side the entire way.

Fate didn't give her to me only to snatch her away again.

She and I were meant for more. Our story was only just beginning. So when I began the transition process, feeding Adalyn both

Pepper's blood and mine, I knew without a shadow of doubt that she would come back to me.

Several minutes later, I felt the moment she started to return. It was a whisper. A gentle caress. A sigh of relief as our bond, our beautiful soulmate bond, slowly knitted back together.

I'm here, it seemed to breathe, soothing away the last of my pain. *I'm here to stay.*

I'd never felt such joy, such *elation* when her heart began to beat again. When her chest slowly rose and fell, relearning how to breathe. And when her golden eyes fluttered open, I was made whole again.

"There's my girl," I whispered, touching her cheek.

As her gaze met mine, I finally allowed my tears to fall.

CHAPTER 35

ADALYN

Something was different.

As Everett touched me, my skin practically hummed with energy. It felt like a live wire was just beneath the surface, and every time he made contact, it sparked to life.

It felt *amazing*.

While his thumb continued to stroke my cheek, I became aware of other things. Smells. Sounds. All of them glaringly familiar. We were in the basement at Faircroft Manor. On my bed. The space smelled *extra* moldy, though, and I couldn't help but wrinkle my nose.

Everett softly laughed. The sound danced across my senses, making me even more aware of my body. Like the fact that I felt like a million bucks. Not just where he touched me, but *everywhere*. I couldn't remember *ever* feeling this good, not even when I'd been high on venom.

Something was different, all right.

I didn't have to adjust my eyes to the basement's gloomy interior. I could see clearly, almost as if sunlight had been allowed to penetrate the boarded-up window above my bed. Everett's eyes shone in a way I'd never seen them before. I could pick out each facet of green in his jewel-toned irises.

As I stared in wonder, a tear fell from one of them. Without even thinking, I reached up and caught it.

Caught it.

Which shouldn't have been possible.

The lone tear was somehow perfectly poised on the tip of my finger, and all I could do was gawk at it.

Something was definitely different.

Something was *wrong*.

"Everett."

His name rasped from my lips, the single word filled with alarm.

"It's okay," he gently said, reaching up to fold my hand into his. "Just take your time. You're doing great."

When he rested our joined hands over my heart, I heard how fast the organ was beating. Not just fast. *Loud.*

It thundered like a drum, painfully bashing against my eardrums. I reached up and covered my ears, suddenly drowning in sensation. My senses were everywhere, dragging me in a million different directions. I didn't know which one to focus on. Didn't know what was *happening*.

As panic flooded me, Everett cupped my face and soothingly said, *Focus on me, Adalyn. Only on me. That's it. That's my good girl. Now breathe. In and out. Listen to my voice. Forget everything else. You're okay. You're going to be okay."*

At the comforting sound of his voice in my head, I immediately felt better.

I did as he instructed, blocking out everything else to focus solely on him. When I did, my senses calmed. Settled. But my mind didn't. My mind was suddenly wide awake, demanding that I listen. That I *remember*. The night's events crashed into me all at once, drowning me in their intensity.

I gasped, tears immediately filling my eyes as I remembered what had happened. "Everett, I died. I *died*."

Sorrow lined his face. "I'm so sorry, Adalyn. I couldn't stop it from happening."

As the truth of his words sank deeply into my bones, another realization hit me. The only one that made sense. With another gasp, I sat up straight. Everett's hands fell away, and I took stock of my body. Nothing felt broken. Nothing *hurt*. I was whole again. Whole and . . .

"A vampire. I'm a *vampire*."

"Yes," he quietly replied. "I couldn't let you go. I'm sorry, Adalyn."

Struggling to accept the news, I stammered, "Y-you turned me."

Guilt trickled through our bond. Still, he looked me in the eye and said, "Yes. We both did."

"We?"

A squeak drew my attention to the nightstand. Fresh tears pricked my eyes as I spotted my mouse familiar.

"Pepper!" She hopped into my waiting hands, and I didn't waste any time snuggling her against my cheek. "I'm so glad you're okay. I was so worried. I tried to come back, but— Oh. You smell different. A good different, but also kind of bad."

When I pulled back with a confused frown, she huffed a laugh inside my head. *Glad to see you're pulling through the transition just fine, Ada. I knew you would. But don't get any ideas about snacking on me. You might have sharp teeth now, but so do I.*

"Sharp teeth?" I lifted a hand to my mouth and felt my canines. They were perfectly normal.

"That'll come later," Everett said. "When the desire to feed hits."

I swallowed. *Hard.*

"So I'm going to start craving blood soon?"

"Yes, but Kenna said that hybrid cravings aren't too bad. She mostly feeds on Loch when the need for blood hits."

My mind began to race again. Not daring to hope, I whispered,

"What are you saying?"

His expression softened. "You're still a witch, Adalyn. You're still you. You're just immortal now and a little less breakable."

My bottom lip quivered. "I'm a hybrid?"

When he nodded, a sob burst from me. Still holding Pepper, I launched myself at him and tightly squeezed his neck.

"Easy," he grunted, almost toppling off the bed from the impact.

I laughed through my tears and loosened my grip a little. "What? Am I too *strong* for you now?"

"No," he said, burying his face in my neck with a contented sigh. "You're perfect."

I sank into the embrace with a small smile. Still trying to digest my new reality, a big part of me expected to wake up and discover this was all a dream.

"Do you hate me for turning you?" he asked after a moment, his guilt returning.

"Of course not," I murmured.

If not for him, I would be dead right now. I *deserved* to be dead.

Unable to keep silent, I made myself say, "Do you hate *me*?"

"For what?" He slid his hand up the bare column of my spine, making my skin burst awake again.

"For betraying you at the ball. For secretly plotting against your family for the past three years."

Pepper jumped onto the bed and scurried away, clearly sensing our need for privacy. I held my breath, waiting for our peaceful moment to shatter. Waiting for Everett to realize what a monster I was.

With another sigh, he murmured against my skin, "No, Adalyn. I don't hate you. You didn't have a choice."

"But I *did*. I chose to work at the club. I *chose* to become a blood whore. I so desperately wanted to pay off my father's blood debt and avenge him that I allowed the rogues to use me and my abilities. I turned your court against you. I almost . . . I almost *killed* you, Everett. After everything I've done, I don't know how you can stand to be near me. I put you and your entire family in jeopardy. You *deserve* to hate me."

Lifting his head, he rested his forehead against mine before saying, "You know what I hate? I hate that you were mistreated by my kind. I hate that the rogues tried to turn you into something you're not. I hate that you had to pretend. That they stole precious pieces of you. I hate when you doubt yourself. Hate when you're not with me. Hate that I didn't tell you sooner how I really feel. I would move mountains just to see that spellbinding smile of yours. I would rearrange the stars just so our paths would align. I was searching for a purpose before I met you, but you *are* that purpose. You're the dream my heart has been wishing for, a dream I didn't even know I wanted. It's not possible for me to hate you, baby girl. You sacrificed yourself for me. You gave up everything to keep my family safe, and for that, you've earned my eternal gratitude. My heart is yours, Adalyn, only yours. Today, tomorrow, and for the rest of my immortal life."

Tears slid down my cheeks as I memorized every single beautiful word he'd uttered. I knew he meant them. They were written in his emotions, emotions he was openly allowing me to feel. Despite the awful things I'd done, he truly loved me. He *forgave* me as I had forgiven him for his past wrongs.

Just like that, the slate was wiped clean. The past was in the past, our futures spanning before us and filled with hope.

My heart overflowed with so much love that I blurted, "I want to kiss you."

His mouth formed a lopsided grin. "My lips are yours, my lady."

As I eagerly kissed him, I was immediately struck by how sensitive my skin was. I'd always enjoyed kissing him, but with my newly heightened senses, the feeling of his lips on mine was *explosive*. I instantly lost myself to the kiss, the good kind of lost I only experienced with Everett. He became my world, my everything. My only desire was him, a desire that was quickly consuming me from the inside out.

When he dragged me into his lap to straddle his waist, the extra contact wrung a whimper from me. He broke the kiss, noting how breathless and flushed I already was.

"You okay?" he asked.

"It's intense," I replied, shuddering when he slid his hand up my spine again. "More intense than . . . before."

Satisfaction pulsed through our bond.

I huffed a laugh, the sound turning into a moan as I felt his arousal press against my underwear.

"Do you want more?" he purred, leaning forward to pull my bottom lip into his mouth. When he sucked on the flesh, my eyes blissfully rolled shut.

"Mmmm," I managed to groan.

He bit into my lip, and heat blasted through me, traveling straight to my clit. At the unexpected zing of pleasure, I jerked my eyes open with a gasp.

He chuckled against my lip. *Welcome to being a vampire.*

Why does it feel so goooood? I moaned back, letting my eyes roll shut again.

Because we enjoy being bitten. Probably more than we enjoy having sex.

Spirits save me.

My mind immediately filled with naughty possibilities. Another chuckle rumbled from Everett, making me aware that he'd peeked into my thoughts.

I can show you many ways in which vampires enjoy being bitten, he continued to purr, lightly sucking on my lip.

Now? I asked in surprise.

If that's what you wish.

Well, that got me all hot and bothered. As my panties dampened, a cloying scent permeated the air. Surprised once more, I sputtered, *I-is that my . . . ?*

Arousal, he finished, pushing me down on his growing erection. The contact sent euphoria unfurling through my body, and I clamped my thighs around him, wanting more of it.

Oh, you poor bastard, I crooned. *My vagina has been flashing a neon sign at you for days, and I had no clue.*

He released my lip so he could breathe into my ear, "It was torture, especially during our picnics. I had to patiently wait for you to finish eating before I could remove your clothes and feast on my own meal."

I burst out laughing. As my head fell back, he took advantage and nipped a path down my neck. When he reached my shoulder, he gripped the strap of my dress between his teeth and slowly tugged it downward.

"Whoa! My bad. I should have knocked first," a male voice suddenly said.

Startled, I zeroed in on the potential threat, a hiss slipping through my teeth. In the back of my mind, I recognized him as Noah Andrews, but my instincts were firmly in control at the moment. When he held up his hands and stepped back, I tracked the movement like a predator assessing its prey. Realizing what I was doing, I slapped a hand over my mouth, but not quickly enough.

Noah's scent hit me like a battering ram, flooding my senses and filling me with a desperate, aching *need*.

His blood. I was craving his *blood*.

"Everett," I whimpered, then cried out as pain bloomed in my gums.

"Shhhh, you're okay, baby girl," he soothed, reaching up to firmly grip my nape. "It's just your fangs coming in."

My gums continued to burn as the fangs slowly descended, invading my mouth and poking into my bottom lip. No sooner were they in than a new pain distracted me, my throat on fire with a terrible thirst.

"Everett," I repeated, the word warbled from my new set of chompers.

"Noah, I suggest you leave before my mate decides to make you her first meal," he calmly said. His grip on me tightened, as if to prevent me from doing just that.

"Got it," Noah replied, slowly backing toward the stairs. "Glad to see she's, uh, feeling better. I'll just go outside and keep a lookout while you two do vampire stuff."

When he started up the stairs, the new instincts flooding my body went haywire. I blindly lunged after him, but Everett didn't let me get far. He caught me about the waist, his powerful arms locking me in place while I growled and hissed my displeasure. The need for blood was all-consuming, and I fought like a wild cat to break loose.

When he refused to let me go, I raked my nails down his arms— or, rather, *claws*. I had claws now. Black, wickedly sharp weapons.

They tore into his skin, leaving long blood trails in their wake. Seconds after I broke the skin, it quickly healed, which drove me into a frenzy. I went for a different tactic, testing to see if I still possessed magic. When I managed to light up my hands like balls of starlight, Everett decided he'd had enough.

With a growl, he threw me onto the bed. I bounced and almost fell off, but he pinned my body to the mattress with his and wrestled my arms above my head. I snapped at him with my new set of fangs, but he only chuckled and darkly said, "Is that all you've got, baby girl? I know you can do better than that. Here. Take out your blood rage on me. Daddy can handle it."

I strained against his hold with a feral growl. He growled back, his eyes bleeding red. Mine were probably equally red, but I didn't care. All I cared about was *feeding*. So when he let go of my arms, I swiftly grabbed his head and yanked it back to expose his throat. The moment I saw the throbbing vein in his neck, I lost all control.

I struck, burying my fangs deep into his neck. He shuddered against me with a groan, pulling me closer instead of shoving me away. His euphoria blasted through me, confirming that he'd *wanted* me to bite him. Spurred on by his pleasure, I took my first pull. My first *taste*. As his blood flooded my tastebuds, I moaned like a hussy and greedily gulped it down. It immediately soothed my raw throat and warmed my insides, spreading through my veins like molten chocolate.

Spirits alive, Everett, I sighed through our bond and took another pull. *I'm addicted already.*

He faintly hummed in reply, clearly enthralled with whatever I was doing to him. Wanting him to feel even better, I focused on giving him my venom. When he released another shuddering groan, I knew I'd been successful.

As our mutual pleasure built, he hiked up my dress and started rubbing me through my underwear. I bucked against his fingers with a breathless whimper, beyond sensitive to his touch. He wasn't even touching my bare skin, and I was already buzzing like a livewire. Sensing how close I already was to coming, he nudged aside my panties and touched my clit. My back arched off the bed, delicious ecstasy whipping through me.

All it took was a few expert flicks of his fingers. He slid two of them through my wetness, then returned them to my clit, rubbing the sensitive nub until stars burst behind my eyelids. Stiffening all over, I screamed against his neck, my fangs still deep inside him as I orgasmed.

"Greedy little thing," he rumbled out loud, clearly pleased by my obsession with his blood. "Take your time. I'm not going anywhere."

Warmth bloomed in my chest. Warmth that had nothing to do with his blood.

Needing to be closer to him, to experience the oneness I so desperately craved, I reached between us and cupped his manhood. *I want you inside me, Everett.*

His cock swelled beneath my touch. "We might break the bed if I do that."

I smiled against his neck. "That's okay. I don't plan to come back to this place after tonight anyway."

"Fair point," he grunted out, clearly struggling to focus while I slowly massaged him through his pants.

Eager for more, I swiftly undid his belt and tugged down his pants, allowing the throbbing erection to spring free. A long sigh shuddered from him when I wrapped my hand around the shaft and squeezed.

You know, I thoughtfully said, continuing to stroke him. *This will be my first time as a vampire. That means you'll essentially be popping my vampire cherry.*

"God, I love how innocently *naughty* that sounds," he groaned.

Pleased by his response, I rewarded him by slicing off my panties with my new claws and positioning him at my entrance. Finally withdrawing my fangs from his neck, I met his eyes and murmured, "Don't be gentle with me, my prince. I want the full vampire experience."

A devilish grin curved his mouth. "Your wish is my command, my lady."

With one smooth motion, he thrust inside me to the hilt. My walls immediately clenched around him, happy to be reunited with him once more. He filled me up perfectly, his body meant for mine. It was magical the way we seamlessly fit together, like two halves destined to become a whole.

He was meant for me, and I was meant for him.

Which meant that he was mine and I was his.

At the realization, I sucked in a breath.

"What is it?" Everett asked, reaching up to brush hair off my cheek.

"I'm yours," I burst out, rapidly blinking as tears filled my eyes.

His expression softened. "Yes, Adalyn. You're mine. But you're still your own person."

I gave him a trembling smile. "I get that now. We belong to each other, but we're still free. I'm still me, and you're still you."

He smiled back, murmuring, "And you're okay with that?"

"More than okay."

He kissed me then, and I kissed him back, marveling at my newest revelation. I was his, but I didn't have to give up who I was. He didn't *want* me to, and that made me love him all the more. I poured that love into our union, making sure he felt it in every way possible as the moment became heated. As he showed me just how unbreakable I now was.

And when we were finished, our bodies humming with contentment and the bed beneath us thoroughly destroyed, I proved my love one more time by whispering, "Yes."

"Yes, what?" he whispered back, brushing a kiss to my brow.

"Yes, Everett. I'll marry you."

CHAPTER 36

ADALYN

It was almost dawn when we arrived back at the castle.

Noah had portalled back a few hours ago, but Everett had wanted me to adjust a little bit more to the transition before we headed back. Not surprisingly, the Faircrofts hadn't returned to the house, so we'd used the alone time to answer each other's many questions. We'd stayed on my broken bed for hours, resting in each other's arms while I told Everett *everything*.

Each word spoken was another weight off my shoulders, a reminder that I was free. Free of thrall. Free of the pactums. Free of my father's blood debt. And, most importantly, free of the Faircrofts.

We had no idea where they'd slinked off to, but at the moment, I didn't care. I was free of them at long last. Free to go where I pleased. Mistress no longer owned me. She was no longer my *mistress*. I could call her whatever I wanted now. She couldn't stop me. Couldn't control me.

She seemed so small now. Small and helpless.

I was no longer the fragile creature stuck in a dangerous world. *She* was.

"We'll get them. They can't hide forever," Everett had assured me as we'd driven off in the Aston Martin, leaving the place that had witnessed the end of my old life and the start of my new one. I'd left it behind without a backward glance, taking nothing with me but the clothes on my back, my familiar, and my soulmate.

The only things I needed for my new beginning.

"You sure I won't burn when the sun rises?" I asked Everett as he pulled into the circular drive at the castle. There were a few cars still parked there, but most of them were gone now. Some of my tension eased at the sight, and I allowed myself to hope that most of the Venturi had survived the fight. They weren't completely innocent in all this, but they hadn't *wanted* this either, something I could understand.

Once he became king, I didn't know how forgiving Everett would be toward the males who'd treated me like a blood whore, but knowing that I would soon be their *queen* went a long way toward repairing the damage they'd caused.

"You're a vampire witch *hybrid*, Adalyn," Everett answered me before killing the ignition. "None of the normal rules apply to you. You're basically a Venturi with magical powers. Nothing about you is fragile anymore, even if you still look like a porcelain doll."

I snorted. "A doll? Come on. I'm not *that* fragile-looking."

He threw me a crooked grin. "You're practically a waif, baby girl."

I scowled at him. "Take that back. I'm not a homeless child."

With a laugh, he opened his car door and hopped out. "You can't deny that you currently look like a street urchin. Kind of like the orphan girl in *Annie*."

I glanced down at my dress, now hopelessly ripped and soiled. Then scrambled out after him and shot back, "Who does that make *you*, then? Daddy Warbucks?"

His smile turned wicked. "I *am* kind of robbing the cradle."

Huffing, I placed Pepper on my shoulder before saying, "I'm almost twenty-one, and you don't look much older."

"Girl, just accept it," a voice called, and we glanced up to see several figures standing at the top of the stone stairs. "Our mates are dirty, old men."

Kade barked a laugh. Plucking his wife up with one arm, he twirled her around and sang, "But you *love* that about us. The older and dirtier, the better."

When he stopped twirling her, Isla batted her lashes up at him and cooed, "If you always look like *this*, I don't mind in the least."

His bottom lip poked out. "I knew it. You only like me for my abs."

"And your pecs," she purred, reaching up to pet his chest. "And a few . . . *other* things."

He grinned a mile wide.

"Sure you want to be a part of all this?" Everett muttered to me under his breath. "If you run away screaming, I won't blame you."

Smirking, I shut the door and came around the car to stand beside him. "I'm completely sure. I think your family is great."

"Aww," Kade said, letting go of Isla to descend the stairs with his arms open. "This calls for a hug. You know it has to happen, so don't even try to stop it, Everett. Adalyn is part of this family and needs to be properly welcomed."

Everett released a disgruntled growl, but when Kade reached the bottom and kept coming with those massive arms wide open, he didn't stop him from drawing me into a bear hug.

"Welcome to the family, sweet Adalyn," Kade murmured, dropping a kiss on the top of my head. "I'm so glad you're safe now."

Unexpected tears sprang to my eyes. Overwhelmed by how quickly he'd accepted me despite all the damage I'd caused last night, I squeezed my eyes shut and returned the hug.

After a few moments, Everett grumbled, "Okay, your time is up. Give me back my fiancé."

"She *accepted!*" Isla squealed, clapping her hands.

We were suddenly surrounded by excited voices offering their congratulations. Isla drew me into a hug next, gushing about how cute Pepper was. Loch embraced me after that, and I sensed that he'd forgiven me as well for all that I'd done. I didn't hesitate to hug Kenna next, but when I caught a whiff of her hybrid scent, my new instincts fired off on all cylinders once more.

"It'll get easier. I promise," she said, pulling back to give me a sympathetic smile. "It helps if you focus on your breathing."

"And don't think of your friends as food," Noah added over her shoulder. He threw me a wink but kept his distance, which was a good thing. As a full-blooded warlock, his scent was even harder to resist.

Sensing my struggle, Everett pulled me back against him, and I immediately felt better, using his closeness to distract me from thoughts of blood.

Is this too much for you? he questioned through our bond. *We can leave and come back later. They'll understand.*

I tipped my head back to look up at him. *Thanks, but I'll manage. I'm used to hunger pains.*

His lips thinned. *Well, that ends now. Anytime you need food or blood, you'll have it. I never want to see you suffer again.*

I smiled at him softly. *That's sweet, but you can't protect me from everything, Everett. I'm still going to feel pain sometimes.*

"Not if I can help it," he said, dipping his head to claim my lips. Pepper squeaked in protest and dug her sharp little nails into my shoulder to keep from toppling off.

"They are so cute," Isla whispered with a dreamy sigh.

"Get a room, you two!" Kade hollered.

"Kade," Loch quietly chastised.

"What? It's time for a little payback, Lochie. Your brother's been sneering at our PDA for *years*. He deserves some egging."

As if to spite Kade, Everett cupped the back of my head and plunged his tongue into my mouth. When he thoroughly tasted me like a man possessed, my legs turned to jelly.

"*Get it*, dude. That's what I'm talking about!" Kade crowed with a wolf-whistle.

"I think you missed a spot," Noah joined in, making Kade laugh.

When the kiss ended and Everett straightened with a self-satisfied smirk, I wobbled unsteadily on my feet.

"Not that this new side of Everett isn't exciting, but we need to head inside before the sun burns my wife to a crisp," Kade said, bringing us back to reality.

"Just a few more minutes," Isla protested, still staring at me and Everett with a dreamy grin on her heart-shaped face.

"No can do, shortcake," Kade replied. "I'm not risking your safety."

She yelped as he threw her over his shoulder in one swift move and started for the stairs. "Overprotective brute," she grumbled with an eye roll.

"Don't forget dirty and old."

"And annoyingly bossy and—"

He reached up and smacked her butt. *Hard.* When she burst into a fit of giggles, Noah muttered, "Now *that* I didn't need to see."

"We should head inside too," Loch said to Everett, sliding his arm around Kenna. "Father wants to see you. We have a lot to discuss."

I noticed Silver at Kenna's feet and smiled at the familiar.

She seems nice, Pepper observed, peering over my shoulder at the fox.

She is, I easily replied, remembering how she'd tried to warn me about Heath last night. *I'll introduce you to her soon.*

But not now. Not when I was about to see the king again.

I recalled his warning to me the first time we'd met, how he hoped I didn't prove to be a disappointment. Nearly stabbing his son and controlling the minds of his court probably fell into the "disappointment" category.

Everett tucked me against his side while we moved toward the stairs as a group, making me feel a little better. But as we approached the spot where my broken mortal body had died, memories of the pain I'd endured flitted through my mind. The spot was empty now, all traces of the horrific event washed away by last night's rain. Even Heath's headless body was gone.

"We burned it," Loch said, noticing where my attention had strayed. "We burned most of the other rogues as well. Only a few escaped."

Everett pulled me closer as if to comfort me. "Any news on the Faircrofts?"

"Not yet, but it's only a matter of time. They'll reach out to their contacts, and when they do, we'll be ready."

"What do you mean?" I questioned Loch, tearing my gaze off the patch of ground to study his profile. "Did you capture some of the rogues?"

"No. They wouldn't surrender, so we didn't spare them. But the ex-rogue, Rocky, has been very helpful."

My eyes widened. "Rocky? He's *here?*"

"Yes. He's been telling us everything he knows. Apparently, he overheard a lot of conversations between Deloris Faircroft and her business partner, Heath Clancy. They were a part of the original rogue revolution six years ago and have been planning this coup ever since. But I'm guessing you already knew that."

"Yes," I replied, ducking my head.

"We don't blame you, Adalyn," Kenna gently said. "I was once taken from my family and used for my abilities too. The important thing is that you learned for yourself what to believe in. You rejected others' definition of you and became your own person. You chose to fight back, despite the personal cost. Your courage saved many Venturi lives last night."

I tried to give her a smile but couldn't quite manage it. Something was still weighing on me, something that would no doubt haunt me until I resolved it. Until I *faced* it.

"My father . . ." I haltingly began. "He was an elder and chose to fight against the royal family in the battle six years ago. I know now that he was misinformed, that you aren't the monsters we were raised to despise. At least, not anymore. But I never found out who killed him. Mistress—I mean, Madame Faircroft—told me that a Venturi did it. Knowing that it could have been one of the vampires I helped save last night, or one of *you*, is still eating me up inside. I need to know who did it. Not to avenge my father's death. I don't want that anymore. But . . . I need closure."

As we reached the top of the stairs, Everett slowed. Studying his brother thoughtfully, he finally said, "You know something."

"I do," Loch replied. "As I said, the ex-rogue told us everything, including who killed Adalyn's father that night."

My heart stopped. *Time* stopped.

Struggling to breathe, I whispered, "Who? Who killed him?"

He paused to face me, his expression solemn. "Are you sure you want to know? Once you do, there's no undoing it."

"Yes. I want to know. I *need* to."

As he continued to stare at me, my heart started to pound. Harder and harder, until I thought it would burst from my chest. He shared a quick look with his brother, but when Everett only nodded, he turned back to me and revealed the truth.

A truth that changed *everything*.

"It was Deloris. Deloris Faircroft killed your father."

CHAPTER 37

ADALYN

Never in my life had I felt this used, this *duped*.

Even when rich, privileged males had used my body for their pleasure night after night, I'd never felt this taken advantage of.

She'd lied to me. She'd poisoned my mind against the Venturi in order to control me. To gain my empathy. To mold me into her *weapon*.

As we entered the castle, I spotted three males: King Ambrose, the older warlock who I now knew was Isla's father, and Rocky. They'd been talking but had paused to face us as we entered the massive foyer. The fallen guards from last night had been removed, and I waited for guilt to surface again. It didn't. I was too busy feeling *betrayed*.

My first instinct was to march up to Rocky and start grilling him. Out of everyone here, he knew the most about Madame Faircroft's secret dealings. He must know of a few places where she could be hiding.

I managed to curb the instinct, though, knowing that I wasn't completely in the clear. Everett tensed beside me, and I knew he was thinking the same thing.

"Father . . ." he began, nudging me a little behind him as he approached the king. *Shielding* me. "She didn't—"

"No," I interrupted and grabbed his arm to stop him. When he turned slightly to look at me, I whispered, "I need to take responsibility for what happened. I'm not afraid."

He opened his mouth as if to argue, but when my gaze held steady, he replied through our bond, *I know you're not. You're strong, capable, and fearless, all traits that will make you a great queen.*

I couldn't help but smile at him. As I stood on tiptoe to kiss his cheek, he turned his head at the last second and kissed me full on the mouth. The move was definitely intentional, an unspoken albeit loud message directed at his father.

The king cleared his throat, and I broke the kiss. Squeezing Everett's arm reassuringly, I plucked Pepper off my shoulder and placed her in his hand.

She started to protest, and I quickly said, *Please, Pep. I got us into this mess, and it's my job to make it right.*

She twitched her whiskers in agitation before replying, *Fine. But be careful.*

I gave her a small smile. *Always am.*

As I turned to approach the king alone, Everett didn't stop me. I could feel his unease, though. I might not be a fragile little mortal anymore, but I'd still brought a war to the king's doorstep. I'd infiltrated his home like a slithering snake and poisoned the minds of some of his most loyal subjects. I'd almost murdered the heir to his throne and started a revolution.

I'd been dangerous even as a mortal witch. As an immortal hybrid, I was doubly so, and the king knew it.

His attention was solely on me now, on the female who'd almost destroyed his family. A few yards away, I stopped and deeply curtsied before him, murmuring, "My king."

And he was. I was half vampire now, which meant that I belonged to his kingdom. This dangerous world was mine now, and I wouldn't run away from whatever punishment their ruler thought I deserved.

As I straightened, he moved toward me on silent feet. Everett stayed where he was, but I could feel his tension like a tight ball in my chest. It made it hard to focus. To remain calm. Still, I stood tall before the king. When he reached up to grasp my chin, I didn't so much as flinch.

His deep red irises bored into mine, studying me for several long moments before he smoothly remarked, "You've been turned into a hybrid, I see. I smell the magic on you. And my son. You fed on him."

"Yes, my king," I replied.

He tilted his head to the side. "You've also claimed him. I can scent your mark on him even from here."

My eyes widened. "Oh. I didn't realize I had. But, yes, I thoroughly bit him."

"Among other things," I heard Kade snicker. Great. Everyone was watching to see what King Ambrose would do to me. Which didn't exactly help me focus.

The king finally dropped my chin, only to pick up my hand next. I stopped breathing when I saw what had caught his attention. Sweeping his thumb over the gold and ruby ring on my ring finger, he murmured, "So, you've accepted my son's proposal of marriage."

"I have," I replied, then threw caution to the wind and blurted, "I love him. I love him very much."

He slowly raised his eyes to mine, eyes that were now glittering with unshed tears. "Good," he whispered, his voice slightly trembling. "That's all I needed to hear."

Just like that, he let go of my hand and stepped back.

I gaped at him in shock. "But . . . but what about last night? What about all the damage I caused? My *betrayal?* I deserve to be punished for what I did. You're my king now, and I committed treason against you."

He shrugged. "If my son has forgiven you, then so have I. We've all made our fair share of mistakes and put this kingdom in danger. At the end of the day, there are only two things I truly care about: my family's safety and their happiness. You kept them safe when it mattered most, and I can see that you make Everett happy, something I haven't seen in a very long time.

"I'm sorry for the horrors you've endured at the hands of vampires," he went on, "but I'm not sorry that fate brought you into our world. I've delayed passing the reins of this kingdom over to my son, sensing that something vital was missing from his life. And that something was you. He needed a strong female worthy of ruling by his side, and I'm thrilled to say, that's exactly what you are."

My own eyes welled with tears, and he smiled at me softly. For the first time, I didn't see him as a powerful vampire king but as a caring father. Not wanting to hide how that made me feel, I let a tear slip free.

"Besides," he added, his tone lightening, "I'm no longer your king. I've officially retired, and the first thing I'm going to do once you and my son have publicly been sworn in is take a long overdue vacation with all fourteen of my wives."

A surprised laugh burst from me, and he joined in, his face alight with amusement. Soon, we were *all* laughing, even quiet Rocky. Arms came around me again, and I gratefully leaned against Everett, his relief mingling with mine.

For the next several hours, we worked as a unit to finish cleaning up the mess the rogues had made. Most of the bodies had already been carried outside to be burned, but there was still lots of carnage left over from the battle. Instead of making the traumatized maids take care of it, we gave them the day off and did it ourselves. Which was a good thing for me, since my new instincts were urging me to take a bite out of them.

King Ambrose had already interrogated the Venturi and had allowed most of them to leave. Only a few were still struggling with the false thoughts I'd planted inside their minds and had been locked in the castle dungeons until their minds were their own once more.

As evening fast approached, Everett and I retreated to his bedroom for a much-needed shower and clothing change. We'd just stepped into the shower together when Loch burst into the bathroom without knocking.

Everett swiftly covered my naked body with his and barked, "Get out, Lochlan."

Loch ignored the command to urgently say, "Rocky got a call. We found her. We know where Deloris Faircroft is."

At the news, Everett's annoyance switched to anticipation, an anticipation that I equally shared.

It was almost over. The dark nightmare that had been my life for the past six years was coming to an end.

All I needed to do was face this last piece. This last terrible piece that I was still holding on to. That kept me from fully moving on.

I'm coming, I whispered, the words eagerly dancing through my mind. *I'm coming for you, my mistress.*

The air was deathly still.

I'd never seen Dreamscape Lounge so lifeless. So devoid of the energy that had sapped so much from me over the years.

There was no music pulsing through my veins. No blinding lights demanding I perform. No bodies writhing on the dance floor and behind the curtained alcoves.

All was silent, holding its breath in anticipation. But, for once, the anticipation wasn't for me.

I was no longer the fragile prey. I was the powerful huntress silently stalking the halls in *search* of my prey.

She was here. With my newly heightened senses, I could hear her thundering heartbeats. A thrill shivered through me, the reaction wholly predator.

My companions were equally as silent, allowing me to take the lead. We'd already planned in advance how this would play out. Noah, his dad, and a few SCA operatives they'd called in had secured the front and back exits, while the rest of us were to confront the Faircrofts head on. If they scattered, we outnumbered them by far.

The numbers were overkill, but it felt good. It felt good to be the one in control for once. To be surrounded by allies instead of utterly alone.

At first, I'd been tempted to face the Faircrofts by myself. When they'd foolishly contacted Rocky to see how their coup had panned out, I'd wanted nothing more than to rush in and seek my revenge.

The club. They'd hidden out in the *club*.

It was too perfect. Too ironically twisted. They were *trapped* just like I had been trapped. Stuck in a dangerous world and unable to leave. The sun wouldn't set for another half hour, which meant that they were going nowhere. Not unless they wanted to burn to ash.

Knowing that they were helpless to flee, my new instincts were practically *singing*. But it was Everett who brought me back to myself, who reminded me that seeking revenge had consequences. Whatever happened next, I would have to live with the outcome. We'd both seen how devastating the aftermath of revenge could be. This was our chance to start fresh, to become the kind of leaders we hoped our kingdom would follow.

As much as I wanted to hunt down and destroy the cruel family that had made my life hell all these years, I let the need for vengeance go. This was about justice. About making things right. Treating the Faircrofts in the same manner they had treated me wouldn't give me closure.

It would only make me a monster.

They already knew we were coming, and that was reward enough. In their arrogance, they hadn't bothered to plan for this outcome. An outcome where they landed on the bottom. Their coup had failed, and it was time for them to face their actions.

Although Isla was also a Feltore, she'd insisted we let her tag along. Every inch of her skin was carefully covered up, even her face. She'd worn dark sunglasses and had carried an umbrella, but had removed them when we'd entered the club. Kade, Loch, and Kenna were also with us, along with Silver and Pepper. I'd wanted Pepper to remain in Everett's room back at the castle, but she'd insisted that she needed closure too.

I was pretty sure she just wanted to see the Faircroft's faces when they realized what had happened to me. I couldn't blame her, though. I was looking forward to that myself.

We soon realized the Faircrofts weren't on the ground floor, and our group silently split up. Loch, Kenna, and Silver took one stairwell, while Kade and Isla took the other. Everett and I headed straight for the elevators, my little mouse familiar perched on my shoulder. Without even thinking, I punched the button for the third floor, fairly certain I knew *exactly* where my ex-mistress and her two daughters were hiding.

I think you might be more excited about this than I am, I told Pepper as we ascended.

Pshh, I'm just excited to be out of that dirty basement, she replied.

I smirked. *Admit it. You want to see the Faircrofts get squished.*

She sniffed as if offended. *Why, Adalyn, I would never be that petty. Inside this cute furry body is an angelic being. We don't condone the act of squishing.*

I rolled my eyes.

Everett caught the movement and reached over to lace his fingers through mine. *You okay?*

I'm great, I easily replied, even as the elevator stopped and the doors slid open. Even as I stepped onto the third floor and headed for the place that had stolen so much from me. Our companions emerged from their stairwells, and no one spoke a word as we strode toward our destination with purpose. The closer we got, the louder Madame Faircroft's heartbeats became.

I knew they were hers. Knew she was *terrified.* As terrified as I had been while under her thumb.

When I stopped outside the room where they were hiding, memories threatened to pull me under, dragging me into darkness once more.

Three years. Three years of abuse lived within those walls.

The air grew thin, suffocating. The need to hide, to shield myself behind a mask trembled through me.

I couldn't go in there. I couldn't go back to that world of pretend.

But before the sucking darkness could claim me, Everett's family crowded in close. *My* family. They surrounded me with their support, their *love,* giving me the strength to shove the darkness away. To rise up and face the root of my nightmares.

As the memories faded, I stood tall once more, squeezing Everett's hand before letting go. I raised my fist to knock on the door, then froze, a wicked grin curling my lips.

Hold on, I said to Pepper, then raised my foot to kick the door in. As the metal gave under the impact, violently flying open to bang against the wall, Everett's approval pulsed through our bond.

That was hot, he purred, making my grin stretch a mile wide.

Twin screeches of alarm reached my ears, and I wiped the grin from my face. As I entered the room, my expression was calm. Poised. *Queenly*. But it wasn't a mask. I'd come to deliver justice as a queen would to her wayward subjects, and that's exactly what the Faircrofts saw when I stepped into the space that had once been my personal hell.

"I'm surprised you chose this room. Feeling nostalgic?" I said by way of greeting. There was a light on in the kitchen, but the rest of the space was cast in shadow, the curtains carefully drawn over the living room window. Madame Faircroft, Georgina, and Octavia were standing in front of the couch as if they'd jumped up at my theatrical entrance. They were still wearing their ball gowns from last night, but their masks were long gone, revealing their terrified faces.

At the sight of me, Madame Faircroft's expression soured. "*You*," she hissed, taking me in from head to toe. "What are *you* doing here? How are you not *dead?*"

I took another step inside, noting the bloodstain embedded in the carpet where Councilman Torres had fallen. The air was still heavy with lavender, incense, and old blood, making my stomach turn. Beyond the doorway of the bedroom, I could make out the remains of my destroyed bed.

Instead of answering her, I said, "I know what you did. I know that you lied to me from the start about my dad. Venturi didn't kill him. *You* did."

She waved her hand dismissively. "An eye for an eye, Adalyn. He took my husband's life, so I took his. In all the chaos, it wasn't hard to catch him unaware. You arrived shortly after that, and I took advantage of a perfect opportunity. One could even call what

343

happened fate."

At how cavalier she sounded, anger heated my blood. Balling my hands into fists, I inhaled a few calming breaths before replying, "When I found out that you killed him, I wanted to kill you with my own two hands. All I could think about was how amazing it would feel to destroy your life as you had destroyed mine. But I don't want to be like you, Deloris. I don't want to be consumed by hatred and vengeance."

Shock contorted her features, and she snapped, "How *dare* you call me anything but Mistress, you little *brat*. How *dare* you betray me like this, after all I've done for you."

"All you've *done* for me?" I roared, so loudly that all three of them flinched. "All you've done is use and abuse me. You treated me like trash and threw me away when you no longer needed me. I was a *child*, and you stole my innocence. You turned me into a *weapon*. You manipulated me into thinking the Venturi were the enemy, when the only one I should have been focused on was *you*."

"Me? *I'm* the victim here, Adalyn, not you!" she shrieked, taking a step toward me. "I've been *stuck* like this for decades, living in perpetual darkness while the Venturi are allowed to walk in the sunlight without consequence. It's not *fair*. This wasn't the life I was promised. Richard said we would live happily ever after. He said we would *thrive*, that the world would be ours. But he was wrong. We've been *miserable* as vampires. I shouldn't have let him turn us, and I hate him for leaving us to face this awful existence *alone*."

"Mother," Georgina gasped, staring at her mother in shock.

"Shut up, Georgina!" Deloris barked, her eyes flashing red as she whirled on her eldest daughter. "You and your sister have been *useless*. You've done nothing to improve our status, and I'm sick to death of your *whining*."

Georgina's chin began to quiver. She stared at her seething mother, then suddenly lunged at her with a feral scream. The two females violently clashed, knocking Octavia down as they slapped and clawed at each other. They tore each other's dresses to shreds, yanking and ripping out hair until I could see their bloody scalps. As they screamed at each other, Octavia sat on the floor and whimpered like a kicked puppy.

"*Enough!*" a male voice thundered, instantly shutting the Faircrofts up. Still gripping handfuls of each other's hair, Deloris and Georgina froze as Everett came to stand beside me and commanded, "Cease this madness immediately. This is no way to behave in front of your future king and queen."

Their faces paled.

"Queen? What queen?" Octavia questioned, looking bewildered. "We've never had a queen before."

"It's her," Georgina whispered, staring at me in horror. "It's always *her*. Mother, do something. Enforce the pactum. *Kill* her. You can't let the troll become our queen. Mother? *Mother!*"

Ignoring Georgina's hysteria, I locked eyes with my ex-mistress and said, "Haven't you heard? The little witch you trapped has become a vampire." Lifting my hand, I willed my new black claws to emerge. "Well, not just *any* vampire. A vampire witch hybrid." Cerulean blue magic danced on the tips of my claws like candle flames. "Since I'm basically a Venturi now, I doubt there will be many complaints when I'm crowned queen."

Her expression morphed from shock, to disbelief, to blinding *rage*.

She didn't hide it. She openly let me see her hatred, and I didn't flinch. Didn't even blink.

"Impossible," she spat, violently trembling from head to toe.

"You're just an orphan. An indentured servant. A blood whore. You're nothing. *Nothing!*"

"Kade, arrest Madame Faircroft for treason," I quietly ordered, finally allowing myself a small smile.

"Gladly," Kade replied and stepped forward.

Madame Faircroft's eyes practically bugged out of her head.

"Enjoy your last few moments of freedom, *Mistress*," I said. "Treason against the crown is a lifelong sentence in a high-security SCA holding cell."

As Kade approached her, she froze like a terrified rabbit about to be eaten. In the next second, she bolted. Not toward us but away. So fast that no one reacted in time. Without a moment's hesitation, she threw herself at the curtained window and crashed through. Georgina and Octavia screamed as their mother disappeared over the edge, as the evening sun sliced through the broken window and hit their exposed skin.

In a flash, I dragged them out of harm's way, then raced to the window—just in time to see Madame Faircroft hit the ground and burst into flames. A wail rose up from the fiery inferno of flesh, but it didn't last long. Within seconds, she was nothing but a smoldering pile of ash.

I waited for the guilt to hit, but it never came.

She'd chosen her fate, just like I'd chosen mine. I'd finished what I came to do, and I could move on now. Could finally *live*.

Pepper was still valiantly clinging to my shoulder as I turned and headed back across the room. Everett opened his arms to me, and I stepped into them with a relieved sigh.

While Loch and Kade secured the Faircroft sisters with cuffs specially designed for vampires, Georgina threw me a scathing glare, her tear-stained face streaked with mascara. "This is all *your* fault."

"Yes, it is," I replied. "I saved you from sharing the same fate as your selfish mother who didn't think twice about abandoning you. You're welcome."

She scrunched her face up in an ugly grimace before looking away.

Octavia stared at me rather solemnly, then quietly asked, "Will they starve us?"

Shockingly, I felt a pang of sympathy for her then. "No, I'll make sure the SCA doesn't starve you," I told her. "And with a lot of hard work and good behavior, you might even earn yourself a few privileges."

Georgina let out a loud wail, but Octavia was surprisingly quiet. Maybe there was hope for her yet. It was never too late to turn your life around.

As Loch and Kade led them from the room, exhaustion finally caught up to me. The moment I sagged in Everett's arms, he bent and scooped me up. I didn't protest, letting my head fall against his shoulder as he carried me from the room after the others.

"I can't believe it's finally over," I murmured, holding a hand up so Pepper could hop onto my palm.

"Oh, this is just the beginning," Everett replied, his steps unwavering as he strode down the hall.

I blinked up at him. "What do you mean?"

"Ruling this kingdom won't be easy. There will be many challenges in our future. Challenges that threaten to tear apart everything we've accomplished today."

Despite his words, I smiled at him.

"Yes," I agreed, "but we have forever together. What are a few measly challenges compared to that?"

He returned my smile with a brilliant one of his own. "You're right, baby girl. What are a few challenges when we have forever?"

EPILOGUE

ADALYN

I stirred awake as a featherlight kiss brushed the nape of my neck.

The lips were warm and soft, slowly trailing down the length of my spine. As the sheet over my naked body vanished so the lips could move farther south, I grinned into my pillow.

"Morning, dearest wife," the owner of those luscious lips murmured, placing a kiss inside one of the dimples on my lower back.

"Morning, dearest husband," I sleepily cooed, then giggled when he swirled his tongue around the dimple. He moved farther down, his kisses turning into tiny nips. As he peppered them over my backside, I started to squirm, eager for more.

"Patience," he rumbled and gripped my thighs to still my movements. "We have all the time in the world, baby girl. There's no need to rush."

I twisted in his grip, exposing my upper half to him so I could bat my lashes and purr, "On the contrary, my prince. Today marks the end of our honeymoon. Duty is calling, but I desperately need a few orgasms first. So chop-chop."

He skated his eyes over my bare breasts in appreciation before replying, "Who says the honeymoon has to end?"

"Oh, just your entire kingdom who expects to see you sworn in as their new king this evening."

"*Our* kingdom," he corrected. "And I'm not cutting our honeymoon short just because we're being crowned king and queen today. As soon as the coronation is over, I'm carrying you up to our bedroom and giving you all the orgasms you desire. But right now, I want to worship your body. *Slowly.* So turn around and stop squirming."

More than a little turned on by his speech, I smirked and did as he instructed. "Whatever you say, solem—"

My words ended in a strangled gasp as I felt his fangs sink into my backside. Ecstasy immediately pulsed through me, and I moaned into my pillow. We'd only been married for a week, but I already knew that Everett loved to use his mouth on me. Any chance he could get, he'd find a secluded spot to kiss or bite me.

Despite how possessive he was, he even allowed others to witness his affection for me, openly kissing and touching me in front of family members, the court, and pretty much anyone else who visited the castle.

We'd decided to remain on Sanctum Isle for our honeymoon, knowing that it was important for our future subjects to see us before the coronation. Word had spread of the failed coup attempt, and we'd spent the past few weeks assuring the kingdom that all was well with the royal family.

During the day, we took time to meet with the council and nobles, including the ones that had been under my influence. Everett still struggled to keep his temper in check around them, but whenever he became short with the males I'd once slept with, I used our bond to send him calming thoughts. That and I sat in his lap, which helped ease his possessiveness.

But we didn't just meet to repair the mental and emotional damage that had been caused. Although we didn't condone what the rogues had done, there was a need for change. Life as a vampire was markedly easier for the Venturi, and they'd taken their privilege for granted. It was time to help the Feltore, to allow them a louder voice. They'd been excluded for far too long, seen as weaker and lesser, when what they really needed was our protection.

Change would take time, but at least we were taking that first step toward making a difference.

News of King Ambrose's abdication had come as a shock to most of the kingdom, but when we'd invited pretty much everyone to attend our coronation—no matter their station—it had gone a long way toward smoothing ruffled feathers.

Our wedding, on the other hand, had been a simple affair. Only family had attended, and the perfect day had ended with the king gifting his eldest son and new daughter-in-law a honeymoon cottage, located on a secluded stretch of beach not far from the castle. We'd stayed there every night for the past week, enjoying the alone time, getting to know each other better, and exploring each other in ways that made even *me* blush.

I'd been bitten more times than I could count in places I didn't even know could be bitten. Knowing that I could no longer easily break had made Everett ravenous, and he'd spent the past several days showing me how to make love as a vampire.

It was addicting. Freeing. Everything I could crave and more.

Knowing that it wouldn't have to end, that Everett had every intention of keeping our relationship a priority when he became king, made my heart flutter happily.

I would miss this cottage, though. Miss how quiet and peaceful it was. While we'd been away from the castle, Everett had arranged for his bedroom to be remodeled. He'd wanted the space to feel like ours, so we'd ordered all new furniture together, adding in a mix of both our personalities. There was even a spot in the corner for me to practice my dancing, which I was super excited about.

Pepper had opted to stay at the castle while we honeymooned, not interested in hearing our "loud humping noises," as she put it. She and Silver had been enjoying each other's company despite the fact that they were technically prey and predator, and I often saw them playing together in the halls.

Wanting to make the most of our last morning at the cottage, I sank into the mattress and gave myself over to the intimate moment. Everett still had his fangs deep in my flesh, and as he fed on me, he spread my thighs and touched my clit. I moaned into the pillow again, gripping it tightly while bliss curled through my insides. He played with the sensitive nub for a few minutes, effectively turning me into a quivering mess, then lazily slid a finger inside me.

"Everett," I panted, lifting my head off the pillow as my pleasure intensified.

Don't you dare orgasm. I'm not done with you yet, he rumbled through our bond, making me laugh.

"I might not . . . be able to help it," I breathlessly said, all but strangling the pillow as he curled the finger and hit a particularly sensitive spot. "Especially . . . when you do *that*."

Oh, that? he chuckled quietly. *That was nothing.*

Inserting a second finger, he plunged them both deeply inside me, making my walls spasm. As he began to pump them in and out, it became harder not to squirm, to chase after my pleasure. It just felt so *good*.

Clearly having heard my thoughts, Everett chuckled again and said, *Squirm, and I'll stop.*

"Bastard," I spat, but the word came out as a whimper.

I might not be patient about many things, baby girl, but I know how to prolong an orgasm.

"I know you do, and it's annoying."

You love it. Admit it.

"Nev—AH!" I cried, bucking against his fingers as he used his other hand to rub my clit. The added pleasure made it nearly impossible to hold still, and I began to shake like a leaf from the effort. "Please don't stop, please don't stop."

You're doing so good, dearest wife, he purred, using praise to further torment me. *And I haven't even given you my venom yet.*

My eyes popped open. "Everett, don't—"

Venom streaked through my veins like lightning, and I completely lost it. Screaming at the top of my lungs, I ripped my pillow in half as an orgasm shot me sky high. Feathers exploded into the air, adding to the epic moment. I was still in the throes of ecstasy when he withdrew his fangs and fingers, only to flip me over and bury his head between my thighs.

As his tongue stroked my center, I nearly lost it again. But my devilishly handsome mate was *cruel.* He slowed his movements, coaxing me back down until my pleasure was a low hum. He prolonged the torture for several moments, taking his sweet time tasting me. Then sucked me deeply into his mouth. My spine bowed off the bed, my breath coming in desperate pants as he started to nibble on the sensitive flesh.

"Everett, I can't . . . I can't . . ."

He bit down, and another orgasm exploded through me. I screamed again, unable to contain the euphoria pulsing from me. I thought he would stop then, but I should have known better. He wrung another orgasm from me. Then another and another, as if his goal was to see how long I could endure the pleasurable assault.

As a mortal, my body would have given out after only a few orgasms. But as an immortal hybrid, my endurance was impressive. After the dozenth orgasm, I stopped keeping count, my only thought on riding out this blissful high for as long as possible.

Everett continued to tirelessly worship my body, filling me up so completely that I could barely stand it. Needing to be close to him in a way I only wanted to experience with my soulmate, I finally breathed, "I need you."

He immediately knew what I meant and stopped what he was doing to crawl up my body. The second he was positioned between my thighs, I curled my legs around him and thrust my hips up. We both moaned as his hardened length slid inside me, our eyes still open so we could watch each other.

When he began to thrust, I stared into his pale green eyes, marveling for the umpteenth time at how beautiful they were. I reached up to cup his cheek, and he leaned into my hand, his gaze remaining on my face as we made love. Even when we were teetering on the edge of release, his eyes stayed locked on mine. And when we fell over the edge together, those beautiful eyes filled with undeniable love.

A love so deep and consuming that tears blurred my vision.

"What is it?" he said, his breathing still ragged as he came down from the high.

Hesitating for a moment, I replied, "I had a dream. A premonition, actually."

He blinked in surprise. "A good one, I hope."

I smiled, but it slightly wobbled. "Yeah. A great one. I saw a brief glimpse into our future, and . . . and we're going to be okay, Everett. We're going to thrive as the new king and queen."

Relief pulsed through our bond. Resting his forehead on mine, he whispered, "Thank God. That's just what I needed to hear today."

"That's not all, though," I started to say, but was interrupted by a sharp thudding noise.

"Unca Evy!"

"Auntie Ada!"

As the twins continued to excitedly pound on the front door of our cottage with their tiny hybrid fists, we started to laugh.

"Hello?" a male voice called, and we stopped laughing. "The door was unlocked. Are you two decent?"

"Of course they're not decent, Lochie. They're on their *honeymoon*. When Isla and I first got married, we could barely keep our clothes on."

"You still can't keep your clothes on," we heard Loch mutter.

Kade guffawed. "True. When it's just me and Isla at the lakehouse, we don't even bother with clothing. You and Kenna should try it sometime. It's liberating."

"What? Walk naked around the castle?"

"Why not? I'm totally fine if we start a nudist colony."

Loch snorted. "Not surprised, but it's not happening. Neither is that foursome you've been pining after."

Kade roared with laughter, and my eyes widened.

"Don't ask," Everett muttered, a faint smirk still on his lips as he lifted off me. At the loss of his warmth—and dick—I stuck my bottom lip out. Chuckling quietly, he bent to whisper against my mouth, "Later."

Somewhat appeased, I watched him leave the bed and search for his pants, which had somehow landed on a lampshade. Before he could put them on, the door to our bedroom started to rattle. With a yelp, I scrambled to cover myself, flinging a blast of magic at the door to keep it shut.

"Evy! Ada!"

As I quickly wrapped a bedsheet around myself, Everett chuckled again and pulled on his pants so he could let the twins in. They burst inside the moment the door was open, buzzing around their uncle until he swooped down and picked them both up.

"No magic," he cautioned them, grunting when Zoey placed a hand on his bare chest.

As her hand glowed red, I flicked my fingers, using my own magic to break the connection. Zoey clapped her hands, oblivious to the fact that I'd stopped her from draining the life out of her uncle. Both she and her brother would be forces to be reckoned with someday. They were already a handful, but I still smiled and watched them use their toddler language skills to communicate with Everett.

Catching my stare, he smiled back, and my heart melted.

"Sorry for the intrusion. Nico and Zoey were restless, so we let them play outside and somehow ended up here," Loch said, poking his head around the door. When he spotted me on the bed, his head vanished.

"Good call, brother," Everett growled, but he was still smiling.

"Married life definitely suits you, man," Kade remarked, wise enough to remain in the hallway with Loch. "You're hardly ever grumpy anymore, even when you sound grumpy. Hopefully you stopped having sex long enough to get a little sleep last night, though. It's your big day."

"*Our* big day," Everett corrected, sliding me another smile. "And our sex life is none of your business."

"You're no fun. Loch tells me about his."

"I do not."

"Well, you should. I could give you a few pointers."

"I don't need pointers."

"You sure about that? You and Kenna have been married for over six years now. Maybe it's time to spice things up a bit."

"Things are still plenty spicy between us."

"Yeah, but how many times do you have sex? Once a week?"

"Of course not. We— Kade, I know what you're doing. It's not going to work."

"Ah, c'mon, Lochie. It's *me*. Share the love with your drothen. How many times, then? Twice? Three times?"

I smothered a laugh as Everett rolled his eyes and shut the door. Kade and Loch continued to bicker in the hallway, a familiar and welcome sound. I'd only been a part of Everett's family for a month, but I was already in love with their dynamic. They deeply cared for each other and always had each other's backs. Even when they disagreed, they always managed to come together at the end of the day.

Knowing that they were waiting for me to get dressed, I scooted off the bed and quickly found my clothing. My coronation gown was in our bedroom at the castle, so we planned to get ready there. Kenna and Isla had offered to help me with my makeup and hair, and although I was used to doing it myself, I'd accepted. They'd so readily included me in their sacred friendship circle, and I couldn't be more grateful.

When I was dressed, we left the cottage as a group, chatting and laughing as we tried to keep the two daredevil toddlers from running off. Eventually, Loch and Everett picked them up and shot toward the castle at vampire speed, to the delight of the twins.

"You look different this morning," Kade remarked, slinging an arm over my shoulders as we followed at a more sedate pace. "You seem . . . calmer. At peace."

I shrugged and gave him a little smile. "I just know that everything is going to work out."

"Oh? Did you have one of your visions?"

My smile widened. "Maybe."

He barked a laugh. "Fine. Keep your Oracle secrets. I'll figure them out soon enough. My wife is a private investigator, after all."

I returned his laugh but didn't respond.

After a moment of companionable silence, he said more seriously, "He's really lucky, you know. You're exactly what Everett needed. You bring out the best in him."

I blinked sudden tears from my eyes. "Thanks, Kade. I'm really lucky too. You've all been so good to me."

"We're happy to have you," he replied, pulling me in for a quick hug. "But we'd better catch up before Everett thinks I'm questioning you about your sex life."

I snorted. "I lost count."

He glanced down at me in confusion.

"I lost count of how many times we had sex this week. If you need some pointers, let me know."

When I winked at him, his mouth slowly fell open.

"Holy mother of Moses," he whispered. "You're going to be the best queen ever."

Laughing, I took off at vampire speed. "Race you back!"

When we reached the castle a couple minutes later, we found it alive with preparations. Everywhere we looked, maids were bustling about with large bouquets of red roses balanced in their arms. The floral scent mixed with human blood was heady, and I paused to breathe in the delicious concoction.

Quiet laughter rumbled from Everett.

He opened his mouth to comment, but a chipper feminine voice beat him to it. "I know, it smells *divine* in here. I already had breakfast but might need a snack soon."

Kade perked up at that. "I'm available."

Isla rolled her eyes at him. "An *on-the-go* snack. We girls have a whole day of pampering ahead of us. How about you boys make yourselves useful and send up some drinks for us?"

"I can send them up myself," Kade replied, then added with a sly smirk, "Clothed or unclothed."

"Kade," Kenna chastised, following her best friend into the foyer. "I already caught you naked in the hallways once. I don't need to see that again."

Kade snickered. "Your face was *so* red, little Kenna. It was like you'd never seen a dick before."

"*Kade*," Loch said, more forcefully. "My children are in the room."

"What? Afraid their newest word is going to be *dick?*"

"Dip!" Zoey chirped, and several groans filled the air. "Dip, dip, dip!"

When a noise that sounded a lot like muffled laughter came from Everett, Kade whirled to point at him. "Aha! Even Mr. Grump thinks it's funny."

Sidling up to her husband, Isla placed a hand on his chest and cooed, "Behave, and I'll snack on you after the coronation."

His blue eyes glittered brightly. "All night?"

"All night."

Grinning like a fiend, he swooped down to kiss her soundly, then lifted his head to mouth at Loch, "*Every. Single. Day.*"

With a shake of his head, Loch passed Nico over to Everett and purposefully strode across the room. In a blink, he grabbed Kenna and dipped her over backward. Her soft gasp was quickly smothered by an open-mouthed kiss, one filled with passion and heat. He gripped her tightly, letting one of his hands brazenly roam over her curves.

When a little whimper escaped her, he abruptly broke the kiss to say, "We'll be right back."

Kade whooped as Loch picked up his mate and hurried from the foyer, his destination more than obvious. "How many times?" he called after them.

"Every single day," Loch called back, and Kade whooped even louder.

After that little delay in our plans, I spent a relaxing morning and afternoon with Isla and Kenna. Pepper and Silver joined us for a little while, begrudgingly allowing us to paint their claws before scampering off again. By the time evening rolled around, I was primped and polished to perfection. But I didn't mind for once. I wasn't putting on a fake persona this time. I wasn't trying to look charming or mysterious or alluring. I wasn't trying to be anyone but myself.

Tonight, I was simply Adalyn, the vampire witch hybrid who was about to become queen.

As vampires from near and far started to arrive for the coronation, I held my head high, truly confident in who I'd become. I wasn't a frightened little witch anymore. Wasn't a servant with a blood debt. Wasn't a blood whore seeking vengeance. I wasn't anyone but who I wanted to be, and words couldn't describe how freeing that felt.

When the coronation began, Everett remained by my side the entire time. We both wore shades of black and burgundy red, the royal family colors. Rubies sparkled at my neck and ears, while little diamonds lined my dress and long train. My hair was neatly twisted into an elaborate bun, held in place by gold combs.

The audience froze at the sight of me and Everett, but for once, I didn't feel the need to put on a mask and perform. They were seeing the real me. Whether they accepted me or not was up to them. All I could do was be myself, and that's exactly what I did as Everett laced his fingers through mine and started toward the dais in the throne room.

His father stood in front of the king's throne, but he didn't sit on it, because the throne was no longer his. And a second throne was now perched on the dais. A queen's throne.

My throne.

At the sight, nervous energy filled me, and the next several minutes passed in a blur. Later, I would barely remember the oaths Everett and I spoke, or the blood exchange we shared with Ambrose as he passed off his power to his heir and newest daughter-in-law. Nor would I remember the excited cheering or the moment a crown was placed on my head.

But I would forever remember the moment when we sat on our thrones, when Everett looked over at me and rose to place me on his lap. "You belong *here*," he murmured in my ear, holding me close to the delight of our audience.

I smiled, not minding in the least that he wanted us to share a throne. I wanted to share *everything* with him, including the premonition I'd had in my dreams last night.

"You're going to tell me now?" he asked, clearly having picked up on my thoughts.

"Yes. But I think I should *show* you," I replied, my smile widening when I felt his confusion. "Bite me, Everett. Bite me, and I'll do the rest."

Excitement pulsed through our bond. "Your wish is my command, my queen," he breathed. Then, not even caring that hundreds of vampires were watching, he buried his fangs in my neck.

As euphoria rushed through me, our connection exploded awake. He knew what I could do, knew that I could control his mind with a mere thought, but he trusted me. He trusted me to use my power for good, to keep him and his family—*our* family—safe. And that's exactly what I did. As he swallowed my blood, I closed my eyes and filled his mind with the premonition. Image after image, I showed him what I'd seen. Shared with him what the Universe had chosen to share with me.

When I'd sent him everything I knew, he carefully removed his fangs from my neck and licked the already-healing wounds clean. As his emotions flooded our bond, I turned in his lap to see his expression. Tears glistened in his eyes, and when one fell, I reached up and caught it.

"Three?" he whispered, staring at me in wonder. "Two boys and a . . . a *girl?*"

"Well, not all at once, thank the spirits," I whispered back with a small laugh. "But, yes. They're our legacy, Everett. Our *future*. Fate has blessed us tremendously."

"That she has, baby girl," he said, gracing me with the most beautiful smile. "That she has."

Many years would pass before the premonition fully unraveled, before three precious children entered our world. But I looked forward to that time, no matter how long it took. Those years meant happiness. They meant *life*.

We were going to be okay. More than okay.

My happily ever after hadn't turned out the way I thought it would. But this version, one that promised everlasting love and an ever-growing family . . .

Was so much better than I could have ever dreamed.

ALSO BY BECKY MOYNIHAN

A TOUCH OF VAMPIRE
Shadow Touched
Curse Touched
Fate Touched
Sun Touched (spin-off standalone)
Forever Touched (spin-off standalone)

WOLVES OF MIDNIGHT
Midnight Vow
Midnight Claim
Midnight Queen

THE ELITE TRIALS
Reactive
Adaptive
Immersive

GENESIS CRYSTAL SAGA
Dawn till Dusk
Fall of Night
Stars till Sun

ACKNOWLEDGMENTS

It was such a joy to write another book in this series! All thanks goes to my readers for asking me to write "just one more book." I don't have any plans to continue the series after Forever Touched, but never say never, right? If enough readers have an interest in more, then I'll make it happen!

For now, I'm saying goodbye once more to my vampires and diving back into the Wolves of Midnight series. The side characters need their HEAs too! FYI, I've had requests for a witch series set in this world and a next generation series. If one or both of those pique your interest, be sure to let me know!

A huge thank you to my faithful beta readers: Melissa, Allie, Morgan, and Kate. You are the dream team!!

Another huge thanks goes to my amazing ARC team. My releases continue to be successful because of your wonderful early reviews, and I couldn't be more grateful!

And to every single reader who takes a chance on my books, THANK YOU for making my author dreams come true!! On to the next adventure!

BECKY MOYNIHAN is a bestselling, award-winning author of paranormal romance and urban fantasy. Her books include the A Touch of Vampire series, Wolves of Midnight series, The Elite Trials series, and the co-written Genesis Crystal Saga.

To stay up to date on new releases, sign up for her monthly newsletter: www.beckymoynihan.com/newsletter

www.ingramcontent.com/pod-product-compliance
Lightning Source LLC
Chambersburg PA
CBHW030551260626
47157CB00006B/2274